Michigan Man

Written by

Amanda MacCormac

About the Author

Amanda Tofield-MacCormac grew up in Dorking, England. She worked for Time Inc., in New York City, Paris, and Brussels, raising two daughters during her time in Belgium and later in Yardley, Pennsylvania. Amanda trained as a Massage Therapist and Stage Make-up Artist whilst in Brussels, and has worked in both fields. Writing is Amanda's passion. Her articles have appeared in a variety of magazines and newspapers. She has had several books published; including poetry, a children's book and numerous short stories. She now lives on the East Coast of Florida with her husband.

For more information contact
maccormacamanda@yahoo.com

Acknowledgements

Thanks to my Dunkin Donut gals, Gloria, Lee, Laura, Gerry, and Susan for believing in me. My gratitude goes to Gerry, for her creative expertise; to Paula and Davita, for their friendship, and last, but by no means least, to Elisabeth for always being there for me. My daughters Kathryn and Laura need to know that without their laughter and constant uplifting of my spirits I would be lost. A big thank you to Dr. Evelyn Bethune, owner of Bethune Publishing House, Inc., my friend and publisher, for her patience and guidance. Finally, to my loving husband, Jack, who endures my silent passion and provides me so much technical support.

Michigan Man

MICHIGAN MAN

I was in paradise in clear, crystal water, dreaming of romance and gardenias, when a rasping voice interrupted my thoughts. This man hailed me while I was swimming. "Do you own your house?" he asked, a sarcastic smile spreading across his face like a melted butter pat.

"Yes, I do; how about you?"

I fervently hoped that he'd say no. No such luck. He turned around, grinning, as he told me that he owned one in this development and two in Michigan. I hoped that my face didn't broadcast my totally disappointed reaction. Who in his right mind would want one house in Michigan, let alone two? I had absolutely no right to be so judgmental, since I haven't been there, but it wouldn't have jarred me one bit if he'd been a tad humble. He was one cocky SOB. He circulated around me, his gut spilling over his, thankfully, elongated swimming trunks.

"Maybe you'd like to come and visit me in Michigan sometime," he said, displaying a set of very uneven teeth.

I'm so glad that I had a reasonable tan, because it would have been obvious that I'd blanched. I was such a snob when it came to thinking that nothing much was wonderful about Michigan or anything else that smacked of cold and snow.

"Thank you so much for the generous offer, but I work full time, and would find it hard to take any time off."

He smiled, telling me that he was getting out as he had to dry off for his usual cocktail hour. He really was the grottiest man I'd set eyes on in a long time. I hoped I wouldn't have the occasion to meet up with him again.

The following Monday morning I decided to take a swim, knowing that it was a good time to avoid all the *folks* (a word I happen to dislike), bopping up and down in the middle of the swimmer's lane discussing inane topics. I had barely started my lap routine, when someone tapped me roughly on my right shoulder. I turned around with a glare, to be confronted by the portly man who had talked to me last week.

"Do you remember me?" he said - like I could forget him in a hurry. "My son is coming down in two days and I would love you to meet him. We aren't that close, but he's more your age, so I was hoping that we could all get together, say the day after tomorrow at noon?"

I wanted to say, *no*, but ended up being feeble and replied that he was in luck, as that was my day off. "Sure, I'll meet you at noon, but where?"

"How about we meet by the pool," he replied.

"That will be fine, but I don't even know your name."

"Oh, it's Mike Sully and my son's name is Bruce."

"It's nice to meet you. I'm Molly Thomas. I'll see you the day after tomorrow then."

Before I got to my car he asked me if my hair was naturally red. "Heavens yes, but it's helped a tad by a bottle."

A satisfied grin came over his face as he walked away. Strange question; but nothing astonishes me anymore.

I kept thinking that I must either have a screw loose or be in desperate need of a decent meal. *How bad could it be,* I thought, as I zoomed off to work. I loved to eat, and hadn't actually been to a restaurant in quite a while. My best friend, Jen, and I usually go out for a meal, or at least drinks, once a week. However, her finances have been lousy since she bought herself a new car.

Wednesday arrived. It was time to get dressed, put on some make up, and head over to the pool to meet Bruce and Mike. I felt a little nervous; although, I couldn't imagine why. This was only a lunch date that would probably be frightful. Time would tell, wouldn't it?

I got to the pool around eleven-fifty, walked over, and spotted Mike with a man who was one of the best-looking males I'd seen in ages. My jaw hung down. Surely this wasn't his son? Mike waved to me and I walked over to where they were standing.

"Molly, I'd like to introduce you to my son, Bruce. Bruce, this is Molly Thomas."

I muttered something back, being somewhat gob smacked. The son had a smile to die for, and then some.

"How about we go to a hamburger cafe on beachside?" Mike asked, but as more of a pronouncement. "We can sit overlooking the ocean. It's such a glorious day that we might as well make the most of it."

We all agreed. Bruce suggested he drive. His voice was like pure, melted caramel. I had just been introduced and was smitten with what I saw. We chatted away on the drive there with ease. I still could not believe that he was Mike's son. The apple certainly fell far from the tree in this case. I asked Bruce how long he was staying. He told me he had a week's vacation before he went back to work. He was a chemist and worked for a large chemical firm on the outskirts of Detroit. He asked me what I did. I told him I was a veterinarian's assistant and was taking a few related courses in college, as well as doing some part time journalism.

I couldn't help but notice him staring at my hair. "You have the most beautiful red hair I have seen on a girl in a very long time," he said.

"Oh, thanks a lot", I replied. Giving my hair much thought, other than I always wanted to have straight hair, instead of the mass of curls I had been cursed with, was immaterial to me at this point.

We ordered lunch, talked about the news, skimming the surface of politics until our hamburgers came. They were the best I'd tasted in a long time. Mine came with blue cheese and mushrooms. I thought to myself that it was certainly worth the effort coming out today. I was having so much fun. Bruce asked if I wanted dessert and I decided to splurge and have coffee ice cream and an espresso. Coffee ice cream and I form a really great partnership.

We left at last, returning to get my car back at the pool. Bruce asked if he could walk me to it, to which I readily agreed. I said my goodbyes to Mike. When we were alone, Bruce asked me if he could take me out to dinner tomorrow night. I didn't hesitate in saying, *yes.* I gave him my address, and he agreed to pick me up at 8:00pm. Driving home I couldn't believe that I had actually said yes to a man I had just met. It didn't seem to matter one bit that his father was fat and boring.

Jen called me at work to find out how my lunch date went. She couldn't believe my enthusiasm, and when I told her that I was having dinner with Bruce tomorrow night, she was thrilled.

"It is about time you started seeing someone again. It's been two years, Molly, since David died. It's time to move on."

"You're right, I know, but it hasn't been as easy as you think. Anyway, he is only here for a week, so it isn't as if it will lead to anything."

The next day we had a lot of dogs to attend to at work, which was a good thing. I couldn't get my mind off Bruce and how much I'd enjoyed his company. I adored my job. It was immensely satisfying to help sick animals heal. I couldn't think of another profession I'd rather be in, besides my journalism, which I did on the side whenever some editing job presented itself.

Five o'clock was upon me, and I decided I needed to hit the beach. I loved to run along the sand, feeling the soft grains trickle through my toes. Such a sense of freedom came over me. After David, my boyfriend, died I came here all the time as I felt his presence here so strongly. I'm not going to rehash his death, other than to say that the drunken driver who killed him was rotting in jail for a long time.

The waves were quite rough this evening, and the sky had a gray tone to it, casting dark shadows on the water. After an hour, I decided that I'd better head home, eat, and get a decent night's sleep as we had a full day at the vet infirmary tomorrow.

Work the next day was busy, but fun. This one dog from the pound that we'd named Skip had stolen my heart. If I thought I could take care of him properly, I would have adopted him in a heartbeat, but knew that, with my schedule and lifestyle, I wasn't ready to commit to him yet.

After work, I decided to take a swim, fervently hoping that I wouldn't bump into Mike. Luck was on my side. There was one other person in the pool, so I was able to really swim laps without any interruption. After about forty-five minutes my stomach was reminding me that I hadn't eaten in a while. Tonight, was cheese, crackers, an apple, and trash TV. What could be better than that?

I slept like a log that night. In the morning, I got out of bed, pressed the coffee button, looking forward to having my usual two cups of strong coffee to energize me into a fully functioning human being. I switched the radio on to the news to be broadside with the gloomy topics of assassination, drought, and global financial disasters. Finally, I changed over to a decent music channel. It was playing Elvis Presley's, *Don't be Cruel*. Boy! That took me back to my childhood when I was about ten years old. My late mother and other singers were perfecting this song for a local theatre performance. Mother had been an opera singer and had done a lot of amateur dramatics. I miss her every day of my sometimes, insane and hectic life. Her philosophy was to do what one loved the most in life. I was attempting that now, with Bruce in mind.

I couldn't for the life of me fathom why I was excited, as well as slightly anxious, to see Bruce this evening. I didn't even know him that well. I was basing my feelings on one meal and his drop dead looks. In Jen's opinion, *it really was time to move on and start living in the real world again.*

Work was relatively calm today, which wasn't such a bad thing. I had a pile of paper work to catch up on, so I seized the opportunity to clear up some of it. Before long it was five and time to go home. All the way back I was going over in my mind what to wear. I finally decided on a purple dress that was off one shoulder. It was very slimming and somewhat alluring. I didn't even have time to get too nervous before the doorbell rang on the dot of eight.

"Hello, Molly. You look absolutely stunning tonight."

"Thank you very much, sir, and so do you." Dumb comment if ever there was one, but it sort of slipped out of my mouth, and furthermore I meant it.

"Well, if you are ready, let's go. I know this great French restaurant called L'Automne. Do you know it by chance?"

"Yes, I've heard of it, but haven't been there."

I didn't want to admit that there were reasons I hadn't been there. One being it wasn't really a place you went without a date and secondly it was rather out of my price range. Our conversation flowed freely during the quick fifteen-minute drive to at our destination.

I had always wanted to eat at L'Automne, as I'd heard the food was excellent. Let's hope it lived up to its reputation. The décor inside was beautiful. The walls were decorated in paneled scenes of France and the table cloths were red and white checkered. We had a table in a corner that was quiet and not directly under a fan – a fixture I usually find irritating. Bruce asked me what I wanted to drink, suggesting I try the house red, if I didn't have a strong desire for a particular label.

"That'll be just fine," I said, whilst perusing a menu that had many wonderful things to choose from. I settled for baked brie for starters, and salmon as an entrée. Bruce had a spinach and feta salad and steak. The evening went by so incredibly fast. We talked about everything under the sun and I felt as if I'd known him for ages. He remembered how much I adored coffee ice cream. Without me knowing, it was served to me with a cherry on the top.

"Oh, you remembered my weakness; you are so sweet."

"My pleasure entirely," he said.

I treasured each spoonful, thinking that if I were offered just one food on this earth to eat, it would have to be coffee ice cream.

On the way home Bruce asked me if I was free to go to the beach on Saturday and then out to dinner afterwards. This whole liaison was moving too darned fast, I thought to myself, yet wasn't unhappy about it.

"Yes. I'd love to," I admitted.

Arriving at my house, Bruce got out of the car to walk me to the door. There he pulled me towards him and gave me the gentlest of kisses. My knees almost gave way beneath me. It was passionate, but at the same time tender. *Molly, take it easy*, I kept saying to myself.

"Thanks a million for this evening, Bruce. I had a wonderful time and look forward to Saturday."

"I had a great time too," he said, as he turned and walked back to his car.

One more day and we would be together again. I couldn't wait to telephone Jen and tell her all about tonight.

I woke up early and decided to go for a run on the beach. It was a still morning and the sea gulls loomed above me, screeching away. Today their cries were downright irritating, so I ran at the water's edge allowing the waves to lap over my feet. I felt somewhat cleansed. The gulls had flown away, obviously sensing my irritation. All that was left on the beach were a few walkers, and out to sea a couple of fishing vessels.

Work was uneventful, but pleasant. I never ceased to be amazed how good I felt caring for sick animals. Somehow caring for humans didn't hold a candle to this. I think it's because animals can't really talk to you and tell you how they really feel that makes them special.

I called Jen in my lunch hour to tell her about last night. She was thrilled for me. I was bloody lucky to have her as my best friend. No matter what, we were always there for each other.

When I got home I decided to watch a couple of movies that I'd rented. One was *The English Patient*, and the other a French movie called *Partir*. I am an ardent fan of Kristin Scott Thomas. Just before settling down with my mug of decaf, the phone rang.

"Hello, Bruce, is that you?"

"Yes, it's me; I couldn't let the evening go by without hearing your voice and telling you how much I enjoyed last night. I also wanted to let you know how much I look forward to spending Saturday with you."

My breath almost left me. I took a deep gulp of air. "Me, too. I had a wonderful time."

"Molly, I'll pick you up at ten on Saturday if that is alright?"

"Perfect, thanks. I'm looking forward to it. Would you like me to make some sandwiches and bring a few snacks to the beach?"

"Oh, I hadn't even got that far, but since you've suggested it, yes, that'll be great. See you then." He hung up before I had a chance to say anything else.

I set my alarm for eight and didn't think that I would sleep that well, but surprised myself as the next thing I knew was the alarm attacking my ears. *The beach will be glorious,* I thought, as I drank my coffee for its nicotine charge. I made cheese and ham sandwiches and threw in some homemade chocolate chip cookies, a couple of apples, water and iced coffee. Bingo, I was ready for the beach by nine-thirty. It gave me just enough time to read the paper and see if anything interesting was going on besides the usual world calamities.

The doorbell rang, and I opened the door to Bruce, who was wearing navy bathing trunks and a pale blue open-neck shirt. *Damn, what a looker*, I thought as my heart missed a couple of beats.

"Hello, Molly. You look so pretty in your beach clothes."

"Thanks", I said, thinking his opening line was a bit cheesy - but I'll take compliments where I can get them.

"You look ready, so shall we head out?"

I nodded my head in agreement, gathered up the picnic basket for him to carry, and grabbed my handbag and a small cooler.

"I'm really looking forward to a whole day at the beach," I said as we walked out the door.

"Well, you can imagine, Molly, that living near Detroit, it's been longer for me, so I am probably more excited than you are to be at the beach. What I suggest we do is eat at the hamburger place on the beach tonight, and tomorrow night we can go out somewhere more up market. That is, if you say, *yes*, to seeing me tomorrow. Anyway, off we go; mustn't miss out on time at the ocean", he said, without giving me time to respond to his suggestion.

I wondered if he gave a thought to the fact that perhaps I actually had a life outside of him, but I said nothing.

The drive to the beach was quick; surprisingly there wasn't much traffic. However, it was still morning. In another hour, it would hot up considerably. I reflected, as I usually did when at the beach, that I couldn't possibly live anywhere that wasn't close to the ocean. My mother had lived part of her life in Spain overlooking the Mediterranean. It was in my blood to crave expansive sand and sea.

The sky was dotted with fluffy clouds that cooled the air somewhat. Thankfully, the car park wasn't that crowded yet. We loaded up the beach cart and decided to sit fairly close to the water. The sea breeze was delicious, and the waves were just perfect for swimming. The surfers wouldn't be too happy. Did I care? No, not really.

I was wearing a ghastly, practical bathing suit. It was a multi colored, two piece that had a skirt. It reminded me of all the matronly ladies that I saw. Today I really should be dressing for a man. I was dressed for comfort, but was wishing that I'd put comfort at the bottom of my preference list. On the other hand, if Bruce really likes me, a dreary swimsuit should not make a difference.

After about an hour of pure laziness, we took a long walk before lunch. We hadn't talked during this time. I guess Bruce felt as comfortable as I did with the silence. The walk certainly made up for the lack of communication. I touched on wanting to be a vet and how I had landed in New Smyrna Beach, due to my mother marrying an American whom she'd met in Spain. The other gory details could wait for a later date. I mentioned that my best friend, Jen, had moved to Florida from New York when her company opened a store in Daytona Beach, twenty-five miles north. New Smyrna Beach was a lovely, artsy beach town, and I was in luck when I found out that the local vet was looking for an assistant when I first looked for a job here. I applied, got the job, and have been living here in

New Smyrna Beach for five years. And while I miss Europe intensely, I know that I can visit from time to time, as finances allow.

Replying to my brief outline, he said, "My life seems to be so mundane after listening to your story. I was born in Dearborn, Michigan."

I couldn't help but chuckle to myself at the name, *Dearborn.*

Bruce continued. "I went to the University of Michigan to major in chemistry and took a year off to travel to Australia and New Zealand after graduating. I then went to graduate school there and got my Master's Degree. As for family life, my mother had a tumultuous time with my father ever since I can remember, until she finally left him for good two years ago. She had a boyfriend or two and talked about traveling the world with one of them, and I haven't heard from her in over a year, which is not unusual for her.

"That doesn't seem dull to me, though rather sad", I said.

He went on, "I returned to Dearborn and got a job as an analytical chemist for a large industrial chemicals company. I have had one serious girlfriend. She walked out on me and I have absolutely no clue where she is today. That is my life in a nutshell. It's really not that exciting. I am glad that I did some travelling when I was younger, but would love to see more of the world one day. Incidentally, you never mentioned your love life, or lack of it, so do please expand on your life a bit."

Before I filled him in on more of my life, I couldn't help but inwardly chuckle once more at the name, Dearborn. I had visions of a pioneer settling in a tiny village and naming it Dearborn after his first child. It was a corny thought on my part and undoubtedly not true.

Reverting to the present, I reluctantly agreed in my mind to do as he asked. But first, I took a deep breath of sea air to calm myself down.

"Before I tell you more of my personal life, let me ask you, isn't this town rather dull compared to Dearborn? With all the hustle and bustle of the car industry etc., you must feel yourself half asleep here."

"On the contrary, Molly, I love this town with its ocean and laid back, artsy feel. I'd move here in a heartbeat."

I thought how interesting that he's flexible. "Are you ready to hear more about my life?" He nodded that he was.

"I was very much in love with a man called, David. I think we probably would have married, but he was killed several years ago by a drunken driver, convicted for DUI manslaughter and now serving a prison term. I lived in limbo for quite some time afterwards, but I'm beginning to realize that I can't live in the past and have to get on with my life. I know that's what David would have wanted.

Before we eat let me give you a brief synopsis of my parents and formative years. Both my parents came from blue collar families. My mother rebelled against my austere grandfather's wishes and trained as an opera singer. Sadly, she had tuberculosis when I was five and was in hospital for a year. She could never have the top-notch roles previously offered to her, but she continued singing with second rung groups, amateur theatres, etc. My dad left school at fourteen and educated himself. He worked on the railroad, progressing to become European Director of the Port of Baltimore, Maryland. He traveled to the States a lot during my preteen years – hence the seed of desire to come here was sown. He was a disciplinarian of the first degree, a very tough critic during my school years. He told me that I should never suffer fools gladly, as there were too many good people around. He was overseas when I was born. Later on, I found out that he was a total shit to my mother, cheating on her even when she was carrying me. She stood by him stoically for fourteen years before bailing out for a life of solitude, far less wealth, hard work, but, with, I guess, a greater peace of mind.

That just about sums it up. Oh, yes, a quotation that has stuck with me is by the famous author, Lewis Carroll, *"If you limit your actions in life to things that nobody can possibly find fault with, you will not do much.* I love it."

"I'm really sorry for you, regarding David. That must have been absolutely awful for you. I can see that you are re-entering the real world. Though, I'm selfishly grateful for that, and I do appreciate having a little more insight into your younger years. Now it's time to chow down, as I'm starving."

"Me too", I said. "I feel as if I could eat a horse. Sea air always does that to me."

Food at the beach seems to taste to better. We ate in silence, as if we hadn't had a square meal in days. Even the coffee tasted heavenly. What struck me was that we both were very comfortable with each other. It had only been a mere two days and I felt as if I had known him so much longer. Incredible!

"Molly, these sandwiches are to die for, and your iced coffee is the best yet."

" Wait till you taste my brownies. Only then will you know that you have truly lived."

"I can hardly wait," Bruce said as he looked at me with what I thought was utter admiration in those drop dead gorgeous eyes.

Stop it, Molly; you are getting very mushy, I told myself. I wasn't willing to give in to my emotions just yet. I suppose I'd steeled myself for so long that it was almost second nature to me to put up this barrier. Jen had told me to go with the flow and open up to Bruce. She kept advising me it was time I dated and socialized with people, rather than cats and dogs. She was right. I would try my damndest to do so.

The rest of the afternoon flew by. We had both taken books with us, so we read for a while, and then decided to take a short walk, followed by flopping into the sea. Bruce pulled me towards him, holding me close, our wet bodies alive with desire. He kissed me with an urgency that unsettled me. He let go of me, looking at me with his piercing eyes. I felt sick with desire for him. I let go of him, trying to regain my composure. We strolled back to the blanket, drying off a bit, before sitting down with a mere inch in between us. I had to break the sexual tension somehow.

"Try my killer brownies, Bruce, they're bloody good."

He ate several of them before grinning and nodding approvingly. "What do you say we go back to your place, Molly, before we go out this evening? That way we can clean up, shower etc."

"That sounds like a good idea", I said, not wanting this day to end.

It didn't take too long to get home. I gave Bruce a towel and pointed him in the direction of the spare bathroom.

"I'm dressing real casual," I said, hoping that was okay.

"Sure, we'll save the fancy gear for tomorrow night", he shouted back.

Then I showered, put this wonderful gardenia cream on my body, and threw on my favorite jeans and purple, short sleeved, silk blouse. I readily admitted that the suntan did wonders for my looks and I actually liked what I saw in the mirror. *Some change this is*, I thought as I went downstairs and waited for Bruce. He was wearing a pair of denim shorts and a blue and white striped short sleeved shirt. He was quite the most handsome man I'd seen in two years.

"Molly, you look absolutely lovely. Is my stunning date ready to go?"

"Yes, I am", I said emphatically and blushing a bit.

The hamburger was superb, and I tested my willpower in turning down the offer of ice cream, opting for an espresso instead. We talked about so many different things that I couldn't begin to relate to half of them. I did know that I hadn't felt this at ease with a man since David. *That was then; this is now*, I told myself, trying hard not to make comparisons.

"I have had a great day and evening, Bruce. Thanks a million. But really, I have an early start at the vet infirmary, so I must call it a night", I said.

"That's fine with me," he replied. "I have a ton of stuff to do before I go back to the suburbs of Detroit next week."

As we left, the sun was setting over the ocean, which gave it an orangey glow. Was there a better sight than this? It was hard to imagine.

Arriving at my house, Bruce stopped the car, got out, and walked me to the door. At first hesitating, he then asked me if I was free on Tuesday for dinner.

"Yes, I'm free", I eagerly replied.

He walked closer to me and neither one of us said a word. Then it happened. He pulled me towards him, kissing me for moments on end, it seemed. I knew he wanted me. I could feel him swell against my groin. But then he pulled himself away hurriedly.

"Molly, if I didn't have such a work overload, I would not be leaving you now; you must know that." His eyes drifted downwards in regret.

"I know, Bruce; I feel the same."

He turned and smiled, then sped off up the road. I walked indoors, a bit miffed. I knew he cared for me, but was it a purely sexual attraction? I knew that I was fiercely attracted to him. I happened to like him as a person, but it was all happening too fast and I felt a knot in my stomach. *Go easy, girl*, I said to myself, as I cleaned up a few odds and ends. I then went to bed and slept better than I had in weeks.

Monday came and went without anything unduly stressful. We had a couple of dogs to spay and several cats for their twice-yearly shots. Otherwise it was catching up on paperwork day. I called Jen during my lunch hour, wondering if she was free to join me on the beach for a walk after work.

"Great, I'd love to see you then," she said.

It was, as always, a marvelous de-stressor, going to the ocean. There wasn't a hint of a breeze and the waves broke gently. There was an almost mystical feel to the evening.

I filled Jen in on my time with Bruce. She, as always, is my biggest fan and was thrilled for me that things were going so well.

"You know, Jen, you are amazing. You don't have any love life of your own, but you're so enthusiastic about mine. I love you for your unselfishness."

"Thanks, Molly. I really appreciate you saying that, but don't worry about my lack of romantic entanglements. I just haven't met Mr. Right yet. One day, I hope, but maybe never."

I had met Jen in London, when I was going to this stuffy, all girls', business, and language school. She came from a family of five, and her parents are still married. Normal!   I, on the other hand, came from a fairly dysfunctional family. My parents divorced when I was fourteen. As I 'd told Bruce, my mother moved to Spain, met an American from New Smyrna Beach, Florida; married him, and lived here until she died five years ago. She originally lived in an adult development which she said was like living on a desert island of senility. My mother and step-dad then moved into a free-standing home which was part of a large development with a pool. She loved the house, as do I. I moved over from London to be with my mother in her final months. I realized that I wanted to stay here and work with animals. I secured my 'green card' that allows me to work in the States. I have been attending Daytona State College concentrating on pre-veterinarian subjects. And, I found a job with a great veterinarian. He pays for me to take classes until I get a degree – a really good deal! Who knows, I may go on to vet school, if my grades merit.

We caught up on pretty much everything and decided that we'd do the same thing again on Wednesday night.

"What if Bruce wants to see you then?"

"I'm seeing him tomorrow night; besides, he leaves the following Monday for Dearborn, and I'm not giving up my life for him. No-one is worth that."

"Alright, Wednesday it is", she replied and then we said our goodbyes.

My life followed a routine pattern most days. It consisted in general of work, the beach, and evening television. It could be a lot worse. Since I'd met Bruce, it was anything but dreary, but I kept telling myself that he was returning home in a week and my life would resume its normality, if there was such an animal.

Tuesday rolled around and I found myself being very distracted at the thought of seeing Bruce again, and erotic visions of Bruce lying stark naked on my bed popped into my head. I lectured myself to snap out of this reverie. I am not usually one to be swayed by thoughts of pleasure when there's work to be done. Before I knew it, it was time to go home and peruse my wardrobe.

A glass of wine was essential in the choosing of the right outfit. I must have thrown a dozen outfits on the bed, tried on about eight and settled on a pair of tight fitting dark pink satin trousers with a black and pink print long blouse. Not bad, I thought to myself as I adjusted my makeup, went downstairs and poured myself another glass of wine. My heart leapt when I heard the doorbell ring. I opened it and practically fell into Bruce's arms. He was wearing a dark blue suit, pale blue shirt, and a printed tie that picked up the blues in his suit and shirt. He looked at me with the same admiration.

"Well, let's get going as I have a reservation at L'Etoile for six-thirty. By the way, you look ravishing."

'Thanks," I said, feeling myself blush again. I was also very excited to go to this restaurant for the first time.

The décor was beautiful, yet understated. The walls were painted pale red, with some exquisite paintings dotted around. The chairs were padded in red satin and the tables had crisp white tablecloths. The glassware was the best crystal money could buy. I prayed the food would match up to the rest.

We started off with a Merlot that was to die for; accompanied by the best pate I had tasted in a long time. I chose the duck a l'orange and Bruce settled on lamb with baby onions. We were not disappointed. I hadn't eaten duck since my time in Europe when we bought Polish ducks. Bruce gave me a taste of his lamb, which was delicious. For dessert, I opted for crème caramel with a raspberry sauce and Bruce had cheesecake. We chatted over coffee, but it saddened me to think that this culinary experience had to come to an end.

As we approached my house I nervously asked Bruce if he wanted to come in for a nightcap, to which he said, *yes.* I wasn't exactly thinking of a drink at this juncture.

"I feel like I should be saying that I will slip into something comfortable."

Bruce laughed, but when I told him that is exactly what I wanted to do, he followed me to the bedroom. No sooner had I opened the door, then he turned me around to face him, looking at me for the longest time in silence.

"Molly, I ache for you. Since I met you I have thought of nothing else than making love to you. Tell me you have been thinking the same thoughts."

"Bruce, I have to admit I have thought along these lines too."

He grabbed my arms, kissing me with a passion that ignited a fire inside me.

"The silky feel of your skin fills my mind, Molly," he said, kissing me again with fervor. He started to unbutton my shirt slowly, touching my bare skin with a sensitivity that made my gasp for air. His eyes held me in his gaze, wanting me, desiring me. I returned the look, taking off his jacket. I then began to unbutton his shirt.

"Are you sure you want this," he asked me. "If it's too soon for you, then I will back away now."

"No, no, please don't stop," I said, feeling as if I would explode inside. Warning bells went off inside me, telling me it was too soon for this, yet it felt so right. Pretty soon I was standing in front of him totally naked. He picked me up and laid me on the bed, and for what seemed like an age, we fondled each other, smothering our bodies with kisses, some hot with passion, others sweet and gentle. We didn't have to speak to know when the time was right for us to become as one. It was a heady moment, neither lasting very long. I knew that the next time we would savor it more. There would be a next time, I hoped. I drifted back to Earth, conscious of his weight on me, but comfortable; feeling as if I had been made just for this. I caressed his back and sighed.

"Molly, this was so much better than I ever imagined. I am sorry that I didn't last too long, but promise next time to take it slower."

I smiled inwardly when he mentioned the next time. There was a part of me that imagined he would think I was just good for one romp in the hay. But it didn't seem like a one-night stand. I sat up and asked him if he'd like a brandy.

"That sounds just the ticket, thanks."

I grabbed a shirt, went downstairs, and poured a couple of brandies, thinking that my life couldn't be much better than it was right now. Bruce was sitting up in bed looking like a Cheshire cat.

We drank in silence, then without further ado, he jumped out of bed, dressed, and announced that as much as he would like to stay all night, he had an early meeting in the morning.

"Are you free for dinner tomorrow?" he asked me.

"Absolutely", I exclaimed.

Before I knew it, he kissed me goodbye and left. I lay on the bed for what seemed like a couple of hours just reliving every moment of this evening. I woke up to the sun streaming in through the windows. I hadn't even closed the curtains last night. It showed how utterly content I was. Too bad I had a whole day to wait before I was with Bruce again.

I got to work and found the most beautiful bouquet of mixed flowers on my desk. The card read, *Until tonight, Bruce.* I was stunned. I hadn't received flowers like this since David's funeral.

Work took on a totally different air from yesterday. John, my boss, came in to say that we had an emergency. A Labrador retriever had been hit by a car and we had our work cut out. I loved challenges. When I saw the dog, I knew we had a huge job on our hands. I prayed that we'd be able to save him. It took us roughly three hours to patch him up. We further sedated him and put him in a doggy bed to recuperate. This part of my job was undoubtedly the best part. *Saving a life couldn't get much better, could it?* I thought, as I wrote up all the particulars for the owner.

I have to mention my boss, John Young. He was a tall, slim, somewhat insignificant looking man with brown hair that was speckled with grey. He had pale green eyes. He was someone who would, I imagine, never light up a room with his looks, but he was pleasant looking, and the kindest, fairest boss I could ever wish for. He was never loud or overly demanding. We worked together in quiet harmony.

I gave Jen a quick call during a break and excused myself from the walk on the beach. She quite understood, and was happy that I was happy. I was truly fortunate to have her as my friend. I thought it would be really fun if I cooked dinner for Bruce, so I took the risk of telephoning him at work. He wasn't there so I left a message and told him to show up at seven if he agreed to my plan. No need to call me back, unless he had a problem. Now I had to put on my thinking cap and come up with a great dinner. My spaghetti sauce was to die for, so that was settled. I'd buy some coffee ice cream as a dessert. Lovemaking uses up a lot of calories! I decided to splurge and open the special bottle of red wine I'd been keeping for a rainy day.

I hadn't heard from Bruce, but assumed that he was coming. Sure enough, at the allotted time, the doorbell rang. I opened it to be greeted with a kiss and a bottle of wine.

The kiss was perfunctory, but once inside he seized me and drew me closer, kissing me passionately. A taste of things to come I hoped.

"Do you want me to open your wine, Bruce, or shall I open the red I've been saving?"

"Oh, go ahead and open mine, as it's not as special as the one you have. We can drink yours later on."

"Let's sit down whilst the sauce is simmering."

I had decided that since I had told him about my previous love life, I was going to get him to divulge his.

"Bruce, do tell me what happened to your last girlfriend."

"Well, there isn't much to tell really. I came home from work one day and there was a note from Valerie telling me that she had decided to break free and return to Utah. It was a shock. I never saw this coming, but there was nothing I could do, and since I never got her address there, I decided not to track her down. The only similarity between you and Valerie is that you both have gorgeous red hair. Before Valerie, I had dated various girls, but there was no one I was serious about. That's about it."

"Thanks for being honest with me", I said.

We sipped on the red wine he'd brought over. I had to admit it was none too shabby, so without further ado I refilled our glasses.

"Dinner will be ready in about ten minutes." I told him and got up to put on the music station that had nonstop hits and no commercials.

"At the risk of sounding corny, Molly, would you care to dance?"

My answer was getting up and walking towards him. We smooched to a Barry Manilow number, feeling the mutual heat of our bodies as they touched. I pulled away saying it was time to eat. I was starving, so had to cool my embers. When I need to eat, NOTHING stands in my way.

"This sauce is spectacular, Molly. You can make this for me any time. Thanks so much for suggesting this as I was getting a bit 'restauranted' out.

"Guess what's for dessert?" I queried."

"I can't possibly guess, so don't keep me in suspense."

I came out with the baked Alaska; naturally the ice cream used for this dessert was coffee. Was there another kind? It was damn good. We ate voraciously until we'd almost licked the plate.

"Care for a brandy now or a bit later?"

"Later would suit me fine, Molly. I was thinking about perhaps lying down for a rest. What do you think about that?"

"Good idea, Bruce; follow me."

We decided to get the dishes done, wanting to get the ugly task out of our way so we could really relax. Once done, we ran up the stairs. You would have thought a tornado warning had been issued, judging by the speed in which Bruce undressed. I glanced over at him. He had a body that many women would kill for. No fat, just pure muscle and those blue eyes. Oh, God, I am one lucky broad, I thought. We fell onto the bed naked, both staring at each other in silence. He cupped his hands over my breasts, causing me to let out a moan. He slid his hands along my thighs and I wrapped my legs around his waist, pulling him towards me.

"We are going to take this slowly, Molly. There is absolutely no reason to rush things."

"I want things to last, but I am not sure that I can wait too long. For God's sake take me now," I said sighing.

He pressed in a little, almost to tease me, then a little more, and without any more hesitation we were suddenly as one. I looked into his eyes not sure what to say, wanting to tell him that I was falling for him.

Before I could blurt anything out he said,

"Molly, you are very important to me and I want to spend as much time with you as possible before I go back to Dearborn. I hope you feel the same way."

"Oh, yes, Bruce I do." I didn't care about the consequences, or how flat I would feel once he was gone. Time together was all I cared about right now. We lay in each other's arms, drifting off to sleep.

I awoke to the smell of fresh coffee. We made love again. It was nothing less than perfect.

"Good morning, Molly, I trust you like burnt toast with marmalade? It was the only breakfast food I could find."

"Sorry my cupboard is so bare. I have to do a large shop today. This breakfast tastes pretty good. Anything I don't prepare for myself always tastes better."

"I was wondering if you might like to go up to St. Augustine for the weekend, he said. "As you know, I have to go home Monday night. I thought we could stay in a bed and breakfast. One of the guys at work knows a good one there."

"Oh, yes, I'd love to. I haven't been to St. Augustine in about three years."

"Well then, it's a done deal. I'll make the arrangements today. We can leave straight after work on Friday."

We both went about getting ready for work in silence. It wasn't awkward. Bruce caught me bending over and tapped me on the buttocks. Truthfully, he squeezed them, wishing me a good day and that he'd see me later. He just assumed that I was free. That didn't sit too well with me, so I told him that I was seeing Jen and couldn't break my arrangement with her. He said he understood and asked if he could come by on Friday around six. "Yes, that'll be great." He turned around, smiled, and was gone before I had a chance to say anything else.

The thought of spending an entire weekend with Bruce really excited me. I adored St. Augustine, and felt chuffed knowing that I'd be a good tour guide. I couldn't think of much else, driving to work. I called Jen to make sure she was still free this evening. We arranged to meet at the beach, take a long walk, and then hit the hamburger joint afterwards. The day flew by because we were very busy. We had an influx of cats to spay and give them their annual shots. For the most part, the cats were very good patients with the exception of this large marmalade cat who hissed when you went anywhere near him. It took two of us to hold him down in order to give him his shots. The day drew to a close and I took off my scrubs, washed up, and headed out for the beach.

The waves were roaring today and surfers were in abundance. They were having a competition in two weeks on the beach, so I imagine lots of them were training. It was exciting to watch the suntanned bodies catch waves. But for me close to shore or on terra firma fell much more into my comfort zone. I spotted Jen who ran down to join me.

"Sorry I'm late, Molly, but I had a huge order that came in, and I just had to process it."

"No big deal, Jen. I have been here only about five minutes and enjoy watching the surfers do their thing."

She had a super grin on her face. It wasn't her usual smile, so I quizzed her about her *happy face.*

"Well, you'll never believe this. Yesterday we had that sales convention I'd mentioned to you last week. My boss wanted me to attend and take a few notes. I walked into a sea of businessmen, feeling quite overwhelmed. Whilst I was collecting my thoughts, someone tapped me on the shoulder, so I turned around and this nice looking young man introduced himself to me as Charlie Davis from Miami."

I said, "Nice to meet you, my name is Jennifer Peele, but I'm known as Jen".

He wasn't movie star good looking, but had huge brown eyes and an endearing crooked smile. Charlie told me that he was in town for a week and didn't know much about this sleepy little place. He asked me if I was interested in coming out tomorrow evening to show him around town a bit. I said, *yes*. Molly, do you realize that I haven't been out with someone of the opposite sex in about nine months? I'm not sure I'll know how to act, but I certainly want to find out."

"You don't expect me to believe that, do you?" I replied.

"Perhaps we could double date, Molly?"

"Actually, Bruce asked me to spend the weekend with him in St. Augustine. I readily accepted his offer as I had no pressing demands on my time. Besides, I really do love being with him. He returns to Dearborn on Monday, so my life will revert back to its routine self soon enough."

She raised her eyebrows, but acknowledged that if she were in that situation, she'd be doing the exact same thing and added, "Go for it, girlfriend. You know it's going to hurt when he leaves, but you might as well enjoy his company while you can. One day at a time with him is evidently a hell of a lot better than no time!"

After hashing out our love life, we walked in silence along the sand, breathing in the salty air, as pelicans swooped down into the sea with a loud splash and sand crabs scurried about their business. There was a never-ending array of sights to soak up. Invigorated, we guessed we'd walked several miles and were starving. The hamburgers, as always tasted great, even greater when washed down with a couple of glasses of zinfandel.

"Jen, be sure to call me on my cell on Saturday to let me know how things went with Charlie."

"Absolutely, but I don't think that my date will amount to as much as yours. However, I am looking forward to being wined and dined even if that's all it amounts to."

We topped the meal off with an espresso before heading home.

When I think about my life in general, it couldn't get much better. It was the best decision of my life to come to the States and live with my mother until I got established. My biggest regret, or should I say sadness, is that my mother isn't around to witness all this excitement. *Switch gears*, I said to myself because I didn't want to sink down into a depression right now. Easier said than done, but with disco songs on the radio I was soon transported to a higher plain.

Death had always terrified me. My mother and David, my step-father, had never feared death. I wish I could somehow be like them, but I couldn't, and I have tried so hard, to no avail.

Driving home I suddenly had an urge to visit the cemetery. Mother was cremated, but Dave expressly wished to be buried in a casket. Lovely that they are together, her urn of ashes set over his coffin. I spent about a half an hour talking to my mother, said my goodbyes, and said a few wistful words to David. I thought I would feel awful, but on the contrary, I felt enormously peaceful and satisfied. Talking to them made me feel better.

As I sped home, my thoughts switched gears to the weekend that lay ahead of me. Spending two whole days and nights with Bruce in one of my favorite cities in the world was none too shabby. When I got home there was a message from Bruce confirming that he'd pick me up at around 6 pm. He was hoping that I could catch him up to speed on St. Augustine whilst driving there. That wouldn't be a problem. I knew its history fairly well.

I stopped off at the fruit and vegetable stand to buy some oranges. Every time I look at an orange it reminds me of the wonderful times I had with my mother in Spain. We would walk through the orange groves, the perfume of citrus permeating throughout the hills. We would often pass this shepherd tending his sheep, and my mother always stopped to chat with him, pointing out his beautiful blue eyes to me, saying she'd seriously consider running away with him, but reality would always kick in. Imagine, my mother flirting with a humble shepherd! Envisioning my mother having romantic thoughts was not an easy effort either.

Work the next day was nothing out of the ordinary, which suited me just fine. I was so excited about my forthcoming weekend with Bruce that I had a hard time focusing to the maximum of my ability. Before I knew it, I was home to get ready. What to pack was not a simple task, but I finally decided to take a couple of dressy outfits, several casual ones, and a floaty pair of trousers and matching shirt for the journey.

I knew Bruce would be arriving at exactly the time he said he would. Sure, enough the doorbell rang exactly at six. I opened it, and was swept off my feet as he hugged and kissed me. After gently putting me down, he asked if I was ready to hit the road

"I'm all set, Bruce."

I gave a cursory look around to make sure everything was in place. It was; so, we were on our way once I double locked the front door. *St. Augustine, here we come*, I thought to myself.

"Are you ready for the guided tour to begin?"

"Yes, full steam ahead", he said.

"Well, first off, a bit of history about St. Augustine itself. It's the oldest city in the United States, and was founded in the 1500's by a Spanish explorer named Pedro Menendez de Aviles. It was named after the feast day of Augustine of Hippo. In the mid 1500's the Saturiwa tribe burned St. Augustine down and it was rebuilt on what is assumed today's site. In the early 1700's the British invaded St. Augustine, and it was handed over to them by the Spanish, in exchange for Havana. In the early 1800's Florida was ceded to the Unites States by Spain. I am not going to further bore you with details, but when we visit the Ponce de Leon Hotel, you can find out more information. As you may know, Henry Flagler, a co-founder of Standard Oil, built the hotel and several others in Florida. He also purchased a local railroad and developed it into a major railway system, which he eventually incorporated as the Florida East Coast Railway, its headquarters being in St. Augustine at the time."

"How on earth do you know all these fiddly details, Molly?"

"Well, to be honest, I know a lot by heart, but I checked on the various dates and wrote them down, so I'm not quite as brilliant as I seem."

"I put the name of the bed and breakfast in my trusty GPS. It's called Raven's Rest, and supposedly they have wicked breakfasts," he advised.

"Just thinking about it is making me hungry. I've got an apple if you want to take the edge off your appetite, Bruce."

"Thanks, that'll do it for me", he replied, as he took my offering.

Before long we approached the city's limits. The bed and breakfast was situated off the beaten track, down a side street that had a view of the harbor. It was very quaint, and the front was gray granite stone. We were led up to our room which was gorgeous. Everything was decorated in soft shades of gray and purple. The bathroom had been totally renovated with pale gray marble and an enormous shower. I could imagine having fun in that.

"Well, I guess we should consider eating, don't you think?" Bruce said; then he added "We can unpack when we get back."

"That sounds good to me, as I'm really hungry. I know this Greek restaurant overlooking the water, if that appeals to you?"

He nodded his assent and kissed me, as always igniting a flame deep in my gut.

Upon arrival, we asked for a table overlooking the harbor. We started off with a nice Greek wine. The food was wonderfully delicious. I had a plate of grilled sardines with a cucumber salad, followed by lamb cooked in rosemary and garlic, garnished with roast potatoes and green beans. Bruce had stuffed vine leaves, and Osso Bucco. We decided dessert would be a fine finish to the meal, so we had Baklava and Greek coffee. It seemed like we had a perfect day. Well, really, I was hoping for an even more perfect end.

Back at the room, Bruce unpacked with alacrity, sat on the bed and looked at me. "Molly, please sit down on the bed with me for a moment." I did.

"Undress please", he said in an almost matter of fact fashion.

Who am I, not to obey orders? I disrobed to complete nakedness. He looked at me and sighed.

"You are so perfect that I want to look at you for a long time before it becomes unbearable for me and I have to take you."

He cupped my breasts in his hands. I could barely stand the heat and excitement I felt. I tugged off his shirt and urged him to undress the rest of the way, staring at him as he did so, almost mesmerized by his firm torso. We touched each other with such urgency. Suddenly he held me very close to him and said that he really couldn't wait a moment longer to have me. I spread my legs and he entered me with such a force that I let out a slight whimper. Before long we climaxed, falling into a relaxed heap afterwards.

"Oh, gosh, Molly, I love you. Maybe it's awfully soon to say it, but I really do."

I was somewhat taken aback, but was happy to hear those words, as they mirrored the feelings I had for Bruce and so I said, "I'm crazy about you, too".

Somehow, I couldn't bring myself to say I loved him. It seemed way too early for uttering these sentiments, although I did feel love for him, or was it more lust than love? Time would tell.

Neither one of us said anything, but lay wrapped around each other for what seemed like an eternity. Finally, the beautiful silence was broken by the phone ringing.

I queried, "Who on earth could that be? You didn't give anyone our number, did you?"

"No, I didn't, but they know where we are staying."

Picking up the phone, Bruce smiled. It was the duty clerk, reminding us that breakfast was from 8 until 10 in the morning and inquiring of any dietary needs. I was glad for the call, because I had forgotten to tell them that I was gluten intolerant, a fact I found out quite a few years ago. I had thought I was having a heart attack, but it turned out to be nothing more than this food allergy. I almost always take my own bread with me, but it had slipped my mind this time.

"Bruce, tell them that I am gluten intolerant, please."

He hung up after explaining my condition and expressed with surprise, "I didn't know about your food allergy".

"Well, it's not something I broadcast. I guess with all the excitement going on I totally forgot about it."

"It looks as if we have plenty of time to rest then," he said, with a huge grin.

Rest was not the order of the evening. We made love again, but this time it was slow and luscious, the urgency having been taken care of several hours prior. I asked myself if it could get better, as each time it seemed to. Now that we had declared our feelings for each other, things seemed so much more relaxed.

What on earth would I do with myself when Monday comes, I thought, but decided to put that feeling aside and enjoy the exquisite moments whilst together. Sleep came softly as we held each other, neither one of us wanting to let go.

I was awakened in the morning by the delicious smell of coffee. I opened my eyes and saw a tray that held a porcelain cup and saucer, a pot of coffee, milk and a beautiful peach rose in a vase.

"Good morning, my darling. I hope you slept well and are ready for lots of sightseeing today," Bruce greeted me.

"Oh, how simply lovely; this is a delicious way to start the day. Thank you so much."

I was tempted to ask him if he'd pinched the rose from the garden as I saw they had a large bush out there, but knew that would be tacky of me to ask. The coffee was not only hot, but very strong and had a hint of hazelnut to it. I could barely wait for breakfast, wondering what delights they would serve us.

"I'm going to have a shower, and then I'll be set for the day."

I didn't linger but knew that the next encounter in this shower wouldn't be alone. I was bound and determined to make that happen. It was wonderful to get dressed in such a deluxe bathroom. Part of the fun of going away was, knowing that I didn't have to worry about dirty flannels and towels. The feel of the cold marble on my feet was quite sensual. I threw on my favorite fuchsia float pants, matching tee shirt, applied some makeup, and was ready for the day.

"You look stunning", Bruce offered.

"Thanks a lot, also for the wonderful start to the day with the coffee and flowers. I'm really ravenous now."

The dining room was almost Victorian in its décor. The walls were of a satin material in a pale shade of red, tassels bound the floral curtains, and porcelain china figurines adorned the mantel piece. More coffee arrived and we were asked if we would like freshly squeezed orange juice. "Yes, for the both of us, please," Bruce said.

The smell of freshly toasted bread permeated the dining room. The owner brought out two plates, gluten-free oat toast for me, and whole wheat toast for Bruce. It was served with homemade jams and butter. No sooner had the toast arrived than the owner's wife brought out a platter with crispy bacon, an artichoke soufflé and fluffy pancakes made, I was told, with brown rice flower. Everything tasted so good. The soufflé was quite different. The tiny pieces of artichoke gave it a kick.

Silence fell upon us whilst we savored this feast. I for one wouldn't want much for lunch, having stuffed myself, but there were plenty of sandwich and snack places in St. Augustine, particularly along the walking streets of the historic district that we planned to explore after visiting the nearby Ponce de Leon Hotel.

"Oh, that was out of this world, more so since I didn't have to make it. Did you enjoy it as much as I did, Bruce?"

"I think you can see by my plate that I enjoyed it as much, if not more, Molly. I can hardly wait until tomorrow to see what's on the menu."

We each had another cup of coffee before freshening up for our tour of the town. Bruce took my hand as we walked over to the famous hotel.

I explained to Bruce that it was built as a hotel for the rich by Henry Flagler in 1888, the first poured concrete structure of its kind. And it had an electric lighting power system designed Thomas Edison. Amusingly, the guests were at first afraid to turn on the lights, so employees were given the task. Anyway, the hotel became the centerpiece for Flagler College at its founding in 1968.

The collage was not in session, so we were able to look around without being bothered by anyone. The inside had a beautiful wrought iron chandelier hanging in the center of the lobby.

"You know, Bruce, the hotel managed to survive the Great Depression, but became a U.S. Coast Guard training center during World War II."

"Everything you've told me is really fascinating", he admitted.

We strolled through some of the upstairs rooms which, as one might imagine, were quite bare. The library was beautiful. It was stuffed with leather bound books; a joy to see in this day and age.

"How about a walk along the old city streets nearby, unless you want to see more of this building," I suggested.

"Enough of the building for now; a walk sounds appealing," he said.

This part of town always excited me. Some of the streets were paved with cobblestone, and full of people from all walks of life. We stopped at the oldest school house in

America. I could only imagine what that must have been like without any form of air conditioning. It was very quaint and rather small, probably holding no more than twenty children. Back when it was built there probably wasn't much else around. *We are certainly quite spoiled today*, I thought. The streets were full of shops and cafes and the touristy atmosphere was awesome. We went into this cute shop that only had merchandise relating to cats and dogs. Bruce bought me a paper weight that read: *Let sleeping dogs lie, and cats tell the truth!* It was corny but cute.

We had done quite a lot of walking and had worked up quite an appetite. There was a café that had tables outside which we opted for. The food was excellent. I am waiting for the time when I have a bad meal. Maybe it won't happen.

"Well, Molly, what's on our agenda for this afternoon?"

"I thought we could go to the old fort and perhaps take a trolley ride around the town. It's fun and the driver gives a running commentary about the history and architecture. Does that sound okay to you?"

"I'm at your disposal, my love."

"Well then that's what we'll do. Bruce, do you mind if I have a cup of coffee before we leave? You will probably have already noticed that I cannot finish a meal without coffee."

Two double espressos were ordered and we split a large almond cookie. What a perfect combination. We spent a couple of hours looking around the fort, which is known as Castillo de San Marcos. By the time we'd finished we were ready to take the trolley and relax a bit. It was very hot outside and we had walked more than our fair share.

The trolley ride lasted about seventy minutes, filling us in on all sorts of details about St. Augustine. It very conveniently dropped us a couple of blocks from the Raven's Rest. By now it was close to five and I for one was pooped, or at least I thought so. As soon as we reached our room at the B & B, Bruce took me in his arms, kissing me gently, yet passionately. Sparks were flying in the air. We didn't waste any time undressing. However, our lovemaking was slow and deliberate. Bruce caressed my breasts, my stomach, and my thighs. I was so aroused that I grabbed him and almost crushed his back.

"Please take me right now, my darling, before I explode in a million pieces."

He followed my orders to a tee. Afterwards, we lay in an exhausted heap, not speaking and I felt tender, happy, and loved. A few minutes later I heard his deep breathing. He was asleep. I was too excited to sleep. My eyes just focused on him. This was the man I really wanted to spend my life with, but it was way too early to think about things like that. He slept for about an hour, woke up and we made wonderful love again. We couldn't get enough of each other. Whilst lying in his arms, he told me he loved me again. I reciprocated. We then switched the subject to food, after being sated by love and lust. Where to eat dinner? We opted to walk around town until we found something quaint.

While dressing for the evening, I mused how drastically my life was changing. But I had just one more day of bliss before he returned to Dearborn. I told myself, over and over, not to be so pessimistic with the idea of not seeing Bruce again, once he left. Bruce, however, brought me back to a happy state. He was laughing about something.

"I give up; I cannot guess what you are cackling about, oh, merry soul."

Still chuckling, Bruce replied, "I was just thinking how funny it is that we go from the bed to the table and back again. Our priorities are at least in line with each other. Let's give dinner a go, before they lock us out for the night."

We found a quaint fish restaurant overlooking the main bridge. It had a pirate-like, old world feeling, with brass telescopes, and fishing nets decorating the walls. It was remarkably quiet. I hadn't, until this moment, really given much thought to how Bruce was dressed. He wore a soft jacket of midnight blue, pale blue shirt and dark jeans, and I again realized just how good looking he was. His dark, cropped hair suited his handsome, tanned features. We were so absorbed in conversation that we didn't hear the waiter ask us what we'd like to drink. If I hadn't been with a man I could have quite gone for the waiter. He was Italian looking, tall, slim and had an amazing smile.

"I'll take a Guinness, please," I said.

Bruce asked for a domestic beer and then we perused the menu. We both decided on the same thing – fish and chips, malt vinegar and two sides of coleslaw. The sun was sinking into the horizon and I decided to get the waiter to take our photo. With the bridge in the background and the sun setting on the water, it looked as if it had been especially ordered.

"Thanks so much, "I said, looking at the two photos he had taken.

They were really good. For me to like a photo of myself was an achievement. Most photos of me ended up in the camera trash bin. My usual reaction reminded me of my cousin, Sossy, who tragically died one month before my mother. She and I were as close as sisters. She used to kid me in our younger days that I looked like a horse when I smiled. I used to have a pony and I had large teeth, but felt that was where the similarity ended.

We had just about finished our drinks when a young waitress, dressed in black from head to toe, with tattoos up her arms, a large diamond stud under her lower lip and one in her nose, arrived with our order. We fell upon the food like starved wolves. For several minutes, not a word was spoken.

Having totally devoured the fish, but still working my way through the large portion of chips, I decided to ask Bruce something that had been on my mind the past few days.

"I've been meaning to ask you about your father. You don't seem to resemble him at all."

"No, you're absolutely spot-on there. I am very much like my mother. I am surprised that my father has any time for me at all, considering how much he seems to despise my mother. She did walk out on him and hasn't seen him since. He never wants to mention her name, so around him, I don't. I really have little to do with my father. He lives a few streets away from me, but we seldom see each other. He is rather pompous and we have very few interests in common, other than he likes the beach. I hope that fills you in somewhat."

"Thanks. I hope you didn't mind me asking, but I was puzzled how someone as great as you could be related to your father. I'm really sorry to be so blunt, but that's my impression. How about we switch subjects and talk about dessert. I am having the coffee sorbet and a decaf. What are you going to have?"

"I am settling on their tiramisu with an espresso. But enough gabbing about my family, I want to hear more about your family, perhaps tomorrow."

"You've got yourself a deal", I offered

My family history was certainly colorful enough for discussion. Dinner over with, we both felt full and satisfied. It was followed by a half hour stroll that concluded an exhausting day. We decide then to return to our room. Fortunately, Bruce had had the foresight to bring a key to the officially closed B & B; otherwise, we'd be sleeping on the porch. Strangely enough tonight we didn't make love. It wasn't lack of desire, but we were both so tired and lying in each other's arms was beautiful and comforting. We both drifted off into an idyllic sleep. I was awakened, yet again, by the smell of coffee. This time there were two roses on the tray. Bruce was stepping up his make-a-girl-happy skills, which was good to know.

"Thanks so much for this great start to another day", I exclaimed.

"Molly, my suggestion is that we have a leisurely breakfast and head back late morning, stopping off somewhere along the coast for lunch. We can, if you like, grab a few hours on the beach before I have to go to the office this evening. I'm sorry to do this to you, but I have a few loose ends to tie up before leaving tomorrow."

"That sounds wonderful, except for the leaving part, but I'll face that sad moment when the time comes."

"Come here, young lady, I want to start the day off right."

Every time he caressed me I felt as if an alarm clock for sex had been set off. My desire for Bruce seemed to increase with each love-making. His kisses were so passionate. I think we both felt we didn't have much time left together. He kissed my face and neck gently, whilst I caressed his back, letting out sighs of happiness. Then we were moving together as one. At last, Bruce rolled over, looked at me, and told me that he was crazy about me. He knew it was a very short time that we'd been together, but he felt so comfortable with me, to say nothing of the great sex that we had together. I echoed his thoughts. We lay there for a few more moments before the idea of coffee called out to me. We brewed a small pot, drank in silence, dressed, and headed downstairs for a gourmet treat.

Fruit salad, strawberry soufflé, crisp bacon, and French toast were the order of the day. I had never eaten a strawberry soufflé before. I hoped it wasn't the last time. I gorged myself, and didn't feel as if I could ever eat again.

Bruce asked, "What shall we do after checking out?"

"I think we've done enough sightseeing around town. How about we take the beach road and stop off whenever the mood strikes?"

"That sounds great. I must admit I don't feel too much like walking the streets this morning."

We sat for a while longer, savoring the moment, before we both jumped up and decided to pack and check out, which we did after thanking the owners for the wonderful accommodations and fine food. Bruce said that we hoped to return one day and took a couple of their business cards.

The B & B was definitely on my list of must-return-to places, if it were with Bruce. I told myself, *stop thinking like this.* I was rushing too much into the future. As the saying goes, *Live for the moment*

We drove south on A1A, the beach road, stopping at a British pub in Flagler Beach. If we hadn't eaten fish and chips the night before, that would have my choice. I wasn't terribly hungry after this morning's breakfast and opted for the fish pate and a light beer.

"Make that two please," Bruce said to the waitress, who looked as if she had had a particularly rough night. I don't think she had even bothered to re-apply her eye make-up which was caked on with black smudges under her eyes. She wouldn't have made the top ten in a beauty contest even if she'd had a good night's sleep.

We sat upstairs overlooking the beach. It wasn't very crowded and the sea was relatively calm. It was almost one, and I know Bruce had mentioned something about working later this afternoon. I mentioned it and he said that he would put in a few hours, but wondered if we could have a late dinner somewhere. I suggested that we eat at my place, which he was more than happy to do.

"Any questions you have about my family you can ask me then. I don't really feel like it right now," I said to Bruce.

"That's fine," he replied. "When our waitress comes around, let's order two large espressos."

"Fantastic," I said, while spotting our waitress chatting up one of the waiters. I beckoned her over to our table, to which she came rather begrudgingly.

"You want anything else?" she asked in a desultory fashion.

"Yes, please. We'd like two double espressos to go and the check."

"Coming right up," she said, in a very non-committal tone of voice.

You win some, lose some, and this would be one waitress I wouldn't mind losing. However, the coffee was to die for. It was thick, rich, and black. I pride myself on being somewhat of an expert on coffee. Living in Europe really got me interested in various types and I fully admitted to being a coffee snob. We lingered over our espressos, gazing out to sea. The sky was flecked with small clouds, as background for circling pelicans and seagulls. We were both reluctant to leave this peaceful scene, but knew that Bruce had office work to do. We drove home in relative silence. I kept dozing off and before I knew it we were at my front door.

"I presume you want to head straight on out, Bruce?"

"Yes, if you don't mind. The sooner I get things organized the sooner I can return to you. I'll call you when I'm leaving for your place."

He took my bags out and put them on the kitchen floor, kissed me with an intensity that aroused me into sexual frustration. I'd have to curb my desires until later on this evening.

"Thanks a million, my love. I had a marvelous time. I'll see you later on," he said.

I blew him a kiss and got on with unpacking, whilst thinking what to cook for dinner. I decided to make the Moroccan chicken curry. I had all the ingredients, which meant I didn't have to go to the grocery store. I'd make a green salad and a strawberry cake that had never failed me. By seven-thirty everything was ready. All that remained was for Bruce to call me. About five minutes later he phoned to say that he would be with me around eight. "Do you want a glass of red or a beer?" I asked.

"Oh, red would suit me, so I'll see you in a bit."

A few minutes later Jen called me with little expectation I would be home. I told her I had just arrived and filled her in on the great weekend. We agreed to meet Monday night at the Irish pub around seven. I told her I wouldn't be in a wonderful mood, since Bruce would be on his way back to Dearborn. She told me that she didn't mind as she would also be alone. Anyway, she couldn't wait to fill me in on the status of her love-life. The doorbell rang as I was finishing talking to her.

"I've got to go now, Jen. See you tomorrow night."

I opened the door to be greeted with a beautiful bouquet of yellow daisies.

"Oh, you shouldn't have done this, Bruce; they're gorgeous", I said, as I handed him a glass of red.

He kissed me in a distracted way, took the wine, and almost inhaled it. I poured him another one and told him dinner would be ready in about twenty minutes.

"Good, that gives us a chance to catch up." He reached into his pocket and brought out a blue box with a silver ribbon around it. "Molly, this is for you. I wanted to get you something that will remind you of me, and perhaps you will feel a little closer to me when you wear it."

I opened the box, and inside was a beautiful, fine gold chain with a cat and dog in gold and sapphires. I was overwhelmed.

"Oh, my goodness, this is just too beautiful. You really shouldn't have done this. The only thing I have for you is a photo of the two of us."

"Come here, Molly", he said, wrapping his arms around me. "You must know how I feel about you. The mere thought of saying goodbye to you is tearing at my soul, but I fully intend to come back in two weeks' time if that's good for you?"

"That would be fabulous, because I, too, feel sadness at the thought of your leaving."

I went to the mirror and put my necklace on. It was so delicate. I wondered if he knew that my favorite stone was a sapphire. He probably didn't, but I loved the necklace and would cherish wearing it.

"Dinner is ready", I announced a little later.

I'd set the table in the dining area. The table looked pretty with my blue and white dishes, blue napkins and the silver cutlery I'd inherited from my mother. I rarely used it but decided tonight was special. The curry was good. Actually, it was better than good. It wasn't spicy hot, yet the mixture of spices gave it an intensely rich flavor. Bruce had two helpings. He grinned before telling me that I wasn't just good in bed, I was a good cook, too!

Then a veritable lull came over the conversation, each of us no doubt contemplating our impending goodbyes, before I said, "Ready for salad, after the main meal, European style?"

He nodded in the affirmative. Bruce again broke our reverie asking me to fill him a little more about my family history.

"How about when we have dessert first; then I will spill more beans."

"That sounds good to me," Bruce said in acceptance.

"Let's have the cake and coffee in the living room."

The strawberry cake was everything I'd hoped it would be. My mother's recipes never let me down.

I continued on with the saga of my life, where I was born etc. My mother was half Welsh, so I later spent a few really good holidays there with my cousins Sossy and Ian, as a youngster.

My parents loved to buy houses, fix them up, and then sell them. I lived in about four before I turned thirteen. The last house we lived in before my parents divorced was fairly small, but the grounds were large with a swimming pool, and it had a huge oak tree that I loved to climb. I spent hours sitting on a large protruding branch reading and it used to drive my mother crazy as she could never get me to come down for meals.

Once I graduated, my mother said she was fed up with the dreary climate in England. She announced that she was going to Spain with her sister, Lily, my favorite aunt from Wales, and was determined to find somewhere to live there. She finally settled on the town of Javea which is on the east coast of Spain between Alicante and Valencia. She bought a home in the hills not far from a mountain called Mongo, with the Mediterranean in faint view.

I got a flat in London with my old roommate Jen and another girl from college. I found work with a pharmaceutical company dealing in medicines for animals. Although my jobs were mostly administrative, I was somewhat fulfilled in working for the good of our furry and feathered friends.

My summer and winter holidays were spent mostly in Spain with my mother, and on one visit, she told me she had met an American at a bridge tournament. He was a frequent visitor to Javea; his name was Douglas and he had a home in New Smyrna Beach, Florida. That part of the world was completely unfamiliar to me.

One summer my mother announced that she was marrying Douglas and would sell the place in Spain and move to the States. Of course, I was very happy for her, but sad about her moving so far away

My dad had remarried and was living in Surrey, England. We saw each other about once a month. He travelled to the States quite a bit, so I knew when I moved here I would see him from time to time, which made the transition somewhat easier.

As I had said before I moved to be here with her as she battled cancer to the end. She was way too young to die and I miss her every day. My dad remained in England until he died from natural causes. We didn't see very much of each other in his later years, but I knew he was well taken care of by my stepmother.

"That is my added family brief," I said as I took a large chunk of cake and followed it with a healthy sip of wine. Rehashing my past was quite taxing.

"Gosh, you really have an interesting family history and I'm thrilled that you shared more of it with me", he said.

Sweet desire was in his eyes, as if he wanted to cuddle me and protect me from the world, then envelope me with his manliness. He suggested we go upstairs. I didn't hesitate to say, *yes*, to that suggestion. I thought he'd never get 'round to it. If he hadn't, I knew that I would eventually make overtures.

I had the strangest feelings come over me. It was almost as if it was the first time we had made love. We looked at each other, removed our clothing, and hugged each other to the point where we could barely breathe. We didn't last very long as Bruce went from gentle to rather urgent in his lovemaking, but I loved it. He fell off me into an exhausted heap, repeatedly telling me that he loved me and hated the thoughts of leaving me. He made me promise to keep the weekend after next free. I told him that it was already engraved in my brain. He said he'd call me every night, except Monday night. He would be getting home fairly late;

besides I was having dinner with Jen. We kissed and held each other in loving embrace for many minutes, as if we both felt we might never be in eachother's arms again. Sleep came fast for us both from emotional exhaustion.

In the very early morning Bruce sat up and said that he had to tear himself away. He got dressed, and I threw on a bathrobe and we went downstairs. He grabbed me, kissed me for what seemed like an eternity.

We both said, "I love you."

I thanked him again for my beautiful necklace, watched him get in his car and roar away. I shut the door and wept. I couldn't stop crying as I got myself ready for work. I felt as if my heart would break into many pieces. Love was wonderful, but it was sometimes hard and cruel. Why did I have to fall for someone who lived so far away? Only time would tell what would happen to us. I fervently hoped that we'd be very busy today at the clinic. We were.

A young girl came in with two of the most beautiful kittens. She said they kept showing up at her doorstep for the last week or so. She was a college student and couldn't possibly keep them. We said we'd give them the necessary shots before sending them to the Humane Society. One of them was a misty gray with longish fur. The other one had gray and white markings, but her fur wasn't quite as long. I had been resisting getting a cat, but was on the point of adopting the long-haired kitty. However, I reminded myself that with all that was going on in my life right now, it wasn't the best decision. If I changed my mind I could always go to the Humane Society. Sadly, the kittens wouldn't be there longer than a month before they were put down. This was not something I really wanted to think about.

The day consisted mostly of giving shots to animals. We had a parrot that had fractured his wing, so we set that. He was quite chatty and highly amusing. What I loved about my job is that it didn't seem like work. How lucky was I to be doing something that I was so passionate about? I glanced at the clock and had one hour before I met Jen, and got the scoop on Charlie. His last name escaped me. I finished up the day by paying a few vendor bills and arranging meds for the next day, all the while thinking about Bruce. He consumed my thoughts and at times it was really hard for me to concentrate on the matter at hand.

I got to the restaurant before Jen, so I took the liberty of getting a table by the window in a secluded corner. I ordered a red wine for me and water for both of us. Jen arrived about ten minutes late, full of apologies.

"It's no big deal, darling," I said. "I haven't been here very long myself."

Jen ordered a white wine and asked, "Do you want to go first, or shall I?"

"Jen, you go first. I am bursting with curiosity to hear all about Charlie."

She filled me in on the three evenings she had spent with him. His full name was Charlie Davies and he was from the Jacksonville office. "We had the best time, Molly. He was easy to talk to, funny and I found him sexy."

"Spill the beans. Did you, or did you not, sleep with him?"

"I actually had made my mind up that I wouldn't sleep with him until I knew him better, but we went back to the company flat and one thing lead to another. It was amazing. I thought that would be it for us, once he went back to Jacksonville, but he called me from there and is coming down this weekend to stay with me. We will see where it leads. I am not in any rush, but I really like him a lot."

"That's awesome. I guess we should order before I tell you about my weekend with Bruce."

We both ordered broiled grouper, and sweet potato fries. When the waiter came we ordered more wine. It never ceased to amaze me that Jen and I had remained close friends. The fact that she ended up in the same town as me, was astonishing. We were so lucky to have each other to confide in.

"Jen, the weekend was truly wonderful. We stayed at this quaint B & B, had the best breakfast I have had in years, a bathroom anyone would kill for, with the biggest shower I have ever seen. We strolled around town, had great food and it goes without saying that our sex life was off the charts. I never thought I would feel anything for another man, but he makes me laugh and I feel very comfortable in his presence. And, I find him incredibly attractive. Of course, the whole situation is a probably a dead ender, but I've decided to enjoy the time we have together and not get too wrapped up in thinking about the future."

Jen responded, "Well, girlfriend, it sounds as if you have a winner. What makes me chuckle is remembering you talking about his father. He must take after his mother, or perhaps his father has hidden talents that you don't know about."

"Who knows, Jen; it does seem weird. From what I gather, he's not that close to his father, although they live two streets away from each other. Perhaps we can double date when you have had a bit more time with Charlie and me with Bruce."

We were interrupted by our waiter who was balancing our meals precariously on a large tray. When he asked us whether we wanted more wine, there was a simultaneous *yes, please.*

"We can walk it off on the beach after dinner," I said. We'd been coming here for a few years and we'd never had a bad meal. We had a ton of restaurants in the area, among them many really good ones, along with the usual fast food chains that were good enough when in a hurry.

After three wines, coffee was in order. We ordered espressos and the check. The wind had picked up and was thick with humidity. We decided to take a walk with the wind at our backs. The moon shone on the water giving it a mystical look. It was almost black with gold shimmers. We walked briskly for about a mile before heading back to our cars.

"I enjoyed this evening, Jen. We'll talk in the week and perhaps we can organize something for the weekend. I don't for a minute think that Bruce and I will be going away again. I think when he's here he'd prefer to go the beach and relax."

"That'll be terrific, Molly. See you, hopefully this weekend."

Driving home I had a sudden feeling of intense loneliness. I don't know why I kept feeling as if this whole affair, for want of a better word, would fizzle out once Bruce got back to Dearborn. I had to cease being so negative, but it wasn't easy. Once home, I put the television on, poured myself a brandy and fell asleep watching some old Clark Gable movie. I was amazed that I slept well. Thank the

Lord that I loved my job; otherwise, the days might seem interminable.

We had a house call to make that morning. One of our clients' horses was poorly so we drove out to the farm to see him. Its name was Bounce, a really dream horse. Outside of my late, beloved Starlight, he had the sweetest nature of any horse that I'd known. He never objected to being examined. In this instance, the vet diagnosed a case of the croup, but was easily curable with prescribed medicine.

When I got back to the clinic there was a delivery on the doorstep. A dozen beautiful peach colored roses in a vase with a message that simply said, "I love you and miss you already, Bruce". My thoughts reverted to our lovemaking. I could feel his soft touch; imagine his kisses, his tongue searching for mine.

"Snap out of it, Molly", I said to myself, as I saw the waiting room with three clients holding three large cats. When my workday day finally drew to a close, I went home, again feeling alone. I'd spent two years by myself and never felt like this. I couldn't be bothered to cook so made myself a sandwich, poured a glass of wine, and decided to become a couch potato for the evening. The phone ran around eight.

"Hello? Oh, Bruce, it's you! I'm so happy to hear from you. Did you have a safe flight back? By the way, the flowers are gorgeous, thank you."

"Darling, I was thinking about you on the plane and realized how much I needed you. I can hardly wait for Friday night, next week, to arrive. I'm glad that work is crazy right now, as it doesn't allow me too much time to think about you."

We went on to chat for about forty-five minutes, when he said, "Well, I'd better go and eat, because right now I am driving myself crazy picturing you stark naked. I can feel your soft skin, your beautiful breasts leaning into me. I just want you so much."

"I want you too", I said. Kiddingly, I added, "I'm going to hang up now before this conversation is overheard by the naughty police."

That broke the sexual tension. We said our fond goodbyes until the next time we spoke. I put the phone down, and heaved a joyful sigh with the anticipation that we would be together again in less than two weeks

Bruce called me Tuesday night, rather frenetic, to say he had a meeting on Wednesday and Thursday and wouldn't be able to call me until Friday night. I hardly had time to say goodbye before he had to hang up. He did confirm he was flying out the following Friday to be with me. So I thought I'd prepare a few meals prior to his arrival to give us more intimate time together.

The weather was perfect at this time of the year. I decided to swim every evening after work. The pool was usually empty around six, which I loved. I didn't have to make polite conversation with anyone. I knew a lot of people by name only. I had one other friend in the development, but not close like Jen and I were. Karin and I played quite a bit of tennis, but she worked at the Racetrack as an accountant, so we generally only saw each other on those occasions. We hadn't played much recently, and now that Bruce was in the picture, no doubt I would be playing tennis with her even less.

The days passed calmly. I managed to get a lot of home administrative stuff done, cooked a few meals for the freezer, did swim every night and was amazed how happy I was, being alone. I had lived by myself for years and couldn't imagine sharing my house with another human being. A dog or cat had been high on the list of roommates until now, but things could change at any given moment.

The designated Friday rolled around and I was shocked how nervous I was to see Bruce again. I deliberated over what to wear. I liked my body. It was somewhat voluptuous, yet decidedly feminine. I picked out a red, snug dress and took forever putting my makeup on - which was ridiculous, as it would be smudged off in record time, if I had my way.

The doorbell rang at the estimated time of arrival. My heartbeat began to race as I opened the door to find Bruce before me. He flung his briefcase on the floor, stripped off his tie, grabbed me, pushed me onto the kitchen counter, ripped my underwear off, and was taking me before I even had a chance to make a fake protest. My breath almost left my body. I had never felt so alive and sexy in my entire life.

When we had come down from the mountain, Bruce exclaimed, "My love, I'm so sorry that I acted like a wild animal, but I have been dreaming of this moment all week.

I promise next time to slowly seduce you and make it last forever, well at least try to."

"No need to apologize, my wonderful lover. I've never been had on a kitchen counter before. Now, getting back to earth, do you want a wine?"

He smiled and asked me for a glass of red. We sat for several minutes in total silence. The air was magnetic.

"I adore you," he said. His voice was low and fluid, and was utterly mesmerizing.

"I adore you too, my most handsome man."

We sat on the couch, embracing each other for some time until I heard a slight snore coming from Bruce. He appeared to be in a deep sleep. I wriggled out from under my exhausted lover, walked into the kitchen, looking at the counter in a totally different light. I would never again be able to think of it solely for kitchen purposes.

I guess Bruce must have slept for about two hours. When he woke up, he looked at me and said that he was bushed and suggested we went to bed, apologetically saying, "I can't promise anything when it comes to love making tonight."

I was lying on the bed in my nightgown, when Bruce proved himself wrong. He pushed my nightgown up over my head, tossing it on the floor. He caressed my inner thighs until I couldn't stand it any longer. He entered me smoothly yet with intensity. I arched my back, digging my finger nails into his shoulders. Our rhythms ended suddenly with a final, deep thrust that caused us to climax together. Satiated, we fell into a sweaty heap. Sleep came instantaneously after. Neither of us awoke until the morning, when the sun was shining through the lavender drapes, giving the room a warm glow. This was another reason I loved Florida so much. The sun shone more often than not, raining just enough for one to do boring chores.

Bruce arose first and didn't disappoint me. I smelled coffee and caught sight of the tray with a small bunch of flowers from my garden, resting in a coffee mug.

"Thanks a million, darling. You have totally spoiled me and I'll always expect this first-class treatment from now on."

"Dream on baby," he said grinning from ear to ear. He passed me my mug of coffee and jumped in bed beside me. "What's on the agenda for today, Molly?"

"Well, we could just take it really easy; go into town, grab a coffee and walk the beach before lunch, then come home for a rest. I have mean lasagna in the freezer that I made during the week for dinner. How does that sound?"

"Just the ticket, if you ask me", he said, kissing my cheek.

We took our time getting dressed for the beach. I threw on shorts and a tank top, Bruce wore shorts and a grey tee shirt. His physique was fantastic and I couldn't help staring at him.

"What's the matter, Babe?"

He caught me off guard with the *Babe* bit. I didn't like to be called that. David was the only person who had ever called me that.

"Nothing, I was just thinking how handsome you look. But to change the subject, I'd prefer that you didn't call me *Babe*, if you don't mind."

"No problem, Gorgeous, I can do that."

After pancakes and eggs we set off to walk the beach. I had thrown a couple of chairs and a blanket in the car and my current novel, suggesting Bruce might want to take a book or magazines. For the number of times I went to the beach, one might suspect boredom setting in. It never happened. The more I went, the more I wanted to go.

We walked hand in hand at the water's edge, letting the cool ripples lap over our feet. Bruce chatted about his job, telling me that he was going through one of the busiest periods; which, in actuality was a good thing. He didn't expect me to understand the intricacies of his world but glossed over the bare essentials.

My job was easy to talk about. Most weeks were basically the same, unless we were called out on a job, as was the case with the sick horse. I adored horses. They reminded me of my pony, Starlight. He had a white star on his forehead and stood sixteen hands. He was the gentlest creature I'd ever known. I had him for almost two years when one day he impaled himself on a tall picket fence trying to jump over it, and we had to put him down. I thought my whole world was over. It seemed that way for several months, until I realized that his spirit would always be with me. To this day I think of him and miss him so much.

We walked several miles, before deciding to hit the coffee shop for espressos. Yes, I was so predictable with my caffeine habit. Whilst we were sipping the strong, hot coffee, Bruce looked at me in an almost awkward way.

I asked, "What's up, Bruce?"

"I'm not going to be able to come next weekend, but I was wondering if the following weekend you could come to Dearborn and I could show you around a little? Not that there is much to see, but I'd love it. I'll pay for your fare. I get a certain allowance for travel. Will you think about it?"

There wasn't much thinking to be done. I said, "Yes", without hesitating.

Bruce look elated and hugged me tight. "That's made my day. Thanks, Molly. I promise to give you a good time."

I suggested we grab a croissant at a nearby cafe. All the walking and fresh air had given us appetites. We ate them with a bit of butter and honey and washed them down with the rest of our coffee. After finishing, we looked at each other with knowing grins, and headed to my house for our well-earned 'rest'.

Once home, we looked at each other expectantly and went upstairs. Bruce slowly took off his tee shirt, all the time looking at me. He stepped out of his shorts, grabbed me, helping me take my shirt and shorts off, before gently pushing me onto the bed.

The sight of his manhood filled my body with such desire, that I begged him to take me.

"I will in my own time," he murmured.

His kisses covered my breasts. I held onto him as if I would fall away. When he finally entered me, he tried to take it slowly, but we were both too eager. In a matter of a few minutes I was screaming. He covered my mouth with his, taking away my sound. We were shaking with sheer ecstasy. He then lay beside me, kissing my entire body, I started to moan again, and he sought my mouth with his kisses.

Suddenly, for some unknown reason, David's face flashed upon my mind and I lost all feeling of desire. I became rigid. Bruce sensed something was awry and asked me what the matter was. He wondered if he hadn't pleased me, or did he do something that I didn't care for. How could I possibly tell him that I was thinking of another man?

"Oh no, it's nothing like that. I just remembered that it was my cousin, Sossy's birthday today. It made me very melancholy." I wasn't totally lying. It was her birthday today. I silently thanked her for her being born on this very day, but was furious that her life had ended so abruptly at the age of thirty-four.

"I'm so sorry, Molly, but thankful it wasn't anything to do with me."

"Don't be ridiculous, everything you do with and for me is more than I could wish for. I cannot believe I have known you such a short time. I feel like getting up and having a glass of wine. Do you want one?"

"Sure, I'll come downstairs in a minute. I'd like to watch a bit of the golf. Do you mind?"

"No, that's fine, go right ahead." What I wanted to say was, *that's one thing I haven't missed at all*, but decided to keep mum. There are worst things than golf on television; football was one, baseball another. I hadn't met a man that wasn't interested in sports, and I thought if I had, perhaps there would be something wrong with him.

I went downstairs and opened a bottle of cold Chablis and poured it into two crystal glasses.

When he came down I gave him his wine and said, "I'm going to take a bath. I'll see you in a bit. I've got a good book right now. Grab yourself something to eat from the fridge if you get peckish."

He barely acknowledged me, which made me somewhat jealous of the game, but I told myself that he was after all, human and a man!

It must have been a darn good match, as I remained upstairs reading for almost two hours. I figured he'd probably fallen asleep. I threw on shorts and a tank top and went downstairs. Sure enough, he was dozing on the couch. He'd fixed himself bread and cheese and taken a piece of the apple pie I'd made the night before. A good sign, I thought. He's a man who doesn't need to be overly pampered. Bread and cheese and another glass of wine sounded just up my alley. It was almost as if we had been together for eons. We were so comfortable with one another. Well, on second thought, I wasn't entirely comfortable about telling him that I wasn't interested in making intimate love, because I had just started my period.

That would take courage to tell him, so I guess I was not totally at ease just yet.

I made short work of the bread and cheese, being ravenous at this time of the month. I heard Bruce fidget. He arose from the sofa, sat next to me and gave me a kiss. I loved it when his lips and tongue met mine.

"Sorry I slept, but I guess I really needed it. How about we go upstairs?"

Now was the time to tell him. "Bruce, I'm not in the mood today. I've got my period and really don't feel up to it."

"That's fine. We can have a lazy time of it, watching television, and cuddling. In fact, we can act like an old married couple."

I gulped. That was rushing it a bit. We spent the rest of the day and evening, slouching on the sofa, drinking wine and picking at the cheese and demolishing the pie I had made. Sunday rolled around and we decided to go to Deland and wander around Stetson University, grab a spot of lunch, before Bruce took off at around five.

Stetson University reminds me so much of a mini Princeton. The main street has many restaurants. We opted for this Greek place. Their feta cheese salad was a knockout. He chose a retsina wine to drink and I braved it enough to order the same.

"I'm going to miss you something fierce these next two weeks, and can hardly wait to show you around Dearborn." Bruce said.

"I'm excited to be coming to Dearborn I'll have to admit."

Bruce packed everything with half an hour to spare. We sat on the sofa, holding each other so tight I could almost feel the breath leaving me. We kissed with passion. Finally, the dreaded moment came for him to leave. I could feel the tears welling up, but didn't want Bruce to see me cry. It was too late, as tears rolled down my cheeks.

"Now, don't be sad, Molly. It's not as if we'll never see each other again. I'll call you every day." He held me one last time, then opened the door and was gone.

Dearborn, here I come, I thought as I went upstairs with a mug of hot, thick cocoa, feeling as if someone had punched me in the stomach. I had two long weeks before we would be together again, and I prayed work would be hectic.

I was right; work was extremely busy. We had an influx of cats and dogs to give shots too, and to change things up, we had two visits during the first week to a local farm whose cows had a virus. I loved these animals. They always seem so soft and appear dumb, but are far from it. They have the most piercing, large eyes which speak to one. We were lucky to be able to give the sick ones' shots and would come back in a week to see how they were doing.

I phoned Jen Monday evening to see how things were progressing. She apologized for not having called me regarding a double date, but Charlie didn't get in until fairly late Saturday night. I told her it was fine as I wasn't feeling at my most sociable.

"Bruce can't come this coming weekend and I am going to Dearborn the following weekend. I'm really looking forward to it. I hope I don't have to see too much of his father. I gather they aren't that close, which isn't surprising really. I'm glad that it isn't winter time, as I don't think I could stand that. August should be pretty nice up there. When are you seeing Charlie again?"

"I'm not sure. He's got commitments this coming weekend and is sailing with a buddy the following weekend, so we are aiming to get together after that. Maybe we'll go to St. Augustine and stay in the same B & B you did. We'll see. It's going well with him, but it isn't as intense as your relationship with Bruce. Anyway, shall we have dinner Saturday night?"

"Great! Why don't you come over around five?"

"Yes, will do but in the meantime, have a great week, Molly."

"You too, Jen. Bye for now."

I decided to do some research on Dearborn. Whenever I visited a place I was always anal about research it first. One would almost suspect me of being an analytical person which I'm not, but have always been intensely interested in knowing something about the place I'm about to visit. I was a tad disappointed when I found out how Dearborn got its name. It was established in 1836 and known as Dearborn Ville, named after patriot Henry Dearborn, a general in the American Revolution and Secretary of War under President Thomas Jefferson. I much prefer my romantic notion that it came from a founding pioneer family who named their village, Dearborn, after their first darling (dear born) child.

The city dates back to a 1929 consolidation vote that established its present-day borders by merging Dearborn and neighboring Fordson which feared being absorbed by Detroit. The area between the two towns was and is today, in part undeveloped.

As I already knew, it was the headquarters to Ford Motor Company The other pertinent piece of information is that the University of Michigan has a campus here, as well as the Henry Ford Community College. It's the eighth largest city in the State of Michigan.

I guess I will get a better feel when I actually go there in a couple of weeks.

The week sped by. Bruce called me every night. We talked for what seemed like ages. It was at least half an hour every night. He told me how much he missed me and longed to hold me which got me quite hot under the collar. We engaged in a bit of phone sex. It wasn't half bad! I didn't really have too much to tell him. My work was pretty much routine. He said that he was busy working on a new solid fuel propulsion project. It was the first I'd heard about this kind of project. It wasn't really surprising considering we'd only known each other for several weeks. There was a ton of information I still hadn't shared with him. It would filter out slowly in time.

Saturday rolled around with alacrity. It was a gorgeous day, so I decided to spend most of it lounging by the pool. The snowbirds would start returning in a month or two and then it would become very crowded. I'd better make the most of it now. I didn't have to cook tonight. I hoped Jen would go along with my plan to eat outside.

I adored swimming. As a teenager, I swam for my county in England. We used to practice four times a week for about an hour and a half. No wonder they called me *thunder thighs"*. *Flabby thighs* would be more appropriate today. I didn't swim with quite the same vim and vigor, but did about twenty laps. It felt wonderful afterwards. I guess like all of us we are very hard on ourselves. *For my age*, I looked pretty good. I don't know who invented that phrase, but I hate it! I was thirty-three, turning thirty-four next spring. It never occurred to me to think that my biological clock was running out. It bothered other people much more than it did me.

I stayed at the pool for about four hours. I'd taken a snack, a drink, and a good book and worked on my tan. Around 3 pm I decided to go home, watch a movie that had to be returned to the library by Monday and get ready for Jen. She showed up with a bottle of chardonnay in her hand.

"You really didn't need to bring that Jen, but thanks anyway. Let's sit outside on the deck as it's so beautiful."

My house overlooked the Inland Waterway and marshes. At this hour, the sunset was magical. Orange and yellow hues bathed the trees and a solitary egret stood in the marshes. He came every evening. I'd named him Sam, regardless of the fact that he might possibly be a she!

"Let's have the scoop, Molly," Jen said, before we'd even had a chance to take the first sip of wine. I had some delicious sharp cheddar cheese to nibble on.

"Well, there really isn't that much to tell you Jen. We had a laid-back weekend. Bruce told me that he couldn't come down this weekend but wanted me to go to Dearborn the following one. I'm very excited to go. The thought of seeing him again is awesome, as I'm looking forward to a change of pace. I haven't been in a big town for ages. I'm nervous about the whole situation, but feel very comfortable with him. He obviously does with me, as he felt no compunction in asking if he could watch the golf. Is there a man who doesn't like sports? Anyway, he's working on some solid fuel propulsion project. That's about it really. I mean how much can anyone find out about someone in a month. There's plenty he doesn't know about me. So, now it's your turn."

We finished the cheese, pouring ourselves a second glass of wine. Then Jen said, "My date with Charlie was great. I only saw him on Saturday. He drove up from Miami in the morning. We went into Daytona and had dinner at The Top of the Hilton. The view is spectacular. We get on very well, but there are some electric sparks flying around but not to the intensity with you and Bruce. I like him a lot, and think that things might hot up down the road. Oh, I know, I slept with him, which was a bit slutty and quite orgasmic. In a way I wish I hadn't, as he expected it after dinner. It was lustful, not romantic sex, but great nevertheless. He's coming up in a couple of weeks' time on Friday and that's the weekend we want to go to St. Augustine, so I'll pick your brains about the bed and breakfast. What say we go and eat? Despite wolfing down that cheese, I'm starving."

"Fine with me; just give me five minutes to go to the loo and I'll meet you at the car. It's my turn to drive," I told Jen.

Dinner was outstanding, just as I knew it would be. We decided to skip dessert and just have espressos.

'I'll flesh out all the details for St. Augustine and call you in the week, Jen."

"Thanks, and by the way, I'm driving you to the airport. No ifs, buts, or maybes."

"That would be super, as I was wondering how I'd get there."

Another fun night had drawn to a close. We've had so many good times together I couldn't imagine my life without Jen in it. I think she felt the same way.

"The plane leaves at seven in the evening on Friday. Will you be able to leave work a tad early?"

"I don't see why not," Jen said as she unlocked her car door.

"See you Friday then," I said, as she started the engine up, waved, and was gone.

I quite liked her two-door Mustang, but my priority was my house. Jen's had always been cars. Her apartment was functional and ordinary unlike the person living in it. Maybe that's why we got along as well as we were quite different in many ways.

Sunday was a lazy, do-nothing day. The highlight was talking to Bruce. We were on the phone for about an hour. I always questioned people who talked forever on the phone and now I was doing the exact same thing. It wasn't as if we had tons to say, but just caught each other up on what we had been doing. Bruce said he would meet me at Detroit airport. I had flown zillions of times but was always a mess before takeoff. Jen picked me up on time and we chatted all the way to the airport, nervously on my part.

"Have a great trip and I'll pick you up Monday night around six", Jen said.

"Thanks a million, girlfriend. I'll be sure to repay you somehow. You have a good weekend and I promise to fill you in when I get back."

With that she sped off, kicking up sand as she disappeared into the amber horizon.

Wouldn't you know it; I had an adult male chatterbox sitting next to me on the plane. It's not that I am anti-social, but I prefer not to talk before I take off. I like to collect my thoughts, and in this instance, anticipate being with Bruce and discovering Dearborn. I responded in curt fashion, hoping he would take the hint. The man was rather portly and very boring. I gleaned that he was trying to pick me up. However, after a few short and sharp replies to his questions, he finally got the hint and shut up.

The flight was very smooth. The steward assigned to our section was efficient and funny. I had a couple of drinks and some nuts to calm my nerves that were frayed a bit because of anticipation and excitement. I had barely settled in when the captain announced that we were landing in ten minutes. The time had flown by.

Since I only had carry-on luggage, I didn't have to go to the baggage claim area. Bruce said he'd meet me as I got off the plane. I touched up my makeup, fussed with my hair, sucking on a butterscotch candy to stop my ears popping. I had butterflies in my stomach. I couldn't remember a time when I was this tense. At least it was a good tense. That counted for something.

I knew Bruce would be there. He was such a punctual guy. Sure enough, there he was, grinning from ear to ear. I walked straight into his arms, being greeted with a kiss so passionate that I could have stayed locked in his embrace, if it hadn't been such a public place.

"Hello, my gorgeous one. It's fantastic to see you. You have no idea how much I have been longing for this moment."

"Oh, I think I do, as I have been looking forward to it as much as you. I am excited to see Dearborn, your house and just having time alone with you."

We held hands, making sure we stayed together, connected as one. Once in the car, it didn't take more than forty minutes to get to his house. He lived in a quaint street of row houses. They almost looked Georgian, with multi colored brick facades with a variety of trees and flowers in front of each house. Cars idled by and children played on the sidewalk. We pulled up outside a red brick house, wider than most town houses I remembered, accented by an array of flowers planted in the small square of garden surrounded by an intricate fence. Bruce opened the car door for me, helped me out, and grabbed my small suitcase.

"Welcome to 110 Blakely Street, Molly. I hope you are going to feel at home here."

"I hope so, darling; the house looks so quaint. I can't wait to see the rest."

He opened the door and followed me inside. No sooner had I put my handbag down, then he took me in his arms, kissing me for what seemed like an age. I was brimming over with amorous excitement.

"How about we go upstairs right now?" he suggested. "We can have a tour of my house a little later on."

"You won't get an argument out of me," I said, unbuttoning my shirt as I climbed the stairs.

By the time we got to the bedroom, he'd taken his shirt and coat off, unzipped his trousers, and let them fall to the ground. I could see how excited he was! He pulled me down onto the bed, undressed the rest of me, caressing my breasts until I let out a cry.

"Take me now, please. I am going to explode with frustration if you don't."

He climbed on top of me taking me swiftly. We were so in sync with one another that we cried out together with intense pleasure.

He looked at me and said, "Welcome to my home, darling".

I lay on my back, feeling relaxed and happy, managing to say, "I'm looking forward to seeing the rest of the house. It'll be so much fun being together for the next few days."

Bruce put on a pair of shorts and a tee shirt and proposed that we finish off the upstairs. He had two other bedrooms that were quite large. They were decorated in a masculine fashion. Both rooms had twin beds, a chest of drawers, and a couple of prints on the walls. Nothing that was memorable. It was exactly as I had expected. We proceeded downstairs to the kitchen. This was somewhat larger than mine and very modern. It included a combination flat top stove and oven, a large microwave and a fancy fridge with an icemaker. The kitchen was painted white and had a white kitchen table and four functional chairs.

We moved on to the living room. It was a warm and inviting room, painted dark beige. There were two brown sofas, a rather large high definition television, and a desk that was quite the most beautiful one I had ever seen. It was surely an antique. There were a few paintings on the walls and in the middle of one wall was a fireplace. It was a cozy room and one that I could envisage sitting by the fireside with a glass of wine on a winter's night. *Winter? Perish that thought!* We finished the tour with the study. It was perfunctory. The dining room was rather dull in comparison to the living room. It had a table, six chairs, and a boring looking sideboard. I guess men don't entertain.

"Bruce, I love the living room, and have fallen in love with the desk. Where did you get it?"

"It was my maternal grandmother's, and I agree with you; it is the best piece of furniture in the house. Now, my suggestion for the evening is that we get changed and go for dinner in the downtown part of Dearborn."

"It sounds wonderful," I said, going up to him and kissing him gently on the lips.

We went upstairs and I unpacked a bit. Bruce showed me the closet and a cleared-out dresser drawer for me. I felt like part of an old married couple in some ways, in other ways, as if I were just another visitor to this bachelor's pad.

"You look stunning, Molly," he said, and followed up with, "But you'd look good in a paper bag".

"Thanks a lot, darling." I was thinking that he looked drop dead gorgeous, but I decided to keep my thoughts to myself for now.

It was almost dark outside, but I asked him if I could see the garden before we left. He opened the kitchen door to a narrow strip of lawn with a couple of flower beds. On the left side was a high wall with a few half dead vines, to the other side a high, wooden fence. It felt somewhat claustrophobic after my garden, but his house was located in a crowded residential area town, and I guess he was lucky to have a backyard. Another thought flashed through my head. There were no photographs anywhere in the house. I didn't feel like saying anything right then, but perhaps tomorrow I would pluck up the courage to do so.

"It's very quaint," I offered.

"You don't have to lie. It's not quaint at all. It has zip character, but it is my own personal space and for that I am thankful. Anyway, let's go for dinner."

I hadn't got a clue as to where we were going. I switch off somewhat when I'm a passenger. Besides, I was tired and really needed something to eat. We came to a square that was bustling with people, lights, and loud rock music. Bruce went around the square a couple of times before someone pulled out and left us his parking spot.

"We are going to this Greek restaurant in front of us. As I seem to remember, you are rather partial to Greek cuisine. It's authentic and the portions are copious."

We were seated at a table in the corner of the room. It was decorated in blue and white with many photographs of different areas in Greece. Bruce ordered two waters and a bottle of house white. The waiter brought bread and butter, which I dived into like a starving waif, after having had a good bit of my first glass of wine.

"What are you going to eat, Bruce? I think I'm going to have the moussaka."

"I'm going to have the lamb shanks with a salad. Changing the subject, I thought that tomorrow after visiting my father, as I promised him, we could do a brief tour of Dearborn in my car. Sunday, if we feel like it, we can pick a few places that you really like and do a walking tour. Just having the weekend doesn't give us much time to really do a lot. The next time you come we can do different things. There will be another time, won't there, Molly?"

"Bloody hell, you're rushing me a bit, aren't you, luv? Let me enjoy this weekend before we plan the next one," I said, trying unsuccessfully to put some humor into my reply.

I regretted speaking a tad rudely, but decided not to apologize. I was feeling a little boxed in right then, despite my feeling crazy about this man. I was not looking forward to seeing his father; however, I did take some solace from the fact that Bruce wasn't close to him.

Before anything else was said, our food arrived and we both ate in comparative silence. I started feel human again halfway through the meal.

"My meal is really good, Bruce. You were right about the food being excellent. Seriously, I am excited to have such a handsome tour guide to take me around. I am also hoping that you can come down for a weekend."

"Don't see why not. My work schedule isn't too loaded right now, so I could probably take a day off and stay until Monday night. How are you fixed for the weekend after next? This coming one won't work as I have a seminar to attend on the Saturday and an industry dinner that night."

"That would work for me. It's not as if I have a full social life. The only person I see on a regular basis is Jen, so I'll mark it on my calendar."

We both decided dessert was a must and opted for the fried ice cream and the obligatory espressos. I hadn't had fried ice cream in ages and had forgotten how delicious it was. I scooped it down rather rapidly. The coffee was thick and strong, just the way I like it.

Bruce leaned over to me and kissed me softly on the lips. "I'm sorry we have to visit my father tomorrow, but it won't be for long. As you know, I'm not his biggest fan, but am his son and have a slight obligation to please him."

"Oh, that's alright, I don't care really. It's not as if we have to spend the weekend with him."

We laughed, swigged the last drop of our coffee, and sauntered out into the balmy night air. The square was quiet now and the moon shone down on the sidewalk, giving it a glassy effect. It was ten o'clock and most of the restaurants had closed. The traffic was somewhat thinner than when we arrived, but still busy. I was imagining this place in the winter with snow on the ground and freezing cold winds, no doubt. Just the thought sent a shiver throughout my body. Bruce noticed it and asked me what the matter was.

"Oh, nothing really, I was just imagining the winter time here."

He grinned. "You really are a hot house plant, aren't you?"

"I can't deny that," I said chuckling away.

We walked arm in arm to the car feeling content with the world around us. Once back at the house, Bruce asked me if I'd care for a brandy, which I accepted readily, and we adjourned to the living room.

He lit a fire that sent flames shooting upward. The orange glow gave the room an even warmer appearance. We sat down on the sofa sipping on the warm brandy. We looked at each other and our thoughts must have been the same. We undressed each other in a frenzy of desire. He kissed my breasts, my back, and my belly moving down to my thighs. I arched my back, digging my fingers into him, responding with deep sighs. Finally, he settled his weight on me and took me with such intensity that I cried out, hardly recognizing my own voice. He was thick, hard, and hot inside me. He covered my mouth with kisses, taking my sounds into his throat. When we climaxed together, we were both shaking, and then laughing at how small the sofa was, but it didn't seem to matter at all. We gently rolled onto the floor on the beautiful, soft animal rug, smothering each other with kisses, relishing the silence, taking in our nakedness with naughty delight.

After many moments of tenderly caressing each other, Bruce got up and went and got us another brandy. He put out the fire that took on a grayness of a winter's night.

"Let's go to bed," he said

I followed him up the stairs, climbed into the bed, put my arm around him, and slept soundly until I was awakened with the aroma of coffee.

"You realize that I shall expect this service every morning in the future."

He smiled, kissed me, and told me that whatever my heart desired, he'd try and satisfy my wishes.

I dressed casually, inwardly dreading going to his father's. We sat outside in the garden drinking our coffee and munching on some French toast Bruce had made. *A man who cooks can't be a bad thing*, I thought. He looked at me knowingly, saying that he knew I wasn't enamored about going to see his dad. I told him that it was perfectly fine and I understood that duty called. We finished our breakfast, did the dishes, and left for his dad's.

"We could walk, but since we are going to do a tour of the town later on, we'll take the car this time", Bruce said.

His father did indeed live very close by! I hope he wasn't going to pester us. Once there, Bruce walked round and opened the car door for me. *A rarity in this modern world*, I told myself as he took my arm and squeezed it. He rang the doorbell, which was answered with alacrity. Standing there, with a grin from ear to ear was Mike followed by this beautiful Labrador mix dog.

"Hello, Molly, this is a treat for me. Welcome to my humble abode."

"Nice to see you, too, Mike. What's your dog's name?"

"Oh, this is Brandy. He's a dear. Now come on in and let's have some coffee and cake."

I wasn't sure what to expect, but once inside I was absolutely dumb struck. The house was magnificent. I couldn't have decorated a place better myself. Pastel walls in the hall, covered with beautiful art work; a magnificent marble and wood occasional table with an antique lamp, decorated what would have otherwise been a boring entrance way.

"Let's do the obligatory tour first before we sit down and eat some delicious chocolate cake that this local baker makes. It's to die for, and I remember your penchant for desserts", Mike offered.

"Thanks, Mike; that would be wonderful", I replied.

We were lead into the office, which was functional, with everything in it reeking of money and good taste. Several beautiful oil paintings adorned the walls. They were pastoral scenes, probably to remind him of what he didn't have here. A beautiful carved mahogany desk was in the center of the room and a leather, studded recliner completed the furnishings. We then moved on to the living room. I gasped when we walked in.

It was probably one of the best living rooms I had ever been in. It was very large. The walls were painted in a very pale red. There were two matching sofas that were red and beige. A coffee table with four animal legs sat between them. The fireplace was artificially aglow, and on the mantelshelf, were gorgeous china figurines. I have a couple of pieces of Lladro, but these were definitely from somewhere else. They had an almost Chinese look to them. There was a flat screen TV that didn't overpower the room, situated between two beautiful red leather recliners.

"Mike, this house is marvelous. I adore the way you have decorated it."

"Oh, I had nothing to do with the décor. Bruce's mother was responsible for all of this."

Once again, I was somewhat taken aback as there were no photographs anywhere to be seen. But, I didn't feel it was my place to comment just yet.

"Well, my dear, let's head into the kitchen for some refreshments. I don't want to keep you, as I know you have a lot of sightseeing to do. The kitchen was as I expected. Everything in it was up to date, expensive, and discretely sophisticated. We sat at the table, talking about this and that and eating the cake, which I did admit was scrumptious.

After about twenty minutes Bruce got and up and said that we really should hit the town, if we were going to see as much as possible in two days. I couldn't help thinking that there wasn't a whole lot to see other than cars. *Prove me wrong*, I thought, as we said our goodbyes.

"Well, that wasn't so bad was it, Molly?"

"No, not at all, but I was so surprised to see how lovely your father's house is. He told me that he owns two, so where is the other one?"

"He just sold one not far from here two weeks ago, so now he is down to just the one in Dearborn and one in New Smyrna Beach. To change the subject, I thought we could visit the Henry Ford museum first. I don't know how interested you are in the history of cars, but we could just take a quick tour of it before we have lunch."

"I'm up for anything," I replied.

The museum was immense. I don't think I have ever been to a museum complex this vast in my entire life. We saw J.F. Kennedy's limousine, the bus that Rosa Parks rode on, and we watched a movie of them building a special type of truck. The number of cars they had must have added up to many hundreds. After a while, my brain told me that it had had enough.

"Bruce, do you mind if we take a quick swing into the gift store?"

"That's fine. We should think about lunch. I know you like hamburgers and I know a wonderful roadside cafe that has the best burgers in town."

Before leaving, I bought a few postcards, a miniature corvette for Jen and a pair of miniature car earrings for myself. The museum was the kind of place that you have to return to over and over again in order to see everything.

On the way to the diner, Bruce was filling me in on some of Dearborn's culture. Surprisingly enough, it has a large Arab population and is the only city in the United States to have its own Islamic cultural museum. He asked me if I would like to make a stop there after lunch."

"That sounds very original and interesting," I said.

I hadn't realized how ravenous I was. Lunch was quite good, if ordinary in selection. We both had espressos to cap off our meal. Bruce leaned over and kissed away some remains on the corner of my mouth, then kissed me again, this time with much more in mind than just cleaning me off!

"My thoughts for tomorrow are that we go into Detroit and take the sightseeing river tour. It lasts about two and a half hours. The tour guide points out all the various places of interest. Does that sound up your alley? I figure we'd both be a bit museumed out!"

"That's fine with me. I totally agree about not going to another museum. I love being on the water, as you know. In fact, I don't think I've ever told you what my four favorite things in life are. They are in descending order: food, Jen, animals and the beach, or even rivers and lakes." Laughingly, I continued, "Food is my choice over Jen merely because food is always around and who knows, Jen may fly off somewhere permanently."

 What are your passions in life, my dear?"

He smiled at me knowingly, before saying that he loved anything to do with the chemical industry, fine dining, the ocean, and me.

"I'm sorry, Bruce. I didn't include you in my passions, but you know that I am very fond of you." *Oh boy, that sounded so old fashioned*, I thought. "What I really mean is that I care for you deeply, but these particular passions have been around long before you." *Talk about digging myself into a hole!* I was saved by the check arriving.

We strolled out of the restaurant, hand in hand, smiling at each and knowing exactly what was on the other's mind.

Bruce suggested that we grab some cheese, good bread and a couple of bottles of wine for later and call it quits for sightseeing."

"Yes, most definitely", I replied.

The air was crisp and a light mist was forming. I knew that I could never live here in the winter, but kept telling myself not to leap ahead so much. It took about twenty minutes to get back to the house, stopping on the way for groceries. Bruce's street was quite charming. As I mentioned before, it had loads of atmosphere with cars whizzing by, the smell of flowers in the yards, and some children playing hopscotch and jump rope.

We lazed around, not doing much of anything, putting off our sexual appetites until later. Finally, in early evening I cut up some cheese and a few ripe tomatoes. Bruce opened the wine and poured each of us a glass of red which we tasted immediately. He found a tray; put everything on it but the wine, which he asked me to carry upstairs.

"I think a night in the bedroom is just the ticket, don't you?"

Damn straight, I thought, grinning from ear to ear.

"First thing is to get comfortable," Bruce said, winking at me.

I didn't need any prompting, but flung my top and bra off, got out of my jeans and jumped on the bed, leaving on my underpants. They were rather sexy hot pink satin briefs. Bruce got the message, lay down beside me, totally naked, and kissed my inner thighs.

"I adore your briefs, but will adore them more when they are off you," he said, pulling them down and chucking them on the chair.

His kisses always ignited a flame deep in my gut. He cupped my breasts in his hands, and grew hard against my groin. He took me slowly into orgasmic heaven.

"Oh, God, you are so good, Molly," he said, rolling over, whilst kissing my cheeks, eyelids and neck.

"You're one hell of a lover," I said, still holding on to him as if I would sink into oblivion, if I let go.

"Are you hungry?" he asked.

I burst out laughing. "Not anymore, but I could go for a bit of bread and cheese and another glass of that wonderful red you bought."

He sat up, grinning at my corny reply, poured two glasses of wine which we drank slowly, whilst caressing each other until the last red drop hung to our glasses for dear life. We had bought an assortment of cheeses, including Brie, Roquefort, and a sharp cheddar. Nothing in the world quite beats cheese, good bread, and wine. I had travelled extensively throughout France with my mother and we got to sample many of the cheeses that France produced.

The thought of those trips now could have depressed me, just thinking how bloody awful it was that Mother was taken from me at such an early age. She was vibrant, funny, and as courageous as anyone I had ever known. But Bruce's strong presence helped defeat the feeling

"What's with the stern look, babe?"

"Oh, I'm sorry, I was just reminiscing about the times I had with my mother in France and how we gorged on every cheese we chanced on. I miss her every day. Enough of that, another glass of wine would really hit the spot, please."

"Your wish is my command, my lady," he said, sitting up on the bed, whilst placing the tray of goodies between us. There was something quite decadent about eating on the bed, stark naked with someone who really turned you on.

We finished the bottle of wine, demolished the bread and cheese, whilst listening to some wonderful New Age music. We both decided to watch an old Cary Grant movie. Good for the digestion.

"I hate to put a damper on things, Molly, but my father is insistent that he takes us out to brunch tomorrow before we do the boat ride. I have to call him back to let him know. I said I wasn't about to commit until I spoke to you"

He looked so serious and intense, but nevertheless sexy.

"That's okay, Bruce. Don't fret; he isn't that bad. Besides which, I love his furniture!"

I'll go and call him now, and then we can get back to relaxing," he replied. The phoning done, he stood at the foot of the bed, staring down at me. It unnerved me somewhat. "What's the matter darling?" I said.

His reply was to gently ease me to one side so that he could lie beside me. "Get on top of me Molly, now."

He was severely aroused, which naturally had the same effect on me. As I straddled him, I welcomed his manhood with exquisite slowness. Finally, nearing climax, he reversed our positions, parted my legs, and took with me a force that I had never encountered before. He repeated my name, over and over, before at last letting the floodgates open. I was transported to a higher plane after a shuddering climax myself. Spent, he rolled to my side and within seconds was asleep. Men have a real knack for falling asleep straight after the most amazing sex, when all we want is to cuddle, talk a bit, and kiss. I got up, took the tray downstairs, and sat for what seemed like a long time, sipping on a brandy before heading back upstairs. I lay with my back touching Bruce's. Sleep came to me gently and quickly.

As was becoming a habit, I awoke to the aroma of coffee, croissants, and jam on a tray accompanied by a beautiful purple iris.

"This is a little something to tide you over before meeting up with my father," he said.

"Thanks, this is wonderful; you are spoiling me rotten. Don't ever stop!"

I gobbled my croissant, swilling it down with a mug of coffee. I kissed Bruce, holding him tight. That did it. Breakfast was delayed a tad!

"Miss Molly, you are really very detaining. How can I get anything else done?" Bruce said, smiling from ear to ear, his amazing blue eyes lighting up.

I finished dressing and decided that now was the time to ask him something that had been niggling at me for a while. "I'm curious as to why you have no photographs of your mother anywhere to be seen, either here or at your father's house."

Bruce winced, hesitated for a moment, and then told me that his father was adamant about removing all the photos of his mother after she left. "I'll show you some photos later on, but right now we should get going as we have just over half an hour before meeting up with my father," he said.

Bruce was spot on about the length of time it took to get to the restaurant which was situated overlooking the lake. The boat trip wasn't taking off until three so we had a few hours to enjoy a meal.

"I want you to be aware that my father likes this restaurant a lot. It's primarily a sports bar, but has a good view, and brunch is exceptional. Otherwise, I couldn't recommend it", he told me.

"That's fine. If you say the food is good, I know it's good. Any meal I don't have to cook sits well with me."

I exaggerated a bit. Spending more than an hour with Mike wouldn't my favorite thing to do, but knowing his son wasn't overly keen either made it easier to deal with. We parked in an underground lot beneath the restaurant, only to hear Mike's loud voice, as we got out of the car.

"Ah, there are my two lovebirds", Mike bellowed.

I gave him one of my sickly, false smiles and said how sweet it was of him to ask us to meet him for brunch. He stared at me for what seemed like several seconds, making me feel totally uneasy. He seemed to gaze at me as if I were a common criminal. It perplexed me. I would have to talk this one out with Bruce at a later date. Entering the restaurant, the awkwardness with Mike was broken by the waiter showing us to our table. He asked us all what we wanted to drink. I opted for a Bloody Mary and water, needing fortification in the worst way. Bruce took my hand under the table and squeezed it, as if knowing how uncomfortable I was feeling.

Mike rambled on about leaving Dearborn at the end of October for about a month before returning for Christmas and the New Year. He would then spend the months of January through March in New Smyrna beach.

I munched on bread and butter, wishing that somehow, he couldn't make it down for those months. I told myself repeatedly to enjoy the time with Bruce and forget that Mike was his father, though easier said than done. Bruce talked about work, until interrupted by our waiter inquiring to take our orders: Eggs Benedict for Bruce and me, and an everything-in-it omelet for his dad. Mike asked Bruce if he could pick up his mail when he left in October. Bruce didn't see that to be a problem. Time passed somewhat faster than I had anticipated.

We ordered espressos to finish off the meal and were fortunate that we only had less than an hour before we took the boat ride. Mike insisted on paying. I thanked him, shook his hand, avoiding him trying to plant a kiss on my cheek. He turned and was gone.

"Molly, what on earth is the matter with you? I noticed the tensions between the two of you."

I replied, "Oh, I guess he couldn't get it out of his head that I am a redhead and possibly reminded him of your mother. Probably that was why he looked at me oddly, but it made me nervous. He asked me when we first met if I was a natural redhead, that's all. It is what it is. Now I'd really like to move on to more pleasant subjects."

"Fine, fine, let's go, he replied. "We need to be at the dock about a half hour before the boat takes off."

Before we got in the car, he took me in his arms, assuring me that everything would be just fine. I wasn't convinced.

I felt somewhat in a haze during the excursion on "The Diamond Jack" along the upper and lower Detroit River. My powers of concentration had temporarily vanished. Bruce was so attentive and sweet; kissing me at intervals, whilst looking at me so adoringly. Why in the blazes, at this juncture, couldn't I get past the fact that Mike, after all, is his father? Was I being unreasonable? I didn't think so. My utter warm and fuzzy feelings for Bruce were not one hundred percent right now. I had been falling more and more for him, but today's time with his father, and remembering the ice cold looks he'd given me before lunch, had unhinged me a bit. Even the thought of love making wasn't at the top of my agenda. *Get over it, Molly*, I said to myself. My mood quickly shifted as a large wave caught the bow! No harm done, but it did jolt me to the immediate present.

The guide was, I am sure, very informative. I am usually such a stickler for facts, particularly about places of interest. But I could see that I would have to repeat this trip to really gain something from it. I must be feeling better. I was thinking about the here and now and the future. *This is a good sign, Molly*, I thought to myself, while squeezing Bruce's hand. I kissed him on the lips and felt so good. Before I knew it, we were docking.

"What do you want to do now? Are you up for more sightseeing?" Bruce asked.

"To be totally honest with you, I would really like to go back to the house. I'm feeling somewhat drained. Is that all right with you?"

"Molly, it's your vacation. I may have forgotten to tell you that I am not working tomorrow so we can do some local stuff if you like, before you catch your flight tomorrow evening."

"That sounds just up my alley; thanks." I gulped. His smile would make the grizzliest of bears happy.

We drove back home in virtual silence, which was good. I dislike having to make conversation for conversation's sake. I was still feeling confused after seeing Mike. I kept telling myself over and over again that there were lots of people I knew who had parents that weren't my cup of tea, so what was so different in this instance? It was a bit weird that his wife, Bruce's last girlfriend, and I were all red heads. In reality it seemed more than just weird. Deep down I felt that he hated red heads for what had happened to him and Bruce. Thankfully, my dismal thoughts were interrupted by Bruce pulling into the driveway.

"Molly, there's a really good, down home Italian restaurant, two blocks away, that we could go to later on tonight. We can walk to it. What say you, as I refuse for you to cook this weekend?"

"Great! Thanks for being so thoughtful. I really don't mind the effort at all, but won't turn down your offer."

The ensuing meal was awesome and we ambled home sated. Once inside we acted like two people who had lived together for a long time. I had come to like his home. It had a real homey feel to it. Bruce poured two glasses of red wine and handed me one from which I promptly took a large sip. Now I really wanted him, and his smile and eyes told me the same thing. It was a long, passionate night, with little talking. We both drifted off into a deep sleep.

Bruce woke me at six-thirty with the usual tray of coffee and a flower, along with newspapers that he'd managed to scatter all over the floor in his haste to jump in the bed with me for early morning sex. I demurred until I could make my way to the bathroom to freshen up, then I scattered the papers even more, showing that I could out-horny him, even if it was with a giggle that I did it.

After some delicious minutes, he suddenly leapt out of bed, sending the tray cascading to the floor, in a hurry to take advantage of the day before I had to fly off to New Smyrna Beach. We both cleaned up the mess and dressed in silence. Tension seemed to permeate the room, both of us knowing full well that the next two weeks wouldn't go by swiftly. Nevertheless, I was returning to the normalcy in my life with balmy weather, my animals, and Jen.

Bruce drove to the airport as if on a deadly mission. He pulled up at the curbside, opening the door for me, hugging me with an urgency of a farm yard stallion,

"Bruce, darling, I really must go now. You know I hate flying, but I promise you I'll call you as soon as I get back home. Thanks again for everything. Don't forget to give my best to Mike."

I almost choked on those words, really meaning to say that I felt like strangling the man. For now, I would be nice.

"I love you too. Call me as soon as you get home," Bruce said in a husky voice.

Before I had a chance to say anything back, he'd gone, leaving me to wipe away my tears. I felt like a limp lettuce leaf and I hadn't even boarded the plane. It wasn't as if it were a long flight. If everything went according to schedule it would take less than 3 hours non-stop to Orlando. After the usual cattle boarding procedures were over without too much pain, I found my seat on the right aisle side, slumping down with a sigh. It seems to be inevitable that I either get the largest person on board or a screaming baby next to me. Sure, enough it was the former, spilling over onto my armrest. The man was fortunately sober and decently dressed, but I didn't want to strike up a conversation - the last thing I needed to do right now. I was missing Bruce like crazy, but something kept niggling at me with regard to his father. I admonished myself to let it go. I was not dating Mike. Fortunately, my thoughts were channeled to the present by a handsome steward offering me a soda and nuts or pretzels.

"I'll take the nuts and with the soda, double vodka on the rocks, please," I replied to the accommodating steward.

"Coming right up, Miss," he said with a darling grin on his face. I wondered how cheerful he really was. I suppose he must be; otherwise he wouldn't be winging along with the rest of us.

I was drifting into sleep, when Mr. Bigger-than-life tapped me on my right shoulder, wanting to start up a conversation. "Howdy. You want another vodka and tonic, Miss?" he said, his beer breath spilling over me.

"No thanks, I am exhausted and want to catch a nap, whilst we are still in the air, but thanks anyway."

He was another one of those insistent types that wasn't going to take no for an answer unless I was rude to him. After the fifth time of poking me, I told him that if he jabbed me one more time I'd call for the steward to change his seat – I actually had pictures in mind of his being banished to the checked baggage hold.

"Well, there's no need to be so snobbish, I was just trying to be friendly. I guess that we Texans are not anything like the English in that respect," he said, as if he were the injured party

That did it. I got up, went to the back and found the steward, explained the situation, and asked if he could move me. As luck would have it, there was an aisle seat close to the refreshments. I promptly ordered vodka and asked if I could pay for extra nuts.

"Sweetie, take these, we have plenty. I hope they'll help make up for your ghastly ex seatmate", the steward offered.

"Oh, yes, more than, and thanks so much again."

I slugged the vodka down, ate two bags of nuts, and fell into a deep sleep only to hear the plane's captain announcing our descent. This was one of the quickest time passing flights I'd had. I didn't even take a tranquilizer. The booze had done its trick.

Since I had a carry-on bag, I got off the plane heading to the transportation area, purposely avoiding any interaction with the Texan. I called Jen confirm my arrival; she had been waiting for me in the off airport waiting zone. I wasn't up to talking much with her during the ride home, except to say Bruce and I had a marvelous time together, details to come later after I was refreshed

Jen came in with me to give me company while I unpacked. I called Bruce to let him know that I was home. Our conversation was brief, but full of tenderness.

I unpacked; then Jen and I ate a quick sandwich. We decided to talk more the following day so she hurried off to her place. I suddenly felt very alone, and quite blue. After a couple of hours, I felt hungry again. I grabbed a small chunk of cheese and a ginger ale, making me a cheerier soul.

I awoke the following morning to take on neglected household chores, having taken off a day from work for that purpose. Midafternoon the phone rang. It was Jen.

"What's up?" I asked.

"Well, I have to tell you about Charlie; besides, I can't wait to catch up on your news. I shall come over this a little later evening, as I think we agreed. See you later."

The phone went dead. There must be something really good going on with her, as she was usually much more composed.

I called Bruce around six pm. The phone rang three times before he picked up. "Bruce, it's me, Molly. Do you miss me yet??

"Darling girl, how could I not? You're constantly on my mind. In fact, I'm trying to picture what you are wearing."

I hesitated, and then said, "Actually I'm sitting in my granny knickers and tee shirt. How sexy is that? What about you?"

"Me, I'm wearing your favorite turquoise tee shirt and my shorts, which are being strained by my desire for you".

I sighed, "Oh, Bruce, you are naughty. But so is this chick. I can feel tingling between my thighs. And as a matter of fact, I am caressing my nipples as we speak."

"Aren't you the one for phone sex? I can hardly bear it", he uttered.

We continued for a while longer with the hot language; then, I heard him groan and knew that I had made him come. Bruce, darling Bruce, I've never had phone sex before, but it's not such a bad second to the real thing."

There was a long pause whilst we both came down to earth. We casually chatted back and forth. He told me about his work and that he had a lab assistant that was slacking off.

Bruce said seriously, "Frankly, I think that he is siphoning funds from the company, but of course, I can't prove anything at this juncture."

"That doesn't sound too good." Changing the subject, I asked him how his father was doing.

"I really don't know. I haven't spoken to him since we saw him together. It's hard to believe that I live so close to him, yet that is about the only closeness we have. I have tremendous guilt for not liking him. He wasn't nice to my mother and I don't blame her one bit for leaving for good. Anyway, back to you. I can come down in three weeks' time. I have ten days' vacation left. Would that suit you?"

"Would it suit me? You sound so formal. I can hardly wait! Yes, yes Bruce; just let me know the exact date. The one problem I have is that I don't think I can take time off again, but you can amuse yourself during the day and have lunch with me. In fact, I'd like you to meet John, my boss, and get a better feel for what I do."

"I look forward to it. Look, I have to go now back to the office. I'm trying to meet a deadline. I'll call you tomorrow night. I love you and miss you more than I ever thought I could."

"Bye my love; talk to you tomorrow night."

He hung up before I could blow kisses through the phone. Was this real love? It was so soon, yet I felt so warm and fuzzy, as well as feeling guilty that David's place in my heart was being taken. Well, it really wasn't being taken, just someone else taking up space in what has been a somewhat lonely and empty heart. I poured myself another glass of wine, sank back in the sofa, for a few delicious moments before dressing and waiting for Jen.

I dozed off, only to be awoken by Jen thumping on the front door. I hate my front door being assaulted, but I have learned to forgive her for the practice. "Hello, friend; how goes it? I assume you'd like a glass of wine before you tell me all about the reason for your frenzied phone call?"

Yes, I'd love one. In fact, have you got some cheese and an apple? I worked late and am starving." She sloshed down the first glass of wine, barely tasting it, slumped down on the sofa, and handed me her glass for a refill.

"Okay, Jen, let's have it. What's going on with you?"

"It's about Charlie. He was in town again from Miami whilst you were away. Things are really heating up between us. I think he is the one. He wants me to put in for a transfer to Miami. I told him that we'd have to see each other a few more times before I made this decision. Besides, I have to give a month's notice and my lease on the apartment doesn't expire until the end of December, which would mean at least four more months of really establishing our relationship. Honestly, Molly, the one stumbling block, apart from leaving here, is leaving you."

I was momentarily stunned. I couldn't imagine living here without her, but it was her life and I had no choice but to think of her well-being.

"That's wonderful, Jen. I'm thrilled for you. Naturally, if and when you go, I will miss you like crazy, but it's not as if you are going to a foreign country. We can see each other often, but I'm not starting to plan my weekend trips to Miami until this transition takes place. Funny, really, when you think that I met Bruce first, yet you are one jump ahead of me."

"Another glass of wine first, pretty please," Jen said, then took another rather large gulp rather than savoring. It wasn't as if it was expensive wine, and even if it was I certainly wouldn't begrudge her that.

"Well, remember the first time he and I met at that conference several weeks back? I went out with him because he was interesting and frankly quite cute, but the sparks didn't really fly the first night. In fact, I was wondering if he wasn't either married or gay as he didn't even attempt to kiss me on the cheek. How wrong could anyone be?"

Jen continued, "The next time he came up he called me at work at asked if I could meet him at his hotel for a drink after work. We had a couple of drinks and it was if I was with a different person. He was affectionate; but something seemed to click between us. He seemed so much more desirable than I ever imagined he could be. He suggested that we grab a bite in the restaurant, which we did. Truthfully, I don't remember tasting much at all. He suggested we go up to his room for a nightcap. We did. Some nightcap it turned out to be. He ripped my clothes off and I had the best sex I have had in forever. That was it. I couldn't stop thinking about him from that night on. He called me every day from Miami. Sorry to repeat I but I'm so excited.

As I previously mentioned, he flew in for two days when you were in Dearborn and we spent the entire time holed up in his room, eating each other up, interspersed with room service food. I have never, ever had such a debauched, yet wonderful time with any man before. There you have it, Molly. I really think Charlie is the one. It seems so utterly uncomplicated. He is thirty-two and has never been married; likes children, plays tennis, and doesn't watch many sports on TV. He seems too good to be true. His mother lives in Miami, widowed since he was 19. He has one brother who lives in London. Naturally he has been around the block, but I am naïve enough to think that I am really the one. Now I need more food and wine please."

Jen got up, pacing around the room as if she had been just let out of a cage, so I said,

"Jen, my dear, I'm thrilled for you and I am not about to tell you to take it slow. I believe that when love hits, it hits and instinct kicks in."

"Okay, enough about me; I want to hear about you", Jen offered.

"Before I get you caught up, how about I fix some spaghetti?"

"That would suit me wonderfully well, Molly."

I busied myself, throwing in some gluten free pasta made from artichokes, poured myself the remainder of the bottle, and told her that Bruce was coming down in three weeks for about ten days. It was my pleasure to fix something for Jen, but I wasn't hungry yet, or so it seemed.

"Naturally I can't take off from work, but we can see each other every lunch hour and at night. He'll probably bring work with him."

My appetite suddenly resurfaced. There were very few occasions in life when I couldn't eat. We made short work of the pasta, sorted out the world and decided to call it a night.

"If you're free this weekend, Jen, do you fancy going up to the outlet mall in St. Augustine? I really could do with a revamped wardrobe."

"Sounds like a plan. I'd rather go Saturday if that's okay. I promised I'd go to work on Sunday and help organize the next conference, which is going to take place in Tampa."

"Done deal, as long as you don't mind driving? I fancy blowing the cobwebs away in that hotrod of yours", I said.

She grinned with that infectious smile of hers, as she headed out the door. "I'll pick you up around ten then." I shook my head in agreement, but knew she didn't see me, speeding off, as if she were trying to break the sound barrier.

The workweek passed quickly. Just like clockwork, Jen picked me up at ten on Saturday, and we again sped off down the motorway. Luck would have it that she didn't get a speeding ticket. We decided to eat lunch before shopping, although maybe not such a great idea to try on clothes on a full stomach. We settled on this cute little Greek restaurant overlooking the harbor with delicious food that took care of our appetites. We decided if our shopping spree was a success, we'd stop for dessert and a glass of wine before roaring back home.

Walking down the wonderful cobbled streets of the old town of St. Augustine, we stumbled on one of the chi-chi stores that were having a clearance sale. I found this skirt that had shades of red and purple, with uneven fringes around the bottom. It fitted and so did a matching tank top in red. I could well imagine a gypsy in the wilds of Spain or even Mexico doing the Fandango. My mind was jolted back to reality, when this snotty assistant came up to me and asked if I needed any assistance. She looked me up and down, as I wasn't exactly dressed like a million dollars. I thanked her, asking her to hold onto the skirt and top whilst I looked around some more. I found a couple of dresses to die for. Both were simple sheathes. One was magenta and the other cobalt blue. Jen found a couple in grey and brown, plus two classic blouses in ivory and white. She was much more conservative in her dress than I was; this would surprise most people looking at the two of us.

We decided to dump our purchases in the car before heading to the hotel for our much-deserved wine and dessert. We'd saved a ton of money so felt quite justified in splurging on a good red and fried cheesecake. We got back around six o'clock. Jen apologized for not wanting to come in. We were both knackered so that was fine with me.

"Thanks for driving, Jen, and I'll call you in a couple of days."

"Great, I've had a blast too," she said as she jumped into her souped-up red mini, masking as a Ferrari, and roared off down the street.

I went inside, dumped my purchases on the sofa and headed for the wine bottle and poured myself a large glass of red wine, before trying on the clothes in the comfort of my own home to see if I really was as pleased as I thought I was. It turned out my shopping spree wasn't a disappointment.

I decided to call Bruce before I did anything else. He wasn't there, so I left a message, telling him he could call me back, up until 11 pm, and that I missed him terribly. I was full to the brim after indulging in the rich cheesecake, and headed up to bed.

Bruce might have called, but nothing woke me. My alarm went off at nine in the morning which really pissed me off as I thought I'd turned it off. Ah, well, the need for caffeine was calling out to me. Sunday is usually the same old stuff. I read the paper, cut coupons, and go to the beach for a couple of hours, but today I wanted to stay put in case Bruce called me. I waited until around two in the afternoon, but got so antsy that I headed to the beach for a run, even though it was mobbed. I ran until the sweat was oozing out of me, then toweled off and headed home.

Three weeks until I would see Bruce felt like an eternity, but I had an awful lot to do. The editor of one of the local newspapers had asked me to write an article about animals and the animal rights etc.; so, I was pretty tied up between that and my day job. Hopefully time would fly by, contrary to my present feeling.

By the time I'd made dinner for myself, and slumped on the sofa, Bruce called. He asked me how I was. I told him that I missed him already. He returned the sentiments then proceeded to excite me with amazing phone sex in which I gladly participated until we both came.

"Wow, Molly", he said. "That was some preview of 'coming' attractions when we get together again, cheek to cheek for real."

I agreed, exhausted, but smug that I was his equal in the arousal department. He said he'd call me tomorrow evening, telling me that three weeks was one hell of a long time before we were together again.

Looking ahead, I said, "The weather will be great, if rather warm, this time of the year, so we can spend our weekends on the beach, but as you know, I have to work Monday through Friday during the day."

"I have a big project that I'm working on so can do that while you're at work. I assure you that between that and you, I won't be bored," he replied.

"Okay then; I was a bit worried as to what you'd do whilst I was working. Dare I ask about your father?"

"I've not seen or heard from him. He doesn't usually call me unless he needs something, which is good in itself." He ended our conversation with, "I love you darling."

The first week passed quickly and uneventfully. I managed to get a few swims in and worked on my article for the paper. Jen was really busy with her job and of course the new man in her life. She called me midweek to tell me that she was going to go down to Miami for the weekend to see Charlie and meet his mother. That sounded like a lot of fun. I love Miami. It's so alive and cosmopolitan. I often thought that if I didn't have my job here, it would be a place I'd seriously consider as I love the Spanish influence. It reminded me a little bit of being in Spain. As much as I enjoy my life here, I feel very European, and always yearn for the European influence. However, life is getting on with the cards you are dealt with, and who am I to complain. My cards are looking like aces right now.

The day finally arrived for me to pick Bruce up at the airport, none too soon. I was breaking out in a cold sweat in anticipation of seeing him again. I parked the car and walked to his gate. As he walked towards me my heart missed a beat. This man was so desirable and I couldn't wait to wrap myself around him. He came striding through, dumped his suitcase on the ground, and grabbed me in an embrace that almost suffocated me.

"Darling girl, am I ever happy to see you."

"Me, too Bruce," I said as we linked arms and walked to the car.

His hand rested on my knee the entire drive home. As soon as I'd opened the door he slammed the door shut, put his luggage down, and hastily undressed, displaying his throbbing manhood, whilst I disrobed with abandon. He threw me on the sofa and took me rapidly. We lay there for a long time, before he made soft and gentle love to me again. Could Heaven be as good as this? I don't think so.

"Welcome to my humble abode, darling." I said, not being able to take my eyes off this man, who filled my heart to an explosive level. He threw on his boxer shorts, sat back against the sofa and was asleep in no time at all. I puttered around, taking his luggage upstairs, all the time thinking that I had three glorious weeks of this man. I was unpacking when I felt something squeeze my buttocks. I spun around and he threw me on the bed again.

"If I could make love to you again I would, but I'm starving and am sure you are. What shall we do for dinner?" he asked.

"I suggest we eat in. There are some ready-made Japanese rice rolls with vegetables and a few other leftovers we might dig into."

"Good thinking, Molly. Let the feast begin."

We ate quietly, devouring everything in front of us, washing it down with a couple of glasses of wine. We looked at each other and our minds were in unison. Upstairs we went with the wine and dessert. It was a night of intense passion. We caressed each other with intermittent intensity and softness. Each time he took my breasts in his hands I felt as if I was going to explode into a thousand little pieces.

"Oh Bruce, you are undoubtedly the sexiest man alive, with the added bonus of being such a great person."

"You are my world," he said gently as we drifted into a deep sleep.

The three weeks flew by. We had a couple of days at the beach, long sensual meals in a couple of expensive restaurants, naturally interspersed with work and daily chores. Bruce called his father once, but never got a reply. I can't say I was sorry about that. I never could get over how very different they were. But these thoughts would depress me if I dwelled on them, so my mind focused on Bruce.

I came home on our last night together to find two dozen roses in a vase, a box of chocolates, two bottles of wine and a card that said, "Let's make the most of this evening, I love you Bruce."

I was totally overwhelmed. I thought this was just the most wonderful gesture that anybody could make. I brushed the tears away from my eyes and before I could even open the first bottle of wine the phone rang. It was Bruce saying that he'd be back in about an hour.

"Darling, that was so lovely of you to spoil me with all these gifts. What time do you think you'll be back?"

"I'll be there around six."

By the time I'd made my face up at least five times, changed my outfit more than once, the doorbell rang and there he stood. He took me in his arms and told me how beautiful I was.

"Oh, by the way, I heard from my father. Naturally he wants something. He wants me to take care of his dog for about four months as he's going to visit a friend in Canada."

"Wonderful! Hope you like dogs. By the way, I've been meaning to ask you, why there are no photos of your mother anywhere to be seen in his house?"

"Darling, when my mother left my father for good, he just switched off and in a rage, told me to get rid of them. So, I just bundled a whole pile of pictures and put them up in the attic. As far as the ones in his house, he probably put them in his garage. I haven't seen my mother in over a year, but it was not unusual   for her to go off many months at a time and leave no word. Now, let's get off the subject, please."

He led me upstairs to make love that took me to utter ecstasy with his deep, undulating thrusts. Afterwards, we lay in each other's arms expended of all energy, yet filled a sweet bliss. Eventually, he jumped out of bed, went downstairs, and returned with two crystal glasses and the remainder of the wine. We talked about everything under the sun, or so it seemed, as we sipped.

"Molly, I won't be able to come down for at least two months, but I have a suggestion that you can mull over. I was wondering if around November you could take a leave of absence from work and spend a month or more with me. I know it's a tall order, but that's what I really would like. I'm not suggesting that you give up your job, I'm just merely suggesting that you think about it, because I can't live without you."

"Whew, that is a tall order since I have only three weeks' vacation. John is a very understanding man, but I'll have to give this some serious thought. It's very tempting. I'd be giving up a lot if I did this."

My mind was in a complete state of flux. Fortunately, I was saved from further contemplation on this offer by the ringing of the doorbell.

"Molly, I ordered food from the French restaurant, because I knew that we wouldn't want to go out; so, I'll go down and get it."

"You think of everything. Thank you, darling."

Dinner was wonderful. He'd ordered smoked salmon followed by the most delicious lamb chops in an orange glaze, baked potatoes with thyme and parsley, and naturally coffee ice cream. What could be better? All the time I was eating I kept thinking about Bruce's suggestion to go to Dearborn. I really wanted to, and felt that he was the man for me, but a stretch in the cold was something I really didn't relish. The next morning, I was greeted with my usual coffee, a flower, and breakfast.

"Bruce, you've really perfected the art of making toast."

"Thank you, sweetheart, and good morning to you," That said, he took the tray and slapped it on the floor, making love to me with the ferocity of a wild animal that had just been let out of its cage.

"I guess the toast is cold now," I said with a big grin on my face. I was hungry so dug in, and sipped on the now cold coffee whilst Bruce packed up his things

He took the tray downstairs and was back in a gif with a piping hot mug of coffee. The time had finally arrived for us to head to the airport.

"Molly, I really don't want you to come inside with me. I loathe protracted goodbyes."

Bruce drove fast, holding onto my leg with the other hand. We didn't speak. We knew what each other was thinking. Bruce pulled up at the curbside, stopped the car, and got out. He held me tight; kissing me so hard that I thought my lips would bleed.

"Darling girl, I am missing you already. Please think about my suggestion. I'll call you tonight. That way you'll have the whole day to think about what I said. I know this is a tough decision, but I don't think I can bear to be without you. It's almost the end of August. What I'll try to do is come down for a weekend at the end of September. I wish I could come before but this is our busiest time of the year. You, of all people, know about being busy. I know that with your journalism and day job you don't have too much time on your hands either, so until the next time my love."

He gave me one final kiss before disappearing into the terminal. He didn't see the tears streaming down my face as I got into the car and drove off feeling like my whole world was collapsing. The trip back home was deadly. Traffic was appalling, and I could hardly see through the tears that were soaking my face. Even the idea of the beach didn't appeal to me right now. My heart was racing and I felt exhausted. Once home I fell on the bed and sobbed for what seemed like an age. I must have drifted off as I awoke suddenly to the phone ringing. It was Jen asking if I was free the following evening. I was glad it wasn't tonight. Tonight, was feeling sorry for Molly night. I drowned my sorrows in a large container of coffee ice cream along with some worthless TV. I was surprised that I slept as well as I did.

Around ten Jen called to say she was on her way. She was so damn cheerful that I wanted to tell her to tone it down, but she actually lifted my crappy spirits more than I'd anticipated. She filled me in on Charlie. She was going to fly down to see him this coming weekend, which I vaguely remembered her telling me about.

Jen said, "Okay, girlfriend. Let's get you out of the doldrums. How about we go and have a large hamburger, double order of fries and watch the world go by?"

"That sounds just up my alley. I was hoping you wouldn't suggest a walk on the beach today. I think I might just strangle one of the seagulls. You know how that goes some days? I am just not in the mood for solitude and sand."

"Grab a jacket and let's go then. You can tell me all the grisly details when we get to the restaurant."

As always, Jen knew exactly how to lift my spirits. We sat on bar stools overlooking the ocean, which was wild and rough. There were a few enthusiastic runners and a couple of yoga gurus. Otherwise, it was calm and fortunately not too many birds were flying around today. I filled her in on Bruce's notion that I take a leave of absence from work in November.

"I just can't wrap my head around leaving here for a month or so for the frozen tundra. I want to be with Bruce, but I have the problem of renting my house out. I can't possibly afford the rent without working."

Jen almost fell off her stool in her rush to get up with excitement. "Molly, I have the perfect solution. My lease is up at the end of October, so I could rent your place for a few months, while taking my time to make future rental arrangements. I'm certainly not moving to Miami in the near future. If Charlie and I do end up together it won't be until early spring."

"I can't believe this, Jen. It certainly would solve my problem. I really do want to spend more time with Bruce. I'm also curious to dig a bit deeper into the mystery of his father's disappearing wife, and Bruce's ex- girlfriend. It's been at the back of my mind the whole time since I spent that weekend in Dearborn. He's calling me tonight, so I'll take the plunge to tell him that I'll ask John at work tomorrow if I can take two months leave of absence. If my boss doesn't agree to that, I'll just leave. I can always get a job somewhere else, but I'm pretty sure John will agree to this plan."

My spirits soared, as did the seagulls that actually thrilled me now. Amazing how one's mood can swing like a pendulum. We ordered a merlot and finished off the rest of our fries. We looked at each other and knew instantaneously what each other was thinking. We got up, giggling away, paid the bill, and walked about three miles on the beach.

"Thanks Jen for hauling me out of the dark tunnel I was in."

"No problem, Molly. You'd do the same for me."

She took off like grease lightening – as usual. It never ceased to amaze me that she hadn't been ticketed more than once. She'd do well in Utah on the Salt Flats.

The following morning, I went to work with knots in my stomach. I was not looking forward to asking John for time off. *Bite the bullet, Molly*, I told myself as I knocked on his office door.

"Come in please. Oh, it's you Molly. I thought it was another vet that had an early morning appointment. What's up?"

Stuttering away, I spat out my request, feeling as if I was going to throw up any moment. He grinned at me with his soft smile.

"No problem! I guess this man has gotten under your skin? I'm absolutely going to miss you, but the job is yours when you return. Now, did you say November and December?"

"Yes, if that's alright with you. It's a bit lengthy, I know, but there you have it."

"Fate must be with us both as this morning an old friend of mine, who happens to be a vet, is in town. He's coming to the office later today. He phoned me last night and asked if I could take on a student or two in a month or so for a number of months, so you see, Molly, it'll work out just fine. And, I can manage alone, or with temps, for a while.

The tenseness in my stomach eased up immediately. "Thank you so much, John. I really don't know what to say, other than that you are the best boss ever." It sounded corny, but it was true. I was bloody lucky. He was such an easy-going man, but not given to divulge his own love life. I often wondered if he had a girlfriend, but never asked about it, in respect for his privacy

"Well, Molly, I think we should get back to work, don't you? We have so much paper work piling up, that perhaps you can tackle that task."

I nodded in agreement, feeling as if a cinder block had been removed from my shoulders. When Bruce called me that evening, I couldn't even wait for him to say more than, *Hello.* I told him that I'd taken a leave of absence for November and December, and then waited for his reaction.

"Darling girl, that is wonderful! Will you consider coming for the entire time?"

"If that's what you want, I don't see why not," I replied.

I was thinking that I could do a lot of investigating during those two months, aside from picturing a frolicsome good time with my man.

We then proceeded to have the greatest phone sex ever. Never in my wildest dreams did I think I could be as wet and excited with just a phone in one hand, while the other hand did its thing. We came in unison. I was a bit frustrated that I couldn't see the delicious creamy fluid eject from his throbbing penis. *Down, girl, you naughty thing,* I said to myself. Once our passions subsided, we talked about when Bruce would be coming down for a weekend.

"Darling, it won't be for three weeks. I mentioned I am super busy right now. We can talk every day which will somewhat ease the separation."

I reluctantly agreed. We touched on world events and then I asked about his father.

"Why do you always have to know how he is, Molly? I told you he has dumped this dog on me, whilst he visits a few friends in Canada. Truth be told, I've grown quite fond of the mutt. What I'll do with him when I travel, Lord only knows. I'll deal with that down the road."

"Does this dog have a name, Bruce?"

"Sorry, I forgot to mention it. It's Brandy. He's a lab mix and really a great dog, but I don't need him right now. "

"Well, think of it this way. When I come to the frozen north, it will give me something to do when you are working. I'll take him for walks, etc., so it's not all bad."

Bruce agreed, told me he loved me, but had to go and finish a boring project. He finished with, "I'll talk to you in a couple of days, my darling. Tomorrow I have an evening meeting so don't miss my voice too much."

I smiled, kissing the phone, muttering sweet nothings and hung up. I was again hot and bothered and gave myself an awesome orgasm before I drifted off into the night.

The few weeks flew by. During that time, we talked a lot and had great phone sex. This kind of experience with Bruce was new to me. I couldn't believe what vivid, sexual encounters we could dream up. Never in my wildest dreams did I think that I could have so much wicked fun, such emotional highs, and such intense orgasms. It made the separation from him almost bearable.

At last, it was time for me to pick Bruce up at the airport. He was able to snatch three days with me. It was mid-September. The weather was perfect. The nights were in the sixties and the daytime in the eighties. The first day we were together we didn't leave the bedroom other than to feed our bodies. I cannot even describe this time together. We explored every facet of each other's bodies. I felt I knew every mole and every bump he had. My breasts were sore with his touch, but it was a soreness that I took pleasure in. It was only now that I felt we really belonged together.

Too soon came the time for more goodbyes. The journey to the airport, the tearful farewells, and promises for the future seemed old hat now. Bruce said he would come in mid-October for a weekend. I told him that in light of taking a leave of absence and packing up to come to Dearborn for two months, I had so much to do that I couldn't come up to see him. He completely understood, all the time holding me close to him. It was difficult to let go of each other. We had no choice. As he got out of the car, he told me that a month would seem like a year. I nodded in agreement. We kissed goodbye, and he was gone. The tears flowed as before, although the pain seemed to have lessened somewhat. I felt that my future with him was looking better, and I knew that I had a million things to accomplish before packing to go north in November.

The next few weeks were so hectic, what with me finishing my article for the newspaper and getting caught up at work on all the veterinarian paperwork. The student who was coming in to help John was going to show up at the beginning of October, so I was busy formulating notes for her.

Funnily enough, the beach took a backseat for a few weeks. By the time I got home each night, fed myself, and talked to Bruce, there was little time for anything else. Our sexual encounters over the phone were something I relied heavily on. It never ceased to amaze me how wonderful he made me feel. And while we were both frustrated not being able to touch each other, we managed to feed our sexual hungers well enough. One night, during a mundane conversation, I asked how Brandy was doing.

"You know, Molly; believe it or not, I am really getting attached to the hound. He is quite the most intelligent dog I've been around and is a substitute companion for me."

"Thanks, darling, I always wanted to be replaced by a Labrador retriever as my stand-in."

We laughed and I was secretly tickled that he had taken to the dog. We changed the subject and discussed current affairs and the fact that Bruce's job was hectic right now. All that I really understood about it was that he was heavily involved in chemicals, but was currently investigating a subordinate accused of embezzling funds. This done with, we both aroused each other with our sexually charged phone hi-jinx. Such fun! We said our loving goodbyes. I was wet and tired.

I was not looking forward to this upcoming weekend. It loomed ahead like a black cloud before the storm. I called Jen and asked her if she fancied a run on the beach, followed by the must have hamburger. She agreed and said she'd pick me up around 11. Before I even had the chance to insist upon driving, she'd hung up. Maybe in her next life she'd become a race driver.

The run did marvels for my spirits. We didn't even talk for three miles, until we were really done in. Even the gulls circling around were soothing with their symmetrical gliding.

"That burger is going to taste so good, Molly, and I can't wait to fill you in on Miami Vice! Let's get a table so we can hear each other talk if that's good with you?"

"Perfect, let's do it", I replied.

We ordered our usual red wine and sloshed the first one down with alacrity. Munching on the warm bread, I told Jen to spill the beans.

"It was an experience meeting his family. His mother is Puerto Rican and speaks English with a heavy accent. At first, she was a bit stand-offish, but after we had broken the ice I really liked her a lot. Charlie's father, on the contrary is a Military man and quite rigid, to say the least. I guess opposites attract. Anyway, we had a really good time. Charlie and I get on so well. He wants me to go down next month for a long weekend, if I can swing it. There isn't much else to tell, other than I feel very good with him, not to mention that sex with him is off the charts.

Our burgers arrived and we ate in silence.

I said to Jen, "Who would have thought that our lives would take such a drastic turn? I can barely believe I am going to Dearborn for two months. At least now I will have a dog to keep me company, plus I am bloody determined to dig deeper into the disappearance of Bruce's mother and girlfriend. I am getting eaten away with curiosity. It will give me something to do other than sightseeing. Enough said, ice cream time, don't you agree?"

We had the largest sundae on the menu, after splurging on another glass of wine.

This was a fine Saturday. Jen dropped me outside my abode, or as she put it, *her soon-to-be new home* and said she'd call me in the week. Before she roared off, I yelled out to her that I was thrilled for her regarding Charlie and his family.

"Thanks, friend, we'll see where it goes, but for now I am savoring the good moments and not looking too far ahead. Unlike you, my life is not about to change too much in the near future."

Time passed relatively quickly and uneventfully. It was difficult to believe that autumn was upon us. Living in Florida, each season just melded into the next without drastic change. At one time, I thought I would miss the seasons, but not a bit. In fact, I was resentful when we had a week of relatively cold weather, confirming in my mind that I'm definitely a hot house plant.

October rushed in. Bruce was coming down for the second weekend which really enabled me to keep my spirits on an even keel. A student, named Marge, came to work almost a month earlier than expected. Marge was sharp, very fast with paper work, and it shone out of her paws, to coin a phrase, that she loved animals. It made my decision to leave for two months a whole lot easier, and I knew John was relieved.

Nothing unusual occurred prior to Bruce's visit. I busied myself packing up stuff in readiness for Jen's moving in. I had so many bills to pay, tradesmen to alert, etc., that I barely saw the beach. I did make time to swim. The pool was now heated and almost free from the summer crowd that had to return to their impending frozen lives.

The week prior to Bruce arriving, I swam fifty laps every day. It was heaven. Thrashing through the clear water with no one to impede me was second best to running on the beach. To say nothing of the stress that seemed to fall away from my shoulders. My body was looking fairly trim and I could hardly wait to be with Bruce. The night before he was due to arrive; we had the best phone sex ever. We came at the very same time, screaming (well, I screamed and he moaned) then panting in unison. I fell on the bed, exhausted in the best way ever.

"Oh, Molly, you are too much; just wait until tomorrow night when we are really together. I love you so, but must rush and finish this darned project."

"I love you, too." I said rapturously - but I don't think he heard me. Anyway, one more night alone wasn't so bad.

A shiver ran down my spine when I realized that I had just over two weeks before I would be living in Bruce's house for two months. I had been reluctantly digging out all my winter clothes, tights, boots and scarves that were in my cedar trunk. *Oh, I don't suppose it will be that bad, cold weather-wise, for a couple of months,* I told myself. *It's not as if I am going to be living there permanently.* My thoughts came to a delicious end and sleep swept softly over me.

The next day at the vet clinic, I felt somewhat displaced as I continued to teach Marge the ropes. I had an empty feeling in my stomach as if I were leaving for good. But I made it through the day and left a little early. Bruce had told me that he'd catch a cab at the airport and would arrive around six.

I had already made a really good chicken in cream sauce with broccoli. I wasn't sure when we would eat our meal, so my mind was not on the kitchen when I arrived at home. Instead, I busied myself choosing a fetching little grey dress that showed off my newly acquired swimmer's curves and retouched my make-up, too many times no doubt, before he arrived.

I opened the door and managed to close it before he threw off his clothes, undressed me and took me right there on the kitchen counter. Whew, another first for me. It felt sinful and very exotic, leaving me sexually sated – for the time being.

"Hello, Miss Molly; it's so good to see you," he laughingly said.

I giggled, grabbed my clothes, not out of vanity, but because I was cold.

"Hello to you, too. Fancy a spot of wine before dinner?"

"Great. But I'm going to take my case upstairs first." He was back in a flash and we ate dinner as if we'd been together forever.

"What's on the agenda this weekend?" he asked.

"I haven't given it much thought really. We can go to the beach if you like."

Yes, I'd like that, plus I want to take you back to that French restaurant called La Crepe, if my memory serves me correctly. We also have a lot of organizing to do before you grace Dearborn with your presence."

I didn't feel elated, which I should have. In truth, I had a mild panic attack, but snapped out of it thinking that I was really looking forward to solving the mystery of the disappearing red heads.

Our Saturday together was idyllic. We made love in the morning. I had my usual breakfast on a tray. We went to the beach and walked in the sea which was cool and delicious. We talked, laughed, and made some plans for my stay. Bruce was booking my flight for the first Sunday in November. We stayed on the beach until the sun set, casting a glow over the water that shimmied like a giant red tinged orange. The view took our breath away. This was something that I'd really miss. Even the birds flew softly above us, singing in a whisper. We would have stayed until dark, but had a reservation at Le Crepe for eight o'clock.

Dinner was wonderful. Our table was in a secluded, dimly lit corner and the meal was nothing short of perfection. Once home, we headed straight for bed. We lay in each other's' arms talking about the upcoming two months. I wasn't as comfortable as Bruce was about this transition, but there was no point in ruining this night.

Our morning was not the norm. Bruce's mind was so distracted with the problems at work that we didn't make love. We acted like a married couple, going about our business until it was time for him to return home.

"Darling, girl, I am so sorry that I haven't been more loving, but I promise you nothing has changed. You know I can't wait for you to be with me in Dearborn."

"Me too; I can't wait either."

The mere idea of being with him for a protracted period of time was damned appealing, but the real rush of excitement came from knowing that I could delve into why his mother disappeared. We ate breakfast, holding each other's' hands as if it was for the last time. The moment of closeness was broken by the honking of the cab outside. Bruce kissed me so fervently that my lip bled a bit. Before he could even see the damage, he'd gone, proclaiming that he'd call me tomorrow night. I blew kisses at the departing cab, but knew that he wasn't looking. It didn't matter, I felt good doing it. I walked inside, locked the door, slumped on the couch, and then felt bloody lonely.

The days were flying by at the office in my frenzied effort to put everything in order for Marge. Then there was the never-ending thought process about what I should or shouldn't take to Dearborn. And, of course, I was saddled with the usual bill paying, re-routing my mail, etc. Meanwhile, Bruce and I spoke on the phone every other night. Our phone sex continued to astonish me. Thank God for that; otherwise, I might have lost my mind.

Jen and I went to the beach on Sunday and had our usual burgers, fries, and ice cream. She was leaving the following weekend for Miami, so we only had another week together to finalize all the boring details of taking over the lease etc. *For heaven's sake, it was only for two months,* I kept telling myself. My last week at work was unbelievably hectic. I had taken several guide books out of the library about Dearborn and the surrounding area, and was now busy reading about my near-term destination. Apart from superficial facts, it was much more interesting than I'd ever have imagined. Now I was getting really excited. I was booked to fly out on Sunday, November third. At 10.30 a.m. Jen and I had a tearful, farewell dinner at "our" home", whilst she unpacked her stuff and I made sure I had everything, especially tranquilizers! We sat up until three in the morning, setting the world right.

"You promise to call me once you've unpacked."

"Of course, I will. Besides, I need to find out how you are making out in my ex house."

There were many giggles between us, before we decided we really should get some shuteye.

The next morning was total chaos. Coffee and a quick slice of bread and marmite did it for both of us. I was always a wreck before flying, no matter how many times I'd been up in the sky. The cabbie rang the bell near eight sharp. We hugged each other, and I jumped in the cab, my feelings rolling all over the place like wobbly jelly. Happy? Yes. Sad? Yes. It was too late for all this sentimental crap. I was on my way to Dearborn and Bruce. Fortunately, this time the plane ride was smooth and I had three seats to myself so I slugged a tranquilizer down with a soda and slept until the pilot announced that we were landing. No fat drunk this time. It took forever going through security. I thought I was in a foreign country, but security has tightened the world over, which isn't all bad. I had two large suitcases to collect, so followed the milling crowd to gate A, carousel 54. My heart soared when, through a thong of people, I spotted Bruce with a dozen peach roses clutched to his stomach. He waved frantically at me. My favorite flowers ever and I wasn't disappointed with the bearer of such good tidings.

He ran towards me, sweeping me up in his arms.

"Am I glad to see you darling girl. How was the flight? No larger than life dudes sitting close to you, I hope?"

"Bruce, the flowers are beautiful, and no, I had three seats to myself. I can't wait to leave here and get back to 110 Blakely Street, my home for the next two months."

"Well let's get a move on, shall we?" he said, looking at me as if he was actually undressing me. That would come later. I had forgotten that it took about forty-five minutes to get to his house. I was bushed and no sooner had I buckled myself in than I fell into a dead sleep until we arrived outside his lovely townhouse.

"Wake up, Miss Molly, we've arrived", Bruce said, gently nudging my elbow.

"I'm sorry that I died on you, but I was exhausted. Jen and I stayed up half the night chatting, drinking a tad too much, and finalizing the handing over of my house. It has worked out perfectly for both of us. I can't believe my luck. Now I feel refreshed and ready for anything."

"Anything?"

"Yes, anything." No need to add another word.

He carried my suitcases upstairs and told me to follow him. We wasted no time throwing off our clothes and devouring one another. I don't think there was a place on our bodies that we didn't explore. It wasn't long before neither of us could wait a moment longer. He plunged into me and took me with such ferocity, that both of us climaxed as one.

"Oh, God; you're so damn good, Molly."

"You're none too shabby yourself, my love." We caressed each other, caught up on our news, and stayed locked in each other's' arms until hunger beckoned us.

"Where is Brandy?" I inquired.

"He's in the basement where he seems quite comfortable. He has his own bed and a window with a view. For my peace of mind, I know he can't wreak havoc with the rest of the house. Not that he's destructive, but I haven't had him that long and why take any unnecessary risks."

"Would you please let him out now?" I asked, then remarked, "Brandy has to get used to me as we'll be spending quite a lot of time together."

He agreed, but said, 'Tonight I want to take you to the Victorian area of Dearborn that has quite a number of good restaurants. Furthermore, I forgot to mention that I have taken the week off work, so we can do tons of sightseeing."

"Fantastic, a whole week together; I am salivating at the thought of it." I kissed him, and that lead to making love again on the kitchen counter.

"Oh, my god, Molly, you are going to be the ruination of me."

"Good, that means I am proving myself to be a successful seductress", I said in an exaggerated southern sexy drawl. We both laughed, and then I continued, "Let's have some time with Brandy, please, before we eat".

Bruce and I went down to the basement to get Brandy. He was very excited to see us both, jumping all over me as if I were a long-lost friend. I happened to see a large box marked photos in the corner of the garage. *Ah, good,* I thought. That's something I will look at when Bruce is at work. I don't think he knew the full extent of my curiosity towards these disappearances. Less said the better. Once Brandy had settled in his basket in the corner of the kitchen, Bruce decided to show me around the house more thoroughly.

"We'll go over to my father's place in the week, as I told him I'd keep an eye on the place. You don't mind do you, Molly?"

"No, that's fine with me." My mind was on being able to look around without Mike breathing down our necks.

The afternoon slid by in comfortable silence. We read the papers, nestled together on the sofa with Brandy at our feet. I kept thinking what a beautiful domestic scene this made. Around five, Bruce jumped up, declaring it was wine and cheese time before we headed out to the Victorian section for dinner.

"You won't get an argument out of me, darling," I said.

The whole setting seemed too good to be true. I felt so at ease with him. We sat sipping our wine and nibbling on crackers and cheese for about an hour, when all of a sudden Bruce got up and said that we should change and get going for dinner. Fortunately, most of my clothes were ready to wear, so I grabbed a pair of tight pants and a floaty top, put on my favorite fake, dangly diamond earrings, and *Bob's your Uncle* (an English phrase "so there it is"), I said to myself, ready to hit the town.

I wasn't one hundred percent aware of where we were going. I was still so darn tired from lack of sleep, excitement etc., so I only heard half of what Bruce was telling me about Dearborn's history. I did catch the part where in 1927 the residents of Dearborn approved a vote to become a city. I was more interested in just looking around at the different forms of architecture. We passed several exquisite rows of Victorian mansions which looked exactly like parts of London. Bruce pulled up outside an insignificant looking Italian restaurant. I was hoping the food was better than its exterior. "Well, darling girl, here we are. This is probably one of the best Italian restaurants around. I hope you're hungry, because I certainly am. You made me work up an appetite."

"Oh, really! You certainly were a contributing factor towards my hunger."

We laughed and walked inside to a small slice of Italy. Fabulous murals of scenes of Venice, Florence, and Rome adorned the walls. All three places I'd been to, so I felt very much at home. I ordered spaghetti carbonara with a side salad. Bruce ordered a loaded pizza. The waiter brought us a carafe of reasonably priced, imported Italian Chianti, along with crusty bread that helped appease our appetite.

"So, Molly, tomorrow I thought perhaps you would like to go to one of the largest Malls in America."

"Frankly, no, I wouldn't. I would rather do something else and leave mall shopping for when you're at work. The trip has left me a bit knackered. Is that okay with you?"

"Good, I was sort of hoping that would be your answer. What about going to the Arab American National Museum? It's quite fascinating as the city has about a forty percent population of Arabs. The Arab Muslim community has built the Islamic Center of America which is the largest mosque in North America, and the Dearborn Mosque. The city has quite a mix of Armenians and immigrants from the Yemen, Iraq, and Palestine, but the Lebanese are the largest group. I know you love anything foreign, so we can devote the best part of the day in this area."

"I love the idea of this. Thanks so much for doing all this research."

"Well, it isn't too much research, since I've lived here many years. We can take a trip on Lake Erie later in the week."

My mouth was full of spaghetti, so I shook my head in agreement. What a week this was going to be, in more ways than one. Naturally, Bruce had ordered coffee ice cream and two espressos.

"Delicious! Thanks, darling, for knowing me so well."

It was hard to believe that we'd been together since the middle of July. *Long may it last*, I thought. But on the other hand, it didn't seem that there was much future ahead for us, as I hated the cold and big cities. *Molly*, I said to myself, *quit being so damn negative.* I think Bruce must have sensed my mood change, as he asked me if I wanted to do anything else before going back to the house.

"No thanks, darling. Bed would be awesome, as I'm exhausted."

"Sounds good to me," he said with a broad grin on his face. He beckoned to the waiter to bring the check. As soon as he paid we got up and walked hand in hand to the car.

The city was buzzing with cars and people strolling in the crisp night air. It was almost eleven o'clock. I was used to places closing by nine in sleepy New Smyrna Beach, except on the weekends. The evening was topped off by Brandy greeting us with much enthusiasm, tail wagging, and smothering us with wet kisses. Bruce got us a couple of brandies, and we flopped on the sofa with Brandy snuggling at our feet. This was almost too domestic, but so comfortable.

"Bruce, I really must hit the hay, before I keel over." He turned the lights off and we said our goodnights to Brandy. Bed felt wonderful. The last thing I felt before I fell asleep was Bruce's hand around my waist.

I awoke to the smell of coffee permeating throughout the bedroom. No tray and flower this time, thank goodness. Routine was boring. I threw on the sexiest underwear and went downstairs to be greeted by two enthusiastic males. Bruce and Brandy were sitting by the fire side. Brandy was licking Bruce's feet, and he was drinking his usual cup of coffee.

"Hello, darling, did you sleep well?"

"Yes, thanks, I did, and feel like a different person. I'm all set for some sightseeing. But to be perfectly honest, do you think that after we've visited the Arab American Museum, I could look through some photographs of your mother? I find it rather unusual that you haven't got any pictures around, but I guess that's a typical man for you."

"If that's what you want to do, baby doll, that's fine with me, but first we must get some breakfast for you."

"I think I'd like toast and marmalade with coffee." I ate my toast as if I'd never eaten before, swilling it down with the hot, creamy coffee.

"Bruce, this coffee is to die for, where did you get it?"

"Actually, I got it at the specialty coffee shop which is two blocks from here. You'll discover it by yourself when I am working, that I'm sure of. We do have a few good things in Dearborn, even though we are pretty much snowed in during the winter months."

I sat next to him on the sofa and he put his arm around me, giving me the look that I knew only too well. We went upstairs and made delicious love. I felt so refreshed.

We laid still for a little while acting like an old married couple, arms round each other, discussing the events of the day

"I think we'd better get a move on, because the museum gets pretty crowded at this time of the year," Bruce said.

I picked out a comfortable pants outfits, tied a scarf around my hair, with matching blue dangling hoop earrings. We went downstairs, filled Brandy's water and food dish in the basement, each giving him a hug before heading out.

The Arab American museum was really manageable after having seen the Henry Ford Museum when I was last here. This museum opened in 2005. Most of the immigrants were Lebanese who moved to the Detroit area in the early 20th century to work in the auto industry. Armenians also settled here. I didn't feel like doing any more walking around, so we finished our tour by visiting the gift shop. I bought a couple of postcards and left it at that. I have hundreds of cards from every place I've visited. One of these days I'm going to decorate an entire wall with them.

We strolled out of the museum, hand-in-hand, looking at each other and knowing exactly what was on each other's mind. No, it wasn't sex this time; it was food. Right next door to the museum was a small Lebanese restaurant that Bruce obviously knew. I'd never eaten Lebanese food before; hopefully, I was in for a treat.

We had delicious unleavened bread with a mixture of eggplant, cheese, and garlic, washed down with a heavy red wine. Without even consulting me, Bruce ordered this delicious flaky pastry prune-flavored flan and coffees that were thick, sweet, and bloody strong. By the time we'd finished it was almost three and we were quite ready for an afternoon nap. We got back to the house and Brandy was asleep in his bed. I couldn't help thinking this was just the kind of atmosphere I relished. We went downstairs and didn't even ask each other what we wanted to do. We knew. We took off our clothes and made love on the rug next to the fireplace. He really was quite the most handsome and sexiest man I had been with, outside of David. I lay there thinking about what I was going to do in the garage. I was really excited about looking through all the photographs. My curiosity was getting the better of me and the sooner I went through this box of pictures the better off I would feel.

Bruce woke up and turned to me, asking if I wouldn't mind if, while I was rifling through the box of photos, he went to work for a couple of hours.

"I have an important project that I have to finish and I will feel much better about it if I do so."

"No, that's fine with me. I'm quite happy staying with Brandy, looking through your photos. And, I will ferret around in the kitchen to see what I can muster up for dinner."

Bruce said, "I was thinking, tomorrow if the weather is good, we could take a boat ride, but it all depends on how warm it is, so let's just play it by ear".

He leapt off the bed with the enthusiasm of a spring lamb, throwing on his clothes. He ran down the stairs, yelling out that he'd see me around six. I threw on my sweats and went into the garage, faithfully followed by Brandy who just sat there looking at me with this curious look. I decided to take the box into the living room where it was more comfortable. I put it on the table and started taking out the photographs. I was dumbstruck. I couldn't believe that on the back of a photograph that I assumed was Bruce's mother was written, *Good riddance*. I really didn't know what to think. I went through a ton of photographs of people that meant absolutely nothing to me and came across a few more of this redheaded lady, with a young boy, whom I assumed was Bruce. On the back of a photo of the two of them was written, *you're out of my life forever.*

Whatever went on between Mike and his wife was a mystery that deserved a lot more exploring. I decided to finish looking at all the photographs, and dug to the bottom of the pile and found a dozen or so photographs of this really lovely girl with dark red hair. She had blue eyes, and was quite attractive in an almost Spanish appearance. There was no name on the back, but I assumed it must be Valerie, Bruce's old girlfriend. I put the photographs away, just keeping out the ones of his mother. I went into the kitchen and made myself a cup of tea, whilst looking around to see what I could rustle up for dinner. Bruce was a typical bachelor. He didn't have very much in the way of decent food. I did find a couple of packets of spaghetti and two cans of tomato sauce. These would do as we'd had a darn good lunch. Having dozed off by the fire with Brandy lying on my feet I awoke to see that it was five-thirty and Bruce wasn't home, so I took it upon myself to pour a glass of red wine and await the return of my master. Bruce telephoned around five-thirty to say he'd be back in under an hour and that he'd appreciate me having a glass of wine waiting for him.

"No problem, darling, but I've already taken the liberty of pouring myself one."

True to his word, he got back at the allotted time, and I greeted him with a glass of wine and a kiss.

"Before we eat I want to just show you a few photographs that I found."

"Okay with me, but frankly I'm astonished that you found anything at all to eat."

We sat down on the sofa with Brandy at our feet and I showed him the photographs of his mother.

"I really can't understand why your father would write something so derogatory on the back of these pictures."

"Molly, my father knew that my mother had had an affair a long time ago. I never told you this as I didn't really think it important. Anyway, when my father found out, my mother apparently walked out on him, never to be seen again. From that moment on he hated her."

I was almost on the point of saying that I didn't blame her one bit, but bit my tongue. Instead, I said that sort of explained her mysterious disappearance, then asked him who was the beautiful girl in these photos?

"That is Valerie. I'd forgotten I had these pictures. In her case, she just left me one day and I haven't seen her since. I tried to call her apartment, but never got an answer, so I have no idea where she is or why she left. To this day it stupefies me. Now that you have gone through the photographs and I've answered your questions, perhaps we can eat whatever meal you have managed to prepare."

The spaghetti with tomato sauce wasn't half bad. It was helped by added spices and several glasses of Merlot. It's amazing how a decent glass of wine can improve even the most mediocre of meals.

"Bruce, you are going to have to show me the stores, so I can stock up this bachelor kitchen. After all, a couple of months are a long time, and I refuse to exist on tomato sauce and wine."

"What say we shop tomorrow morning and go to the beach in the afternoon?

"Fair enough," I said.

We cleaned up and went to bed rather early. Neither of us was very sexed up this evening, which was fine with me. I had just started my period and Bruce was bushed from working. We lay in each other's arms until the morning light streamed through the bedroom window.

Molly, I've stopped bringing you a tray with breakfast, a flower, and coffee simply because I don't want you to expect it on a daily basis. I wouldn't want you to be totally spoiled."

Spoiled, but not totally spoiled, I mused, as a smile spread over my face. I cleaned up in the bathroom and threw on my favorite purple sweats, and headed downstairs, the aroma of strong coffee calling me. Brandy greeted me enthusiastically. I threw four slices of bread into the toaster, found the last of the butter, and a jar of tired looking marmalade. I also poured Bruce a cup of coffee for which he thanked me.

"I see you've found the butter and marmalade. I am not the world's best chef, or shopper, as you have already surmised," Bruce said, apologetically.

"No problem, I'll have this place licked into shape in no time," I replied.

I wasn't quite sure how I was going to fill two months here, but I'm sure with my curious mind, time would fly by.

"Perhaps we can take a walk by the lake today, after grocery shopping. I'd like to swing by my father's tomorrow, and then Friday we can go to Frankenmuth. I figured with your European background you would really like this town. It was named by 15 settlers from the Franconia region of Bavaria, a state in Germany. They settled in the Saginaw Valley in the 1800s and named their settlement, Frankenmuth, which means 'Courage of the Franks'. This town has the largest Christmas store in the world which is open every day of the year, and since we are approaching the holiday season I thought you might enjoy Michigan's small slice of Bavaria."

"Sounds like a plan to me," I replied.

I suddenly realized that I'd be with Bruce for Christmas. A shiver ran down my spine. I'd spent every Christmas with Jen since I'd been alone in New Smyrna Beach. Ah, well. I'll cross that sentimental bridge when the time comes. After finishing breakfast, we drove to the local supermarket whose name escaped me. I wasn't paying much attention to where or how we got there safe to say it was huge and reminded me of European mega grocery stores. I went berserk over the selection of cheeses and meats. Naturally we went overboard, stocking up on everything imaginable.

Afterwards, we hit the coffee shop a few blocks away. Now this was living. I walked in and almost had an orgasm. The smell was out of this world. They must have had at least fifteen varieties of coffee. I chose a hazelnut cappuccino. It was to die for. The rich cream spilled over the side of the cup. Bruce got up and said we must get going in order to take a walk by the lake, but not before buying a bag each of hazel nut and chocolate almond coffee.

Traipsing along the river was mentally refreshing and at the end a bit tiring. Finally, we drove back to Bruce's home. Along the way, I couldn't help thinking there must be a connection between his ex and Valerie's disappearance. My dad always said I had an overly curious mind, given to fanciful speculation. He was right. I suppose that's why I love investigative journalism. I was going to do lots of digging into this mystery, even though it might be of my own making. It took us a while to unpack and put everything away, and for me to become a bit more familiar with his kitchen. It now looked more like a normal kitchen rather than just a bachelor's pad. I made a couple of ham sandwiches and we decided to splurge and have a glass of wine for lunch before heading out again.

"You'd better grab a sweater, Molly, as it will be mighty chilly this time of the year," Bruce advised.

"Where are we going?" I asked.

"It's a freshwater lake called Lake St. Clair. It's situated about six miles northeast of the downtown areas of Detroit and Windsor, Ontario. It's quite a large waterway, most of it located within Canada. I'm taking you to St. Clair Shores, which is actually situated in the suburbs of Detroit. Along the southwestern portion of the lake are many wealthy suburbs such as Grosse Pointe, Tecumseh, and Lakeshore. In this exclusive area, only residents are allowed to moor their boats. You can read more about it yourself later on."

It took about forty minutes to get there as traffic was somewhat heavy. By the time we arrived it was rather chilly. The temperature had dropped into the forties and I was glad I had thrown on a scarf and gloves; otherwise, I would have felt like I was turning into a block of ice. We walked along the shoreline admiring the view, after which I felt quite invigorated. However, it was a big change from the warmth I was used to, and not a temperature range I'd want on a permanent basis.

After a few hours of walking and gawking, Bruce asked me, "What do you say we head back to the homestead?"

"Sounds good to me; so, what would you like me to fix for dinner?"

"Absolutely nothing, as I'm going to spoil you this week, while I'm on vacation. You can become majorly domestic once I start back to work." He said, then continued: "Do you fancy seafood this evening? If so there's a great seafood bistro in Dearborn."

"That sounds just the ticket. How should I dress?"

"Naked would suit me, but since you're asking, casually elegant. I'll leave that up to you, but for now Miss Molly let's head to the bed, I'm in dire need of your body."

Our lovemaking was pure perfection. The more we made love the better it became. By now we knew every crevasse of each other's body. Next week would be a comedown after being spoiled rotten. I just hoped that I could find enough to keep me busy. The forecast was for heavy snow in a few days, so we had to make the most of things before we got hemmed in.

For dinner out, I wore a red two-piece pants suit and discreet fake stud diamonds. I couldn't see the point of wearing the real McCoy. I'd live in dread of losing them.

Bruce was right; the restaurant was quite lovely inside. The walls were dotted with stylized fish and nautical memorabilia. I opted for baked cod, French fries, and a medley of vegetables. Bruce ordered trout baked in a cream sauce with linguini and carrots. We had a bottle of white Sancerre (a wine made from the sauvignon blanc grape grown in the Sancerre region of France). It was citrusy and refreshing with its zippy acidity, and certainly pleasing my palette.

During the meal, we talked about tomorrow. We were going over to Mike's house. I felt an adrenalin rush with thoughts of looking through his garage and hopefully finding more photographs and whatever. Bruce hadn't heard from his father, but said he'd wait until he opened the mail and call his dad afterwards. Speaking of his father, why was I imagining Mike being involved in the disappearance of Bruce's mom and Valerie? My suspicions had no foundation, other than my feeling that there was a dark side to this man.

Bruce brought my focus back to the present with, "would you care for dessert, my love?"

"I could go for a crème caramel, if that's all right with you."

The waiter came by to clear our plates and Bruce ordered two crème caramels and two decaf coffees.

"This has been a perfect end to a brilliant day. Thanks, darling", I said after dessert.

He gave me a smile that sent a pleasant sensation throughout my body. He really was an amazing catch. Being rather tired Bruce asked for our bill, which he paid, then we gathered up our coats and headed to his house for a good night's rest.

The following morning was much as I'd expected. Coffee, toast, feeding Brandy, and off to Mike's house. Both of us seemed to prefer to make love at night. If we only had a few days together it would have been morning, noon and night, but we were more relaxed knowing that we were going to be together for quite some time to come.

"Molly, we'll take Brandy with us. We could actually walk to my dad's, but since we have mail to get etc., we'll drive this time. You can walk there when I'm at work. It'll give you something to do, and Brandy could sure use the exercise. I know you haven't forgotten that tomorrow we are going to Frankenmuth. It'll take about an hour and a half to get there. It's approximately seventy-five miles from Dearborn, but it all depends on traffic. I know you'll love that town. You can always drive me to work sometime and go there by yourself. Anyway, that's down the road. Today is mundane stuff."

I had forgotten how tastefully decorated Mike's house was. That in itself was a surprise. Bruce collected the mail which was quite substantial.

"Molly, why don't you go and fish around in the garage for pictures? I know that you are itching to find out more about my family. It's going to take me a while to go through the mail."

"Will do, darling, so on that note, let's get going, Brandy", who barked enthusiastically, as we went into the garage to begin my search.

Unlike the rest of the house, the garage was a mess. I spotted two large boxes on a shelf at the back marked, *Photos and Memorabilia.* Rather than go through them in the garage I decided to take one box at a time into the kitchen.

There were masses of pictures that had faded with time, which made it impossible to identify who they were. As I got towards the bottom, I saw an album marked *The Three of Us.* The pictures were obviously of Bruce and his mother. Several were marked, *Greta and Bruce.* That was the first time I'd seen her name written down, or come to think of it, mentioned. Bruce must have been about ten. The entire album was of the two of them. Underneath were more photos. I came across one of Greta by herself and written on the back was, *Greta, the whore.* This one made me feel quite sick. I uncovered several more of her with the words, *Greta, the unfaithful.* I wondered if Bruce had any idea about these photos or the writing on the backs of them, but assumed he didn't; otherwise, I was sure he would have mentioned it. I decided to put them back in the box, and took it back to the garage. I would discuss my findings with Bruce later. The second box would be reserved for next week. No sooner had I returned to the kitchen than Bruce came in, planting a kiss on my cheek and asking me if I was satisfied with what I'd found so far.

"Well, I wouldn't say satisfied is the correct word, but I learned a bit more about your life and that of your mother. I never knew her name until now. Why did your father call her the whore?"

"What are you talking about, Molly?"

"Well, written on the back of one of the photos was *Greta, the unfaithful* and on another was *Greta, the whore.* Can you explain what this means?"

Bruce looked at me very awkwardly, shifting from one foot to another, and then paced up and down the kitchen seemingly very perturbed.

"My mother was apparently unfaithful to my father and that is all I know, Molly. If there was anything else to tell you, I would, but there isn't. I'm sorry that I never told you her name. It didn't seem that important at the time. I hope your curiosity has been satisfied?"

"For the time being, yes, I suppose it is," I replied.

"Now let's change the subject, Molly. How about stopping at the corner diner for lunch? We can slouch around this afternoon as tomorrow we are going to Frankenmuth."

"Suits me! Why don't you call your father whilst I re-arrange the photo boxes in preparation for my next visit to your dad's garage?"

I knew there was more to this scenario than met the eye, but next week I would start some serious investigating into Greta's and Valerie's disappearance.

The remainder of the day and evening were uneventful. The next morning, we had a leisurely breakfast and set off for Frankenmuth around ten. It took about an hour to get there. Bruce was right; I really felt as if I was transported back to Europe. By the time we had wandered around and I had a flavor for the place, it was time to eat lunch. We settled on a German Brew Haus and Grill which had a mixture of finger foods, delicious bratwurst sausages and the like, plus warm beer.

"I'm definitely coming back here, Bruce, with or without you. I know I will just love browsing around the Christmas store. I'd read about the Bavarian Inn Glockenspiel Tower that plays a selection of melodies followed by a presentation of carved wooden figures depicting the life of the Pied Piper of Hamelin."

"I'm not going to stop you, but am glad to give that particular trip a miss. Shopping for Xmas stuff is not my bag."

"I quite understand good sir. Besides, I need to find lots of fun things to fill my snowy days when you are at work."

I didn't want to tell him what my real idea of fun was. Less said the better. We walked back to the car, feeling very satisfied with the meal we'd just had and quite tired from the day's activities. I did my usual and fell asleep on the trip back to Bruce's.

"Wake up, my sleepyhead," he said.

"I'm sorry, Bruce, but I don't seem to be able to stay awake as a passenger. That has always been my weakness."

"No problem, I'm sure you'll make it up to me later on."

That evening I made it up to him in spades. We had what I would describe as ferocious sex on the living room sofa. Bruce fell off to my side and sighed with utter satisfaction - as did I.

"Golly, Molly", he said in exaggerated rhyming fashion. "You were absolutely spot on. You certainly did make it up to me. What do you say we retire to bed for a good night's sleep?"

"Good idea. But then, you are always full of good ideas. So, what is your idea for tomorrow?"

"I really haven't given it much thought. I'm sure we'll fill the day quite successfully."

We undressed in silence, both slipping into bed and reading for a while. Bruce fell asleep before I did. I read the guide book on Michigan which didn't really do much to keep me awake either. Another night of blissful sleeping, arms wrapped around each other.

The next morning, I awoke to the usual smell of coffee coming from a mug on the bedside table. I thanked Bruce for my morning jolt of caffeine as he came out of the bathroom. He told me that the weather had made our minds up for this long weekend.

"We have about a foot of snow outside, so Molly we are going to have to have a lot of sex, and home cooked meals."

"Sounds right up my alley," I said, as I drank the strong coffee, gradually wakening to the day.

After my morning ablutions, Bruce and I hopped into bed and made leisurely love. It might sound corny when I say that it was a very relaxing and comfortable experience. The urgency of sex at the beginning of our relationship had changed into something more intimate and less rushed, so natural, yet wildly arousing at times. We lay together for an hour or so, before deciding that more coffee and toast was in order.

Bruce was dead right about the order of this weekend. Once we fed ourselves and Brandy, and viewed the beautiful wintery scene, we went upstairs and made love. Again! This time we acted like wild animals, devouring each other, kissing each other, digging our fingers into each other's' shoulders, and coming together with such an explosion that we gasped in unison and fell to the wayside of sleep. We never got dressed. The day drifted by in a delightful haze of eating, reading and committing sexy acts.

At one of the intervals, Bruce said he was going to make tuna melts and that I should take my wine into the living room, start a fire and he'd bring the sandwiches in when he was finished.

"You're not getting an argument out of me. I'm rather famished", I said.

"I prefer to be in the kitchen by me; besides, it will give you a break before next week rolls around and you become Miss Domestic," he offered.

The sandwiches were delicious enough; although very different from any tuna melt I'd had in the past. I was grateful for my glass of white wine with which to wash them down. There was a particular spice that Bruce had put in that didn't quite suit my taste buds, but far be it from me to mention that to him.

Saturday sped by in somewhat the same fashion as yesterday. We never got dressed. We made love several times, sat and read by the fireplace, and agreed that tomorrow we really should take a walk in the snow. As much as I hate the cold, it was a novelty and I knew I'd probably enjoy it. The last time I remember playing in the snow was when I was five.

The next morning, I dressed in more layers than I thought a human being could put on. I felt bulky, fat, and very uncomfortable. Bruce looked at me and burst out laughing.

"I know that I look like the abominable snow lady. Please let's get going before I am crushed under the weight of these clothes."

I had to admit that what awaited me outside took my breath away. It was certainly a magical winter wonderland. The trees had icicles hanging down from their branches and were swaying in the brisk morning air. The snow was deep and fresh and came up to my knees. We slowly trampled through it to the end of the block, before I couldn't stand the freezing cold any more. Beautiful it was - to look at, not to experience first-hand.

"Bruce, I need to go back. NOW! I'm so bloody cold, I can't endure it."

"I didn't think you'd last more than a block or two, but you have to admit it is very picturesque."

"Yes, I can't deny that, but I think I'll admire it from inside, if you don't mind?"

"He slipped his arm around my 'Michelin' attire, kissed my frozen nose and dragged me back inside.

"Hot chocolate with a touch of brandy is in order, don't you think?" he asked.

I nodded in the affirmative as I stripped off my layers, finally feeling more like me than a roly-poly orphan of the cold.

"Double up on the brandy, if you please, Bruce. I'm going to put my comfy sweats on."

There was no way in Hell I was moving to this part of the world on a permanent basis. I didn't care how much I loved this man. This morning had made my mind up. It was warm weather or remaining single for the rest of my life. I took off the three sweaters I'd piled on and got comfortable in my grey sweats, but touched up my makeup and combed my hair which had become a wet frizzy mess. I hated my curls but understood that I probably would have paid a fortune to have then put in. I felt so much better, both mentally and physically, knowing that my mind was made up about my residential future.

"Now you look more like the girl I fell in love with than some arctic moon gal," Bruce said with a huge grin spreading over his face.

"I feel more like the girl you know and love so well too."

I suddenly felt in desperate need of sex, so I went over to Bruce, kissed him passionately, and started to undo his shirt buttons. Dear God, he didn't even have time to take his shirt off before I felt him swelling inside his trousers. He took me on the kitchen counter with an urgency that almost frightened me. It felt as if this was the last time we would ever make love.

"Molly, you're a piece of work. I think I will venture out in the snow again with you. Obviously, the cold weather does something for your sex hormones."

I laughed outwardly, but felt a trifle sad. This was the last day of Bruce's vacation, but looking on the positive side, tomorrow I'd be able to start delving into the mystery of the missing Michigan women – well, misplaced ones at the very least.

I awoke to a tray of hot coffee, a rose, toast, and delicious French raspberry jam placed on the bedside table. Before I could even thank Bruce, his enormous erection told me that I'd have a cold breakfast. It was worth it.

"Oh, by the way, the cold toast is really good with this jam. Thanks for spoiling me darling." He smiled and jumped off the bed like the virtual athlete I'd come to know.

"I'm going downstairs, so I'll await my highness when she is ready".

I smiled from ear to ear. I think he was beginning to understand that as much I really loved him, I also relished my solitude and hoped that he would come to really understand that side of me. In the meantime, I ate the dry toast, threw on my sweats, and spent way too long making up my face. He was worth the effort, as much as I loathed makeup.

"Molly, what shall we do for the rest of the day?"

"Nothing other than what we do within these walls." Sex for three hours after breakfast was perfect. It was long, incredibly exciting, yet, at the same time, slow and utterly transforming us onto another planet. Our sweaty bodies intertwined for quite some time after our orgasms, in the cool silence of the bedroom. Lunch was pasta, marinara sauce and a couple of glasses of Australian Merlot. We shot the breeze in a warm, but messy kitchen. After the perfunctory job of cleaning up, Bruce brushed my cheek with his moist lips and beckoned me towards the living room. We sank down onto the fake fur rug and lay together, whilst Brandy gave us wet kisses until we faded into a deep sleep.

I awoke suddenly to Brandy's obvious urgency to pee.

"Off we go, Brandy." Damn, I thought, I've got to throw on a few layers before I face the frigid outdoors. Brandy rushed outside to do his business. Both our noses went blue.

"Okay, Brandy, are you done? Enough of this tundra climate for me, so let's move it."

He smiled at me, showing his large, but cute doggy teeth, and brushed against me with earnest affection.

"Hey, buddy, we're going to have so much fun", I said as I entered the warmth of the house I almost called home.

Bruce was up and dressed for work.

"Molly, my love, I got an urgent call from my CEO wondering if we could go over a few details later this afternoon, before tomorrow's meeting. I could hardly say no. Hope you don't mind? What I thought I could do is bring back some Chinese for dinner."

"Perfect, and no, I don't mind. It'll give me time to finish reading a guide book on the area. After all, I've got seven more weeks here. Don't get me wrong, it's magical, and Brandy and I'll have some good bonding together, but I'll miss you whenever you are not with me."

"I'll call you when I am heading back," he said, then freshened up before leaving.

Funnily enough I was quite anxious for Monday to roll around as I wanted to go over to Mike's house and do some serious digging around. My intuition was telling me that his dad had a very dark side, and I was going to try and prove myself right. On a lighter note, I envisioned a visit Tuesday or Wednesday to the Edsel and Eleanor Ford House, at Grosse Pointe Shores. I had always been fascinated with this house after reading up about it, particularly since it was styled after houses in the Cotswold's of England, which is one of my favorite areas back home.

Around five o'clock I decided to take a long bubble bath. I hadn't had the luxury of taking time for this in eons. Bruce had called to say he'd be back around 7:30 which gave me time to spoil myself. I poured myself bourbon and found a couple of magnolia scented candles. I decided to let Brandy come up with me. I wasn't sure whether he was allowed in the bathroom, but I wouldn't say anything. What the eye didn't see the heart wouldn't bleed over. Brandy sat by the side of the bath fascinated with the bubbles. He kept putting his nose on them and making the strangest of noises. I could almost swear that he was laughing.

Bath time over, I dried off, slapped a mild magnolia cologne over my body and put on my purple sweats - my favorite casual clothes. Applying some makeup, I glanced in the mirror and was pleasantly surprised at what I saw. The bath had done wonders for soothing my mind and body. I went downstairs and settled into the comfy armchair in the living room, no sooner to hear Bruce unlocking the front door. I got up to greet him and took a couple of the bags of Chinese food he'd bought and put them in the kitchen. "How many people are you feeding?" I asked with a big smile.

"Well, I figured that if I bought enough for today and tomorrow you wouldn't have to do any cooking, so wasn't that nice of me."

"Yes," I said. Nice was a word that my mother disliked. She felt it so bland and nondescript, which was far from describing the Chinese food that Bruce had brought back with him. He had picked out fried rice, sweet-and-sour pork, which a while back I'd mentioned was my favorite, and a beef dish with mushrooms. It was delicious, accompanied by my bourbon.

"Molly, I've not seen you drink bourbon in a long time. You usually drink red wine."

"I know, but I decided to treat myself while in vacation mode. I'm not going to be overindulgent, because I definitely will clean your house when you're at work, and naturally I'll look after Brandy. By the way, it's my plan to go over to your father's tomorrow to pick up his mail and plow through some of his photographs. I know I have this over curious mind, but there's something that doesn't ring true about your girlfriend and your mother, so allow me to do a bit of delving. Okay? And something else is niggling at me. I know I haven't been here long, and our relationship is relatively new, but I've never ever heard you talk about your friends. I assume since you've lived here a long time that you do have friends? I know that I only have Jen in New Smyrna Beach, but have a lot of contacts through work, plus my other three closest girl friends are in Europe."

"That's really funny that you should bring up this topic. I was going to ask you if you wanted to meet one of my gym friends Nigel and his girlfriend Sally. I've known him for about five years, but you know guys; we tend not to communicate very well. Anyway, he'd mentioned perhaps getting together for dinner this weekend."

"That sounds good to me, darling. I'm quite excited really. I was beginning to wonder if you weren't living a monk like existence."

"I'm really sorry, my love. I guess I was being selfish not disclosing more of my life here. But now that I am pretty certain that we're a steady item, or at least I'd like to think so, I really want you to meet some of my buddies. I have two really good friends at work, Doug Williams and Colin Close. They are department heads in the bio-chemical research division. We've worked together for several years, but got friendly by going to the company gym. In fact, the company is having our 'Winter Games' party in two weeks. I was hoping that we could attend and you could see where I work and meet all the gang. Does this idea appeal to you?"

"Yes, sure, but what exactly does the 'Winter Games' entail? If it means dressing up in Michelin layers and sliding on toboggans, count me out. Otherwise, I would love to do some socializing."

"No. We just have fun indoor stuff like table tennis, cards, and the like. So that makes it a go," he offered, then said, "Molly, what say we call it a night?"

"Right on, as I'm knackered."

Bruce looked at me weirdly. I don't think he'd heard me use this word before. We went about our ablutions like an old married couple and were in bed and asleep in less than half an hour. As I drifted off I was actually excited at the prospect of being commander in chief for a week.

The next morning, I woke up to find my usual tray of coffee on the dresser and a note saying that he loved me, wished me a great day and that he'd be back around eight.

I really did relate to the famous Wordsworth poem "I wandered Lonely as a Cloud" - especially the line: *for oft when on my couch I lie, in vacant or in pensive mood, they flash upon that inward eye, which is the bliss of solitude.* It sums up to perfection the necessity for alone time. Many poets, writers, and artists feel this need. Lord Byron, for one, certainly had more than his fair share of alone time. He spent twelve years incarcerated in the Chateau de Chillon in Switzerland, simply for being a writer, where he died of tuberculosis, confined to a room with a slit window, overlooking Lake Montreux. Who wouldn't succumb in that damp and dreary place, despite a magical view – good for a day or two maybe, but not the only view for a lifetime. Memories of walking there with my mother flooded into my head and I had to busy myself lest I got too morbid.

I decided to call Jen around lunch time to find out what was going on back in the tropics. How I yearned for that warmth. The best part of this morning was that I didn't have to wear makeup! I threw on my purple sweats, which had been washed numerous times already, and went downstairs to let Brandy out in the backyard. It was freezing. I could barely catch my breath while I waited for him. After a leisurely breakfast of oatmeal and toast, playing with Brandy and cleaning up the house, which even entailed vacuuming - in my mind, a necessary evil. I called Jen at work after my turn at domesticity. She was excited to hear from me and we talked for about forty minutes.

Her love life was going well, work was busy but great, and when she told me it was in the eighties, I sighed, "You lucky bitch; it's so cold here, I wouldn't stay another week, if it weren't for Bruce and his father's dog, Brandy. Anyway, Jen, I'm going over to Mike's house today to do some serious delving into the disappearance of Bruce's mother's and his old girlfriend. Do you think I'm crazy?"

"Molly, I think that you should check to see if there is an affordable detective agency that could help with your investigation."

"Jen, I'm amazed at your idea, because I was thinking the exact same thing. At this stage, if I lose Bruce over this, so is it. My curious nature has to be satisfied. That aside, I really love him, and am getting majorly attached to Brandy: a beautiful, friendly chocolate Labrador. It's so darn funny; really, that everything related to Bruce is awesome, except for the man who fathered him. But I've come to the conclusion that there isn't a single normal family on this planet."

Jen replied, "You're on the nose there, Molly. Changing the subject, I really miss our walks on the beach."

"Thanks a lot for that info whilst I'm freezing my rear end off. This area is so beautiful, but winter time; forget it. Anyway, you've inspired me to move right along with my crazy ideas. I've got some money saved up that will pay for this. I'll call you next week and let you know what I've done. Say hello to Charlie, and when you dip your feet in the ocean, think of me. Bye girl friend, it's been great talking to you."

"Likewise. Good luck with your ventures and have a great time with Bruce. And when you trudge through the slush, think of me." She laughed and hung up before I got a chance to say anything else.

Bruce got back around ten thirty as expected. I was already ensconced in bed reading a trashy romance novel. He shouted up the stairs to ask me if I needed anything.

"No thanks, I'm waiting for you." He came in ripping off his shirt, throwing it on the chair and headed for the bathroom. Afterwards he leapt into bed for love making that was brief but very satisfying. We hadn't uttered more than a dozen sentences between us before he fell asleep. I continued to read for about half an hour before my eyes couldn't stay ajar any longer.

Miracles would have it that I got up before he was even awake, so I was able to let Brandy out for his usual morning business. It was still so bloody cold outside. I made coffee, threw four slices of bread in the toaster and feeling like a naughty schoolgirl, I took a swig of brandy. At least I knew I wasn't on the road to becoming an alcoholic. Too many people in my life had been heavy imbibers and it was nauseating to me. I sounded like a real hypocrite. I wasn't. I had been shit faced drunk twice in my life and that was twice too many, so from now on it was social drinking and staying in control of my faculties. *Okay, girl, enough of being so sanctimonious*, I said to myself.

Bruce came downstairs dressed for work. "Sorry, Molly, no time for loving right now. I'm already running late for an important meeting."

He grabbed a piece of toast and his coffee mug. He kissed me passionately and promised he'd make it up to me this evening.

"I love you too, Bruce, I said, shutting the door and relishing the warmth of the kitchen, which was normally not my favorite room.

I finished up the usual kitchen cleanup chores, dressed in layers, fed Brandy, and put his leash on as he wagged his tail and gave me his wonderful grin. I locked the kitchen door, glanced around the kitchen to double check that all the necessary appliances were switched off, and headed off to the car with Brandy tugging at his leash. It was about twenty-five degrees outside. I bundled him into the backseat and set off for Mike's house, which I actually admired. Its attractiveness grabbed me every time I went there. But I reminded myself that it was his wife who had decorated the place.

I collected the mail, setting it in three piles: bills, magazines, and junk stuff. After taking a drink of water, which should have been brandy to give me Dutch courage, I finally took the plunge to dial information for Utah from my cell phone.

"May I help you, ma'am?" a female voice asked.

"Yes. I'm looking for a Valeria Pickens in Utah, but unfortunately I don't have a specific town for her."

"I'll see what I can do. Please hold the line." A couple of minutes went by before she got back to me. "I have a listing for a Valerie G. Pickens of Salt Lake City, Utah. The number I have is 435-823-4579."

I thanked the operated, hung up, then took the bull by the horns, and dialed the number to hear the words I didn't expect to hear, "This number has been disconnected." My heart missed a beat. I was no closer to solving her disappearance; although this gave me the feeling something wasn't kosher. She had either moved or was missing. I was snapped back into the present by Brandy wanting to go outside.

Mike's garden was covered in a thick layer of snow. Brandy peed, leaving a visible mark on the pristine snow. He suddenly started running around like crazy. He was sniffing at a particular patch of snow, trying to get rid of it, continually scratching away at this particular spot.

"What's with this area that makes it so interesting, Brandy?" I asked him, as if he really understood me. Finally, my canine companion calmed down.

"Come on; let's go inside before we both become frozen fixtures."

I decided this was enough snooping for one day. I began to feel quite uneasy, even a tad claustrophobic, to say nothing of my stomach telling me I needed to eat.

"Let's get going Brandy."

He wagged his tale in agreement. I checked the locks before leaving. Tomorrow was my goof off day. I had decided to visit the Edsel and Eleanor Ford House in Grosse Pointe. Then Wednesday I was coming back here to continue serious rifling through the photos. My adrenalin was pumping. I almost forgot a major reason I was here in Michigan. I felt like a sleazy, third rate private eye, but I needed something other than sightseeing and dog sitting whilst Bruce was at work.

Back at Bruce's, I engrossed myself in leafing through the yellow pages looking for a private detective close by. I found two: One was about ten minutes from Mike's house, the other was smack in the middle of town. I called both from my cell phone. My mind was easily made up as to which one I'd go with. The one close to Mike's charged $125.00 an hour. The other one, had a message that ended with, *I'll find just what you're looking for in little time at only $65 an hour; my name is Bri.* I couldn't leave my number, but knew that this was my man.

Bruce called to say he'd be back around eight and that he wanted to go out to eat.

"I was hoping you'd say that, so I'll see you this evening."

We went to this awesome French/Lebanese restaurant. They had the best beef and chicken pitas. For dessert, we both chose a sweet pastry filled with ground nuts, topped with whipped cream, accompanied by a sweet Muscat wine. Once back at the house, Bruce grabbed me in the kitchen, taking me again on the counter. It was clean, but I wouldn't have cared if he'd shoved everything on the floor. This counter would never look ordinary to me again. Bruce was so masterful at giving me the best climax I'd ever experienced, and we went up to bed, content. I was secretly thrilled that he didn't ask me about my day. He said that he'd call his father later on in the week. I told him I was going to the Edsel and Eleanor Ford House tomorrow.

"You know, darling girl that I've never been there, so I expect a full report."

"Absolutely, Bruce, I promise." I was so lucky to have found him. He'd even rented a car for the time I was with him, so I'd be mobile. If that wasn't love, what was? I felt even worse about deceiving him about my darker suspicions, but I'd convinced myself it was for him that I was meddling.

I didn't even hear him leave the next morning. A tray of coffee, a donut and a note saying, *I love you, see you tonight, my love,* was on the dresser. The coffee was stone cold, but the aroma sent me downstairs to nuke it. It was strong and had a hint of ginger to it. Two cups of it with toast and a banana set me up for the morning. I dressed decently, threw some makeup on, filled Brandy's water and food up for the day, and then let him out. I felt a bit mean shutting him in all day, but he did have the doggy hatch to let himself out and in when nature called.

The trip wasn't bad to Grosse Point. Without the GPS system, I'd have been up shit's creek. I wasn't a person who could be told to go North, East, South, or West. Left or right was my kind of directions. I wasn't disappointed. I opted not to take a guided tour, but amble around by myself. The house was exactly like the ones in the Cotswold's in England. In fact, the Fords traveled to England with their architect, Albert Kahn, to build an exact replica of one. Theirs was built in 1926 and had the traditional moss and ivy growing on the outside of the house. One thing that struck me as sensational was the kitchen counter that was made of sterling silver. The house was lavishly decorated, keeping totally in the English style. It was quite majestic. The garden more than lived up to its reputation. Even with snow on the ground, the flower beds had been cleaned off. Poinsettias lined either side of the meadow leading to the reflecting pool, along with a beautiful array of trimmed bushes. I could well imagine how magnificent it must be in the spring when all the snow had gone and spring flowers were in full bloom. I bet it was really crowded at that time of year. I had visited the Cotswold's with my dad for a holiday just before I left for the States and had fond memories of staying in this beautiful hotel on the main road. Now that experience seemed a life time away.

I had brought snacks, so opted to buy a coffee from the self-service restaurant. I reviewed the brochure to find Edsel Ford died in 1943, and Eleanor Ford lived here until her death in 1976. I decided not to go to the basement, but ambled through the rest of the home until I was tired; it was almost three-thirty. I hoped to return with Bruce and perhaps take a guided tour. Deciding to leave I hopped into my rented vehicle and turned on the GPS. I simply followed instructions back to Bruce's, but didn't have a brass clue as to how I got from A to B. I would get back in time to relax, let Brandy out and decide on dinner.

True to form Bruce had left me a phone message saying he would be back around seven and was sorry that it was so late. Brandy was waiting anxiously next to the kitchen door, but he was wagging his tail. I guessed he wanted my company while outside, rather than just using his own door.

"Alright, buddy, let's go. Molly is tired and wants to have a glass of wine and thaw out before she gets Bruce dinner."

I swear he understood every word I said, because he did what he had to do, sniffed around the snow covered back garden for a few moments, and ran back inside with me to retreat from the cold.

I opened a bottle of Merlot, cut up some cheese and went into the living room and built a fire. In no time at all, I had it roaring. Brandy jumped on my lap and we settled into domestic bliss together. I was ravenous and ate all the cheese, deciding that I needed another glass of wine. I would make veggie omelets for dinner. I wasn't in the mood to spend a lot of time in the kitchen anyway. The cold, and wine had a really somniferous effect on me. Yes, I dozed off. The next thing I knew was a hand tapping me on the shoulder. "Hello, darling girl, you look the picture of peace and tranquility. I'm sorry to have woken you up."

"Oh, Bruce, I apologize, but the sightseeing and cold really wiped me out. The house was magnificent and I can't wait to go back with you and take a guided tour. How was your day?"

"It was very busy. We had lengthy meetings, but nothing that I really want to elaborate upon. I'm just happy to be home with you. I'm going to pour myself a glass of whisky. I feel I deserve it. Do you want another wine?"

"No thanks, Bruce, I've had enough already. Tell you what, why don't you sit in the kitchen with me whilst I make us a killer omelet."

He nodded in agreement. It wasn't a killer omelet, but it was quite tasty. We sat chatting about the office party that was coming up this weekend. It would be really fun to meet the people that Bruce interacted with on a daily basis. I did the dishes, whilst Bruce let Brandy out for his nightly sortie. Once the kitchen was in order, Bruce suggested we retire to the boudoir. In so many ways I felt as if I had been with him forever. Everything between us was so amazingly comfortable. We went upstairs to bed. In a matter of minutes, Bruce was fast asleep. And I was not far behind.

The next morning, he woke me with a mug of coffee, then said that he'd be back around three and that he wanted to eat out tomorrow.

"You won't get an argument out of me on that one, Bruce. I'm going over to your dad's, to go through some more photos. I haven't looked at the big box in the garage. I've had enough sightseeing for the next few days."

He chugged his coffee down, patted me on the back, blew me a kiss, and was out the door before I could offer any reaction to his caress.

Once at Mike's, I did the usual perfunctory job of getting the mail and sorting it out. I then picked up a box of photos from the garage and put it on the dining room table. I was hoping that I'd really learn more about Bruce's life. I tipped the box out onto the table, somewhat overwhelmed by the sheer quantity of pictures. I started sifting through one by one. There were many of Bruce, Mike and his mother, otherwise known as Greta. As I turned over more recent ones I read on the back, Bruce, Mike and the bitch. What on earth was that all about? The rest of the photos were of scenes and people that I didn't recognize. I can't say I was any further along with my investigation. I put them back in the box and returned it to the garage. I'd brought a marmite sandwich with me. I was ravenous and it tasted really good. Brandy was sleeping on the kitchen floor next to me. I took the bull by the horns and called Bri.

"This is Bri, may I help you?" he answered.

"Yes. At least I hope so. I'd like to make an appointment to see you. Do you have any time tomorrow by chance?"

"As luck would have it, I have a cancellation at 11.30. My address is 120 Clover Street, and you are?"

"My name is Molly Thomas. I'm actually staying with my boyfriend and I'd prefer for this to be strictly confidential between the two of us."

"No problem, Molly, so I'll see you at eleven-thirty tomorrow. Do me a favor and call me if you can't make it, please."

"I'll do that, but is your name really Bri?"

"Well, my actual name is Brian Stevens, but I answer to Bri. Let's hope I'll be able to help you tomorrow."

I hung up satisfied to know that I had started my formal investigations. Brandy woke up wanting to go outside. I threw on my parker and walked around the garden whilst he relieved himself. He went to the same spot that he'd nosed around the other day and kept scratching away at the surface of the snow.

"What's with this particular area that you are so intrigued by, Brandy?"

He kept digging away with his paws. If it hadn't been so damn cold, I might have stayed and helped him, but I was not enjoying this at all.

"Come on boy; we are going inside."

We got back to Bruce's around five. I had a feeling that if I weren't doing this investigation into the disappearing ladies, I would become a trifle bored. I missed my work and with the crappy weather here I couldn't really get out and about very much. I had six more weeks to go. I questioned myself as to whether I would last that long. Love is one thing, but filling the hours when my lover is at work is quite something else. I was excited to meet Bri tomorrow and start my investigation. I didn't have too long to be in a down mood. Bruce walked into the house in a wonderful frame of mind.

"Well, darling, I trust you had a good day without me?"

"As a matter of fact, I didn't really do much of anything other than go over to your father's, sort out the mail and look at the entire box of photos. Did you have a good day at work?"

"I had a great day. By the way, the company is bringing forward their company winter games do to this coming weekend. As I mentioned before, the function consists of indoor games and catered food. It will give us something to do Saturday night."

"Sounds good to me, and now monsieur, dinner is served."

I had made some pea soup with crusty French bread accompanied by a damn good merlot. When Bruce gave me that certain look, I knew it meant one thing only. We went upstairs and had the best sex. We lingered over every touch and he took me as if it were for the first time.

I woke up the following morning with Bruce having already left. As usual a mug of coffee was on the dresser with a note saying that he loved me and would be back around six. I swigged the coffee and thought excitedly of meeting Bri later in the morning. I wasn't sure what Bri could do for me, but at least it was a start. I dressed decently, but not in my best. I didn't want him to think that I had tons of money – which, of course, I didn't. I went downstairs, heated myself another mug of coffee, let Brandy out, and ate a couple of pieces of toast. I jotted down in a notebook the questions that I wanted to ask Bri. By the time I'd done the usual mundane chores it was time to leave.

To re-iterate, I don't know what I'd do without the GPS. Well, I managed before, and didn't think anything of perusing a map, but this made life so easy. I set the address and sped off. I was amazed to realize his office was less than five minutes away. I parked and rang the doorbell. I could see why he was cheap. His office was perfunctory. The man was probably in his thirties with long hair that could have done with a comb. He had an adorable smile and he was clean shaven, a good sign.

"Hello, I'm Molly Thomas and assume you must be Bri."

"Your assumption is correct. So, let's get down to brass tacks, shall we?"

I filled him in on Mike and Bruce and the mysterious disappearances of Bruce's girlfriend and mother. "I tried phoning Utah where Valerie Pickens lived, but the number had been disconnected."

"No worries, I have friends in the police force in many states, so I can dig deeper. Now, the main question is, who do you want me to investigate first?"

"Well, I think it would be a good idea to first find out what happened to Valerie Pickens. The main thing is to keep this whole matter strictly between you and me. I think that she split up with Bruce about a year ago. It would be a good start to find anything out about her."

"Alright; give me a couple of weeks. But I'll call you as soon as I've made meaningful progress. I'll do my best to keep the cost down. It usually adds up to about four or five hours of work, or about $240 - $300 for Ms. Pickens. Is that about what you expected to have to pay?"

"I really didn't have much clue to be perfectly honest, but that sounds about right to me. Thanks so much, Bri. I'll call you in a couple of weeks, if you have not contacted me."

"You bet. But in the meantime, I'd like a retainer fee of $200 as security that you don't disappear into thin air."

"Not a problem," I said, as I wrote him a check for $200. "Thanks in advance for your efforts."

"Bye, Molly. I'll do my utmost to come up with something concrete to tell you. Have a good couple of weeks then."

I walked to the car feeling really sleazy. I felt as if I was cheating on Bruce, but I really wasn't. As I drove back I passed this bakery which called to me. I stopped and bought two meringues with cream fillings and a cappuccino to go. With the taste of the warm, creamy coffee, my spirits soared. Back to Brandy and Bruce and what was my temporary home.

Friday came and went with nothing much out of the ordinary occurring. I was beginning to get restless and wondered how on earth I was going to fill my remaining time. I hadn't been out of work this long in forever. I wasn't good at being idle. Looking after Brandy, the house and Bruce was great, but there was a hole. I would have to fill it somehow. Dealing with the private eye wasn't enough.

Saturday morning was the usual ritual of coffee, toast, and marmalade brought up to me. We drank the hot, strong coffee in bed, reading the papers like an old married couple. It was hard to believe that we'd only been together just less than six months.

"What time is the do tonight, Bruce?"

"It starts around seven. It should be a lot of fun."

He was right. We got there a tad after seven and he introduced me to Doug Williams and Colin Close, the department heads he had spoken of. I was then introduced to so many people in the company that I was lucky if I remembered their faces. I met his secretary, Sally, who was a very likeable girl. She wouldn't set the world on fire in the looks department, but had a tremendous personality. Bruce had mentioned her name to me on one occasion, but I dismissed her from my mind.

The food had been catered by a local Italian restaurant. We had pizza, pasta with cream sauce, meatballs, bread, olives red wine, and tiramisu for dessert. In between eating we played table tennis.

It took me back to my school days. I was quite good back then, but had had no practice and it showed. But I had a blast. We stayed until about eleven that evening, having eaten more food than I possibly thought imaginable. We said our goodbyes to many of his co-workers. I was tickled to have met them.

"Next weekend, Molly, we are going to meet up with my gym friend Nigel Dexter and his girlfriend Sally Alcott. I think you'll really like her. In the meantime, we have to think of something to do tomorrow. With the weather being so bad, it's not really conducive to doing much of anything outdoors. But we could go out to brunch. I know a great place overlooking the water."

"Yes, that sounds appealing, Bruce. I have to tell you that I am getting somewhat restless. I haven't been on holiday for this long in ages and I am getting a little itchy footed to do something. Is there a vet around here that I might be able to volunteer my services to whilst here?"

"I'm not sure, but we can look in the yellow pages. It sounds like a great idea for you. If the weather were better you probably wouldn't be as bored."

He went into his office and brought back a phonebook. There was a vet not too far away. Bruce called to explain the situation and asked if they needed help. It was my lucky day. One of their staff had the flu so an extra hand would be appreciated. He passed the phone over to me and I filled them in on my credentials.

"Can you start tomorrow? Before you answer, my name is Cliff Benton and I am the resident vet here. We aren't usually open Sundays, so you were lucky to catch me. I came in for a few hours to catch up on paper work."

"My name is Molly Thomas and I would be thrilled to start tomorrow." He gave me the address and said that he'd expect me around nine.

"Thanks so much for this opportunity, Dr. Benton."

"Just call me Cliff. And you don't need to thank me. I should be thanking you, Molly. You have no idea how wonderful this is going to be not to be short staffed. I can't pay you that much, but enough to cover your travel expenses."

"That's fine. I'll see you tomorrow, Cliff." I put the phone down and let out a loud *Yes!*

"Are you alright, Molly?" Bruce asked in startled fashion.

"Am I alright? You better believe I'm alright. I'm so thrilled to know that I will have something else to do around here. Don't get me wrong, darling, but I'm not someone that likes to be totally domestic day in day out. Now you were talking about brunch somewhere, because I'm ready to rock and roll."

Bruce's idea of rocking and rolling was not exactly what I had in mind at this particular instant. He grabbed me and started undressing me with the urgency of our first time of love making. We threw our clothes all over the place and he pushed me down on the rug in front of the fire place, taking me with rapturous, deep slow thrusts. Once we both had exploded, he rolled off me and we looked at each other with deep love. I knew that Bruce was the one for me. And no matter what happened with this investigation, I would do my utmost to keep him close to me.

"Wow, Molly; that was fantastic! Now I really have an appetite for food. Let's get dressed and go brunching."

I recognized the place as Bruce drew up and parked. It was just as Bruce had described it. It was essentially a sports bar with umpteen televisions inside, but the view of the water made up for the media invasiveness. After lunch, we strolled around for a bit, and decided to head back. The rest of the day was really uneventful. We relaxed in more ways than can be imagined. Bruce accompanied Brandy outside whilst I decided to write a few notes for my work in the morning.

I was so lucky to have a car to drive. I can name a lot of guys who wouldn't be so generous. Monday morning the GPS lead me to Green Street in less than twenty minutes. I rang the doorbell. It was answered by this drop dead gorgeous male. If I wasn't in a relationship, I would have plotted to be in one with this man.

"Hello," I said. "You must be Cliff."

He replied, "And you must be Molly. Pleased to meet you. Come on in and I'll show you the ropes. I gather from our short conversation yesterday that you work at a Vet's back in New Smyrna Beach?"

"Yes, I do.   And I can't thank you enough for this opportunity to help you out, but it's helping me out more than you can imagine.   I am not very good at doodling around the house, particularly since it isn't my place.   I have been working for quite some time at my present job, so am fairly current with most procedures."

"That's great. Today we have a few cats to spay and one dog that broke its leg. There is not much else, besides the usual boring paperwork. No need to involve you that task at this stage. Also, I was wondering if you could stay for two weeks. And if I ever need you again, may I call you?"

"That would work for me and, yes, by all means call me if you need extra help, bearing in mind that I'm staying here in Dearborn for about another month."

The day passed by quickly as I was very busy helping to spay and neuter cats, and also assisting in the surgery of a dog whose leg was broken. Before I knew it, it was five and time to leave.

"I'll see you in the morning, Molly, and thanks so much for everything," the good-looking vet said.

"You're welcome. Thank you for slotting me in. I'll see you tomorrow."

The week flew by. My mood had soared. Bruce and I acted as if we were married. A couple of nights we didn't even have sex as we were both so tired, but our relationship was full of love in a most comfortable way.

"Molly. Do you remember that we are meeting Nick and Sally this weekend? I thought we could meet in town for dinner and have them back for dessert, if that sounds good to you."

"It is perfectly okay with me. I'll admit I'm happiest when my schedule is mostly full, including preparing dessert. And I'm really looking forward to meeting Nick and Sally.

"Settled then, I'll call Nick from work today."

I enjoyed the week at the animal shelter. It wasn't the same as my usual job, but it certainly made the time fly and when I got a check for $150.00 my mind flew to knowing that most of Bri's expenses for the first part of his investigation were covered.

Saturday morning was my very favorite part of the week. When I was last to wake up there was always a mug of piping hot coffee on the dresser with toast and marmalade. Bruce would come up some time after I'd drunk it and eaten my toast and we would have the best sex of the week. It seemed like every time we made love I thought it was better than the last. I was getting quite used to being here and Brandy had captured a corner of my heart.

"When is your Dad getting back from his travels, Bruce?"

"I think he comes back in about ten days. Why? Have you missed him?" he asked and chuckled - he knew darn well that I had little time for him.

"No, not at all, I was just curious. Where are we eating tonight?"

He replied, "I thought we'd go to this steak house right in the middle of Dearborn. It's really good and I haven't been there in a long time. Does that suit your palette?"

"Anything that doesn't involve the stove is good with me, Bruce. You should know that by now. How about if I pop out to that bakery and get some desserts for tonight?"

The snow had started to melt a bit and it was almost bearable outside. Since the bakery was only two blocks away, I decided to brave the elements and take the dog with me.

I informed Bruce, "Brandy's with me. I should be about an hour as Brandy and I are in need of some exercise. If I don't come back, you will know that I have become a frozen snow lady."

Brandy was tickled to be taken for a walk. He sniffed around the sidewalks and I could sense, that like me, he was excited to stretch his muscles. Arriving at the bakery, I bought some meringues, profiteroles and an apple pie that look quite scrummy. I ordered a small coffee and a napoleon for myself to eat on the spot. Brandy was so good. He was exhausted and sat really still whilst I enjoyed my guilty pleasure.

Bruce was sitting by the fireplace when I got back with a tray all prepared for lunch, consisting of a variety of cheeses with crackers, and a glass of merlot for each of us.

He said, "I figured the walk would have made you hungry and we might as well start the festivities early. We are meeting Nick and Sally at seven so that gives us time to chill a bit."

I looked at him knowingly. Some chilling this would be! How right I was. We ate the cheese and crackers rather hastily, washing it down with the fruity red wine. Bruce got up and put the tray on the kitchen table and led me upstairs where we stayed until almost six o'clock. We were so relaxed in each other's arms that we were almost as reluctant to get up, despite looking forward to this social occasion.

We found Nick and Sally sitting in the bar area of the Steak house. I knew immediately that we were going to get on famously. There was an ease about Sally that I liked and we chatted away as if we'd known each other for a good while. Nick was delightful. He had a wild mop of short, curly, black hair and eyes of green that reminded me of a Swiss lake in winter time. It was obvious that he worked out as he didn't have an ounce of fat on his body.

"Now, what do you do for a living, Nick?" I asked.

"I'm a surveyor. Not exactly a profession that one can talk a lot about, but it provides me with a good living and the benefits are great. Bruce has filled me in on what you do. I gather you even managed to get a part time job at the local vets. How lucky is that!?"

"Very! It saved me becoming totally housebound and too domesticated."

After some more small talk, Nick and Sally followed us back home for dessert, cognac, and hazelnut decaf. We chatted away until well past midnight. At the end of our conversation, Sally asked me if I wanted to meet up with her in a couple of weeks when I wasn't working, to which I warmly agreed. She gave me her card and we said our fond farewells.

What a fun evening we'd had. But I was too tired for a romp in bed. Bruce, for once, couldn't understand why. We had our first row and probably not our last. I said I was sorry, with insincerity, and went downstairs to sob. Brandy licked the salt from my cheeks, sensing I needed to be comforted. It almost worked. I finally went up to bed and silently cried myself to sleep, while my partner snored lightly beside me – seemingly without a care.

Sunday morning Bruce was up way before me. However, there wasn't the usual tray of coffee, toast, and marmalade waiting for me. Instead, there were six peach roses in a lavender vase, with a note that said, "I love you,

Molly. See you downstairs whenever you're ready to go out for breakfast."

Enough thought about toast and marmalade. I dressed and went downstairs. Now this was beginning to feel like a *real* relationship! Sunday passed by much too fast. Of course, Bruce's previous irritability due to no sex was rectified.

Monday was upon me, and for the first time since I'd been here I was more excited than I could have ever imagined. I knew that apart from being insanely in love, I had a real purpose to my day besides wielding a feather duster and cleaning carpets.

Cliff was happy to see me, as was I. We chatted for ten minutes before the work day began. He told me that they had a program he was starting that pairs a dog with a prisoner who trains the dog for a couple of months to perform a number of tasks. In turn, the inmate gets fresh air, a sense of purpose in life and a possible career on the outside. The program is called, *Prison Pups and Pals.*

"How exciting?!" I replied. "However, you're in a metropolis. I'm not sure there is such a program in the local jail system where I live. Anyway, this gives me a good reason to find out when I return home. Thanks for sharing this heartwarming information. Now that I have rambled on, put me to work please."

It was busy, more fun than I'd ever imagined it would be, and Wednesday was upon me, not soon enough, as I had an appointment with Bri regarding the missing women. I'd asked Cliff if it was okay to come in just Wednesday afternoon, which he readily agreed on. I called Bri about an hour before the allotted time just in case he'd forgotten, or had a more urgent case. "Look forward to seeing you Molly in less than an hour."

Thank goodness, again for the GPS, although I think I could have managed to find the place on my own recognizance. 120 Clover Street was less than five minutes' drive from Bruce's. I rang the bell and was buzzed in. He really was a jolly fellow. I'd taken an instant liking to him the first time, but having spent a few hours with him, was so glad that I'd picked him. He was cheap and cheerful.

"Molly, I have some news for you. I called Valerie's number several times to no avail. I tracked down all the Pickering's in her code area and with the process of elimination finally got hold of her parents. I pretended to be an insurance adjuster. They said she'd moved to Michigan and had met someone called Bruce. They said she'd called them several times a month until a year ago when all calls ceased. They never heard from her again "

Weren't they anxious to know where she went to Bri?"

"Her Dad said she'd left home at eighteen and had roamed around the country. Apparently, she wasn't at all close to her mother. They had clashed something fierce all throughout her teenage years, so their level of curiosity wasn't that high. There we have it. That's about as far as I can go without involving the cops."

"God forbid; I don't want to dig that deep; well at least not just yet Bri. I'm going to look at more pictures and memorabilia before I ask you to do any more delving. All I know is that nothing adds up. I'm working full time for two more weeks, but if I phone you towards the end of the second week, would that work for you?"

"No problem Molly. I'm sorry that I didn't come up with anything more conclusive, but this is just the beginning and I have a good feeling that between the two of us we'll solve this mystery."

"Me too, Bri, I'm really glad too, so I'll call you the week after next after I have gone through more photos, etc. Now, to the nitty-gritty of our relationship; do you get paid now or is it an "I trust you," deal?"

"Since you paid the retainer fee of $200.00 you can pay me when we have come to a more conclusive ending to our working together." I'll get in touch with you and thanks so much again for what you've done so far."

"My pleasure entirely Molly," he said as he got up and showed me the way out.

My heart was racing as I drove back to Bruce's. I was so excited to be doing something I considered really useful as well as necessary, but on the other hand, I felt such a heel for doing this behind his back. I would eventually have to tell him, but now wasn't the time. Bruce came home around seven and we had a great evening, eating pizza in front of the fire, demolishing an entire bottle of merlot before hitting the sack. Bruce was so utterly thoughtful towards me, always waiting for me to climax at the same time as he did. Afterwards we looked into each other's eyes and I felt as if I could squeeze him to death. Damn, he was one sexy man!

"Molly, before I fall into a dead sleep, I thought we might make a return visit to the Edsel and Eleanor Ford's House in Grosse Pointe. I'm anxious to go there and the weather doesn't seem like it will be too cold. Does this idea appeal to you?"

"Absolutely, I am dying to return and take a guided tour."

We slept like babies and I woke up to the smell of coffee, but no tray. A note was on the dresser.

"Sorry darling girl, no time for frills this morning." A large grin came over my face. He was slipping into normalcy, finally!

I worked my but off for Cliff, both Thursday and Friday, which I didn't begrudge at all. He was almost as great to work for as John. The week drew to a close and we said our goodbyes. Cliff asked me if I could just come in Tuesday through Friday next week, which suited me better as I could really recoup from the weekend.

"Thanks again Molly for everything. It's worked out beautifully for both of us, hasn't it?"

"Yes, for sure. You certainly saved me from going stir crazy. I love being with Bruce but I am not in my natural element in the cold, so doing what I love most and getting paid for it is a real bonus. I'll see you Tuesday morning. Have a great weekend."

"You too, he said with a smile that would have melted many a heart. Back at Bruce's I found the usual domestic scene. I let Brandy out for as long as it was necessary for him to perform his bathroom duties and have a bit of a scamper around the still snow laden garden. He wasn't that thrilled to be out long either. I made myself an herbal tea and decided to make fettuccini Alfredo. Bruce called to say he was due back around six. If I wasn't in the early stages of a love affair I could have convinced myself that I was already married. Slow down girl, I said to myself. Dead on six, Bruce came home, ripping his tie off as he came in the door. He looked at me with lust in his eyes, pulled me towards him, simultaneously undoing my blouse. His enormous erection pushing into me told me this would be a fast and furious love making. He took my hand, and we fell onto the rug. He pulled off my panties and took me with such force that I screamed. This was an orgasm to beat all orgasms.

"God gal, you are so damn sexy. Just looking at you stirs my groin."

"I had notice that, and I'm not complaining. You are one heck of a lover." We lay together for a while before I decided it was time to fix us dinner.

"How was your day Bruce?"

"It was quite busy trying to find out where the missing funds have gone to, otherwise nothing untoward occurred, but it's all rather scientific and I don't feel like giving a lesson right now. How did your day pan out?"

"It was really busy with Cliff, but I don't have to go in until Tuesday which thrills me. I think on Monday I am going to your dads to pick up the mail and look through some more photos." I got up and went into the kitchen to finish making the linguine with a delicious cream and onion sauce. I'd made a tossed salad and bought a French baguette yesterday which I heated up in the oven. We sat at the kitchen table, eating away in virtual silence.

"This is delicious. You really shouldn't have gone to all this trouble."

"It really wasn't any trouble, besides this is one of the easiest recipes known to mankind. Do you want a decaf, Bruce?"

"Yes, that would be great. Tell you what; I'm going to hop in the shower so if you'd bring it upstairs that would work for me."

"Right on, darling; two decafs are heading your way."

I cleaned up the kitchen and within twenty minutes was wending my way upstairs. Bruce was lying stark naked on the bed. I was utterly mesmerized. He had a body to die for and I couldn't help but put the coffee down and jumped on top of him. He responded beautifully. He never ceased to totally satisfy me and I fell off him, utterly sated.

"Two cold coffees coming right up, my love." Too late, he was dead asleep.

I guess we'd forgo coffee until the morning. Some night this had been. The next morning, I assumed Bruce was already downstairs. I assumed correctly. I threw on some sweats and went downstairs. Bruce came over and kissed me good morning.

"Oh, by the way, I forgot to mention that Nick and Sally want us to come over to his place on Sunday for brunch. I said I'd check with you first before I got back to him."

"That sounds wonderful. I'd love to meet up with them again. I really enjoyed their company and hope that we can become really good friends.

"Good. While you're getting us breakfast, I'll give him a call."

"Bruce, breakfast is ready, such that it is."

Believe it or not, my efforts tasted really good. It is amazing what appeals to one's taste buds when one is really hungry. I ate my French toast with alarming speed, gulped more coffee, and told Bruce that I was going upstairs to get ready for the day.

By the time we'd let Brandy out and cleaned up it was almost ten thirty before we headed off to Grosse Pointe. I was really excited to revisit this place. It reminded me so much of England, which, of course, it was meant to. We opted for the 1 pm tour which gave us time to walk around the grounds. The snow was starting to melt and the poinsettias were in full bloom, lining the path to the reflecting pool. It was truly a magnificent sight. Prior to the tour we were told that the rooms inside were fully decorated for Christmas. Bruce was a bit aghast at this but I reminded him that it was November and Christmas was only five weeks away.

One room was more lavish than the next. The paintings were a collection from around the world. There were a couple of Singer Sergeant's and several from the 18th century Dutch school. The furniture was mainly Italian with a few classic English pieces here and there. One word could describe these rooms and that was 'opulent'. We went to the kitchen and I pointed out the sterling silver counter to Bruce. He was amazed at such lavishness. Afterwards we decided to eat out. Bruce suggested a seafood place in Grosse Pointe Farms and we were not disappointed.

Brunch with Nick and Sally turned out to be so much more fun than I'd anticipated. Nick's town house was very modern but delightful. Sally had a sense of humor that matched my own and I knew we would become firm friends. We had a salmon mousse with scallop potatoes and a dry white wine which hit the spot. We chatted for hours before finally getting up and leaving. I mentioned to Sally that I would be working for a couple of more weeks, but the week before I went back I was free. We planned to meet on that Wednesday for lunch, but would be in touch with one another to firm up the date and restaurant where we'd meet.

At the end of our delightful afternoon I said, "Thanks a million, Nick and Sally; the food was delicious and the hosts great. I'm so glad that Bruce introduced me to you both. I'm sure we shall be seeing a lot more of each other. At least I hope we shall. Again, many thanks."

"Oh, we had a blast too, Molly. We're happy you and Bruce were both able to come over," Nick replied, holding the front door open for us as we echoed our final goodbyes.

We got back around six and let Brandy out who was chomping at the bit to go outside. Bruce looked at me with that knowing look which meant one thing. Yes, our lovemaking was as usual phenomenal. I wasn't sure how I felt about leaving him and going home. I was dying to walk on the beach and feel the warm sun on my body, but being alone without him was something I didn't want to think about right now.

I awoke Monday morning to find Bruce's side of the bed empty. There was no coffee or a note and judging by the way his clothes were flung all over the place he must have been in one heck of a hurry. I picked everything up and put them away, then went downstairs to get my morning coffee. The pot was brewing and the aroma gave me a mini high. There is nothing like the smell of coffee in the morning to get me going. It tasted as good as it smelled. After my usual toast and marmalade, I took Brandy outside. It was still frigid and snow was on the ground. There didn't seem to be any sign of it melting either. We stayed out for about ten minutes before going back inside. Boy did the warmth of the indoors feel good. The phone rang and it was Bruce apologizing profusely for not having left me some coffee, but he'd overslept." No sweat, darling. I'll see you this evening." I ran the vacuum over the house, picked up the kitchen, got Brandy's lead, and once he was in the car, set off for Mike's house. It took me about ten minutes to get there. Once there, I let Brandy out into the snow laden garden. For some bizarre reason, he kept going to the same spot and started digging away again.

"Come on boy, let's go inside for now." He wagged his tale knowingly and followed me inside. After picking up the mail, I headed for the garage, Brandy in tow, and heaved a couple of boxes down from the shelves. I brought them into the kitchen and started with the first box. There were tons of photos of Bruce with his mother and father when he was probably around twelve years old. Nothing was written on the back so I placed those to one side. They were no help to me whatsoever. I then came across several of his mother, in what one would only deem to be very provocative poses. On the back was written, *Greta doing her usual thing.* Then to my surprise I came across a couple of photos of Greta with her arms around a man. It wasn't Mike. There was no name on the back, so I had no clue as to who this was. I put them to one side to take home and ask Bruce. Perhaps he knew this stranger, or, maybe he wasn't a stranger. The rest of the photos in this box were of scenes and people I had no clue about. They didn't seem to be of interest to me in helping solve her disappearance. I decided to take a break for lunch. I'd brought my own sandwich so ate it rather fast, hardly tasting it. I was keen to get my hands-on box number two. The first batch was of unidentifiable scenes, but in the middle, I struck gold. There were photos of Greta with *You bitch, you slut and marriage breaker,* written on the backs of several of her poses. Why would Mike keep all these photos of her, since he hated her so much?

I couldn't make sense of it, so I decided to call Bri. I was surprised to get hold of him.

"There's nothing really new from my end, Bri," I said, "other than I keep discovering photos of Greta Sully with vulgar descriptions on the backs. I wish I knew what to make of all this. I'll have to ask Bruce what her maiden name was and perhaps you can start to track her family down."

"That sounds like a plan, Molly. For my part I have no particular news. Anyway, we'll keep each other posted of any developments. I have a client coming in less than five minutes, so I'll have to hang up."

"Thanks a lot, Bri. I'll give you a ring in a few days."

I got back to the house around four and had hardly walked in the door when the phone rang. It was Bruce suggesting we eat out.

"There is a great neighborhood restaurant that we can walk to. They have the best burgers in town. It's at the end of my street. I don't know why we haven't eaten there before, but I thought we should give it a try."

"Sounds wonderful, Bruce; see you later on."

I made myself a cup of herbal tea and took Brandy outside. *When is this snow ever going to melt?* I asked myself. Brandy didn't seem too much in favor of being outside for long either.

Bruce was right; the café featuring hamburgers was amazing. I would definitely be coming back here. I had a blue cheeseburger to die for, with the best curly fries ever. I decided to swill them down with a lager, which tasted heavenly. It wasn't very often that I had a beer, but when I did, it tasted so good. Back at the casa, neither of us felt like sex, but cuddled for quite a while, mulling over plans for the week. I was working, and outside of that nothing was going on. Bruce said he had to work late Wednesday but would be home early on Friday night. We both drifted off into a comfortable sleep. We woke up at the same time, which was a first. I said that I'd go down and make the coffee, whilst Bruce used the bathroom. In all the excitement of going out to eat last night I had totally forgotten to show Bruce the photos that I'd found. Ah well, it would just have to wait until tonight.

Work was good. The day sped by with several spaying of cats and a couple of dogs that had had accidents of one sort or another. Pretty soon it was five o'clock and I was heading out the door for home, well my temporary home for now. I poured myself a glass of wine for Dutch courage and put the photos on the coffee table for Bruce to see. He was back by six. I shouted upstairs to see if he wanted a drink, to which he replied, "Yes I'll have a scotch on the rocks please darling. I'm taking a quick shower so will be down in about ten minutes".

True to his word he was down in twelve minutes and I handed him his scotch.

"Bruce I've got some photos of your mother I want you to see. By the way, what was her maiden name?"

"Her maiden name was Weis. Her parents were German, but came to this country before she was born."

I handed him the photos, pointing out what was written on the backs of them.

"I just don't get it, Bruce, why anyone would write such stuff. Was this the work of your father by chance? Do you know who the mystery man is with your mother?"

"To be perfectly honest I haven't got a clue. The only way we'll find that out is to ask my father when he gets back in two weeks. You'll get to see him before you return to New Smyrna Beach, which I know thrills you no end."

I chuckled at that comment, before I announced that I was going to cook dinner. "I'll call you when it's ready, so just relax in the meantime Bruce."

Dinner consisted of pork chops, apple sauce, spinach, and sweet potato fries. Everything was delicious and I decided to have another beer. I had recently become fonder of beer than I needed to be. Not only did it make me fat but I really didn't like the headache I got from it the next morning. *Ah, what the heck, a couple of times won't kill me,* I thought. Whilst I cleaned up, Bruce was making a fire in the living room which sounded mighty enticing. He pulled me down onto the rug and we made love for a very long time. We never made it upstairs but spent the entire night on the rug, intermittently sleeping and screwing. Brandy lay close to us in a deep sleep oblivious to the two sex pots next to him. Morning came too soon. If I had a coin, I might have tossed it to see who was getting up to get coffee. Anyhow, Bruce was sleeping so deeply that I didn't dare wake him. And since I only had a part time job, it was only fair that I moved my butt into the kitchen.

"Coffee's up, Bruce," I yelled. He woke up and rolled over, looking somewhat surprised that he was on the rug and not in bed.

"Some night that was, Molly! I need a large mug of strong coffee to get me going, and do not come close to me right now or I will definitely be late for work", he said, jumping up and running upstairs.

In less than ten minutes he was downstairs, dressed like the corporate officer that he was. He took my breath away. I handed him a couple of pieces of buttered toast and told him to at least sit down and eat them in a civilized fashion. He ate them as if he hadn't seen a square meal in forever.

"Sexy lady, you really give me an appetite. But I must run now, so have a great day and I'll see you this evening."

He kissed me on the cheek and was gone before I could say a word. I let Brandy out, tidied up, and got dressed for work. In my lunch hour I'd call Bri and see what he could do for me, if anything. I always had a sick feeling in my gut as I felt I was betraying Bruce. I wasn't sure when I was going to tell him what I was doing. I figured it was early days yet. I really didn't have enough concrete evidence for him to work with, but at least I had Greta's maiden name, so perhaps he could make some inroads with that. Work was pretty much the same as back home. We had several cats to spay and a few animals that had cuts and bruises from falls or fights. In my lunch hour, I took my cell phone into the kitchen area and called Bri. I was lucky to actually get him on the phone. I filled him in on the current status and gave him Greta's maiden name.

"Perhaps you can see if there are any Weiss's in the area; otherwise I really don't have anything for you to work with."

"I'll see what I can do and will call you next week. Since you're not too rushed, I'll attend to an urgent case I have. I'll try and call you midweek."

"Thanks, Bri. I really appreciate what you are doing for me, so until our next chat."

I felt as if I was hitting a brick wall, and began to wonder if this private eye thing was worthwhile. I'd call Jen when I got back to the house and see what she felt. Someone else's opinion is what I needed and since I couldn't say anything just yet to Bruce, Jen was the next best thing. It had been a while since I'd spoken to her and I was anxious to catch up on things back home. I got back around five-thirty, poured myself a glass of wine, and dialed Jen. Thank goodness, she was home.

"How goes it, Jen?"

"Better now I am talking to you. I miss you Molly. It's kind of empty without you here. The weather is to die for. It's been in the low eighties and my walks on the beach are just not the same. Work is good, and Charlie and I are very much an item. I am seriously thinking that he might be the one for me, Molly. We get on so well together, to say nothing of how great our sex life is. Otherwise, not much is going on really. What's with you?"

"Well I did hire a private eye, who so far hasn't come up with a damn thing. I'm beginning to think it's a waste of time and money. The weather is dreadful, and if it wasn't for having a small job here at the local vet's, and naturally for Bruce, wild horses wouldn't keep me here. Do you think I should continue with prying into the disappearances Jen, or hang it up and let sleeping dogs lie?"

"No way, Molly; you have to keep going. Perhaps after the holidays you can resume your investigations. In the meantime, do give my love to Bruce. I'm sorry, but I'm going to have to cut you short as Charlie and I are going out to dinner and I have to get ready. Call me next week around the same time if you can. Bye for now and enjoy the rest of the week."

I felt a whole lot better after talking to Jen. Somehow, she always lifted my spirits. I missed home even more and the weather in particular. I was deep in thought trying to figure out what to cook for dinner when the phone rang and Bruce said he was picking up pizza on the way home. I sighed with relief as cooking was not high on my agenda this evening. The pizza was good and what followed was even better. Need I go into elaborate details?

"Molly, I thought we could go away this weekend. I'm working on a few ideas as to where to go, but would that appeal to you?"

"I'd absolutely love to go away, darling. What do we do about Brandy?"

"I thought I'd ask Nick and Sally if they could take him for the weekend. If they can't take him to their house I'm sure they would be happy to come in twice a day to let him out and feed him. He is the least of our worries."

I must admit I was really excited about going away. I think my mood would lift a lot with a change of scenery. It was even more thrilling as I didn't have to think about where to go. All that would be left up to Bruce. My job was packing and being ready on time. I slept like a proverbial baby that night, waking up just before the alarm went off. Bruce was gone but the usual mug of coffee sat on the dresser with a note saying that he'd see me this evening and to have a great day. Two more days of work this week, two the following week, and then I'd be finished for good. I'd been so lucky to have this opportunity drop in my lap. I busied myself getting ready and actually looked forward to going to work.

The work day sped by. I was in the mood to create something really good for dinner and decided on nut encrusted salmon, sun dried tomatoes and pasta in a cream sauce. When Bruce got home I was waiting with a glass of red wine and a kiss.

"Wow. Whatever I smell in the kitchen is really enticing. I must admit I only had half a sandwich for lunch so I'm starving."

Dinner was every bit as good as I hoped it would be. We sat at the table mulling over the day's events, and discussed the upcoming weekend.

Bruce said, "I thought that we could go to Lansing for the weekend. It really isn't beach weather, and since you live by the beach a little culture won't go amiss. It's about an hour and a half away and we can stay at a hotel that was recommended by someone at work. Apparently, it has a bistro in the hotel which has a European atmosphere. While there I suggest we visit the Michigan Capitol building. There are a number of museums to visit if we are so inclined, ranging from the Women's Historical Center to the Impression and Science Center. Old downtown Lansing has fun shopping and they have the City Market which is open on a Saturday. How does this sound to you, darling girl?"

"It sounds a treat to my ears. I could do with some culture. Oh, by the way, I called Jen who sends her love. She says the weather is fabulous and her love life seems to be great. I told her that I'd be back in three weeks, which I find hard to believe. I have one more week at work, then two weeks to relax before I head back. It would be awesome if you could come for Christmas, but I don't want to rush things."

"I was thinking the same thing the other day, so you aren't rushing things at all. Perhaps this weekend we can go over our schedules and come up with a long-term plan. In the meantime, let's head upstairs."

Our lovemaking this evening was intense. There was urgency in the way Bruce took me, as if to suggest it was our last time. Perhaps just talking about my going back home made him sexier.

Work was relatively slow, so Cliff told me to leave early. I thanked him, wished him a great weekend, and was thrilled to be going back to Bruce's early. Nick and Sally were picking up Brandy around five, which gave me plenty of time to get my bags packed and organize everything they needed to care for him.

When they arrived, we exchanged pleasantries and then I said, "Thanks so much, Nick and Sally, for taking care of Brandy. A weekend away in Lansing should be a wonderful experience, thanks again to you."

Bruce added, "We should be back late Sunday afternoon, but we shall call you when we are on our way to pick Brandy up".

Brandy didn't seem in any way upset to be leaving us. I had a pang of envy run through my veins. I had become so attached to him and would certainly miss him when I returned home, but that was a ways off, so I managed to put that negative thought on the back burner.

We left around five, checking into the hotel close to seven that evening. The hotel was lovely and our room was beautifully decorated. We had a four-poster king size bed, a sofa, two recliners and a bathroom the size of my downstairs at home. All in all, a real treat. When Bruce suggested that we order room service for our evening meal, I was more than enthusiastic. I was imagining making love in this wonderful bed. We both ordered steak and asparagus, a bottle of red wine and some cheesecake. The meal was to die for and the cheesecake one of the best I'd tasted. We sat on the recliners like an old couple, finishing our wine. To the contrary our lovemaking was nothing like I imagined an elderly couples' lovemaking would be. We came with such an explosion of lust and love that we fell away totally sated and quite exhausted.

"God, Bruce; you're something else!" I uttered, as I thought back to his massive hardness.

"Molly, I adore you. You are sexy, fun and I never want to lose you."

He had a smile on his face as he drifted off into a peaceful sleep. Certainly, my face must have had a serene look as I passed into temporary oblivion.

The next morning, I heard someone knock on the door. It was room service. I opened the door to find a young man holding a tray loaded with a large pot of hot coffee, two croissants, two baguettes, various jams, and butter. After thanking and tipping the attendant, I called to Bruce to wake his lazy self.

The coffee was strong, fresh, and quite delicious. "What a way to wake up to the day Bruce", I said as he slowly came to.

His first intelligible words were, "Well, my love, I suggest that after our continental breakfast we go down town to look around, check out the open market, and then grab some lunch. In the afternoon, we can go to the State Capitol building. Sunday, we can possibly visit a museum in the morning before we have a leisurely lunch and head home. Does that meet with your approval?"

"It sounds perfect", I answered enthusiastically.

I poured myself another cup of hot coffee and put on one of my pant-suit outfits. I dressed up fairly well. Bruce wore jeans and a long-sleeved shirt. Naturally we had to have heavy jackets as it was still mighty cold. We set off for the Lansing City Market. It was huge and fun. I found a very delicate necklace with a tiny opal for fewer than ten dollars. I don't think the vendor knew what he had, but it was fine with me. It was beautiful and would be a constant reminder of this weekend. We wandered around for about an hour, and then sauntered into the old town. It was much more attractive than I'd had imagined it to be. I don't know why I have it in for big cities, which is an unfounded prejudice of mine. Neither of us had any desire to go into the big department stores. For lunch, we settled on a Chinese restaurant. I drank more hot tea this time than I had had in a week, preparing for the frigid outdoors. Our next step was visiting the state capitol building which naturally reminded me of the US capitol in D.C. After all, Michigan's capitol building was modeled after the national one.

By the time we'd looked around it was almost four o'clock and Bruce suggested we go back and rest before dinner. Our rest was delicious slow sex on the amazing four poster bed. For some reason, it made me feel more decadent than ever and I experimented with Bruce's body in ways I'd never done before. Two hours of utter bliss. We both agreed that we were starving and decided to go to the restaurant in the hotel. Supposedly it was decorated to look European, and that it did. While there, I noticed a brochure advertising a zoo.

"Bruce, you know what I would really love to do, if you don't mind, is go to the Potter Park Zoo. Here's the brochure. I love zoos and haven't been to one in years."

"Going to the zoo sounds good to me. I wasn't too excited at the idea of traipsing through a museum. We can have a leisurely breakfast at the hotel then head off. It'll be good to be outdoors despite the cold, but at least we'll get our share of exercise. I'm glad that's decided. Now can we relax with a drink?"

"Yes, please", I replied.

We sat for about forty-five minutes digesting our meal and sipping our decaf. Bruce said that he couldn't believe that it was less than three weeks before I went back to New Smyrna Beach and only one more week of temporary work. And I expressed my own disbelief.

By the time we returned to hotel room, it was gone ten and we were pooped. It was less than twenty minutes before we were both asleep, nestled in each other's arms, ready for a new day to begin.

It began very nicely, thank you. I woke up to the smell of strong coffee and trundled to its location on the counter. Evidently room service came without my waking up. Bruce was sitting on a recliner drinking his coffee and reading the paper. I planted a kiss on his lips and went for my caffeine infusion, before planting myself in the other recliner and thinking about our next foray.

"Darling, the reason I think I'm so attracted to zoos is my passion for animals. I know zoos are considered taboo by many environmentalists, but some zoos are really very considerate with their inhabitants. This zoo is a member of the Species Survival Program that emphasizes natural habitats for its roughly 500 animals. Anyway, Potter Park Zoo has snow leopards which I have never seen, so I am psyched about our visit today. It opens at ten so that gives us plenty of time to have breakfast, pack up snacks, and head out."

"Miss Molly, your mind is organized this morning, I must say. I'm looking forward to our 'safari'. In the meantime, would you kindly pour me some more coffee? I intend to finish this newspaper if it kills me." It didn't kill him, I am happy to report.

I knew we wouldn't be spending hours there as it was still freezing outside, but one of the game keepers told us that if we were interested a snow leopard or two had been spotted outside not long ago. We hot footed over to the spot where they were supposed to be. Sure enough, sitting on the manmade rocks was two of the most elegant, beautiful large cats I'd ever seen.

"Oh, Bruce, aren't they magnificent? It was worth coming just to see them. Now I know why I love zoos. I was fortunate enough to have my camera so got some great shots of them. They didn't seem in the least bit perturbed by our presence, and certainly didn't seem unhappy in their surroundings. We hung around for about fifteen minutes then decided to take a swing around the rest of the zoo. We saw monkeys, elephants, various birds, and a few penguins. We decided to skip the aviary. Birds in close quarters were not my thing.

"Have you had your fill, Miss Molly?"

"Yes, and thanks darling for humoring me and bringing me here. It's been the highlight of my weekend seeing the snow leopards. Now you know why I work with animals."

It was time for lunch. We had driven about five minutes when I spotted an Irish pub. I am sure they had good food, and on a cold day a relatively warm Guinness appealed to Bruce and me. The food was typical pub fare. I had a pork pie with pickles. Bruce had a ham sandwich.

"Thank goodness it's less than a two-hour drive, but I think we should take a short walk before getting in the car, he said."

A short walk it was, and way enough for both of us. I wasn't the only wimp in the cold, it seemed to me. I called Sally and Nick when we were about fifteen minutes away.

Upon our arrival, we were told that they had had a blast with Brandy and said that they would keep him any time. They were seriously thinking about getting a dog after this weekend. We offered encouraging words, but I privately thought they would have to be rather lucky to find a dog as spectacular as Brandy.

Sally invited us to dinner. I said that if it was no trouble we would love to, but we preferred to go home first. Whereupon we agreed to return about seven that evening.

Bruce advised me that he wanted to stop by his dad's to check on the mail. Then he added, "I forgot to tell you that he's coming back on Thursday and wants to take us out to dinner on Saturday. I know this is not your most favorite thing to do, but at least we'll let him pick up the tab."

"Whatever you say, besides, I want to ask him about the man in the photo, so it'll kill two birds with one stone."

"One way of looking at it, I suppose," he replied.

I dozed on and off for the rest of the journey, not even realizing Bruce had made the mail stop.

"Wake up, sleepy head; we're here."

"Sorry about that. It must have been the freezing cold fresh air at the zoo that made me conk out."

We had a couple of hours before we had to leave for Nick and Sally's. We unpacked with an urgency that was so obvious. We couldn't wait to have sex again. It was, as always, fantastic.

Brandy was over the moon to see us after our interlude. He couldn't stop wagging his tail and planting his wet kisses all over us, but was not a happy camper when we had to leave. I promised to spoil him on our return. What was I going to do when I returned home in a couple of weeks? I had forgotten that Mike didn't own Brandy, but was looking after him for a friend who had retreated to the warmth of St. Lucia for a few months. I had the feeling that this friend wasn't smitten with his dog, so I was keeping my fingers crossed that Brandy might end up permanently with us.

Our meal with my new-found friends was very pleasant. We chatted about our weekend; they told us about theirs, which consisted of lots of walks with Brandy and more naps than they were accustomed to. Sally and I arranged to meet the Wednesday after next for lunch, as that was her day off and I would be done with work. One more week after that and I would be heading home for the sub-tropics.

It was close to midnight and we suddenly realized that we all had to work the next day. We were having so much fun that time flew by much too quickly.

I said, "Thanks again so much for a fabulous evening and I'll see you, Sally, in ten days."

We said our final goodbyes and sped home to our warm bed and deep sleep.

The next morning, I plopped myself down on the sofa in the living room, opened up my cell phone, and to my utter amazement there was a message from Bri asking me to call him at my earliest convenience. My heart was racing as I dialed his number. Miracle upon miracles he picked up.

"Hi, Molly. I have some interesting news for you. I did some research on the name Weis and called about fifty people. I succeeded in establishing that Greta's parents are dead, but I did track down her aunt who still lives in Dearborn. She is in her eighties but was very helpful. She said that Greta was extremely unhappy with her marriage and had met an acquaintance of her husband's, with whom she had a long off and on affair. Mike found out about it and supposedly kicked her out of the house well over a year ago. That was the last she heard from of Greta, but Greta was known to go off without saying where. A complete disappearance is suspicious, but, of course, I am still delving."

"Bri, I am so grateful to you and will get your retainer check off in the mail. Unfortunately, I don't think there's a whole lot I can do at this juncture as I'm going back to New Smyrna Beach in a couple of weeks, but am having dinner with Mike Sully on Saturday and will confront him with the photos of the man in the picture with Greta. I'm bloody sure I'll be coming back again, so we can continue on with this investigation. Keep in touch and I'll do the same." He mumbled something but hung up before I had a chance to catch what he said. Now, I was really excited about pursuing this matter. The worst part was how secretive I have been. I was bursting to say something to Bruce, but now wasn't the right time.

The weekend was upon us and Bruce told me that we were going over to Mike's house first and then out to dinner. "Dad asked me if I could keep Brandy for the time being. I don't think he's that keen on having him back. That suits me fine, as I've become very attached to the mutt, and he'll be great company when you head back home."

We got to Mike's around six. He opened the door and was very enthusiastic with his greeting.

"I can't thank you enough for taking care of my mail and house while I was gone. Thanks so much, both of you. Let's have a celebratory drink before we head out to eat. I thought we'd go to the steak house down the street. They have the best ribs in town."

Bloody hell! He still had that disgusting cheesecake grin. I swilled my wine down, accepted another one, and got up enough Dutch courage to confront him with the photos.

"I hope you don't mind, Mike, but I was looking through your photos and came across these. I was wondering if you could clear up the mystery of the man in the photo with your wife."

He blanched, then said, "Oh, him," with a distinct smirk on his face.

"That is Philip Glaston and he worked with me. We used to be reasonably good mates until he set eyes on Greta and that ruined any friendship there was between us. They had a long, well-kept secret affair from me, until one day someone from work saw them together in a restaurant in a more than cozy pose. When I confronted them together, there was no going back. They admitted that they were very much in love and Greta packed her bags and moved out. She came back a couple of times to pick up the rest of her stuff, but I never saw her again. As for Philip, he died a couple of years ago of a heart attack." *Good riddance*, he thought. "Hope I've answered all your questions, Molly. Now perhaps we can concentrate on having a good dinner together."

Dinner was good, fast and devoid of much conversation. We returned to Mike's house around eight. I felt quite satisfied to know the truth about Greta and Philip, but still couldn't work out exactly why she'd disappeared. That was a matter for Bri down the road. For now, I would have to satisfy myself with the facts in hand.

Towards the end of our meal I said to Mike, "Thanks for filling me in on the photos. But let's move on to brighter subjects. What are your plans for the immediate future?"

"Well, first off, my friend asked me to take care of Brandy on a permanent basis as he's purchased a house in St. Lucia and doesn't want to return. I told him point blank that I am also interested in purchasing somewhere in St. Lucia so would check to see if my son wanted Brandy. What do you say Bruce? Are you interested in keeping him? The alternative is to take him to the SPCA, but I am reluctant to do that."

Bruce looked reflective, then a little unsettled. "Dad, you give me no choice. If you think that I'm going to put

Brandy somewhere where he'll have a death sentence hanging over his head, you're crazy. Yes, I'll keep him. I've grown quite attached to the pooch, and I know that Molly loves him. You are one lucky man, Dad. You owe me big time."

"Why did I suspect you'd say that?" Mike offered.

"On that note, I suggest we adjourn back to my home and split a bottle of champagne. I am going to be here for about a month then plan to go back to St. Lucia to really look around with the intent to purchase something."

Was God answering my prayers and taking him far away? I asked myself.

At Mike's, I agreed to a glass of champagne and clinked glasses in a toast by Bruce to his dad – an insincere gesture on my part to a less than endearing human being. I was more determined than ever to get to the bottom of what happened to Greta and Valerie.

We chatted awkwardly until around ten-thirty. Bruce jumped up suddenly, saying that it was late and we had to get back. I thanked Mike for the dinner and said that I was sure I'd see him before I left in two weeks' time.

"You betcha, Molly, I look forward to it, and Bruce, thanks for taking Brandy off my hands. You have no idea how much I appreciate that. I am keeping my house here until I find something in St. Lucia. I realized when I was in New Smyrna Beach that the cold weather is not for me, plus I have a friend there, so a new start is just the ticket."

How wonderful to think that if Bruce and I remained an item we wouldn't have to see Mike again. I walked to the car in a wonderful frame of mind. But we drove back in silence and I sensed that Bruce wasn't in the greatest of moods. When we got back to a warm greeting from Brandy, I turned to Bruce and said that he was one lucky man for inheriting such an adorable dog.

"You're absolutely right, Molly. My gut told me that Dad wasn't really keen on keeping Brandy. I must say I'm somewhat surprised that he's decided to look on the island of St. Lucia for a house. I suppose it makes sense, because his good buddy lives there. There really isn't anything much here for him. I suppose eventually he'll sell the house. Now, if you don't mind, I need to unwind in front of the TV."

"No. I don't mind at all. I'm surprised, as you haven't watched more than a half an hour since we've known each other."

"To be truthful, I watch quite a bit at night."

We poured ourselves a final glass of wine and went into the living room. He turned the set on and flicked though the channels until he came to the one he wanted, a Jon Stewart re-run.

"I'm going to bed to read, so I'll see you when I see you."

"Don't you want to watch this with me?"

"No, I don't, but thanks for asking. He's just not up my alley. I'll see you later."

That is one thing we don't have in common, I thought as I climbed the stairs, excited at the prospect of Mike leaving, and doubly excited about continuing my investigations.

I never heard Bruce come to bed, as the next thing I knew, I was waking up to the smell of fresh coffee. Naturally, I raised my head and saw a mug of steaming coffee on the dresser. *What a great way to start a Sunday,* I said to myself, as I dragged myself over to the dresser, took the mug, and sat up in bed sipping the strong brew. I'd just about finished when Bruce came into the bedroom, took my nearly empty mug, and then proceeded to arouse every fiber of my body. It seemed like a long time before either of us spoke.

"Happy Sunday, Miss Molly. What is your pleasure for the rest of the day?"

"I think a walk with Brandy would be nice, followed by a late brunch somewhere, and then relaxing at home, well your home, for the remainder of the day. Does my idea meet with your approval?"

"It sounds perfect," he said and added, "Let's eat a light breakfast snack before we face the elements. I hesitate to tell you that it's freezing outside. Anyway, my little hothouse plant, this hot man is going down to make toast. I'll see you in the kitchen in a few minutes."

He always brought a smile to my face. I dressed in my uniform of sweats and made my face up. I looked in the mirror and was pleasantly surprised at what I saw. It must be the regular sex that I was getting that gave me such great skin tone. The toast and marmalade hit the spot. It's amazing how simple food can really satisfy one's appetite. I drank another cup of hot coffee, patted Brandy, and stuck my nose out the door. The cold gripped me in a breathless, frigid stranglehold. *So, this was winter time in Michigan? I don't think so*, I said to myself quickly shutting the door. I sunk into a cozy, but well-worn armchair, wondering how people managed to survive during the winter.

"Where were you planning on going for brunch, Bruce?"

"I thought we could go to this omelet place two streets away. Now, if it's really too cold for you to walk there I'll take the car, but I think we should brave the elements. It'll work up an appetite. This place serves the best omelets in town"

"I'll brave the elements, Bruce, if you promise that it's really only two blocks. It's mother cold out there right now. I suggest that you take Brandy out whilst I clean up the kitchen. We can read the papers before we leave."

He replied, "Good idea, darling. I'm on my way out. Come on, Brandy, let's go."

The dog jumped up, wagging his tale with great enthusiasm. I knew that would wane in a hurry once he went outside. My bet was that he'd be back in about ten minutes. I was almost on the button. It took nine minutes, to be precise. Brandy ran towards the fireplace and slumped down in a heap. We lounged by the fire as well, reading the paper and drinking what seemed like endless cups of coffee.

The time came to bundle up and faces the outdoors. I was beginning to wonder what sandals felt like as I hadn't worn them in so long. The walk wasn't as bad as I'd thought it would be. The place was aptly called, *The Omelet House.* Normally I wouldn't opt for eggs. I wasn't much of a fan but I had a smoked salmon and cream cheese omelet with the best fries ever. Bruce had a spinach and mushroom omelet. Once our appetites were sated we lingered over coffee before walking home. The rest of the day passed by in a delicious haze of dozing, reading and cuddling. Another weekend had almost come to an end. One more week left working here, and one final week of doing not much of anything before I returned home. I was filled with mixed emotions but decided not to concentrate too much on the negative right now.

Work the next day was good. It was bizarre how well I jelled with Cliff. This was the second constant about my stay in Dearborn. I honestly don't think that I'd have lasted this long, if I hadn't found this job. I would have been bored out of my tree. As it was I'd started reading some books on personality malfunctions. The first one I'd finished was written by a prominent psychologist and it confirmed my belief that someone evil could give birth to someone totally normal. It went into all the ramifications as to why, and how, which I glossed over. I felt better having this knowledge under my belt.

During my lunch hour, I called Jen who was thrilled to hear from me. I filled her in on all the comings and goings. I told her about Mike's imminent move to St. Lucia and how excited I was about coming home, and how freezing it was here. She didn't make matters any better when she told me that it was in the eighties and the beach was awaiting my return. Her love life was going well. Overall, her life seemed a lot less stressful than mine. I knew that I was in love with Bruce, but there were so many issues to resolve and I wasn't convinced about a long-distance romance.

Towards the end of our talk, Jen said, "I can't wait to see you, Molly, I have missed our walks on the beach so much."

I replied, "Rub it in, won't you? Next week I'm not doing much of anything except lunching with a really fun girl who goes out with a colleague of Bruce's. Life is very restricted here because of the cold. I'll call you next week. I miss you tons and love you."

"I miss you too, Molly. Hurry home, but be sure to let me know if you want to be picked up at the airport."

"As soon as I have my flight details, I'll call you. I'll be in need of major moral support and wine."

We both laughed before hanging up. Thank goodness for Jen.

The week seemed to evaporate. Bruce and I had steadily grown into an informal routine. He would come home and we'd have a couple of drinks and eat dinner, then sit by the fireplace for a while. We'd change and have great sex before he went downstairs to watch some man television. I would read and fall asleep, the majority of times, before he did. It was a very pleasant routine. I felt almost married. *Don't jump the gun Molly*, I said to myself. We had a long way to go before that event would take place. That is to say, if it ever did take place. I wasn't really keen on the idea of tying the knot. I didn't want children, so I couldn't see much purpose other than financial stability. We'd decided to go out to dinner both Friday and Saturday nights to celebrate my last weekend here for a while.

"Where do you fancy eating, Molly?"

"I'd like to go back to the steak restaurant and the other night I'll leave up to you to surprise me."

"Well, that settles that. My dad is going to be around and insists on coming over one-night next week to have drinks and say goodbye to you. I know you don't like him, but it'd mean a lot to me if you could remain civilized towards him."

"Oh, don't worry, Bruce. I'll be sweet as apple pie nice to him, I promise you."

The mere idea of having to make pleasantries with him didn't thrill me one iota, but I wasn't going to let the prospect of a fabulous weekend ruin it.

"Molly, I have just come up with an idea. Since this is your last week here, I'm sure you must want to buy a few trinkets to take back with you. My suggestion is that we go into downtown Detroit on Saturday afternoon to the GM Renaissance Center where there are many great stores. The attractive part of this place is that we can wander around the RenCen's five story atrium and enjoy views of the rejuvenated downtown waterfront. There's also a Hard Rock Café there with rock'n roll memorabilia. For dinner, we are going to really splurge. I'm making a reservation for Saturday night for a restaurant called, *By Candlelight*. It's probably the most expensive restaurant in town. I went there a year or so back with clients. The view is spectacular."

"That sounds wildly extravagant, but you know me and fine dining - any excuse for putting my fineries on instead of the usual uniform of sweats. Thanks so much, darling, for planning my final weekend with you."

I woke up Saturday morning to discover that it was snowing. Not fine snow, but large white flakes, and the ground and bushes were completely covered. It looked magical, but the thought of venturing out in it was not my idea of fun. I threw on my dressing gown, leaving Bruce sleeping, to start the coffee and take Brandy out.

My canine friend put his nose out, did his business, and came back inside. It was not just cold; it was frigid and uninviting to me despite the beautiful snowfall. I felt even happier about going home considering the weather. Bruce came downstairs after about an hour, by which time I'd had my mandatory toast and marmalade and several cups of coffee.

"Good morning, sleepy head", I said, looking at him with such love in my heart.

"Hello to you to, too, and what's the weather like outside?"

"You mean you haven't looked out yet? It's snowing like crazy. Will you be able to drive into Detroit in what to me looks like a blizzard?"

"Don't worry about that. This is a civilized area. The roads will be plowed in no time. Nothing is going to stop us from doing what we'd planned. Coffee please," he said as he hugged me and planted a gentle kiss on my cheek.

The snow finally abated by eleven. It must have dumped between six and ten inches and there was a magical stillness in the air. I opened the door and the cold almost froze my nose off, or so it felt. I was glad we would be inside most of the day. Shopping was never at the top of my priorities, but I had to admit that I was quite excited to go to this mall. It sounded very up market, plus I'd never been to a five story one in my entire life. I'm all for new experiences.

"Bruce, I have an important question for you. Are we going directly from the mall to the restaurant? If we are, then I have to dress accordingly."

"Yes, I thought we would. I managed to get a reservation for six. I know it's a tad early, but that was all they had, and I really wanted a table by the window. If we leave around two thirty that gives us plenty of time to shop and look around. We can stop for tea or coffee during our shopping."

"Perfect. I know exactly what I'll wear. I have these brown leather trousers with a matching silk blouse and leather jacket. I'll wear a silk undershirt so I'm sure I will be warm enough to face the elements for the short amount of time we'd be outside."

By the time I had taken Brandy outside for his last foray outside, it was time to leave. It wasn't as if he couldn't go out by himself as he did have the doggy door, but it wasn't quite the same as going with him. Finally, I changed into my finery and was happy with what I saw. Bruce was even happier.

"Molly, you look amazing. Brown is definitely a good color for you"

Bruce wore a black shirt, navy blazer, and grey pants.

"You look very handsome, darling. If we weren't going out, I would attack you on the spot."

He grinned from ear to ear.

"Alright then, Miss Molly, are you ready to face the elements?"

"Lead on Mac Duff."

The snow lay evenly and the air was biting. By the time we'd got in the car my face felt frozen. It took about forty minutes to get to the Mall. Bruce was right, it was massive.

"Well, I guess we'll start at level one and work our way up, what do you say, Molly?'"

"That sounds good to me."

I was somewhat dumbstruck by the enormity of the place. And the views of the river were breathtaking. There was what seemed like chunks of ice floating around.

We wandered in and out of several clothing stores. I bought two tank tops for Jen. One said, *I love Michigan* and the other said, *Dearie, I'm in Dearborn*. I bought a sweatshirt for John and a couple of tank tops for myself. I wouldn't need thick clothing. I didn't have anyone else to buy for so we just browsed around finally reaching the third level, when we both decided it was tea time. Tea time consisted of cappuccinos and a couple of white chocolate chip cookies which melted in our mouths. We didn't want to totally spoil our appetite for this evening. I was quite excited to go to the number one restaurant in Detroit. What a treat. We meandered around the remaining floors. I did break down and buy a couple of boxes of chocolates that were locally made.

We were good and ready for dinner. I wasn't totally convinced that I'd like to shop in a mall this size again, but it was certainly a place worth visiting, just for the architecture alone. It didn't seem too crowded, but was sure it would fill up closer to Christmas.

We got to the restaurant smack on six o'clock. A waiter in what looked like evening wear took our coats and led us into a dining room. My mouth dropped. I don't think I have ever been in such a beautiful room. Every table had white silk table cloths and in the middle, were exquisite vases of gardenias and roses that gave off a delectable perfume. The walls were a pale rose color, filled with paintings of romantic locales around the world. Everything was done with exquisite taste. Our table was right by the window. We had an amazing view of the Detroit skyline and, as I was informed later, the Ambassador Bridge.

Bruce broke the silence by suggesting we order a bottle of Merlot to start us off. Our waiter came over with a basket of piping hot breads of every variety and a plate of butter pats, carved in the shape of roses. What a way to start the meal. We perused the menu which, as I had suspected, was exotic, making my decisions difficult. I decided on fish pate to start with and a rack of lamb for my main course. Bruce ordered mussels and sea bass.

"Cheers, Molly. Here's to a memorable evening," Bruce said in a toast to us both.

"I can't thank you enough, Bruce. If the food matches the ambiance, then we can't go wrong."

The appetizers were brought out. Now I've had fish pate in my life that was good but this was to die for. The presentation was out of left field. It was in a fish shaped dish, swirled in a fin pattern, lightly dusted with parsley, and an assortment of gluten free and regular crackers on a smaller fish plate.

"How are your mussels, Bruce?"

"Do you want to try one?"

"I think I'll stick to fish pate if you don't mind. The two just don't seem to go together and I don't want to spoil the taste in my mouth. Thanks anyway. Now, if you want some of mine feel free."

"I'm good," he said, downing another mussel followed by a sip of merlot.

What I really appreciated about the waiter was that when I ordered my lamb well cooked, he didn't tell me that lamb should be rare as they do in a lot of restaurants. He nodded and went about his business. Neither one of us was disappointed with our main course.

Bruce said his fish was cooked to perfection and the vegetables were al dente, just as he liked them. We didn't have too much to say to each other as we were so busy eating. I finally looked at him half way through mine telling him this was a wonderful way to spend my last weekend here.

"Last weekend this go-around, but not your last weekend here, Miss Molly."

"I'd like to think that I'll be coming back again when warmer weather hits these parts, whenever that will be."

He grinned and said, "You really are a hot house plant, aren't you?"

"I told you I was and I'll never change. By the bye, I'm having dessert as well. What about you?"

To that he answered, "I'm having Crème Brulèe and I can bet my bottom dollar you'll have the white chocolate cheesecake. Am I right?"

"Spot on, darling. You know me a lot better than I think you do."

The waiter came over to take our dessert orders, asking if we wanted coffee. We ordered two decafs. The room was filled with happy diners, but it wasn't noisy due to good acoustics.

I would remember this meal for a long time to come. We chatted about Thanksgiving. It wasn't a holiday that I celebrated, for obvious reasons. I usually got together with Jen, but now that she had a man in her life I wasn't sure what I'd be doing.

Bruce said, "I'm going to take a few days off at Christmas and if it's fine with you, I was planning on coming to New Smyrna Beach".

"That sounds terrific. I was getting nervous already about when I'd see you again but this makes me feel quite relaxed, knowing that we'll be together for Christmas."

"Hopefully it won't be our last one together," he said holding me briefly and giving me a tender kiss.

Leaving the restaurant, I had forgotten how cold it was outside. We turned the heater on in the car and were glad when we finally arrived outside Bruce's house. Brandy was anxious to go out for a bit, and Bruce stayed with him whilst I went in and lit the fire. I was so full and felt pleasantly drowsy. Brandy came charging in and got his prominent spot close to the fire. Bruce put his arm around me, kissed me passionately, and told me that he was head over heels in love with me.

"I love you too, but I can't believe that this time next week I will be basking in the Tropics!" I said, kiddingly serious.

"You don't sound too upset about that part of returning home, I must say."

"I'm not, and to be honest, I'm really looking forward to getting back to my regular work. This has been a wonderful holiday for me, but at times I feel like a fish out of water. It's hard to explain, but I think you know where I'm coming from."

"I do, Molly; trust me, but I don't want this time together to end, so we'll have to make the most of it."

After an hour or so, we meandered up to bed. Neither of us was in the mood for sex. We were so full from the dinner, cuddling was the order of the night. We drifted into blissful sleep, only to be rudely awakened by the alarm clock the next morning. I turned over, saw that it was seven, and decided that I could laze around for another half an hour. Bruce jumped out of bed, ran downstairs, and switched the coffee on. He came back with my usual mug, laid it on the dresser, got back into bed and we made love. "Now I'm ready for work," Bruce said, as he kissed me on the cheek and proceeded to get ready.

What on earth was I going to do all week? I had lunch plans for Wednesday, otherwise nothing scheduled. Maybe I should think about doing some more sightseeing, but the freezing weather wasn't exactly enticing me to do much of anything. I decided to slouch around the house all morning then take a walk to a neighborhood restaurant, return, read and take Brandy out. This way the day would pass by fairly painlessly.

"Don't bother to cook tonight, Molly. I have a business lunch today. *Catch as catch can,* as they say, will suit me nicely."

"Right on, so I'll see you tonight."

I felt downright depressed. I think it was the letdown from the marvelous weekend we'd had, but also, I was getting itchy to get back to my real life. I called Jen at work, but unfortunately, she wasn't there, so I left her a message to call me after four in the afternoon, or I would try her later in the day

I decided to go ahead and confirm my flight home for Sunday. I had managed to get a one o'clock flight back, which would get me in at approximately four-thirty, if all went smoothly. It was a good time for Jen to pick me up and we could possibly grab some dinner. Once that was done, I was ready to hit the frozen tundra for lunch by myself.

I took Brandy out for a few minutes and found a biting wind, so I knew my lunch destination would be the omelet restaurant only two blocks away. I had an idea to go back to the Edsel and Eleanor Ford House either tomorrow or Thursday. I'd fallen in love with the place and I could do with a third visit. How the rest of my week panned out depended on when Mike was coming over, but Bruce and I could sort that out this evening.

Morning chores done, I made my way to the omelet place with a near frozen face. It was a treat to enter the warmth inside and sit down. Good old comfort food on a bleak day like this was just the ticket. I got a top up on my hot chocolate and checked my messages. No one had called, but then who would? I have one close friend in New Smyrna and although I have lots of acquaintances, I wasn't really expecting any calls this time of day. Bri might have called me on the off chance he had made some more progress. However, I'd told him I would call him when I returned home to discuss the next stage of his investigation. There wasn't anything more he could do right now. I lingered over my hot chocolate delaying going outside again. The bundling up was a royal pain and I couldn't wait to wear shorts and a tee shirt.

I got back frozen to the gills and decided to light a fire. I had no sooner settled into the comfy armchair than Brandy jumped onto my lap and we both snoozed for quite a long time. I looked at my watch. It was four-thirty. Nothing like a full stomach and the cold to induce a good sleep, but it was time to get moving. I redialed Jen and was surprised when she picked up.

"Do you have a moment to talk, Jen?"

She replied, "Yes as a matter of fact I do. We're slow today, so what's new in the frozen tundra?"

"Don't laugh; its ghastly here, weather-wise that is. I'm really looking forward to getting back to shorts and a tee shirt. I don't know what I would have done if I hadn't picked up the temporary job at the local vets. As much as I adore Bruce, I'm going quietly insane not being able to get

out and about as much as I'd like. Bruce's father is back.
I've seen him once and he's coming over one night this week
to say his farewells. He's decided to look for a house on the
island of St. Lucia. He's willed his newly owned dog,
Brandy, to Bruce. We both love Brandy and I'll miss him
when I come home. Apart from wonderful food and great
sex, nothing much else is going on. What's up with you?

"Charlie and I are going strong. But I miss our girly
walks on the beach like crazy; otherwise, life ticks along at
a rather boring pace. Now, have you booked your flight
home?"

"Yes, I get in at about four-thirty on Sunday afternoon.
I was wondering if once I've dumped my stuff at home we
could grab a bite?"

"That sounds awesome. I'll meet you Sunday, but in the
meantime, enjoy the rest of your time there. Call me if you
change your plans for coming back. Bye for now and say
hello to Bruce for me."

Now I was really anxious to get home after speaking
with Jen. I fished around in the kitchen for something to
make for dinner and decided I'd make chicken with peppers
which were easy, but unexciting, and then realized that
Bruce had told me he was eating out, so I put it in a
Tupperware container ready for tomorrow. A glass of red
wine was the order of the night. Bruce called to say he
would be in late and not to wait up for him. I was secretly
happy as it was that time of the month and I felt decidedly
out of sorts. I never even heard him come to bed, but
awoke the next morning to the smell of coffee. There was
my usual mug on the dresser, steam emanating from it. He
was so good at spoiling me.

The day passed by uneventfully. I was in a sluggish
mood. Apart from letting Brandy out, I lolled around the
house, munching on toast, reading, and being excessively
lazy. The morning slid into the afternoon and it soon
became time to resurrect the dinner, heat it up, and make
it reasonably appealing. Dinner was edible, not memorable,
ruined partially by Bruce telling me that he'd spoken to his
father who was coming over Thursday night to say goodbye
to me. God only knows why, as he must know that there is
no love lost between us. The mere fact that he was Bruce's
father meant I really had to make an effort to be pleasant.
I'd made plans to meet Sally at the Steakhouse on

Wednesday around noon which I was psyched about. We'd hit it off and it was fun to be able to shoot the breeze with another female for a change.

"What's going on, Molly? You don't seem yourself tonight," Bruce said.

"I'm not myself. I've got my period and feel quite drained. By the way, I'm having lunch with Sally tomorrow. And I've decided to drive out to the Edsel and Eleanor Ford house one more time. I thought I'd go Friday. It's hard to believe that the end to my time here is almost up."

"I feel a lot better now I know the reason for your being blue, which if far from our usual state. As I said, my father is popping in after dinner Thursday night, but he won't be staying long. He mentioned that he intends to leave for St. Lucia in about a month. He's staying with his friend for a while and if he isn't lucky enough to find a place to buy right away he'll look around to rent somewhere."

"Great! Well, I'm off to bed Bruce. I'll see you upstairs. Bruce knew that lovemaking was out of the question tonight.

I woke up to an empty bed and the usual smell of coffee, with my mug strategically placed on the dresser. My mood was brighter today as I was having lunch with Sally. I sat up in bed sipping my coffee, relishing every mouthful and switched on the news. I'd hardly watched television since I'd been here. I don't know why; as I'd had plenty of time to do so. I guess it was being in a different setting. Besides, I'd made the most of reading as much as I could. I bundled up and took Brandy outside. It was no better than yesterday. We spent about ten minutes outdoors before both of us couldn't wait to get back inside. More coffee and toast was the order of the morning. I rarely ate anything else, but some habits are hard to kill off!

By the time I had done the usual chores, I decided against my better judgment to call Bri. Lucky for me he was in.

"What's up, Molly?"

"Nothing much Bri, but I decided to give you a jingle to tell you that I'm going back to New Smyrna Beach on Sunday. I really wanted to find out whether you thought we could do anything else about Greta and Valerie's disappearance or just leave things well alone."

I think it's better to do nothing at this juncture, Molly. Give me a call when you return to Michigan. You don't need to give my any more money until I do more for you. Stay in touch and have a safe flight home."

"Thanks, Bri", I said, feeling so much better now that I'd phoned him.

I was relaxed and ready for a good, chatty lunch. I met Sally at noon at the Steak House. We picked a booth that was tucked away in a corner and ordered a glass of red wine before ordering off the menu. Sally worked at the Ford museum in the administration office. She'd been there three years and liked the ambiance, plus the fact that she got free passes to a lot of other museums, and the work wasn't exactly taxing.

"I don't seem like someone who has much ambition really, but I owned my own dress store for nine years and became burnt out with the long hours and tremendous amount of responsibility, so for now I'm perfectly content with a menial job that pays well for what I do. I'm also tickled that we met, as outside of Nick and a few friends at the gym, I really don't have many friends here. I feel so comfortable with you and must admit I'm sorry you're leaving on Sunday, but don't blame you for wanting to get home. Having a man in one's life is fantastic, but it isn't everything. And while I'm thinking of it, would you and Bruce be free to go out on Friday night?"

"Oh, I'd love to Sally. I'll check with Bruce and get back to you."

We chatted about all kinds of things, girlie and otherwise. I really felt as if Sally would become a good friend, but at this stage not close enough to share my suspicions about Mike.

"Fancy a dessert, Sally? I think I'm going to splurge and have a hot fudge sundae."

"Now you're talking; make that two."

The sundaes were large and delicious. There were no guilt feelings on either of our parts. Something this good was worth the extra calories. If I were at home, I'd run along the beach or take a swim to shed the surplus, but here I didn't thee options. We settled the bill and walked outside to Sally's car.

"Want a ride home", she chuckled, knowing full well it was short distance away.

"I think I'll brave the elements, thanks all the same. I can work off a few calories too. I'll get back to you about Friday, but as far as I'm concerned, it's a date. I'll call you later this evening, Sally. I had fun and thanks."

"I had a good time too, Molly. I'll miss you when you go, but we can stay in touch by phone."

The walk back to the house was invigorating, however really cold and uncomfortable. Once inside the cozy house I poured myself a brandy, sat down in the living room, and snoozed the afternoon away. I was awakened by Brandy whining to go outside. It was five o'clock and high time I got my ducks in a row. I'd make Bruce an omelet and salad. He came home in a jolly mood, dumping his briefcase down and grabbing me fiercely. I knew what was coming up. The kitchen counter was a favorite spot of ours when Bruce was feeling particularly randy. Afterwards, I could have sworn that I was slightly hungry. *Desist, girl; wine and a salad will suffice. You had a big lunch!*

"Wow, Bruce, great as ever", I exclaimed.

On a calmer note, I said, "I assume that your day went well. For me, I had a lovely lunch with Sally. She wants us to get together with Nick and herself on Friday night. I said I'd call her back when I'd spoken to you. It suits me personally."

"Sounds like a good way to start the weekend, Molly. I say go for it."

"Good! Then I'll give her a quick buzz before we eat."

It was six before I knew it. Mike was coming around seven. I'd rustled up some hour's d'oeuvres in place of dinner. Sure enough, on the dot of seven the doorbell rang and there he was, larger than life with a sickly grin on his face.

"Hello, Molly, good to see you again", Mike said and nodded to Bruce.

"Likewise, Mike", I replied. "Do come in and have a glass of wine."

Insincerity was oozing out of every pore of my body, but I managed to stay focused at being artificially pleasant. The couple of hours that he was with us went quickly enough.

At the end Mike said, "I don't suppose I'll see you again, Molly, so have a safe trip back to New Smyrna Beach. I'm sure you are looking forward to getting back to the warm weather again."

"You bet I am," I said grinning from ear to ear. "Have a safe trip to St. Lucia and who knows, I may see you in the New Year."

I hugged him, avoiding any form of kissing, and followed him to the front door.

After our goodbyes, Bruce said, "That wasn't so bad was it, Molly?"

"No, it went a lot better than I had anticipated."

We both slumped down in an armchair, after pouring ourselves another wine and polishing off the remaining appetizers.

"Two more days, Molly, and I'll be alone. I can't bear to think about it. I actually took the liberty of taking two weeks' vacation today around Christmas and plan on spending it with you if that works for you?"

"Oh, that'll be fabulous, Bruce. It'll make the time pass by so much quicker, knowing that you're coming for the holidays."

I jumped up, sat in his lap, and kissed him with an intensity that led to us making love on the rug – his thick engorged member, as usual, sending me into throbbing, loud ecstasies. And I did my part to make his rise to climax an explosive one.

Once we were relaxed, he said contentedly, "I'm going to make the most of you over the next few days, so watch out".

With that, we went upstairs, him to watch news on the TV, I to read a magazine, until we both fell asleep. It was rather late in the morning before I awoke. Bruce was already at work. The Ford House visit would have to wait until next time around, as there did not seem to me to be sufficient time to get ready, drive there and enjoy an unhurried visit.

It looked like the day was going to be rather mundane, except that I had the prospects of a fun evening with Bruce, Nick, and Sally on the horizon. I busied myself with miscellaneous chores, read some, ate more than I should have, and took Brandy out for a couple of short snorts outside.

Bruce was home around five which gave us some time for some top-notch lovemaking. I decided to gussy myself up for a change and wore my favorite red satin trouser outfit with a pair of ruby earrings that my mother had given me. Bruce looked at me and his mouth dropped.

"You look stunning, Molly. I'm a lucky man."

"Thanks! That makes me feel really good, as I seem to spend almost all of my life in sweats, other than at work and the occasional fancy meal out. I'm looking forward to this evening. Sally and I get on so well which is an added bonus."

As agreed, we went to Nick's place for drinks and snacks, before hitting a restaurant of our mutual choice. A unanimous decision was made to try a new Chinese restaurant within walking distance of Nick's. We chatted about all sorts of topics before realizing that if we wanted to get a table and be served we'd better hot foot it to the restaurant.

The place provided us a wonderful culinary experience, slightly more up market than we'd imagined it would be.

After dinner, it came time to say my fond, but sad, farewells, realizing that I only had one more day left here. Part of me was really unhappy to leave, but the other part was excited and anxious to return to my normal life.

"I promise to call you, Sally, when I've come down to earth a bit."

"Thanks, Molly, I'd like that", she replied.

I was excited that I'd met another female outside of Jen whom I related to, even if she was miles away. But it was time for us to say goodbye to her and Nick with handshakes and air kisses.

At his house, Bruce asked me what I wanted to do tomorrow, but I told him that outside of packing, I'd really like to stay in and order pizza.

"That suits me," he said giving me a hug that almost rendered me speechless.

It was less than two weeks to Thanksgiving and Bruce would be flying to New Smyrna Beach on the fifteenth of December. I'd probably just get adjusted to being home alone before he showed up

Morning was delicious. We lingered over the newspapers for quite some time. All of a sudden, Bruce jumped out of bed as if he was on a mission. He was, returning with a tray of toast, marmalade, brie cheese, a pot of coffee and steaming milk in a jug.

"This is the way to go, Bruce. I must leave you more often," I said chuckling as I chomped on a piece of toast.

Breakfast done with, Bruce put the tray on the dresser and stood by the edge of the bed, looking at me. I was stark naked and he stared at me with adoration in his eyes. What came next doesn't need to be put into words. After a long period of lying cradled in each other's' arms, I decided that reality must set in. I had a lot of packing to do and didn't want to leave everything to the last minute. I got up, leaving Bruce lying there and jumped in the shower. Once dressed in old sweats it took me less than an hour to pack my bags. All that was left was the essential toiletries and last-minute stuff. I took the tray downstairs and encountered Brandy ready for some human company. I threw on one of Bruce's anoraks and went outside with him. Did I ever want to get back to the warm weather, and how? We stayed outdoors for about ten minutes before my face was telling me that enough was enough. Inside, more hot coffee and some serious thawing was in order.

I had just finished lighting the fire, when Bruce came downstairs, and threw already read newspapers in the collectible bin.

"Molly, I think slouching around will suit me perfectly. I'll order pizza with everything on it, and while I think of it, I'll chill a bottle of champagne that I've been saving for a special moment."

"Sounds wonderful," I said curling up in the other armchair. Brandy didn't waste any time in joining me. It was a perfect domestic scene.

The afternoon drifted by, interspersed with naps, reading and fire gazing. Bruce looked at his watch. It was already five o'clock!

"Time for pizza I think, but first toast," he said, as he brought two of the best glasses out.

"Here's to the best girl in the South."

"Here's to the best man in the Frozen North," I replied.

We demolished the bottle and brie cheese with ease, realizing that we'd both worked up quite an appetite. Pizza arrived in less than thirty minutes. It had everything on it but the kitchen sink, and we wasted no time tucking into it. After our meal and dishes done, we put out the fire and headed upstairs to bed. Another perfect end to a not so bad day!

I woke up to coffee and the realization that I really was leaving today. Panic set in. I jumped out of bed, showered and went downstairs to find Bruce immersed in the newspaper. I flung several pieces of bread in the toaster. Bruce didn't even look up at me.

"Hello there, darling; what gives? The article must be really juicy for you to be so into it. Do you realize that I have exactly three hours before we have to leave for the airport?"

"He looked up, gave me one of his drop-dead smiles, put the paper down, and planted a kiss on my forehead.

"My, you're dressed and organized at such an early hour, Molly."

"I'm always rather twitchy before I fly, as you have by now discovered. Everything is packed and ready to go. I can't believe that I'm actually going home. I have a weird sensation in my stomach, but knowing you will be with me in just over a month makes it so much easier to take."

"I know what you mean. It will be so darned quiet when you've gone."

The dreaded hour was upon us and we drove to the airport.

"Please don't come in with me, Bruce. I'd much prefer to say goodbye to you at the curbside if you don't mind?"

"If that's want you want, so be it."

The time really had arrived to say goodbye. I got out of the car, followed by Bruce who almost swept me off my feet in a fiery embrace.

"I'm going to miss you like crazy, Molly. Call me as soon as you get in."

"I'll do that, but I'm having dinner with Jen, so will have to make it short and sweet. Tomorrow night we can talk more, if that's all right?"

"That's fine. I quite understand."

"I really have to go," I said, as the tears welled up in my eyes. "I'll see you in just over a month."

"I love you, my darling girl. Have a safe flight."

"I love you too, my handsome brute," I said, trying to be funny, as I turned and walked into the terminal feeling utterly sick.

I turned to wave goodbye, but he was gone. It was in my unsettled mind that the flight had better be on time, and I'd better not have anyone obnoxious sitting next to me. Luckily, going through customs was painless and I boarded about thirty minutes before the scheduled takeoff. I had an aisle seat, so far so good. But then a mother and a bratty looking toddler took the seats next to me. At least it wasn't an overweight drunk. It turned out the little boy was quite the exception to the terrible two's rule. His name was Jake and he was chatty and very cute. The trip turned out to be smooth and seemingly quick. When I got up to get my bag, Jake gave me a kiss goodbye. Toddlers weren't as bad as I'd imagined them to be, or maybe he was the exception. I waited about twenty minutes for my luggage and spotted Jen jumping up and down with excitement. I grabbed my bags, shoved them on a trolley, and walked towards her.

"Am I glad to see you, Molly! You look quite pale, but interesting."

"Thanks a lot, girlfriend. I'm pale anyway; however, I'm more interested in stripping off some of these clothes when I get in your car. Thanks so much for picking me up."

We walked outside and the warm air hit me in the face. I really was back where I wanted to be, climate-wise, that is.

"I thought we'd drop you by your place first, have a glass of wine whilst you arrange your stuff and change before we go out to eat. Does that sound good?"

"Yes, I'd like to do that, particularly since I said that I'd call Bruce to let him know that I was home safe and sound. He knows we are going out to dinner so doesn't expect a long call."

It took a little over an hour to get back from the Orlando airport, with not much traffic. I felt quite discombobulated. One moment I was freezing my butt off, the next, sweating with the weight of my winter woollies. I opened the door and felt a whole lot better. The first thing I did was to fling off all the upper layers and my trousers and chuck them by the washing machine, then ran upstairs and put on a pair of shorts and a flimsy top.

"I'll be right down Jen, unless you want to bring two glasses of wine up here whilst I unpack. First of all, I'm going to give Bruce a quick ding to let him know I'm back."

He wasn't home, so I left a message telling him I'd call tomorrow night and that I missed him already. That was actually a bit of a white lie because I really hadn't had time to miss him. It didn't take me long to put everything away. How wonderful it would be not to have to look at a sweater again for a long time, apart from going to the movies, which

I didn't do a lot of as it was always so freezing inside. I almost inhaled the glass of wine that Jen brought me.

"I'll be ready in ten minutes, Jen. Be a dear and refill my glass."

"No problem. Take your time; I'm not going anywhere."

Jen returned with my refill and said, "Charlie knows that I'm with you tonight; besides we don't live in each other's pockets, which is a good thing. We both have our own space and when we are together it's fabulous. Fancy a steak, because I do?"

"Sure thing," I said as I put my suitcase up in the closet. "Let's finish our wine off downstairs. I have so much I want to tell you and I'm sure you do, as well. Shall I go first?"

"Yes, fire away," Jen said with a grin on her face.

"It's so good to be home and not have to contend with the snow and freezing cold. I had a wonderful time with Bruce, and I adore him, but somehow the whole time felt unreal to me. I felt as if I were dancing in limbo. If I hadn't got the temporary job at the local vet's, I think I would have gone balmy. I did meet a couple of super friends of his, Sally and Nick. I really like Sally, as I am sure you will. We had lunch a few times, and outside of you, felt she could become a friend if we lived in the same town. We went to some amazing restaurants, but in all seriousness the weather was a deterrent. As I mentioned to you, I finally called a private eye who goes by the nickname, Bri. He's a hoot.   He's smart and cheap and found out some information re Bruce's mother and girlfriend. I am now at a total standstill until I return, if I return at all. I haven't had the guts to tell Bruce yet what I've done and will wait until he comes down for Christmas. I feel really sleazy doing this behind his back, but the timing wasn't right to tell him. His father is moving to St. Lucia and has bequeathed the dog he was taking care of to Bruce. Brandy is the dog's name and he is a real treasure. Otherwise, I don't have a clue as to what our future holds. Once I tell Bruce what I've done, it might be the end of a beautiful romance. We'll see. So that's it in a nutshell, Jen. Now it's your turn."

"My life has been quite normal. Work is going well. Charlie and I are very involved. He works in Jacksonville, so it isn't quite so difficult for us. He travels a fair amount and could get a transfer to the Ormond Beach office should the occasion arise. I told him flat out that I'm not moving to Jacksonville. Fortunately, he understood that sentiment very well. I've missed our girlie walks and run on the beach and can't wait to resume that part of my life. Now regarding the private-eye you hired, I wouldn't let it keep you up at night right now. Of course, you have a much more complicated relationship than we do, especially since you are so far away from each other, but I do believe that if you are meant to be together, then you will be. But enough of this philosophical clap trap, let's go eat."

We went to a local steakhouse. We decided to splurge on the wine. It was, after all, a special occasion. After the meal, we lingered over decaf and if it hadn't been a work day we would have had dessert and stayed longer.

"What are you doing after work tomorrow, Molly? If you're free, I thought we could hit the beach for a run or walk."

"Oh my God, I've had withdrawal symptoms, so the answer is, of course, yes. I'll pick you up at home around five. How's that?"

"Perfect, and sorry that I haven't removed all my stuff from your home, but know you'll fully understand what it means to be in a somewhat transitional phase," Jen said as she got in the car.

"Thanks for everything. I don't know what I'd do without you," I replied.

"Likewise; so, I'll see you tomorrow, and have a good first day back at work."

She did her usual speeding off before I could say another word. I went inside and it felt so quiet that I immediately turned the television on. I had such a weird feeling in the pit of my stomach. I almost felt as if I hadn't been gone at all. I had for a long time been used to living alone and fully understood the difference between loneliness and solitude. The former was oppressive, the latter invigorating. I absolutely abhor the popular consensus that people who live alone remain isolated from life's experiences. Tonight, I felt lonely. I had lived by myself for so long and couldn't have imagined my life to be any other way. Now that Bruce had entered it, things were topsy-turvy, and I wasn't sure what lay in store for me. I sat down and balled my eyes out until the tears had exhausted themselves. I felt better. I went upstairs, got my clothes ready for the morning, and settled down in my bed.

It felt strange to be alone in it. Utter exhaustion took over and I slept like a baby until the alarm awoke me at seven.

What a rude awakening. No coffee, no Bruce, no dog, just me. Things could be worse. I busied myself making coffee and toast and was excited to see John once again. The silence in my house hung like a ghost in the air. I relished quiet but this was a heavy quiet, so I put the radio on and listened to some wonderful Latin pop music, which was my favorite. It reminded me of Spain. My mood lifted and I realized that I'd only an hour before I had to leave for work. I picked up a few things, put the dishes in the dishwasher, and headed out the door. John was happy to see me. He flung his arms around me and told me that the animals had missed me so much.

"And what about you; did you miss me at all?" He laughed out loud and told me that he had truly missed me and that the temp was not even close to my outstanding abilities. Then he asked, "So Molly, are you ready for the day ahead?"

"You bet," I said with genuine enthusiasm. Let's have at it."

It was a busy day. We had a couple of dogs that had met with unfortunate mishaps and a bunch of cats that had to be spayed. Then there was the usual pile of paper work that had to be attended to in the quiet moments. It was great to be back at work in familiar surroundings and working with John was such a pleasure. As I noted before, he wouldn't set the world on fire with his looks, but he is just a really decent man and the best sort to work for.

I couldn't believe how the day sped by and that it was time to go home. Once home I changed into my jogging gear and went to pick up Jen.

On the way to the shore, I said, "Isn't this a slice of Heaven, Jen? I couldn't possibly live in a big city."

"Me neither; that's why I told Charlie that I could never move to Jacksonville.

We arrived at the beach to a calm sea and just a few bathers in the water. We walked along the water's edge allowing the salty water to dabble over our feet. The air smelt quite refreshing, so we kicked up the pace and before long were running along the hard sand. Adding to the scene were an abundance of seagulls and several pelicans bopping up and down in the sea. We must have run a couple of miles as we were both dripping in sweat. We slowed down and walked the rest of the way back to the car.

"Want a drink at my place before you set off home, Molly?"

"Sounds like a pregnant idea. I have to call Bruce this evening and funnily enough I really haven't had much time to miss him. It was strange waking up to an empty bed, with no coffee and no dog, but I reckon I'll adapt. It just feels so good to be home, and be warm again."

"I know what you mean, Molly. I'm not sure I could ever live in the cold weather. I've grown so used to this climate that I cannot imagine anything else."

After a quick glass of wine, I declared that I really had to get home and do a bunch of domestic stuff before settling down for the evening.

Jen asked in response, "I can't make the beach tomorrow, but how about Wednesday?"

"That sounds good to me", I replied

Jen then said, "I'll pick you up around five-thirty then, and it's fabulous that you are back".

"I'm glad to be back", I said as I got in my car and waved goodbye.

Once home, I started feeling terribly alone. I had been used to being with another human being for about four weeks and it would take some getting used to. The best way to alleviate this feeling was to get busy. I did a load of laundry, had a sip of wine and did the final round of unpacking, sipped on more wine, then reached the decision that dinner would be a frozen pizza. I hadn't even been grocery shopping since I got back, other than to go to the corner store for milk. By the time I'd finished eating and had cleaned up the kitchen, it was almost eight-thirty. It was time to give Bruce a jingle. He picked up on the third ring and sounded genuinely thrilled to hear my voice.

"Hello, darling Molly, how the hell is you? It's so darn lonely here without you and Brandy misses you too."

"Tell him I miss him as well. This morning was so weird waking up to no coffee, no you and no Brandy. I've become rather accustomed to having my coffee waiting for me. Most of all I miss you being in bed with me, to say nothing of our love-making. I cannot believe that I have to wait four weeks and three days before I see you again. I think that

I'll be more than ready for a romp in the hay by the time you get here. You are still coming for the holidays, aren't you?"

"Absolutely, do you honestly think that I would cancel my trip? I miss your giggle, your cooking, although I know women don't like to be told that, but most of all, I miss you. And, of course, making love with you is amazing. I wish I had a lot to tell you. Work went well, and I did find out something fairly interesting today. If I wanted to get a job in your area, I have a promising possibility at Cape Canaveral. It's something to put in the memory bank at least. I'm going to the gym with Nick tomorrow. I figure some vigorous exercise will help get rid of some of my excess energy. I haven't spoken to my dad yet, but he plans to leave for St. Lucia in the near future. So how is it to be back at work?"

"Great! Being back in familiar surroundings and working with John is so rewarding. I don't really feel as if I am actually working. By the way, Jen and I went to the beach for a jog on the beach today after work. To be back by the ocean in the warmth is wonderful. We are going again Wednesday evening. Otherwise, I feel a bit out of sorts. On one hand, it's as if I never left, but on the other hand it feels so weird being by myself again. Hopefully, time will fly by, what with Thanksgiving, and then getting ready for Christmas. Jen said that it looks as if Charlie will be with her, so maybe all four of us could spend Christmas Day together, that's if it's all right with you?"

"Why wouldn't it be? I think we'd have a lot of fun. Nick and Sally said they'd take care of Brandy while I'm gone, which will really make things easier for me. Poor dog, he's being buffeted about so much. One of these days he'll be able to settle in one place, I hope. Well, darling, I think that about does it for me. I miss you so much. When I go to bed there is a gaping hole without you."

"I know what you mean, Bruce, and I miss your coffee, too." We chuckled, and said we'd talk again on Wednesday night after I'd come back from the beach.

"Eat your heart out, darling, while I loll on the beach," I said as I signed off.

The following day, Tuesday, proved to be a very busy work day. Lunch time rolled around too quickly. Neither

John nor I had time to even think about unnecessary paper work today, which in some ways was good.

After work, the grizzly task of grocery shopping reared its head. I had to do a big shop, as I had virtually nothing to eat. By the time I'd finished the weekly grocery chore, it was almost seven-fifteen, and I was starving. I decided that a frozen dinner, for two, finished off in the microwave, would suffice to be accompanied by some good, mindless television, and a couple of glasses of white wine. Now I was beginning to feel like the old Molly, the Molly who really enjoyed living alone. So, I settled down to a rather pleasant evening. But I did miss Brandy's company a lot, as he always nuzzled up to me. Ah well, such is life. I'm sure he would adjust to being without me. Of course, once in bed, I would yearn for another, sexier nuzzling.

Wednesday at work was relatively quiet so John and I tackled the mountain high stack of paper work in between appointments with quiet efficiency.

"I think you and I should go out for lunch today, Molly", John informed me. We have earned this much. Besides, I would really like to talk to you more about your trip. And, I can fill you in a little more in depth about what has been going on here."

"I'm game, boss; you know me and eating out. Have appetite, will travel."

There was an excellent fish and chip restaurant on the water. It wasn't in the slightest bit fancy, but the food was really good. I settled on none other than fish and chips with coleslaw. I was tempted to order a beer, momentarily forgetting that I was on duty. However, when John ordered a beer I didn't lag far behind in ordering one for myself. We had a lovely lunch. Conversation flowed between us. I hadn't really missed too much in the way of excitement at work. The same old stuff really, but it was good stuff. I filled John in on my visit with Bruce. I told John that I was very keen on him, but the weather up there sucks, and I'm not really a city girl at heart.

"Oh, I do have one other bit of news for you, Molly. I've met someone. Her name is Jessica Tate. I met her at the gym while you were gone. She is everything that I could ever want in a woman, and I do believe that we will end up together. It's early days yet, but she is coming into the office tomorrow, so you'll get to meet her and be able to give me instant feedback."

"I'm so happy for you, John, and I'm excited to meet your Jessica."

We lingered over our one beer each, until the realization came that we had to get back for afternoon appointments, so John paid the bill and we headed on back to work. What a pleasant break that was. It was the first time that John had ever asked me to lunch. Perhaps his wanting to tell me about Jessica had something to do with this new luncheon experience, but who was I to wonder why?

I picked up Jen after work and we headed to the beach. I filled her in on my lunch and she told me that she was heading to Jacksonville for the weekend.

"Hope you'll be all right by yourself, Molly."

"Of course, I will be, but thanks for caring. I was thinking that I might spend one entire day at the beach, taking lunch and a good book, then the other day I'd reserve for dreary chores. The weekend will come to an end too soon, anyway. Actually, I am going to start back swimming. I don't think the pool is that crowded at this time of the year.

The waves were pretty rough and there were a number of surfers riding them. The pelicans were in full force, circling around us and dive bombing into the water. What magnificent birds! They have an awkward majesty about them.

We walked at a decent pace for just over an hour. Dusk was approaching and the sun was beginning to set on an amber sea. It was a magical time. However, it soon would be dark at this hour and we probably would have to cut out our beach walks after work. In its place, I thought about the pool in my development. The beauty of it is that I could go any time as it was lit and heated.

By the time I dropped Jen home it was close to seven and I realized how famished I was. I made myself a cheese omelet and a salad and decided on a bourbon and ginger as the beverage of the evening. Not a bad life really.

I knew that Bruce was working late, so I called him around eight. He was so loving and sexy that before long, I had my first phone orgasm since I'd returned. From the sounds coming down the pipe I think he might have had one too. I didn't ask him.

At last, I asked him, "What are you doing this weekend, darling?"

"I'm going over to my father's place to help him pack up his stuff as he decided to leave next week for St. Lucia. Outside of that, nothing spectacular is going on. Oh, I forgot; Nick and Sally are taking pity on me and having me over for dinner on Saturday night. Sally said to be sure to say hello to you. And what are your plans this weekend?"

"Tomorrow it's an entire day at the beach. Sunday will be filled with house chores and a possible trip to the Mall. I can't believe that Christmas is in four and a half weeks. You'll be here before I know it. So, I've decided to start back swimming in earnest to prepare myself for your advances. Luckily the pool isn't too crowded at this time of the year."

At the end of our chat, Bruce said, "I'll catch up with you Sunday night, if that suits you, Molly?"

"Sounds perfect, and don't forget that I love you and look forward to your call on Sunday", I replied.

A mild depression came over me upon hanging up, so I busied myself cleaning and running the vacuum. It's truly amazing what physical activity can do for the mind. In the evening, I took my drink to bed and watched television until I couldn't keep awake a minute longer.

The next morning, I was going over patient files just before noon, when in walked this petite blonde with an award-winning smile. Her hair was golden blonde and her eyes were dark brown with a sense of mystery. She was truly lovely. She wasn't overtly sexy, but had an allure about her that was quite mesmerizing.

"May I help you?"

"Not as a patient", she smiled. "I'm here to see John. He may have mentioned me, I'm Jessica Tate."

I hope she didn't see my jaw drop.

"Hello, Jessica; how lovely to meet you. I am Molly, John's chief assistant. He told me you would be coming in today. Have a seat and I'll get him."

I was somewhat shocked that John had managed to captivate such a beauty. It never ceased to amaze me how men who weren't obviously good looking ended up with real show-stoppers.

John was preparing for the next onslaught of animal kingdom patients, when I interrupted him, "Jessica is here. How come you never told me how adorable she is?"

"I never gave it much thought to tell you the truth. She is the sweetest girl I've ever met. Let's hope she sticks around. You don't mind if I take a slightly longer lunch today, Molly, do you? Besides, the appointment schedule allows it", smiling as he said it.

"Why would I mind? After all, you're the boss."

His smile turned into a grin from ear to ear. It was obvious that he was excited to see Jessica.

After my lunch break, an unscheduled emergency patient was brought in by its owner. It was a fat marmalade cat that had been caught in some wire that left him with bloody scratches. He didn't flinch at all when I cleaned and bandaged his wounds. Such a calm demeanor this cat had. I swore he smiled at me after I'd finished with him, but I've always been convinced that animals can smile in their own way.

Jessica and John came back a little later, both in very good moods, possibly with the first flush of love. Jessica said goodbye, adding that she looked forward to seeing me again. She gave John a lingering kiss and sashayed out of the infirmary. Things really were heating up for my mild-mannered boss.

I was right to hit the beach on Saturday. It was a perfect day without a cloud in sight. I packed a sandwich, a bag of chips, and a couple of diet cokes. I treated myself to a soda or two at the weekends. The rest of the week it was juice and green tea. I was reading a particularly good mystery book so the time would fly by. There weren't too many people on the beach, so I took my beach cart loaded with my chair, food, towel, and blanket to the hard sand, very close to where the waves were gently lapping. The seagulls were soaring and a couple of smaller birds were walking at the edge of the sea. *How in my right mind I could ever give this up*, I said to myself, as I opened my chair and arranged my stuff for the day.

I went for a long walk just before lunch time and by the time I got back to my chair I was ravenous. Those malt vinegar chips should really taste good. And they did. I ate my cheese sandwich with the first coke and settled back in my chair with my book. I must have drifted off as I woke up to my book falling onto the sand. I looked at my watch and to my utter amazement it was three o'clock. I decided to stay until around four and would swing by the pool at my condominium to have a swim.

I was alone in the pool and able to put heavy effort into my lap work, which, of course, worked up my appetite. Tonight, it would be junk food. I decided upon crackers with the rest of the gorgonzola cheese, followed by a large dollop of ice cream. I didn't even feel like wine this evening. I cleaned up, settled into my comfy bed, and watched television until way past midnight. I had no reason to leap up in the morning, so I didn't really care what time I turned the light off. But I couldn't get to sleep. I felt very restless and somewhat wired. Then I remembered that the last coke I consumed was around four. No wonder I couldn't sleep with all that caffeine. I turned the light on and read until I was really spent.

I woke up around nine to a room with no coffee aroma. *Damn, I'd have to get up and make it myself,* I thought. There were definite perks to having a man around. Once it was brewed, I grabbed the newspaper from the driveway and took my steaming mug of coffee with two cookies upstairs and stayed in bed until almost midday feeling pleasantly decadent. I decided that I'd hit the mall for a couple of hours before returning to do some housework. It was amazing how many excuses I could find for not cleaning. My admiration went out to cleaning ladies.

I finished a small yogurt and set off for the Port Orange mall. To my utter shock all the Christmas decorations were out. I wasn't geared up for this as Thanksgiving wasn't upon us yet. I found a couple of two-piece bathing suits and two casual yet smart dresses for me and a couple of shirts and ties for Bruce for the holidays.

Thinking of Thanksgiving, I recalled that Jen had asked me to spend the holiday with her, despite the fact that this holiday was not a British tradition. Still it didn't hurt to be thankful and we liked an excuse to stuff our faces on turkey, stuffing, and cranberry sauce. I wasn't sure at this juncture whether Charlie would be around for the holiday, neither did I care.

I got home around four, and spent about an hour cleaning the house. I poured myself a glass of merlot, settled down on the couch, and called Bruce. He wasn't home, so I left him a message. He called back in less than fifteen minutes, apologizing that he was in the shower and couldn't get to the phone.

"I'm glad, as I do love a clean man," I said chuckling.

"You sound jolly, Miss Molly. Sorry! That was a pathetic form of poetry. How was your weekend?"

"Apart from having to make my own coffee and do a considerable amount of housework it was really very relaxing. I did some Christmas shopping and bought myself a few items of clothing. Otherwise, it was the same old, same old. What about you Bruce?"

"My meeting lasted until about ten on Friday, so Saturday was a lost cause. Dinner with Nick and Sally was wonderful. I changed seeing my father until Sunday and spent the better part of the day helping him pack up stuff for his move. I said I'd take care of the mail until he had a permanent address. I was sort of sad to say goodbye to him, but thrilled that he'd finally decided to do something for himself. I knew that he detested the cold weather. The real push for him was having a great buddy living in St. Lucia. There you have it."

"Before I forget, Bruce, I meant to mention that my boss has a girlfriend. She is a cute blonde. I was shocked when I met her. I would never have expected him to find someone quite so adorable. I'm happy for him as he seems smitten. Anyway, that's my weekend news. As for being smitten myself, I miss you, love you tons, and am counting the days to your visit."

"I love you too, darling girl. We'll talk in a couple of days, right?"

"Yes, indeed. Tomorrow I'm hoping to go running on the beach with Jen. We're trying to do it as much as possible before it gets too dark. On that note I'm signing off, as I have to take a shower. Bye, darling; talk to you on Tuesday."

"I look forward to it and before I forget, Brandy sends you lots of licks."

"Great, send my kisses back to him. I truly miss his cuddly self."

I don't know why I felt a strange knot in my stomach after hanging up. It was a slight surge of loneliness that was creeping into my heart. Enough of this, a good hot shower would really help, plus another glass of wine. I let the steaming hot water cascade over my body, standing under it for a lot longer than usual. It was terrifically soothing. Finally finished, I dried off and turned on the television to the news. But I decided not to be depressed by all the negativity in the world. I found an old movie and hunkered down for the night. *Life is good, Molly; don't ever forget that,* I said to myself.

The days sped by. What with work, numerous walks on the beach, and the usual daily crap that has to be attended to, Thanksgiving was now only two days away. I called Jen and lucky for me she was home.

"Are we still on for Thanksgiving, Jen?"

"You bet we are", she said. "Why don't you bring some turkey and cranberry sauce? I'll provide the rest. Oh, perhaps a bottle of wine would be good. Charlie can't make it, by the way. His favorite aunt is coming to Jacksonville, so they'll be spending it together. It'll mean more to them than to us anyway. It's a good reason to eat a lot." We both chuckled at the same time.

"If you want to come in the afternoon at your convenience, that'll be fine with me", Jen said.

"I'll mosey on over around three-thirty. I'm looking forward to it, girlfriend. In the meantime, if you think of anything else you want me to bring, give me a holler."

"Will do," she said, hanging up before I could actually say goodbye. There's nothing in the world better than a close girlfriend. I'd spoken to Bruce the night before for about two hours. What we had to say to each other wasn't memorable, except for the amazing phone sex. I never knew remote control orgasms could be quite this good. I told him to call me the next day so we could exchange food information.

I added, "Give my love to Sally, Nick, and Brandy, and have a wonderful dinner, darling".

"You too, Miss Molly. I miss you more and more each day. Just think it's only twenty-seven days before we are together again."

"I know it's hard to believe. We're always so busy at the clinic a couple of weeks before Christmas, but I've got a head start on present buying so I'm good. Now I have one question related to food on the big day. I've always cooked roast pork, cracking and all the accompaniments for years, so hope that you'll be happy with this arrangement. I couldn't imagine having turkey at Christmas."

"That's fine. Just being with you is all I ask for. Tons of hugs and have fun tomorrow with Jen. I'll catch up with you the following evening."

"Have a good dinner and don't forget I love you."

Instead of buying a whole turkey I bought about eight slices of cooked turkey, heated it up, and poured the cranberry sauce into a plastic container. I'd made some stuffed mushrooms, which were quite yummy. The filling was a mixture of breadcrumbs, an assortment of herbs and chestnuts. I grabbed a couple of bottles of Merlot and headed off to Jen's.

By mutual decision we decided to have a glass of wine and the mushrooms as a starter. It was a beautiful early evening as we sat outside on Jen's patio. She had a splendid assortment of potted plants and hanging flower pots. The sun was beginning its descent and the purple glow lingering over the garden was nothing less than magical.

"One thing that's bugging me, Jen, is when to tell Bruce about the private eye. I was thinking that perhaps I'd wait until after Christmas day, as it might ruin things if I told him beforehand. What do you think?"

"I think you're right. Leave it until after the big day. You know it can go one of two ways. He'll either break off with you and you know darn well he'll be furious. However, if he's really serious about you, I don't think there'll be a major breakup. Time alone will tell."

"I'm glad you think along the same lines as I do. Well, at least we've got that stressful subject out of the way. We can now settle down to some serious eating and drinking."

I was spending the night with Jen which meant I didn't have to worry about drinking too much wine. By the time we'd finished the mushrooms and the first bottle of wine it was almost eight-thirty and the turkey and trimmings called to us. Along with the second bottle of wine, we polished off everything in sight. What we talked about couldn't be repeated. So many topics, ranging from clothes, sex, food, men work, etc. We were never short of conversation. Around eleven we decided to clean up the kitchen and have a brandy before hitting the sack.

"Thanks, Jen, for a lovely evening."

"My pleasure", she said. "Let's take our brandy upstairs and we can sit on my bed until we decide to call it quits.

The brandy hit the spot and before too long we were both dead beat, so I said, "I'm going to say goodnight now. See you in the morning. I'm not setting an alarm. Perhaps after breakfast we can go to the beach and spend a couple of hours there."

"That sounds perfect. Have a good night's sleep, girlfriend", she replied.

"You too," I said as I climbed into the very comfortable bed in Jen's spare room.

This was a perfect Thanksgiving as far as I was concerned. I didn't have time to miss Bruce beside me. The bed was small and two people in it would have been way too cozy. It was gone ten when I got up and went downstairs to get coffee. To my amazement Jen hadn't even surfaced yet. I knew my way around the kitchen enough to put the coffee on and sauntered outside to test the day. It was beautiful! The sky was azure blue with a few mottled clouds dotted about; the air was warm and inviting. Back inside, I made toast and poured a large mug of strong coffee, before returning to sit on one of her comfortable outdoor patio chairs. This was living.

I was daydreaming whilst sipping my coffee when I heard Jen's voice.

"Are you outside, Molly?"

"Yes, I'm waking up to a magnificent day, so come and join me."

"I think I overdid the booze last night," she said looking a little worse for wear. "I'm thinking that the beach would be the perfect place to cure my hangover. What do you say we grab breakfast out, so we don't have to drag a bunch of food down on the beach with us?"

"Great idea, but in the meantime, I'm getting myself another cup of coffee. Three cups and I become human and I'm only on cup number one."

Jen was on the phone when I returned to the patio.

"I'm talking to Charlie, so won't be too long", she said as she disappeared inside. At this instant, I began to miss Bruce. I'm sure he'd had a good Thanksgiving, but I wouldn't be talking to him until this evening. Jen returned to say that Charlie would definitely be spending the holidays with her, so all four of us could be together.

"That sounds like a wonderful idea," I said. "How about this year we have it at my house? I'll cook the roast pork, cracking, and vegetables and you bring dessert."

"If that's what you'd you like, it's certainly okay by me. I'm getting hungry so let's hustle to a breakfast place."

Once we'd eaten, we both felt much more like human beings and headed off to the beach with renewed enthusiasm. We were not disappointed. There was a gentle breeze and the air was comfortably warm. There was stillness to the ocean that we hadn't seen in a while. It attracted a host of birds that floated on the surface. It called out to me to do the same thing. I wasn't up for swimming today, just relaxing. Jen came in and we enjoyed the quiet that the day brought us. We stayed about three hours before returning to her place.

"This has been an amazing holiday, Jen, and to think that we have the whole weekend ahead of us. Aren't you going to Jacksonville?"

"Yes, I'm heading there tomorrow after his aunt has left, and will come back on Sunday. What are your plans?"

I said, "I don't have any, which is good, so I'll do a fair about of slouching around."

I gathered up my overnight gear, gave Jen a hug, and sped off home. I'd forgotten that this weekend there was a minor bike festival for two days, smaller than Biketoberfest and very much smaller than February's Bike Week in February, when over 500,000 bikers appear. I hated travelling with thousands of bikes and the associated traffic nightmare. Here I am, almost 34 years old and sounding like an old fogey, but I really didn't enjoy doing errands when they were around. Fortunately, there weren't too many on the roads and it was less than ten minutes from Jen's house to mine. Within a couple of hours of being home I started to feel a bit feverish and by the time the evening had set in I knew I was coming down with the flu. I felt like hell. I took some medicine and made a hot toddy and went to bed. Bruce called me and I told him that I was feeling crappy, but did have a wonderful time at Jen's, and that I'd call him during the weekend when I was feeling more like a human being.

"I'm sorry, darling girl, that you aren't feeling well. Do take good care of yourself, drink lots of hot fluids, and I'll check in with you tomorrow night. And, yes, I had a great time at Nick's. Sally is almost as good a cook as you are."

"Flattery will get you everywhere, but I'm signing off now as I feel awful."

It was a long, very disturbed night, tossing around the bed, sweating like a pig one minute and the very next freezing cold. I'd just have to be patient. I hoped I'd feel better by Monday, but if I didn't I'd just have to miss work. I hadn't been sick in three years so that wasn't a bad batting average. I managed to get some sleep and woke up around ten, feeling a little better. Coffee, however didn't appeal, so I managed to crawl down to the kitchen to make some herbal tea, and forced down a couple of pieces of dry toast, before going back to bed. I dozed on and off all afternoon and felt somewhat better with a glimmer of light at the end of the tunnel. I was pretty sure it was just twenty-four-hour flu, so with any luck I should be ready for work on Monday. I certainly wouldn't push it, as I didn't want to be infectious to John or the animals. Dinner was toast and marmalade and more herbal tea. I slept well and woke up Sunday morning feeling almost healthy. Thank goodness, as I was a lousy patient. I would stick around the house and not exert myself as a precaution.

Bruce called me around six. We didn't talk for long and I wasn't feeling like sexy talk, so we kept the conversation to perfunctory stuff.

"I'm so glad you are feeling better, Molly."

"Me too, as I'm not too good at staying at home for long, but I'm sure I'll be able to work tomorrow. I'll call you tomorrow night."

"I won't be home tomorrow until late. I promised Nick I'd work out with him and catch a bite afterwards, so Tuesday might be better."

"That's okay with me. I love you, miss you, and look forward to calling you Tuesday. I'll bid you goodnight, my prince." Gosh, that was so corny, but I just felt like saying it.

There was a distinct pause at the other end of the phone, followed by "Goodnight my fair princess and I love you, too."

Fortunately, I felt perfectly fine on Monday so went to work as usual. I decided that I wouldn't hit the beach or pool, but would coast for a few days. Jen understood perfectly and said that she had a lot of catching up at home as she was gone most of the weekend.

"How was your time in Jacksonville, Jen?"

"It was fabulous, but like you, I am not a city girl. We ate out all the time and had so much fun together. But now I'm behind on domestic crap, so how about we make a date to hit the beach on Thursday?"

"That sounds perfect, Jen; that'll give me a few days to really be on top of my game."

Thursday was a pretty slow day at work, so, like most slow days I waded through paperwork. I was deep in thought when a very sensual voice asked me if we could take a look at his dog who'd cut his front leg. I looked up and thought that I must be dreaming. If I weren't already in love, I would be infatuated now. This tall, slim man, with a mop of black hair and eyes to match, smiled at me. One could really get lost in those dark pools.

"Yes sir, absolutely. Why don't you follow me into the surgery?"

He introduced himself in a rather foreign tone as Antonio Miller.

"You seem to have an Italian accent. Am I right?"

"My father is American and my mother is Italian. We moved here about three months ago. My father has a job in Orlando, but they decided to buy a house in New Smyrna Beach to be near the ocean. And, I'm staying with them until I get established."

"Oh, forgive me. I'm Molly Thomas, and pleased to meet you Mr. Miller."

"Please call me Antonio."

My gaze kept flitting to those dark eyes. I couldn't believe the feelings he'd stirred up in me, and I felt rather guilty. But I defied any female not to be attracted this man. I introduced him to John.

We were able to patch up his dog and told him to return in one week when we'd take the stitches out. He thanked us and shook my hand. It was a firm handshake and when he smiled at me my heart missed a beat. *Molly, for goodness sake, cut it out,* I said to myself. I called Jen right away and told her. She told me not to sweat these normal feelings, and not to give it a second thought. Later on, at home I called Bruce, still feeling somewhat guilty for my feelings earlier in the day. As soon as I heard his voice, any guilt disappeared. We had the best long-distance sex. I will never again look at a telephone in the same light. We talked about seeing each other in three weeks and general news topics.

"What would you like for Christmas, Molly?"

"Nothing but you, my darling man; thanks for asking."

"I'm getting you something, so if you have no ideas, you'll have to trust my choice."

I asked how Brandy was doing. He was fine and he loved being with Nick and Sally, so Bruce didn't have to feel guilty about leaving him there for three weeks. He hadn't heard from his dad, so no news was good news, although he hadn't really expected to hear from him. After more than an hour on the phone we agreed it was time to go to bed.

"Goodbye, darling; I'll talk to you during the weekend. I love and miss you more than you know", Bruce said.

I replied, "Me too; I love you bunches and have a good night's rest".

The next day at the beach with Jen after work was nothing less than perfect. As usual our hamburgers lived up to their reputation. This relaxing, yet invigorating time renewed my spirits and I felt on top of the world.

"I'm going Christmas shopping tomorrow, Jen. Do you want to join me?"

"I'll give it a miss, if you don't mind. Charlie is taking me out to dinner so I'm going to stick close to home during the day. We could do it another time, but thanks for asking. I hope you have lots of success. Shopping this time of the year doesn't thrill me, but you're smart to go this early before the crowds get too ghastly. I'll call you during the week to see if you want to walk the beach."

"Have a great dinner with Charlie. This has been so much fun as always."

My shopping day went very well. I found a necklace and matching earrings for Jen and a shirt for my boss, John. We had been exchanging gifts for a couple of years now. I found a few inexpensive sets of earrings for my neighbors on either side who look out for me. I really don't know them that well, so it was more of a thank you than anything else. Shopped out and tired, I opted for a cappuccino that revived me enough to make my way home. I was too tired to cook, so I dragged a ready-made pizza out of the freezer to heat and munch on, while watching a bit of television before turning in. I was ecstatic that I'd finished my Christmas shopping. Definitely a load of stress had been eradicated and I slept like a baby.

I'd totally forgotten to call Bruce over the weekend, but moreover, he hadn't called me, so we both were quits. I finally called him around eight Monday evening.

"Molly, I don't know how to apologize enough for not calling you. The weekend got the better of me and I realized late Sunday evening, that I hadn't spoken to you."

"Don't feel bad, because the same thing happened to me. I spent Saturday at the beach with Jen so was tired in the evening, then yesterday I spent the better part of the day at the mall, so by the time I got home, ate and cleaned up it was late, but we can make up for lost time now. How was your weekend?"

"It was above average. I hit the gym on Saturday and met Nick for dinner, and then Sunday I went into the office to clear up a lot of paper work that was long overdue. We have the CEO coming in tomorrow and I had to get a jump start on a project. That sums it up. Nothing really thrilling, but the time flew by. And believe me, I thought of you so much."

"I thought of you too. By the way, I am sitting on the kitchen counter and cannot help thinking of the wonderful love making we have had on it. Touch yourself, Bruce, and give me an orgasm."

I could hear his groans and pictured his erection, which in turn, made me feel utterly aroused helped by my own physical manipulation. I couldn't contain myself any longer and screamed out loud as I exploded with pleasure. I lay down on the counter and almost kissed it. How amazing to think that kitchen counters and telephones had such magic.

Finally, we both expressed our love and said goodnight, promising to talk with each other every night.

Thursday was upon me more quickly than I had expected. It was the day that Antonio was coming back with his dog to get the stitches out. I don't know why I should be feeling excited at the thought of seeing him. Only yesterday I'd had some of the best phone sex ever. As I was wrestling with my guilt feelings, he walked in and smiled at me. Is it possible to fancy two men at the same time?

Loving one and fancying one maybe, but I felt utterly confused. So, confused I'd remain.

"Hello, Molly", he said with a smile that would melt anyone's heart. Those eyes were penetrating and he had the perfect set of teeth to offset his smile.

"Hello, Antonio. How's your dog today?"

He's doing fine and I'm sure he can't wait to get the stitches out as he's been trying to scratch the area quite a bit."

"Bring him on through to the surgery and I'll take a look at him."

The dog was healed enough for stitch removal. Since John was out on a field call, I asked Antonio to help hold him down while I removed the stitches. The canine was so good and didn't flinch at all.

"I forgot to ask you what his name is, Antonio."

He's called Wimp, since he's just the opposite of his name. Thanks, so much Molly. I was wondering if you don't have anything to do this evening, would you care to have a drink with me."

This can't be happening, I said to myself. I wanted desperately to say yes, but my will power kicked in.

"I'd love to, but I am in a relationship; otherwise I wouldn't hesitate. I'm flattered by your asking me."

"Oh, that's too bad. Anyway, if the relationship falters, let me know."

"I will, Antonio. It was good to see you and bring Wimp in if there are any other problems with him."

"Will do, so goodbye for now", he said as he turned and walked out of the surgery.

I asked myself, *darn it, why does everything happen at once?* For two years I hadn't met or even seen a man that interested me. Now, I'd met two within the space of six months. What a shame I didn't have a girlfriend I could introduce him to, but I don't think it would take him long to hook up with someone.

Fortunately, our office got very busy in the afternoon, which helped take my mind off the sentiments I had been feeling towards Antonio. However, I eventually admonished myself, *Molly; you have a great man so put this one out of your head right now.* It was easier said than done, but I figured a run on the beach after work would take care of some of this stress. I was right. The waves were raucous today and I ran about three miles. By the time I'd finished, my soul felt cleansed and I knew that the feelings I had were normal. It was time to go home, eat dinner, and call Jen. She was in total agreement with how I felt. She also made the observation that I hadn't been in a relationship with Bruce that long and who knew what lay ahead of us. Bruce was arriving in two weeks on Saturday and the time until then would pass quickly enough. I was going to paint the bedroom and decorate for the holidays.

Indeed, I finished painting the bedroom a subtle shade of purple and treated myself to a new set of sheets and a duvet cover in varying purples. All in all, it transformed the rather drab room into a peaceful place.

My two little trees were now decorated and by the time I had put all my Christmas stuff out, the place looked rather festive. I loved decorating for this holiday season, although it has bittersweet memories for me. My Mum died just after Christmas and my closest friend, who happened to be my first cousin, died two weeks before, so I try especially hard to have a jolly season feeling in my home. This year wouldn't be hard at all, as Bruce would be with me.

I didn't see Antonio again, and as the days passed he didn't feature in my head so much. It was now the Thursday before Bruce was arriving; just two nights before we'd be together again. I made sure I had all the food necessary for the holidays and I decided to make the apple crisp, so that I'd have very little left to do when he was here. That way I could give him my undivided attention. He called me briefly to say that he was psyched about the trip and that tomorrow was a killer day in the office, so more than likely he'd see me at the airport around three on Saturday.

"I can barely wait, Bruce. I'm so excited to see you, even if it's at Orlando International among thousands of travelers," I said half joking. "Have a wonderful trip and give hugs to Brandy from me."

He said in reply, "Will do, darling. I can't wait to see you, too."

I didn't go to bed until past one as the pie took me longer than I'd anticipated. It was worth it. It looked marvelous and smelt fabulous. I had one more day of work and all of next week I was off. Now this is what I call a sweet deal.

On my way to the airport, it flashed upon my brain as to how he would take the news about me hiring a private eye to look into the disappearance of his mother and girlfriend. I didn't, for one moment, think he'd be thrilled, but it was done with his best interests at heart. I would wait until the day after Christmas, what we Brits call Boxing Day, to tell him. I felt sick with excitement as I walked towards the gate, and then I saw him. He was looking drop dead casual and so handsome in navy trousers, a pale blue shirt, and a matching blazer. I knew at that very instant that he was the man for me. He blew me a kiss when he saw me and rushed up to me, lifted me off my feet and gave me a huge hug whilst smothering me with kisses.

"Molly, it's so great to see you. You're looking more wonderful than ever."

When he finally put me down on terra-firma I told him that I was so happy he was here. We waited for his luggage which only took about fifteen minutes, and chatted about this and that until it came sliding towards him. He grabbed it, took my hand and we headed off to the car. It was a really easy trip back with very little traffic, which surprised me as it was the holiday weekend. One never knew with Orlando. We were home in under an hour and twenty minutes.

Once inside, Bruce literally threw his case down, stripped off his tie, jacket, and shirt, and lifted me onto the kitchen counter where he took me with the ferocity of a tiger that'd been released from his cage. After we'd both come down to earth, he picked me up and we headed upstairs for a brief cleanup and to bed. We didn't get up for over four hours.

"Bruce, I think it is time we had some dinner and wine, don't you think?"

"Good idea," he replied.

"Let's go downstairs and sit in the living room. I've saved a particularly good bottle of red for tonight", I offered.

We sat on the sofa, his arm around my waist, whilst we indulged ourselves by slathering crackers with strong camembert and brie. It didn't take very long to finish the wine.

"Are you still hungry, Bruce?"

"Hungry for you, but not for food", he said, with a pseudo leer. "I'm pretty sure that I couldn't satisfy you again this evening, but there is always tomorrow. Let's go up so I can unpack and we can shower together."

"I'm game for that," I said wondering if he would get another erection in the shower.

We had a long, steamy shower and sure enough he took me again. What it is to have a young stud as my man. We dried off and were both exhausted in the best kind of way. Sleep was long and luxurious. With the morning light came the aroma of coffee.

"Bruce, you are not only drop dead sexy, but a coffee maker par excellence. I've missed that part of you more than you'll know."

He passed me my steaming mug of coffee as we sat up in bed, reading the paper like an old married couple. It felt so good. I had a flash of what Boxing Day might bring when I told him about the private eye, but I did my utmost to dispel any more negative thoughts regarding this subject. Christmas day was two days away and we were going to have a wonderful time. The start to the weekend was stupendous. Three cups of coffee with breakfast in bed, followed by slow love making that seemed to last for an eternity, then the reality of Mars and Venus kicked in – endless boring sports and loud bright lights. At one-point Bruce came upstairs where I was reading and decided to talk. I was bush-wacked, but loved him so much that I sat up in the dripping bed and listened to my man.

"Molly, I can't get enough of you. Not just from the sexual angle, but being with you is so relaxing and we have fun together. You make me laugh and that is so good for my soul."

I responded with my own pronouncements of lust and love. And so, we cooed back and forth until sleep took us.

My day started around eight-thirty with lots of coffee and two croissants, smothered in butter and blueberry preserves. The combination probably gave me a minor case of acid reflux. His day started more slowly. Once he awoke, with the sun high in the sky, I told him how amazing he was and asked if he wanted to take a walk on the beach this afternoon before dinner?"

"That sounds perfect, darling girl. How long do I have before I have to get some clothes on?"

"Well, it's almost noon, so what say we head out around three?"

"That sounds perfect. Do you have any fancy cheese left, as I could really go for some brie right now?"

Oh, God, more shopping, flashed through my brain.

"There's no brie left, but I have some cheddar. I know; I'll go down and cut up a couple of apples and some cubes of cheddar and I have a bottle of good cider to go with them. I'll be right back, so don't go anywhere,"

I came back up with reasonable portions of cheese, crackers, apple slices, dried apricots halves, raisins, and two glasses of cool apple cider. We sat up in bed munching away and sipping cider. Afterwards, we cuddled until we couldn't keep it together and Bruce took me with wild abandon. Someday this had been and it wasn't even evening yet. We chatted about Christmas Day and that reminded me to give Jen a call to finalize arrangements.

Jen responded to my greeting over the phone with, "How are things, Molly?"

"Better than you could ever imagine, Jen. I just wanted to check and make sure things were still on for Monday."

"Absolutely! You might plan on showing up around eleven, if that's okay with you two."

I replied, "Sounds like a plan. So, have a merry weekend, and see you on Christmas. Say, 'hi', to Charlie for me."

"Will do, and the same from me to Bruce", Jen said.

Obligations over, it was time to throw some clothes on and head to the beach. It was, as always, better than a therapist. We strolled hand in hand, waves lapping at our feet. I'd a gut feeling that the shoreline would be fairly empty, and I was right. It seemed everyone was shopping or cooking.

"Isn't this just perfect, Bruce?" I said squeezing his hand and giving him a peck on the cheek.

"It certainly is", he replied. "Nothing much beats a walk along a deserted beach. I suggest we come for the better part of the day tomorrow, unless you are going to become too domestic and make stuffing or some such thing."

"No way! Let's take a picnic basket like before."

Take advantage of our tomorrows while we can, I thought, as I kissed him on the cheek and turned away for fear of him seeing me shed a tear. Men usually hate to see their mates cry, because they can't figure us out - well at least the ones they are currently living with.

The next morning, because Christmas was almost upon us, I briefly had maudlin thoughts about my mother, cousin, and various friends that had passed through my life never to be seen again. But it was to be too good a day to waste in sadness. We made our way to another brilliant day at the beach and later exchanged gifts, because we were spending most of the day in the company of Jen and Charlie.

It was now Monday, the day of Christmas. We didn't make love in the morning, mainly because we were preoccupied with getting everything ready to spend most of the day at Jen's. If it had been just Jen and I, we would have eaten off paper plates and curled up in front of the tele, but this was a special day and I was going to make sure that Bruce, Charlie, Jen, and I would remember it as such.

We arrived at Jen's a few minutes after eleven in the morning. Of course, Charlie was already there. Before long we each had a glass of bubbly in hand, chatting up a storm, and nibbling on some starters that Bruce had bought earlier.

On pretext of reviewing the menu, I dragged Jen back into the kitchen and told her that she looked glowing.

"I'm in love, Molly. Charlie is definitely the one."

"I can see that", I said. "It's obvious."

I then told her how bloody nervous I was about my impending conversation with my private eye."

"You'll be fine, Molly. It'll go one of two ways as we talked about before. Anyway, I think you'd better have another glass of champagne, or two."

"How can I ignore such sage advice?" I asked, *tongue in cheek*, as they say.

Our conversation was cut short by the fellows coming for more goodies to munch on.

"So, cutie pie, what have you girls been talking about?" Charlie inquired of Jen.

My instant reaction was slight nausea at the use of *cutie pie*, but if the endearment pleased Jen, so be it.

Jen answered with, "This and that, Charlie. Nothing that would interest you guys."

It was agreed that we sit down for the main meal at about two-thirty.

"If you fellas want to watch football beforehand, have at it", Jen suggested, and I seconded her idea.

Bruce came over and, kissed me grinning from ear to ear. Charlie did likewise to Jen. That settled Jen and I settled into finalizing the meal, and talking. When it was time we called the guys to the table. Neither Jen nor I had much of an appetite as we'd already had done considerable taste-testing of brandy butter for our special pudding dessert.

The meal was a success, up to dessert, that is.

When Jen and I put it before the men, Charlie asked, "What on earth is that black blob with white sauce all over it?"

Jen said, "Its English Christmas pudding with brandy butter poured on it. Try it; you might like it, and if you don't, that'll leave more for Molly and me."

He took a bit of it and got up and went into the kitchen, to assumedly spit it out. Bruce tried it and seemed to like it. Charlie's reaction did not hurt our feelings. Jen and I felt that one or both might not care for our English Yuletide tradition. After all, not all Brits were enthralled with this heavy pudding. Anyway, we had small apple and pumpkin pies in reserve, to which both guys helped themselves.

With coffee and dessert out of the way, Jen asked, "A glass of Port by the fake fireplace anyone?"

I was the first to respond, "Sounds wonderful, Jen, but let's do the dishes first and leave the guys to their own devices, once they help us clear off the table. It won't take long."

We could have demanded their assistance in the kitchen, but I wanted and succeeded to get Jen off by herself.

"I must say, Charlie is quite cute, and charming, even if he did not like the pudding. No wonder you are smitten, Jen. Luckily, you don't have the added complications that I have."

"We'll see, Molly; it's early days yet."

Our conversation centered on Bruce and Charlie while we finished cleaning up. We then joined them to enjoy a Portuguese $20 bottle of Croft Tawny Port Reserve, the cost of which was split between Jen and me. Port is a fortified wine produced in Portugal, though producers in other countries use the name for similar wines.

Sipping the Port was a very fine experience that mellowed us all. As couples, we smooched for a while, before Charlie jumped up and said that he had a bit of office work to do.

Before leaving, Charlie asked, "I've been meaning to ask you, Jen, what is the meaning of Boxing Day. That's the day after Christmas, right?"

Jen explained, "In England, in the days when servants lived downstairs, on Christmas Day they tended to the needs of the upstairs family and had no time for their own celebration of the holiday. The tradition developed that the family of the house, as a thank you, would invite their household staff upstairs to the main house the next day to give each one a box of goodies and the day off. And so, the day after Christmas became known as Boxing Day.

Both Charlie and Bruce appreciated the explanation. Charlie left and I said to Bruce that we really should get going as well. We told Jen what a fabulous time we'd had, and agreed to have her and Charlie over for dessert and coffee tomorrow afternoon around three to help celebrate Boxing Day.

Once home, Bruce said, "Let's go upstairs, baby girl".

"I think you have been watching too much television calling me that. I prefer *darling* or *my love*, if I have a choice."

"I'll store that in my chemical brain", he said, as he chased me upstairs.

It was a wonderful end to Christmas, being swept away in what seemed like endless lovemaking. I didn't have much time to think about tomorrow, which was just as well, as it was probably going to resemble a real fight; at least I fervently hoped it wouldn't.

Bruce woke up first and brought me my wake-up mug of coffee. I had hardly opened my eyes to be greeted by something long and hard – it wasn't dried toast!

"Thank you darling", I said. "That was a great way to begin the day, which looks to be a shiny one, so we'll be able to hit the beach for several hours."

"I can hardly wait. I'm going to jump in the shower", he replied as I went downstairs to gather stuff for a picnic on the beach.

Suddenly I felt quite sick thinking about when I should tell Bruce about Bri. My cowardly side told me to wait until after the beach. I would definitely need a sherry in order to broach the subject. Before I could dwell too deeply on it, Bruce snuck up behind me, squeezed my bum, and wouldn't you know it, took me on the kitchen counter, sweeping aside the various cold cuts before entering me.

"Wow, where on earth do you get this stamina from, Bruce? Are you taking Viagra?"

"No, I'm not; you just arouse me something fierce, but don't expect anything more until tonight. I'm virile, but not a robot."

We both roared as I re-cleaned the counter in order to make sandwiches. A sandwich would never be a normal sandwich again! I opened the cupboard door to get the mustard out and screamed bloody murder I had been invaded by sugar ants crawling all over the place. *Bugger, this is really what I need today*, I thought, as I proceeded to take everything out, running into the garage to get the spray and ant traps.

"What's going on?" Bruce asked, as he came downstairs, ready for the beach.

"I'm sorry, but sea and sunshine are going to have to take second place right now.

I've been invaded by ants and they are all over the place. I was so pissed that I took the bottle of wine that was sitting on the counter, surrounded by the little monsters and took a large swig.

"Want a swig, Bruce?'

"Sure thing," he said as he helped me grab everything out of the cupboards.

It took us several hours to apparently get rid of them. We piled everything up on the kitchen table. I called the pest control company, but as I suspected they were closed until tomorrow. Sod it. Once we'd got everything out of the cupboards, sprayed them and wiped them down, the kitchen looked as if we were either moving in or out.

"You know what, Bruce? We might as well go to the beach. We can't do anything more until I call pest control in the morning. I'm positive we haven't killed them all."

"I'm up for that and we'll grab a bite out. No way are you going to cook with this upheaval."

I nodded in agreement.

"I'll just be a sec, as I'm going to have to cancel Jen and Charlie coming over later," I said, as I ran upstairs and put on a bikini. There'd be none of this matronly swimming gear for me today. When I came downstairs I knew exactly what Bruce was thinking, but there was no space on the kitchen counter.

"Wow, you look sensational, Molly."

"Thanks," I said, feeling extremely nervous. "Shall we get going then if we want to have time on the beach?"

"He pinched my boobs, as he gathered up a couple of towels. He drove. We didn't say very much at all. I didn't even have to tell him how to get there anymore. He had it down pat. As I suspected there was only a smattering of people here today. I knew most people would be out picking up bargains or returning gifts they really didn't want.

"Molly, we have the beach almost to ourselves again", Bruce said in amazement.

I smiled in return, as we unloaded a few essentials and headed in the direction of the ocean.

"Bruce, let's sit really close up today, since the sand is firm and dry."

"Good idea."

Once ensconced, we fell into our chairs and remained totally silent for ages. I was so preoccupied with what lay ahead that even the sound of the waves lapping gently at my feet were irritating, instead of soothing. I jumped up and said that I felt like taking a jog.

He replied, "I'll come with you. I really need to work off yesterday's food".

We ran at a steady pace for about forty minutes. I still didn't feel any better.

"Is there something wrong, Miss Molly? You don't seem your usual self today."

"Oh, I suppose it must be the ant situation in my kitchen", I said with a nervous smile, feeling ill about how dishonest I was being.

I grabbed the cooler and passed over a couple of sandwiches to Bruce which we ate in virtual silence. We both grabbed our books and read for a while. I looked at my watch and it was almost four o'clock.

"Don't you have to get up early tomorrow, Bruce?"

"Unfortunately, I do, so I suppose we'd better head back as you have the ghastly job of dealing with the ants while I am attending to some work."

We packed up the car and Bruce drove back to my house, neither one of us uttering a word. His tension was totally different to mine.

I opened the door to the kitchen with trepidation. *Oh, shit,* I uttered to myself. The bloody ants were swarming everywhere. There was a black mass in all the cupboards. I got the ant control, my mask, and sprayed the heck out of them, then slammed all the cupboard doors shut.

Bruce remarked, "When you move, you really move. What can I do to help out?"

"Pour me large bourbon with water, and let's sit down in the living room. I have something that I have to tell you."

I swigged the first drink down behind his back, discretely pouring myself another large one. *Here goes,* I said to myself, taking a large gulp of air.

"I can't imagine what you have to say to me, Molly, but I'm ready to listen."

"There is no easy way to tell you, so I'm going to plunge right in. You know that I have a very curious mind, having trained as a writer before I went into studying to be a vet?"

He nodded, looking quite perturbed.

"Well, I became really concerned about the disappearance of your girlfriend, Valerie and your mother, so I took it upon myself to find a private investigator to help me in the search for them."

Bruce got up, paced around, and flung his hands in the air in utter disgust.

"You did what?!" he shouted.

"I know it seems so underhanded, but I thought long and hard before I decided to hire a relatively inexpensive detective. Please understand that I undertook this project because I felt so sorry for you not knowing what happened to your mother and former girlfriend. I'm sure now you are really pissed with me, but I promise it's because I love you so much that I wanted to get things sorted out."

He looked at me with momentary anger that flared from his beautiful blue eyes. My stomach turned over and I took another large swig of bourbon.

After some moments he said, "I'm not sure I can take all this in right now, Molly. I'm going to bed. Don't follow me, because I have to digest this project of yours. I love you, but feel betrayed right now."

He turned and ran up the stairs. I sat down and sobbed for a long time until I fell dead asleep, until four am. I went upstairs and climbed into bed beside Bruce, who was fast asleep and never woke up, for which I was thankful. Finally, I drifted off and when I got up the next morning there was a note saying that he'd gone for a long walk. He hadn't left me any coffee, or toast, just an empty void. The silence hung like a Halloween web in the room, and I cried again, until I became ravenously hungry and had the beginnings of a caffeine withdrawal headache.

My symptoms forced me to go downstairs and make some coffee. I hesitated to open the cupboard doors, but carefully opened the china closet to find more live ants, which I naturally sprayed to death.

I managed to make coffee without ants floating around and I rescued a bagel that I had protected from the ant horde. It wasn't yet time to call the pest control people. I had another hour to go and felt really fidgety. I couldn't very well call Jen just yet, particularly as Charlie was staying with her. All my phone calls would just have to wait. After a couple of cups of strong coffee and the buttered bagel I felt much better, physically anyway. Time sputtered slowly forward until eight-thirty when I managed to get the pest people. They said a rep could come in the afternoon, if that worked for me. I readily agreed and then I tried Jen at work, but got her answering machine.

"Jen, it's me, Molly. I told Bruce about hiring Bri. Call me in your lunch hour, if possible, so I can elaborate."

Now what am I going to do for the rest of the morning I thought? I'd first attack my laundry and then clean the upstairs. I poured myself another cup of coffee and before I'd even gone upstairs the phone rang. I nervously picked it up to find Bruce on the line.

"Molly, it's me. I know this is going to be hard for you to understand right now, but we have an emergency at the factory back home, so I'm flying out tomorrow morning. We can go out for dinner if you'd like."

"Thanks for the offer, but I really don't feel much like going out. If it's okay with, you we can order pizza."

"Okay by me. Sorry, but I've got to run, so I'll see you around seven." He hung up without even saying my name, darling, or any other endearment.

I didn't know whether to believe him, and frankly I wouldn't blame him if he was using the office emergency as an excuse to go back to Michigan. What a mess I'd made of things. Now I really wished that I'd not meddled in his affairs, but deep down knew that I was glad to have hired Bri. Even if Bruce and I split up, I'd still pursue my investigations. I sat down at the kitchen table and cried. The phone rang again, and I grabbed it, trying to muffle my tears.

It was Jen and she knew that I'd been crying.

"Let it go, Molly; don't hold back on my account. I 'm on my way over right now, so is there anything I can get you?"

"No thanks, but I will be so happy to see you."

"I'll be there within ten minutes", she replied.

True to her word, I heard her car roar into my driveway. I went outside to welcome her, but burst into floods of tears as she climbed out of her car.

"God, you're a mess. Let's get some coffee inside you with a shot of brandy."

Once we'd got our laced coffee and grabbed the cookie jar, we plonked ourselves down on my wonderfully threadbare, but comfortable sofa. It had been my grandmother's, inherited by my mother. And now it was mine, threadbare in spots, but still very comfortable, standing the test of time. I bet it could tell a tale or two.

"Jen, I told Bruce about Bri and my digging into his affairs. He was furious, and I don't blame him. He barely spoke to me, taking off to his office here, which was sort of what I'd expected. He called me this morning and said that he'd have to go back to Dearborn early tomorrow as there was an emergency in one of the plants. I don't for a moment believe that's the real reason he's going home. What a cock up I've made of my life with him, but I can't be anything other than this nosey journalist. To tell you the truth Jen, I'm not sorry for my actions. Even if everything fizzles out between us, at least I will have done something positive."

I felt much better having let everything out.

"Do you want another laced coffee before you go back to the office, Jen?"

"Yea, sure, but hurry up and I can give you my tack on things."

I dug out the rest of the brie, dumped it on a plastic plate, and sat opposite her on my favorite sickly green rocking chair.

"I'm all ears", I said.

"Molly, I personally think you did the right thing as far as Bri goes. Time alone will tell how things pan out, but you really have to get on with your daily life. If Bruce really loves you, and I'm convinced he does, he'll work through this. As for Charlie and me, he asked me if I would consider getting engaged in another six months"

I didn't give her a chance to say anything else, as I let out with, "Oh my God, you have totally turned this black day around for me. I'm so thrilled for you, and somewhat envious at the same time."

I leapt up and hugged her. We both shed some tears before she realized that she'd be late if she didn't leave right away.

"I'll call you tomorrow night, Molly, and don't dwell too much on this state of affairs, although it's easier said than done."

I handed her a doggie bag with bagels, cheese, and a bar of chocolate, as she tore out to the car.

"Thanks for my afternoon snack", she said as she buckled up and sped off.

The pest rep came on time and sprayed the whole house. I retreated to the back deck to avoid the pungent odor, but if it killed the buggers once and for all, it was worth it.

I telephoned John and asked him if I could return to work on Friday and he was overjoyed. He wasn't enamored with the temp that he'd been sent to cover the Christmas Holidays.

My house seemed too silent, which I would normally relish, but not today. I changed into my bathing suit and headed off to the pool. There was only one other person swimming, so I was able to really lash through the water. Twenty-five laps really helped with my mental fatigue. Bruce showed up around seven. He kissed me passionately on the lips, but I didn't feel the real warmth that usually exuded from him. I busied myself getting the pizza and poured him a glass of wine and asked about his work.

"Molly, work was hectic and I have a couple of hours still to go, so if you don't mind I'm going to eat and finish up odds and ends before we go to bed. I have a 9:00 am flight out of Daytona Beach, by the way."

"You've got to do what you've got to do, Bruce. I understand completely, so after I've cleaned up I'll wait for you upstairs." I filled him in on the ant situation, told him I'd had a good swim, and went upstairs feeling very distant from him. I took a long shower, but that didn't help. I tried to read but couldn't. I just lay there feeling sad.

"Oh, you're still awake, darling girl", he said with a grin that somewhat lifted my spirits. We did make love, but there was something missing. Maybe it was my imagination, but I wasn't into it, and before I had time to get into it he sighed, rolled over, and was asleep. It seems that men are able to sleep through any emotional crisis, from what I've read, plus my own limited experience dealing with the male race. I watched the clock go through the hours, until the sun peeked through my Belgian lace curtains. I was convinced that this was his way of saying *sayonara.*

I feigned sleep as he ran downstairs, I assumed, to make coffee. My assumption was correct. He brought me my favorite brown mug of steaming coffee. He'd perfected the amount of creamer I liked, but there wasn't any toast or a flower.

"Sorry, that I am so distracted, but I've ordered the cab for seven", he told me.

It was six thirty already and my heart was beating faster than I wanted it to.

"Will you call me when you get back, darling?"

"You bet I will, and I'm going to spend some time thinking over what you told me.

"I love you so much but-------."

He'd jumped in the shower before he'd even completed the sentence. He looked so handsome in his business suit. I threw on my favorite sweats and accompanied him downstairs.   No time to feel maudlin, as the cabbie discreetly honked his horn.

"Goodbye, my love, I'll see you soon."

"Adios, Bruce; have a safe flight and I love you."

He was gone and my world was crumbling around me. I sought refuge on my well-worn couch, and sobbed until exhaustion got the better of me. I dozed off for almost an hour. I'd almost forgotten that I was going in to work today, which was a blessing. The last twenty-four hours seemed like an eternity. It was more like a surreal nightmare, but unfortunately, I was waking up to reality. I just hoped that we were super busy at work. I knew John would be really sympathetic when I told him what had happened, but I was paid to attend to animals, not to have a free psychiatric treatment. John was great, but we were not intimate friends. I loped downstairs, turned the coffee on, and looked over at the kitchen counter, which I had renamed, *the sex slab*. At least I had experienced something new with Bruce. I drank my coffee with gusto, ate some dry bread with butter and marmite, poured my second cup of coffee, went upstairs, and got dressed. It was pretty amazing that I got to work in one piece as I drove there like a robot. When I walked in the smell of animal pee was amazingly comforting.

"Molly, is that you?"

"Yes, John, it's me and I'm ready to work to make up for lost time."

He came out of the office, took one look at me and exclaimed,

"You look awful. What's going on with you?"

"You really want to know?"

"I wouldn't have asked you, if I didn't need to know, but unfortunately we have to wait until lunch time as you have to make up for what Miss Drippy failed to do. Her name was Miss Diplock. I complained to the agency about her. I told them that she'd have been more suited to a biker bar serving drinks than working as a vet's assistant."

"That's funny John, and I'm so happy to be back. Tell me what needs to be done before our lunch break."

Two beautiful golden labs had to have their annual shots, and a little white mouse had a bad cold. How anyone could have a pet mouse was a little beyond me. My love of animals did have its limitations. Mice, gerbils, and snakes were not high on my list. In fact, if anyone came in with a snake I'd make a hasty retreat. John discovered this the first time someone brought in their pet anaconda and I almost had a coronary. From that day on he always dealt with them. In our lunch break I told John what had transpired between Bruce and me.

"You have been a bit of a meddler, Molly, but true love triumphs. Not that I know anything about love up until now. But if your relationship is that solid, I think you'll get past all of this. Who knows, the outcome may be very positive. On that note, we have six cats to deal with before we quit for the day."

"Thanks, John. You are the best boss and I appreciate your input. I'll try my utmost not to let my emotions get the better of me here."

He smiled, but raised his eyebrows in mock disbelief that I could control my expressive self. Then he hustled off into the crowded waiting room. The day was a blur of clients that made the day pass rapidly. At the end John and I said our goodbyes and I rushed home to an empty house, except for a few residual ants that had escaped the poison. I sprayed the heck out of them until I defied anything to live through that deluge.

There were no messages for me, but it was barely six o'clock. So what else can a dejected girl to do, but busy herself fixing dinner and turning on the TV in an effort to get on with the evening? I had switched on the news, but that depressed me even more, so I hopped over to the cheesy movie channel to see what I could find to distract me. About seven the phone rang. I rushed to answer it to find Bruce on the line.

"Hello, Molly. I'm sorry that I didn't call you sooner but I had to finish this project that I mentioned to you. I'm not going into all the details, but my feet have barely touched the ground since I got back. You'd hate it right now darling, as it is freezing outside. Is everything all right with you?"

I took a large gulp of air. He sounded as if he expected everything to be just fine.

"I'm not sure, Bruce. Have you given any thought to what I did without your permission?"

"To be perfectly honest with you, I haven't really had much time to digest what you did, but I will think about it over the weekend. I still love you, Molly, but I just never expected you to be in any way dishonest with me. I understand that you had my best interests at heart, but it's not something I can mull over with all the problems at work. I have to meet up with the project manager in an hour, so I'll call you Saturday morning. I've got to dash, so until Saturday."

I didn't even have time to say goodbye and I began to cry my eyes out, but at least he'd phoned which was more than I'd expected. I called Jen, but there was only the answer machine. My self-imposed misery leads me to devour an entire bag of M and M's. I just couldn't get Bruce's slightly cool attitude towards me out of my head. Since I had to get up early for work I resorted to a sleeping pill; otherwise, I knew I'd be wired all night long. I slept like a log, waking up to the buzzing of my alarm, and was thankful that I had to go to work.

Meanwhile back in Dearborn, Bruce woke up around six, as restless as could be. His mind wasn't on work, but on Molly. He'd woken in the night with a hard on which dissipated quickly. He knew that he couldn't live without her, but felt so betrayed. He ran downstairs, made some hot coffee, drinking it as he headed towards the shower. He felt better after the water had streamed over his body, clearing his head somewhat from the excess wine he'd drunk the previous night. He threw on his suit and tie, ran downstairs, grabbed his briefcase, and went outside. It was damn cold. The snow was coming down fast, but it was little more than a dusting of white powder that swirled in wave patterns on the sidewalk. He buzzed open the car, and sunk down into the warm cloth seat, knowing how much Molly loathed this climate. He had a fully charged day, but would call Nick and pick his brains over a game of squash. That always de-stressed him after a day at work. He knew Molly would be at the vet's, so he'd call her later in the evening. As for business, he was having a hell of a time trying to figure out why an exorbitant amount of company money had seemed to have been embezzled; so much so that his brain was becoming fried. He dialed Nick's number at work and fortunately Nick picked up on the third ring.

"Hey, bud, do you fancy a game of squash and a couple of beers this evening? I need to de-stress and swing something by you."

"Sure, that works for me. I'll meet you at the courts after five-thirty. I've got to run, so see you later."

Around five-thirty Bruce hung it up for the day, grabbed his squash gear, and headed for the racquet club which was about ten minutes' drive from the office. It was a swanky club, but fortunately for Bruce one of the perks of working where he did was that the company picked up the yearly tab; otherwise, he'd have thought twice about joining. He ran down to the courts to find Nick warming up. They played for a solid hour, sweating profusely, but downed a couple of bottles of water each to compensate. When finished both of them sank down into comfortable chairs overlooking the courts.

"That beer is going to taste mighty good Nick, and thanks for meeting me here. I needed to de-stress big time, and there is nothing quite like a fierce match with you to work out the kinks."

"Well, I'm happy for that, so now let's get changed and head to the pub."

They found a booth in the corner away from the pool table, and immediately ordered a couple of beers.

"We'll decide on what we're going to eat when you come back with our drinks," Nick said to the waitress, who had a killer smile. He thought to himself that if Sally wasn't in his life he'd definitely want this girl's number.

"All right, let's have it, Bruce. What's going on with you and Molly?"

"Everything was perfect until Boxing Day when she told me that she'd hired a private investigator to look into the disappearance of my ex-girlfriend and my mother. I feel totally betrayed. Why would she do that without asking my permission?"

Nick smiled, brushed his curly hair out of his eyes, and gave Bruce a look of amusement.

"Is that it? I thought it was something much more serious. For God's sake, Bruce, it's in her inquisitive nature. She was a journalist of sorts at one time, was she not? Admittedly, she should have told you first, but probably was afraid you'd say, no. From what you tell me, she regrets it and was waiting for the right time to say anything, worrying how you'd take it. Do you mean to tell me that you are contemplating throwing away the best thing that's happened to you since Valerie?"

"I thought you'd say just that and I'm really trying to wrap my head around this whole scenario. I adore the girl and don't want to lose her, but feel that having done this behind my back, who knows what else she'll get up to."

They were interrupted by the waitress returning with their beer and asking if they'd decided on what they were going to eat.

"I'll have the fish and chips with extra vinegar and mayonnaise for my fries, thanks, and you Nick, what's your pleasure?"

"Make that two orders, but leave off the mayonnaise, thanks."

Their waitress flashed a winsome smile at them and asked if they cared for another beer when she returned with their order.

"Yes, sure, unless we are in need of one sooner; thanks", Bruce replied.

Nick continued the conversation, "So my friend what are you proposing to do about this mess?"

I'm going to call Molly this evening, and upon your advice, think that I'll tell her if she insists on continuing with this investigation, then she's got to do it with me."

"Now you're talking; thank God for that. So, when do you intend seeing her again?"

"I've got to stay here for at least a month, and she's busy with her job; besides, she'd hate the weather right now. So, I guess we'll have great phone sex until the next time we get together."

That settled, they talked about work and, politics until they'd finished their order of fish and chips and second beer.

"Nick, thanks for being such a good mate, and you can put your wallet away. Consider this my donation for a therapy session."

"I'm not going to refuse. So how about a return match in a couple of days?"

"That sounds like a plan. How about we meet at the gym on Thursday at six? Oh, yes, say *hello* to Sally for me"

"You're on, and when you talk to Molly, give her my best."

It was dark and very cold outside. Bruce felt so much more at ease with the whole situation now that he'd hashed it out with Nick. He was anxious to get home so he could call Molly.

Back in the warmth of New Smyrna Beach, Molly had survived the work day in a perfunctory haze. Even John noticed how distracted she was and told her to finish up the paper work and head out early.

"I think a run on the beach will do you a world of good, Molly, so scram as soon as you're done."

John was right, of course. I headed for the beach and ran a good mile and a half one way along the shoreline. The ocean was calm and a few pelicans flew overhead. Before I turned to run back, I stood still on the water's edge embracing the warm, salty air which cleared my lungs and calmed my ragged nerves. *Damn*, I thought, *I am so lucky living where I do and even if Bruce and I don't remain an item, I have a pretty good life here.* Relaxed now, I ran the rest of the way back to the car. I was starving and couldn't wait to get home, shower and have a glass of white wine with my pizza and wait for the dreaded call. I was on my second glass of cheap chardonnay, and had abolished an entire mini pizza. It was about eight o'clock and the phone hadn't rung, so I decided to clean up in the kitchen, get the coffee ready for the morning, and head upstairs with a full glass of wine. I was no sooner ensconced in bed, feeling rather mellow when the phone rang. It startled me somewhat. I picked it up on the third ring.

"Hello there, who is it?"

"Hello Miss Molly my darling, I'm missing you terribly already"

He sounded like a totally different man, which took me by surprise.

"I've been thinking about what you did behind my back, and have talked it over with Nick. I think that if you intend to carry on with this crazy private eye thing, then I am going to back you all the way and be part of the search for answers."

I started to cry, which was apparent to Bruce as I sniveled over the phone that I loved him, was so sorry that I'd hurt him, and was elated that he was now supportive.

"Was it Nick that really influenced you, or did you come to this conclusion before you chewed the fat with him?"

"Well, I thought about it long and hard, but knew that I couldn't afford to lose you. Besides, you'd never do anything intentionally to hurt me."

"Oh, Bruce, you've made my night. I've been so upset since you left for fear of losing you. I can now go to work without looking like a sheepdog. Now for the sixty-four-thousand-dollar question, when will I see you again?"

"Molly, you'd hate it here right now. It's so darn cold and we've had a lot of snow. I am really tied up with this embezzlement case right now, so won't be able to come to

New Smyrna Beach for about a month. I know it's an age, but we'll get through it, that I'm sure of. Now as far as this investigation of yours, can this wait for a couple of months?"

"I guess it will have to. I'll call Bri tomorrow and keep him on a retainer basis, if you're in agreement."

"I don't suppose I have any option other than to agree, do I?"

"No, Bruce; at least I hope not. I really have to get some shut eye, which I haven't been able to do since you left. I adore you and look forward to tomorrow night when we can speak again."

"Unfortunately, I can't call you tomorrow, but will call you after nine on Thursday night. Tomorrow we have a big department meeting followed by a business dinner, and Thursday evening I'm playing squash with Nick. But don't forget that I love you to pieces, my Southern girl. Sleep tight and dream of me."

I didn't have a chance to say another word. But that was okay. My world was looking much rosier now. I'd call Jen in the morning to see if she wanted to run on the beach and have dinner tomorrow. I read a few chapters of my sleazy novel and passed out.

The sun shone through my lace curtains awaking me before my alarm. I was feeling very energetic and sprung out of bed, and raced downstairs to turn the coffee pot on. I looked at the kitchen counter with renewed enthusiasm. I knew that my sexual appetite would warrant another session on it. Coffee tasted good, but not quite as good as when delivered to me on a tray with toast and marmalade. Such are the joys of being in a loving relationship. I opted for a bagel and cream cheese and turned on the television to catch the morning news. I decided to get to work early and surprise John. He hadn't arrived yet, so I unlocked the door, heading straight for the office to get a jump start on the paperwork. I recognized John's whistle as he came into the office.

"My Goodness, do I ever see a change in you from yesterday", he said. "You look like a normal human being, so what happened."

"Briefly, I spoke with Bruce and he has decided to go along with my investigation. We both acknowledged that we can't live without each other, and he realized that I did everything with his best interests at heart. I can't tell you how ecstatic I am. I won't be seeing him for several weeks, as he has a heavy work load and won't be able to come down for a while. And, we both agreed I would loathe being in Dearborn right now as the weather is arctic like. So, now you'll have a hundred percent of me, John."

"I'm thrilled for that. Your mental outlook had me quite worried."

"Yes, no more worries", I said with a smile in my voice. "Moving right along, I brought you a Dunkin Donuts coffee and a blueberry muffin to start the day off right."

"Thanks, Molly, for thinking of me. If I am going to indulge, this is the way to go."

We both intermittently dunked pieces of our muffins into the rich, dark coffee.

The day was passing by uneventfully. I called Jen in my lunch hour and got hold of her.

"Do you feel like a run on the beach after work today, followed by dinner?"

"Yes, that sounds great, so what say we meet in the car park around five-thirty?"

"Perfect, Jen. I can't wait to catch up with you   See you later on."

I heard her agreeing, but then the phone went dead. Work called to us both.

Arriving at the beach, it was cloudy and rather breezy. The waves looked angry as the surf swelled up before dying at the water's edge. It was perfect for running as we didn't get too hot. We'd agreed to keep to just casual conversation until dinner time. We managed five miles, lagging somewhat at the last half. The birds were circling around in a frenzy as if something was about to happen. Suddenly out of nowhere about six dolphins leapt out of the water, obviously searching for fish. I wish that I'd had my camera because the silvery light reflecting on their backs was a sight that could only be held in my memory.

"What an awesome sight, Jen."

"You better believe it. Its times like these I know I'm living in the right place. I am more than ready to eat now, so let's hop in my car and I'll bring you back here after we've eaten."

We decided to go to the Steak house about a mile away. Somehow sitting on bar stools overlooking the water is magical but we wanted a bit more privacy and comfort. We'd had our fair share of magic and views for now. We opted for a booth in the corner. No sooner had we sat down than our waiter came over and asked us what we'd like to drink. We knew each other so well that Jen ordered a carafe of merlot and two glasses of water.

"It'll be right up, girls," he said with a movie star grin.

We decided to focus on what we were going to eat before we started gossiping. We both decided on steak, fries and creamed spinach. Once we'd downed a glass of merlot, I filled Jen in on what had transpired between Bruce and me.

"I knew that things would work out between you two. You have too much going for you both to squander a wonderful relationship. When is Bruce going to grace us again with his presence?"

"He's really busy with some embezzlement stuff right now, but plans on coming in a few weeks. Anyway, that's enough about me; how are you and Charlie progressing?"

"He told me two days ago that he wants to marry me, but would like to wait until the summer time when we can celebrate by going away. I was taken aback a bit, but I think that I'm going to take the plunge. When I do, you are going to be my maid of honor."

We chuckled, worked on another glass of merlot, and chatted about this and that until our food arrived. We ate in virtual silence. That run had given us fierce appetites. We got the check, skipping coffee and dessert and got in the car, heading back to the beach car park.

"If you feel like repeating this on Friday, Molly, give me a buzz."

"Sure thing, Jen. It's been so much fun and that run really cleaned out the cobwebs. I'll call you in a few days."

Miss Mercedes roared off into the orange haze.

I drove home thinking that life couldn't get much better, other than having Bruce here, but I was looking forward to talking to him in a couple of hours. In all the excitement, for want of a better word, I'd completely forgotten to ask about Brandy. I know that Nick and Sally were temporarily taking care of him, but wondered if Bruce had got him back. Before I had time to ponder the question, the phone rang.

"Hello, darling girl. How are you?"

"Great, and thanks for asking. By the way, have you got Brandy back with you? I meant to ask you that the last time we spoke, but there were so many other things on my mind that I totally forgot?"

"As a matter of fact, I picked him up last night. He's mighty happy to be back and I know that he misses you. Now tell me which room are you in now?"

"I'm in the kitchen, but why do you ask?"

"I'm picturing you naked against the kitchen counter. Your boobs are hard with desire for me and I can hear you quiver. I miss caressing you and can feel your wetness against me."

"Oh, Bruce," I said, having an orgasm there and then. "You have captured my heart, and I miss making love to you, darling man. I heard him groan as he came slightly after I did.

"How many more weeks do I have to go before we are together again?"

I think I can swing a long weekend in three weeks. In the meantime, I guess we'll have to do with good old phone sex. Have you been on the beach since I left?"

"Jen and I ran five miles this evening and are going to repeat the performance the day after tomorrow. I'll be honest, Bruce, the thing I miss about Dearborn is being able to walk to the coffee shop, and be part of the hustle and bustle of daily life; although, I know that I could never live anywhere that wasn't close to the beach. Work has resumed its usual pace and I've had a lot of paper work to catch up on. Otherwise, life ticks along in a rather mundane fashion."

"If I weren't so busy, Molly, I would miss you even more than I do now and that is saying something. My father is still in St. Lucia and will probably return here around the end of May. He is very serious about selling the house and buying a property out there. It makes good sense to me. I have no desire to take care of his house on a long-term basis while he's gone. Well, that just about sums things up for now. I'll call you in a couple of days, darling. I adore you."

"I love you too, Bruce; talk to you soon."

The kitchen seemed bare but quite sensual. I headed upstairs feeling quite content with life.

Bruce felt elated after speaking with Molly, so much so, that he decided to take Brandy for a much-needed walk. He threw on his overcoat, wrapped a scarf around his neck, put a lead on Brandy who was jumping around with excitement. It was beyond cold, so the pair walked at a swift pace on the sidewalks which still had traces of snow. The sky was blue black, studded with many stars that threw a silvery light on the streets. After about twenty minutes, Bruce about turned and the two headed for home. If that walk hadn't done Brandy in, it had certainly worked its magic on Bruce. Once inside, Brandy flopped into his basket and within minutes was asleep. Bruce took a glass of water upstairs, turned on the television, watched about an hour's worth of CNN, and slept like a log.

Days turned into weeks and the Friday that Bruce was due in New Smyrna Beach was upon me. I was going to leave work early in order to pick him up at the airport around six thirty. I was more than a little excited. I stood waiting just outside the arrivals line, and then I saw him. My heart missed a beat. He was drop dead handsome and sexy as well. He ran into my arms and I didn't want to let go.

"Bruce, it's so good to see you. How was your flight?"

"It was nothing out of the ordinary. You look as if life is treating you fairly well. Judging by your tan you've been frequenting the beach quite a lot in my absence."

"You better believe it, darling, and I'm hoping that we can both go whilst you are here, albeit it a long weekend."

The traffic wasn't bad at all and we were home in just over an hour. No sooner than we were in the door, Bruce grabbed me and started ripping my clothes off with an urgency that I'd forgotten. He stared at me, totally naked with such lust in his eyes that it didn't take him long to strip off, throwing me down on the kitchen counter, taking me so fast that I barely had time to breathe.

"I've missed you something fierce, Molly, to say nothing of dreaming about this moment more than you'll ever know. I'm starving for food now, so what've you got up your sleeve for dinner?"

"I made eggplant with a meat sauce. I'll go and heat it up, but whilst I'm doing that, do you fancy a glass of wine?"

He nodded in agreement. It didn't take us long to devour dinner. Bruce said he was going up to take a shower whilst I cleaned up, if that was all right with me."

"Sure thing, darling; go for it, and I'll be up in a bit."

He was sitting up in bed with a pretty sizeable erection. It seemed made love for ages, re-exploring every inch of each other's bodies. Afterwards, we lay entwined, at one with the world.

"Welcome home, darling", I said, but Bruce was fast asleep. I wasn't far behind.

I awoke in the morning to the delicious aroma of coffee on a tray, as per usual.

In appreciation, I said, "My, how I've missed my morning coffee and breakfast in bed. You are a dream."

"It's my aim to please my princess," he said, chuckling as he is climbing into bed, balancing the tray between us. Then he added, "What's on the agenda for today?"

"I thought we'd take lunch and head to the beach as I'm sure you're in need of some rays. This evening we could go out to dinner if that's good for you."

"That sounds like a perfect way to spend a Saturday. It's been dastardly cold back home, so some sea and sun are just what the doctor ordered. I've been meaning to ask you, what is going on with the investigator you hired?"

I took a deep gulp of air, wondering when this subject would rear its ugly head.

"I've got him on a retainer fee. I'm paying him fifty dollars a month so that when I, or should I say we, decide to go ahead with more in-depth investigation, I don't have to go through all the preliminary stuff again."

"That sounds like a very reasonable amount of money for retaining this guy. Now, for planning ahead, I thought that I'd come back down in February and perhaps towards the end of March you could get a few days off work and come to Dearborn when the weather should be more spring-like. We could really get going with the investigation at that time. What do you think, Molly?"

"It sounds okay to me. I have three weeks' vacation a year and I could take a week in late March. It's not worth coming for less than that. Now that we've somewhat sorted out our travel plans, let's get organized for the beach. I've made some roast beef sarnies –that's English slang for sandwiches. I've also cut up some cheese and have a thermos of coffee and some chocolate chip cookies for us to take."

I'd already dressed in my bikini and had grabbed a couple of towels so with the goodies prepared we were ready to rock and roll. Bruce jumped in the driver's seat of my car without asking if it was okay. We had our roles down pat, so no questions were necessary. It didn't take long to get to the beach as traffic was pretty light this morning. We unloaded everything into the handy beach cart and headed for our favorite spot fairly close to the water.

"Let's take a swim first before anything else," Bruce suggested.

We ran into the not too cool surf, letting the waves engulf our bodies. We swam for at least a half an hour in earnest before heading towards the shore. We flopped down on our towels giving each other a passionate kiss.

"I've been thinking about this moment ever since I left you, Molly. It's perfect."

We lay there soaking up the sun's rays, enjoying listening to the birds flying above us, until we decided it was time to have some lunch. The sandwiches tasted awesome, washed down by iced coffee, followed by a couple of cookies each. It felt like I was on holiday today. We lay for a while digesting our food before deciding to take a slow stroll along the water's edge. Our beach day was truly blissful.

That evening we had steak for dinner and then made love again. Most of Sunday was spent in bed until it was time for Bruce to start getting ready to return to Dearborn.

"I can't wait for you to return, darling man", I said, feeling a lump in my throat.

"Don't be unhappy, Molly, my love. We know that we will be together some day forever. It's just a matter of time before we decide where it will be."

I was on the point of saying that in my mind it would never be Dearborn, but my thoughts were distracted by the door bell ringing.

"I guess that's my cab for the airport. I'll call you this evening, Molly. I adore you and cannot wait to be with you again in less than a month."

We kissed passionately before he disappeared into the cab. This time I didn't cry. We'd had such a great time together and my spirits were lifted.

I got to work early and gave Bri a call and explained about Bruce's involvement now and said, "Look, I'll be coming to Dearborn for about a week in March, so maybe Bruce and I can come to your office and go through what we need you to do in more detail, if that sounds good to you".

"I'm fine with that, because right now I am working on two messy divorce cases and am quite busy. I look forward to hearing from you next month then, Molly. Thanks for giving me the heads up."

"You're welcome, Bri, and I am putting your retainer check in the mail today."

After hanging up, I thought about how I loved my work. Although it wasn't super exciting, it was very satisfying and pleasurable to work with animals. They have such powers of non-verbal communication that are difficult to explain to lay people. We had many varied clients today, so I barely had time to eat. Lunch consisted of snatching a yogurt in between surgeries. Paperwork would have to wait.

And so, it went each workday, taking care of our animal patients, and their often clueless masters, with administrative duties tended to in spare moments. I talked to Bruce almost every night.

During one call, he told me that his father would be returning to Dearborn at the end of March for a couple of months to see if he could sell the house, before returning for good to St. Lucia.

"He's not leaving you the house, is he, Bruce?"

"Now what on earth would I want with his house as well as my own? I think it makes ultimate sense for him to sell his place before leaving Michigan for good"

"I suppose you're right. You weren't too keen on his house anyway."

Most of our conversations revolved around our work, what we did on the weekend, and climaxed with great phone sex *(pun intended)*. It certainly beat complete abstinence.

At last, Bruce was set to arrive the next day. I decided that it would be a neat idea if we went to a bed and breakfast place in Flagler Beach. I didn't want to go back to the one in St. Augustine, as I preferred to retain those wonderful memories without confusing them with new ones. I called around and found one place right across the road from the ocean. It had three guest rooms, one was deluxe with bathroom en suite, and so I went ahead and booked it for Saturday night.

Bruce decided to get a service from the airport instead of having me pick him up. This allowed me to greet him at the front door in a sexy negligee with a big grin on my face. Upon seeing me, he threw his suitcase on the floor, undressed, and took me again on the kitchen counter, which was becoming a favorite spot for our first-time encounter after being apart. Neither of us was in any way disappointed. He pushed me back a bit and looked at me up and down several times.

"Do you know how incredibly sexy you look in that outfit, Molly? How could a man resist you wearing that?"

It didn't take him long to make love to me again, this time slower and more deliberately. He actually laid me down on the counter, climbed on top of me and took me slowly, both of us crying out together. When we'd both come down to earth, I told Bruce that I'd booked a night at a bed and breakfast at Flagler beach for Saturday.

"That sounds wonderful and different. I'm looking forward to it, but in the meantime, let's get dressed and go grab something to eat. Do you fancy a hamburger? Because, that's what I was thinking about on the plane, secondary to ravaging you, of course."

"I'm game", I said as I headed upstairs to put on one of my favorite pants outfits.

Hamburgers were up to snuff and we both treated ourselves to dessert. Mine, as one might guess, was coffee ice-cream. Bruce opted for a crème brulèe – not on every hamburger joint menu. That meal over with, we returned to my place undressed, slipped into bed, and passed out until after eight the next morning.

We were somewhat slow in moving, and I was the first one downstairs to set the coffee machine in motion. I stuck two steaming mugs of coffee on a tray and headed upstairs with breakfast included. Bruce was just coming to as I came into the bedroom, setting the tray down on the dresser. I took him his mug of coffee, but breakfast was somewhat delayed. Do I need to say why? The coffee tasted even better afterwards, and our appetite for the toast and jam had increased. We packed our bags and headed out the door by eleven. I drove us to the B & B in Flagler

Beach. It had a very original name, *The Flagler Beach Bed and Breakfast Inn.* The room I'd booked turned out to be way better than I'd imagined it to be. It was indeed overlooking the beach and endless ocean.

After settling in, we took a lengthy, but leisurely stroll along the water's edge, mulling over Bruce's work situation and when I could take a week off to fly to Dearborn.

"I think that the third week in March will work for me, Bruce, as that's our least busy time. John doesn't want to get temporary help to replace me, as it is more work for him in the long run. I'll ask him on Monday if that week will still work for him, and I'll go ahead and book my flight. I think I have enough air miles for a one-way ticket."

"You're not paying a dime for your flight, my love. Whatever the difference is, I'm footing the bill, no argument."

"If you insist, then I give in", I replied

The sun was beginning to set, and cast a beautiful purple hue on the coquina rocks. I never have my camera when I need it. We went and sat on one of the larger ones, drinking in the sheer beauty of the exotic, marbled sky.

"Where shall we go to eat, Molly? I don't have a clue about this area so I'm leaving it up to you."

"How about we check out one of the restaurants overlooking the beach? There are several close to the pier."

"I leave it to your nose for finding good eating places", Bruce said with a smile in his voice.

We ambled back to the room, flopped on the bed, and made delicious love. With our sexual desires sated, we decided to satisfy our stomachs at a steak restaurant, which turned out to be a great find. Breakfast the next morning at the B & B was from eight until eleven which gave us plenty of time to wake up properly. Bruce's flight wasn't until the next morning, so we had the whole day to fritz away. Breakfast consisted of a variety of omelets, an assortment of breads and jams and delicious strong coffee. We decided to take a walk on the beach before heading home. Once the bill was settled, we packed up the car and headed to the beach. It was deserted, all but a few pelicans flying above us. We walked for about an hour, deeming it necessary to burn off some of our breakfast calories.

We got home around two in the afternoon and did absolutely nothing outside of reading the paper and making love, off and on, before deciding to make a few sandwiches to eat in bed while watching TV. It was hard to believe that it was, again, almost time for Bruce to leave. Next time it would be my turn to travel. At least the parting was getting easier each time, as we just knew we'd be together permanently before too long.

To my utter surprise I woke up to find Bruce had left and I never heard a peep. He'd left me a note saying that he'd had the best time, would call me that evening, and hoped my day went well. The usual mug of coffee was set on a tray, with a croissant and jam. I was so spoiled, but wished I felt happy, for right now I had that empty feeling in my gut. Thank goodness, I had to go to work today; otherwise, I'd be floundering around.

The days came and went by rather quickly. I'd debated whether to renew my subscription to the gym, but decided to wait until after I returned from Dearborn. No point paying for time away and they didn't honor holidays. I would content myself with the pool and beach. I went to the gym mostly for social reasons.

It was a week away from my leaving for Dearborn and I was busy at work. The paperwork had piled up and I knew that I couldn't leave John with a stack, so stayed late most nights to get everything caught up. We were hectic in the animal department too. I'd planned to have a farewell dinner on Thursday night with Jen. It wasn't as if I was going to be gone for long – just a week – but it seemed I had so much planning to do that I opted to skip our usual run and just head out to eat, to which Jen readily agreed.

Over dinner I explained to Jen, "I'm really looking forward to returning to Dearborn, but apart from seeing Bruce, I'm also really excited to see Brandy. As for Bruce and me, I'm not sure how long we can continue this long-distance romance, but for the time being I have to be satisfied with this arrangement with the idea that it won't be long before we will not be separated. Oh, yes, we are both going to meet up with Bri whilst I'm there, to push along the investigation."

Dinner was excellent, another sumptuous meal down the hatch, accompanied by lively conversation, and fine wine – for our price range. At the end of our meal, Jen insisted on taking me to the airport for my evening flight which would certainly save me time and the hassle of having to find a parking space.

"I'll be round at five tomorrow afternoons, Molly, so until then have a great last day at work. It sounds as if you are never coming back when I say it like that!"

The next day at the vet's zipped by. I'd cleaned up all the paper work so there was nothing left for John to do in that area. That brought a smile to his face as he gave me a perfunctory hug, told me to have a glorious time, and not to think of work at all.

The flight was smooth and I managed to doze off a bit, waking to hear the captain announce that we were landing in about twenty minutes. I had just a carryon bag so didn't have to wait for luggage. Bruce was there to meet me at the arrival area. As always, my heart skipped a beat when I saw him. This man had definitely won me over, hook, line and sinker. I just hoped my hooks were in him as deeply. He gave me a hug and a passionate kiss, telling me how happy he was to see me. It took about forty minutes to get back to his house. Sure enough, Brandy was waiting in the kitchen and showered me with wet kisses. We had definitely bonded and I couldn't think of my life without him in it.

Bruce had roast pork, and a mean Chardonnay for dinner. We were both ravenous and knew that in this instance food took precedence over our sexual appetites. That came later! We demolished everything with great gusto, cleaned up and took our wine upstairs. The drinking of which was much delayed and need I say why. Our lovemaking was always fantastic and each time I thought that it couldn't get any better, I was proved wrong.

After our interlude I said, "Bruce, I've made arrangements to meet up with Bri on Wednesday afternoon, if that works for you? I know you said you've taken a few days off, but wasn't sure which ones."

"That suits me, as I'm taking Wednesday through Friday off. I thought that tomorrow you could take it easy, and possibly take Brandy for a walk. If you have the time and inclination, I'd really appreciate you going to my father's and picking up his mail."

"I don't mind doing that at all", I replied, considering as well that the weather was almost bearable outside.

There was still a thin remainder of snow, but it was melting as the day time temperature had risen to the forties. *Whoopee to that,* I said to myself. Properly bundled, it would not be an effort to take walks with Brandy or visit a coffee shop and various stores on foot; although it couldn't compare with walks on the beach at home.

On the following morning, I decided to brew the coffee, defrost a couple of bagels in the microwave, and take the quick breakfast with condiments on a tray to the bedroom. To my surprise Bruce was ready for work. He grabbed a mug of coffee, gave me a bear hug, and said that he had a mountain of stuff to do, since he was taking time off.

"I'll see you tonight around seven, Miss Molly. Have a great day with Brandy."

"Thanks, I'll work on that."

"By the way, Molly, there is a new French restaurant in town called Les Fleurs. It sounded very interesting, to the point that I've booked a table at seven for Wednesday. I thought we could start the mini vacation off with a bang."

"That sounds wonderful, my good man. I'll see you this evening, then."

He was out the door as I finished my last sentence. I hopped back into bed, and Brandy followed, making him comfortable beside me. I finished off my coffee and breakfast watching the local news, such that it was. I decided that we'd walk to the café up the street for lunch, then in the afternoon we'd saunter over to Mike's place and pick up his mail. The morning slipped away from me as I dozed off, but I finally awoke and dressed before noon. Brandy and I went downstairs, as he wagged his tail off, very excited at the prospect of going for a walk.

"Off we go boy, we are going to get me some lunch and if you're lucky you'll have a few left over's."

After lunch, good as always, I was thankful that I had put my GPS into my handbag. Putting it into pedestrian mode, all I had to do was entering the address, 116 Nutley Street, and follows its directions. I had remembered that it wasn't that far from Bruce's house. Arriving there, I emptied the mail box and let myself and Brandy inside. It felt weird being in Mike's house. What secrets did it have?

Brandy went to the backdoor wanting to get outside. I followed him into the backyard to find him fascinated with one area in particular, which was puzzling to me. He kept sniffing around in the same spot relentlessly trying to dig up something to no avail. The ground was rock solid. I would definitely do some serious excavating when the earth warmed. Brandy's nose must have been very cold, I guess, because he finally retreated to the back door waiting for me to let him in. I wasn't about to hang around Mike's, so I did a quick check of the place before I locked it up and headed back to my lover's much more welcoming home. We got back around four, so I decided to call Bri just to confirm our appointment for tomorrow.

He said, "That's a good time for me, Molly. I look forward to seeing you and to meeting Bruce."

I decided to make pasta for dinner, and read my sleazy novel until Bruce showed up. He kept his word and rolled in around seven-fifteen.

I greeted him with, "Well, my darling, I'm sure you are more than ready for a glass of wine and dinner."

"Yes, I have to admit I'm super hungry", he said, with a naughty grin on his face, double entendre no doubt intended. Again, he captured my heart and set my sexual desires on fire. However, the meal did come first and we teased ourselves with a quiet interlude afterwards, before challenging our lovemaking imaginations.

Wednesday morning slipped through our lazy fingers. In preparation to meet with Bri, Bruce told me to wear something dressy for the evening, as the restaurant was quite up-market. I did have a trouser suit on, but I said I would prefer to come home to change into something more elegant before going out to dinner.

We got to Bri's on time, an office on the first floor of the building. It was a pretty dingy looking place, but he was mentally sharp, had a pleasant personality, and was inexpensive, and that mattered most to me. I knocked on the door to hear his cheery voice telling us to come right on in. Once the introductions were done, Bri told Bruce pretty much what he'd told me. Valerie had left home at an early age and wasn't close to her parents, so that when they didn't hear from her, it didn't faze them. He couldn't give us any more information than to say that she'd simply disappeared off the face of the earth. He would dig around some more regarding Greta's disappearance. His research did reveal that she'd left Mike for this new man of hers, Philip Glaston, who died of a heart attack in the summer of last year. But what happened to Greta after his passing remains a mystery.

"I'm sorry, Bruce and Molly, but that is as far as my research was able to take me. If you wish to continue to retain me, I'll be happy to assist any way I can. Perhaps you can feed me more info to work with."

"That would be great, thanks", I said as Bruce nodded his head in agreement. "Thanks so much for your time. We'll stay in touch, Bri."

We walked back to the car in silence. It hadn't been a very successful meeting, but at least Bruce had met Bri and knew with whom I was dealing.

After we returned to Bruce's, he asked, "Fancy a walk before dinner, Molly?"

I replied, "Sure, the exercise would do us some good, and we can take Brandy with us".

"Good idea; you wait here and I'll get him."

Brandy was very happy to be out and about. We trekked for about three miles around the streets of Dearborn. It was fun, gazing into all the stores, and observing the people around us. The big city atmosphere was something I didn't have back home, but I had warm weather and the beach that more than compensated for these attractions.

We got back with about an hour to spare before dinner reservations. We took a shower together which was torrid to say the least. I'd decided to put on my favorite red velvet dress which I must say really did do me justice. Bruce looked at me with utter admiration in his eyes.

"You look a million dollars, Molly. Am I ever a lucky guy?!"

"You don't look too shabby yourself, my prince charming."

The restaurant was beautiful, its elegance understated. We had a table in the corner. The tablecloths were of beige linen and each table had a single cream rose in a crystal vase. Bruce ordered champagne, which stunned me for a moment. I didn't think this was a special evening, but maybe he just felt like splurging since he was on a mini vacation. The champagne duly arrived and we toasted each other.

After reviewing the menu, Bruce asked, "What would you like for an appetizer and entre, my lady?"

"I think I'll start with the coconut shrimp and mango sauce followed by the salmon and garlic mashed potatoes."

Bruce opted for oysters and a steak. Once the waiter had left with our order, Bruce got up from his seat and came over and sat next to me. He looked very awkward. Suddenly he got down on one knee and told me that he couldn't live without me, wanted to marry me, and hoped that I would like his choice of rings. He opened the ring box and took out the most spectacular ring of sapphires surrounded by diamonds in a gold filigree setting.

"Will you do me the honor of becoming my wife, Molly?"

I burst into tears, telling him that I would definitely marry him. He put the ring on my finger and kissed me passionately.

"You have made me one happy man. I love you, Molly, with all my heart and then some."

Now I understood the champagne. I took another sip and had to pinch myself for fear that I was dreaming. I kept looking at the ring that sparkled on my finger. I couldn't wait to telephone Jen and give her the news.

Dinner was wonderful. We laughed a lot and I couldn't imagine being any happier.

I told him, "This was such a thrilling shock, my darling. I didn't imagine anything like this in my wildest dreams. When this has all sunk in, we'll have to talk about when and where we'll get married."

"Let's not rush things, Molly. We must enjoy the moment, don't you think?"

I smiled in agreement. We lingered over dessert and coffee before heading home to some of the best love making that I could ever remember.

Before going to sleep, I murmured, "This has been some night, Bruce. I hope I won't wake up to find it was a dream."

"I think, my princess, you will know it is real when you look at your ring finger."

I had absolutely no intention of taking off the ring for the night. I wanted it to re-assure me when I woke up in the morning that I was a princess engaged to a gallant prince.

It wasn't in my nature to wait until Jen got to work to give her the news. It was around eight in the morning and she'd still be at home.

"Jen, it's me, Molly. I have some fantastic news to tell you and I couldn't wait another moment. Bruce proposed to me last night. Naturally I said, *yes*. The ring is gorgeous, it's a sapphire with little diamonds surrounding it on a filigree band of gold, and just so you have plenty of time to get used to the idea, you are going to be my bridesmaid."

She congratulated me with much enthusiasm and told Charlie who was with her that I'd just become engaged to Bruce.

I was happy to see that her relationship with Charlie seemed to be on solid ground. A double wedding maybe? I think not. That's not something that's ever appealed to me, no matter how much I adore Jen. And she probably feels the same way.

"I get back home Sunday night around six and I'll call you shortly after, Jen. I'm sorry to have called you this early, but I couldn't contain myself."

"I'm glad you did. News this spectacular shouldn't be held in. I look forward to your call on Sunday. In the meantime, enjoy the rest of your engaging time with Bruce." I heard her chuckle as she said this.

After I hung up Bruce asked, "So what would my future bride like to do today?"

"I know it sounds really dull, but I'd like to go to the mall and buy a couple of outfits, because the clothes selection seems better here. If you'd rather not come with me, I understand completely."

Bruce replied, "I will come with you as I need a couple of pairs of shorts for the gym. We can have a leisurely morning and go shopping after lunch. There are a few halfway decent restaurants in the mall where we can snatch an early dinner after shopping.

"Bruce, I'd love to have a celebration with Nick and Sally either Friday or Saturday night, if they're free."

"I'll give Nick a call after breakfast to set something up, but before that, would my future bride get back into bed with me. I have something I have to do."

Bruce made love to me with such passion that, in fact, he was a bit on the rough side, but I lapped it up. I dug my fingers into his back and growled like a tigress until we both exploded. Exhausted, he laid himself beside me and gazed at me with the eyes of an adoring puppy dog.

"I'm one lucky man to have you as my future wife", he said as he caressed my breasts.

"It works both ways you know. I can't say that I am too unhappy about the situation myself," I said as I rubbed my fingers over my sparkling ring.

The morning was enjoyed in slow motion. We drank our coffee in bed, munching on some toast with marmite. I'd introduced Bruce to marmite and he actually liked it. Not too many Americans did. We took a shower together which wasn't just any ordinary mutual cleaning exercise, so that delayed us even more. It was definitely time to get dressed; otherwise, we'd never leave the house.

I found two pants outfits at the mall. One outfit consisted of tight bronze colored pants and a floaty top that had some interested black beadwork on the front. The other was all red, again with tight pants and the top was plain, but had billowy sleeves. Both were flattering and cheap. Bruce found his shorts and bought a couple of matching tee shirts. We were happy as it hadn't taken us very long to do what we'd set out to do.

"Oh, I forgot to tell you, Molly, but Nick and Sally are free on Saturday night. I suggested they come over for drinks and appetizers and we could figure out somewhere to go."

"That sounds like a good idea", I said, but silently thinking it was strange to have an engagement ring on my finger, the reason for our upcoming get together.

While shopping, we decided to go to the steak restaurant in the mall. The choices were limited, but the steaks were phenomenal. It was amazing how shopping gave one an appetite. We tucked in to our food as if we hadn't eaten all day.

During the course of the meal, I said, "I'm so happy that we both found what we wanted here in the mall, Bruce. The prices are more reasonable and the selections are better than where I live. All in all, I'm tickled."

"If you are tickled, my fair bride to be, then I am tickled; so tickled that I suggest we skip dessert here and head off home. I have a great idea for dessert in mind." He chuckled like a naughty schoolboy and my mind went straight to the kitchen counter.

We got back and sure enough I was right. Bruce began to undress me as soon as the door was closed. It may not have been the most comfortable place to make love, but it was one of the sexiest. We didn't last too long before we came together, both of us laughing after we'd come down to earth. Why it should have struck us both as being humorous, I don't exactly know.

The next morning, after our usual coffee and toast, I decided that I'd go to Mike's place to pick up his mail. Bruce mentioned that he had to make a lengthy conference call to work, so that would work out well. I also decided to buy some snacks for when Nick and Sally came over this evening. After a quick shop, I took a few minutes to pick up Mike's mail and put it on the kitchen table with the rest, and to take a quick look around to make sure everything looked as it did before. It did, so I left.

Bruce was still on the phone when I returned, so I busied myself in the kitchen getting things organized for later on, poured myself an early glass of wine and went and made myself comfortable in the living room. After about half an hour he joined me.

"Sneaking an early one, are you, fair maiden?"

"I'm on my vacation, so I can cheat somewhat, don't you think?"

"It's amazing how you can find an excuse for your weaknesses", he said with a sarcastic grin on his face. "I think I'll join you. After that long call, I need something to calm my nerves. I put it to my supervisor that I wanted a recommendation for the Cape Canaveral position once my findings and resultant actions are completed. I told him I planned to relocate to New Smyrna Beach in the summer or early fall. He was somewhat taken aback, but I reiterated that's what I've decided to do.

There is no way the princess will move to the land of ice and snow; therefore, the prince will have to move his tent to the temperate land of his princess. Seriously, I'll be able to get a good job in the physics or chemical arena with my background, and with the references that I'll get."

"I don't really know what to say, Bruce. Naturally I'm thrilled that you have made this decision, because I was having nightmares about moving. What are you going to do with your house?"

"I plan on keeping it for a couple of years. You never know, we may decide to spend a few weeks in the summer here. We'll see, but the market isn't that great for selling right now. Our lives are taking major turns, all for the better I feel. It does seem we need to decide whether we are going to stay in your house or move."

"I can't see any reason for moving right away. The place is plenty big enough for us now and you may not realize that I am less than one hundred percent in favor of having children. We need to get married first before we take too many leaps, don't you think?"

"I agree, Molly. Let's drop the decision making for now and instead just kick back and relax before Nick and Sally show up. Well, we do have one more decision. I thought we might try this new seafood place within walking distance of my house, if that sounds good to you?"

"You know me and seafood. It sounds perfect and I'm sure it'll suit Nick and Sally."

"Good, I'm glad we've settled that. I'm going to get us another glass of wine and bring in the snacks. Don't move, just stay put, and relax. You have to fly back tomorrow, so I want you to reserve your strength."

He laughed as he disappeared into the kitchen. I knew what my strength was being reserved for and I looked forward to it.

Nick and Sally brought a bottle of chilled brut champagne along with the biggest grins this side of Texas.

"We are so thrilled for you both, Nick said. Let's drink to the happy couple."

We made short shrift of the bottle and snacks, while catching up on each other's affairs. The following dinner at the seafood restaurant was excellent, we all agreed.

"Do you want to come back for a nightcap, you two?" Bruce asked as the tab was being paid.

Nick replied, "If it's all the same to you we are going to head off. We are going to visit one of Sally's cousins tomorrow and it is about a two-hour drive, so we need our beauty sleep."

"Thanks so much for the Champaign, you two. I'm thrilled that Bruce introduced me to you both."

Farewells done with, we walked back to the house. I needed every ounce of strength I could muster as Bruce made love to me for a wonderful eternity. We fell asleep in unison. My last thoughts before I drifted off were that life couldn't get much better than this.

I awoke to the usual coffee on the dresser and a vision of Bruce in his running gear.

"I hope you didn't mind that I took a run. I felt like I had a lot of pent up energy and you were sleeping so deeply that I didn't want to disturb you?"

"That's fine, Bruce. You've got to do what you've got to do. I want to stay close to home today, since I have to leave around three for the airport. In the meantime, I'm going to go down and make breakfast. I'll bring it up when it's ready."

Once back in bed with eggs, bacon, toast, and coffee we started to talk about the future.

"Molly, I've been thinking about the months ahead of us. What I'm thinking is that I'll come down to you for a couple of weekends in April, and then you can come North in May. I think that my father plans to leave for good sometime in May and I know he'd like to say goodbye to you. I plan to stay here from June until packing up and leaving Dearborn for good, no later than the end of September. I am going to try to set up interviews for April inside and outside my company. I don't want to leave everything until the last minute. Does this sound reasonable to you, darling?"

"I'm glad that you have it all worked out as it makes my job easier. The only issue on my mind is, when we should get married. I would love it to be in October. Otherwise, I have no plans to do anything differently. I'm still going to work and not much will change, other than the fact that I'll have a permanent roommate."

Bruce grinned at that comment and said, "I never thought of myself as a roommate, but I'll take it. I'm glad we've sorted out some of the nitty-gritty. Now we can relax for the better part of the day."

We had absolutely no problem with the relaxing part. Breakfast finished, we lay in the bed, intermittently drifting off. It culminated in some rough sex which wiped me out in a good way. I took a hot shower afterwards and proceeded to finish off my packing. Before lunch we took Brandy for a walk around the block. It was a very pleasant experience, as all the dirty snow had finally melted away and the smell of Spring was in the air.

During our jaunt, I said, "Oh, one thought, Bruce, and that is about Brandy. He has to come with you and get used to the beach. Do you think he'll adapt? There is a particular beach that allows dogs and he would be in his element. I couldn't think of my life without him at this juncture."

Bruce didn't answer me, but that was okay. His mind was probably on work.

I made sandwiches for lunch and we sat like an old married couple reading the Sunday paper before it was time to head off to the airport. All this back and forth crap was really getting old and I couldn't wait until we were finally in one place.

We hugged each other at the departure curb, and I promised to call as soon as I got home. Bruce was parked in a very awkward spot. A security officer asked him to move the car, so he left without even waving goodbye, which suited me. I hated protracted goodbyes.

The flight was uneventful and we landed on time. I took the airport bus to where I'd left the car, and within an hour and a half I was happily back home. It felt good. Bruce's place was lovely, but somehow it wasn't home. I dumped my stuff on the stairs and headed for the kitchen and the wine bottle. I called Jen to see if she could have dinner tomorrow evening.

"Absolutely, Molly, I'm dying to see your ring."

I had almost forgotten that I was wearing it. I asked, "Do you fancy a walk on the beach before dinner?"

Sure thing. So how about I come and pick you up around five-thirty?"

"That sounds great Jen, and I can't wait to see you."

I went outside and gazed upward at the beautiful moon. The otherwise dark sky was lit by the moon's pale, eerie glow. It was ethereal. I was swept up in the moment, so much so, that I'd almost forgotten that I'd promised Bruce to call him when I got back. I had to stand in the yard for a few more minutes to drink in this magical sight before calling.

I spoke to his answering machine, "Bruce, it's me, Molly. I just wanted to let you know that I got back safely. I'll call you tomorrow evening after I get back from dinner with Jen. I love you, my handsome devil." I didn't know where he was, but at least he'd get the message and knew I'd got back in one piece.

I went to work the next morning feeling so different. How could something as simple as being engaged make me feel like someone new? I walked into work with a Cheshire grin on my face. John noticed it and asked me what was up. I flashed him my ring.

"Well goodness me, Molly, you have been a busy bee while you were gone. I'm delighted for you, but fervently hope that this doesn't mean you are moving to Dearborn."

"Are you crazy, John, in even thinking that? Bruce knows only too well that I would never live in such a climate. He's moving here for good this fall or sooner, and I'll keep on working."

"I think we should celebrate this momentous occasion. What do you say about having dinner with Jessica and me this weekend?"

"That sounds lovely, John. Thanks very much."

"We'll make firm arrangements later on in the week. Shall we say Saturday night then?"

"I'll pencil it in my busy diary," I said laughingly. It was so good to be back at work with John and the animals.

The day passed quickly. It wasn't overly busy, just a constant stream of animals needing their shots. I got back home a few minutes before Jen showed up. She ran up to me and took hold of my left hand.

"My, that's some ring! How lucky you are that Bruce bought you something you really like. It could have been a disaster, if he hadn't known your love of sapphires"

"It pays to have a big mouth", I said. "Let's attack the beach, shall we? I must say, I miss the ocean when I'm in Michigan. Thank goodness Bruce is moving here. He knows me so well climate-wise. His father is buying a house in St. Lucia, so Bruce won't have that bother. He's keeping his house for a couple of years as the present real estate market isn't that great. We'll probably go there in the summer for a few weeks. Anyway, that's all down the road."

We strolled along the water's edge, loving the feel of the cool salty sea tickling our feet. There was a light, but warm breeze blowing, and the ocean was very calm. After an hour of walking one way we turned around deciding we were really hungry. We went to a nearby hamburger joint and sated ourselves on juicy burgers and fries.

"You have yet to tell me about you and Charlie, Jen."

"There isn't much new to tell you. We are going along as steady as can be. We won't get engaged for quite some time. Charlie has a cash flow problem right now, and I'm in no rush. Have you decided when you're getting married, Molly?"

"Yes, I thought I like to get married in October. The nineteenth is the day that I have temporarily picked out. That has always been my lucky number."

We chatted about other topics before heading home, deciding that we'd repeat our seaside walk Friday after work.

"Thanks for being you, Jen, and thanks for the ride. Have a great week and it's my turn to fetch you for our next beach walk."

"Night, Molly", she said as she tore off in her usual madcap fashion. What would I do without her? I hope I never have to find that out.

During the week, I had busy work days, evening walks on the beach by myself and nightly long phone calls with Bruce that usually culminated with excited phone sex. Jen had to cancel Friday night, as there was a work project that needed her presence. It was not a disappointing development, particularly since I was going out with John and Jessica on Saturday night.

My mind was working in overdrive as to where we should get married, have the reception, and where we might have the honeymoon. I decided I'd like to get married on the beach and have our reception at some lovely outdoor restaurant. We would decide on which one down the road. As to a honeymoon that remained to be discussed at length. I had absolutely no ideas right now. I'm sure we would come up with something splendid.

I decided to give the beach a miss today, particularly since it is more crowded on the weekend. Lounging around the pool was the order of the day. First, I did perfunctory household chores and made a quick run to the grocery store. Once my purchases were put away, I made myself a couple of sandwiches and a mug of green tea to take to the pool. I swam my twenty laps in a nearly empty pool before relaxing with a good book.

Towards the end of the afternoon I left the pool to get ready for my dinner date with John and his new girlfriend, Jessica. I was quite anxious to see how that would work out. John had arranged to pick me up around six-thirty and he was on time.

The three of us said our hellos and John gave me a kiss on the cheek, telling me how much they were looking forward to this evening.

In reply, I said, "Me too, John. I can't wait to get to know you and Jessica better."

The evening was a resounding success. There were no awkward silences and I felt sure that when Bruce was here we would be doing this on a more frequent basis. John refused to let me pay, telling me that it was an engagement gift to his wonderful assistant.

I said, "Thanks so much for everything. It was a lovely dinner and I hope that when Bruce moves down here we'll be able to double date."

Jessica nodded her head in total agreement, gave me a hug, and said that she looked forward to seeing me again soon.

The next few weeks seemed to evaporate into thin air. I couldn't believe that Bruce was arriving in two days. He had lined up a couple of interviews at his company's Cape Canaveral facility, so he'd be staying until Monday morning, a real treat to have him this long in my part of the world,

Everything in my life was perfect, almost. At the back of my mind, I still felt uneasy about the disappearance of Bruce's mother and his former girlfriend. It didn't seem as if anything further could be done in regard to the investigation. Still, I anxiously decided to phone Bri.

"Hello, Bri. It's me, Molly. I was wondering if there was anything else you could do to further this investigation?"

Bri replied, "Frankly speaking, there doesn't seem to be a damn thing more I can do. I've followed up on the leads that I had and now find myself at a dead end. If you find out anything else, then maybe I can forge ahead, but right now, Molly, we are at a total standstill. Stay in touch with me and let me know when you are returning to Dearborn. I'd like to meet up with you again."

"I'll do that Bri. I know you are right, but I'm getting so impatient. I'll let you know when I head up to Dearborn again. It'll probably be at the beginning of May. In the meantime, I'll send you a check for your month's retainer fee. Thanks for everything."

"My pleasure, Molly; so, take care of yourself, and we'll be in touch."

I don't know why I felt better after speaking with Bri, but I did. I think he reassured me that there really wasn't anything further that I could do right now, so I must not let niggling thoughts interfere with the enjoyment of my life.

The day finally came when Bruce would be with me again. I had stocked up the fridge, bought some decent wine and invited Jen and Charlie over for dinner on Saturday night. I hadn't even consulted with Bruce about this. I knew he'd be happy to see them both. Waiting for his arrival I fidgeted around making up my face, over and over again, as if this were my first date with him. At least I'd only changed my outfit three times! When the doorbell rang, I flung open the door and threw myself into his arms.

"Well, this is some greeting my love", Bruce responded, "I suspect this is just a taste of things to come."

He was right. After excusing himself to freshen up, we headed straight for the kitchen counter and devoured each other like starving animals.

"Wow! Now I'm really ready for a drink and something to eat", Bruce exclaimed.

"Your wish is my command", I said, grinning ear to ear.

I poured two glasses of red, brought out a tray of slightly more exotic cheeses and some crackers, instead of the usual cheddar and walked into the living room with Bruce in tow.

After some moments of casual conversation, I said, "A couple more wines are in order, don't you agree? I've made lasagna, which is heating up in the oven. Do you mind if we slum it and eat in the kitchen?"

"No, that's just fine with me, as I'm rather beat and look forward to heading to bed after we clean up the dishes.

We ate in relative silence. I think Bruce's mind was concentrating on the job interviews he had tomorrow and the next day. Pretty understandable really, when you think that his whole life was doing an about turn. I was so thrilled that I'd met a man who was willing to relocate. It usually seemed to be the other way around, woman following the man. Our relationship had reached the stage where we didn't feel the urgency to talk all the time. In fact, after we'd eaten, we cleaned up in silence and headed upstairs. I turned the television on and we watched a couple of sitcoms before settling down to some serious cuddling and sleep.

Bruce was up and dressed long before I'd even opened my eyes. He had brewed the coffee, which was sitting, as usual, on the dresser. He had two interviews, one this morning and another one in the afternoon.

"Good luck this morning, darling", I said, as he finished dressing, then grabbing a second mug of coffee as he took off.

Bruce hurriedly replied, "I'll call you when I'm done. Perhaps we can head out to the beach afterwards."

"That's a brilliant idea," I agreed. "I'll put together a picnic basket."

He called me around one-thirty to say that the morning interview had gone splendidly and the job was his if he wanted it. It would be as part of the managerial team of scientists working on new space projects. It sounds really fascinating, but I'm not making any decisions until I check out the other opening. That interview has been put off until tomorrow. I'll be back in about forty-five minutes. Be ready to head out then, darling."

"I'm thrilled for you, and I'll be ready to kick back at the beach for the rest of the day."

True to form Bruce was back in less than forty minutes. He raced in, ran upstairs, and was down in a flash, ready for the beach. I never ceased to be amazed by his manly body. Down girl, you must wait until later, as the beach is calling us. We had a wonderful time strolling along the water's edge, lazing around until it was almost five o'clock and we were both getting pretty hungry for a proper meal. We'd decided earlier that we'd grab a hamburger on the way home. What a perfect end to a perfect day.

Jen and Charlie were coming over, so I couldn't afford to be entirely lazy, just a little. Nevertheless, our morning, as usual, started off with hot coffee, steamy sex, and lazing in bed, reading the newspapers. Chores came later, which were tended to somewhat haphazardly as I still could not shake the anxiety I felt about the disappearing Sully women. I was agitated about getting more meaningful information about their disappearance than I cared to admit. For sure I would arrange my visit to Dearborn to coincide with Mike being back in Dearborn before he went to St. Lucia as a full-time resident. My mind shifted gears when Bruce asked me what I was cooking for this evening.

"I've got roast pork and I bought a cheesecake for dessert", I replied.

"That sounds positively mouthwatering. What you do say we take a swim and have an hour or so by the pool?"

"I could certainly go for that, Bruce. On a more serious note it's been in my mind that I would really like for us to get married in October on the 19th. October is so beautiful here and nineteen is a good luck number in our family. How does that timing suit you?"

"That sounds wonderful, Molly. Have you any thoughts now on where to hold the reception? Perhaps we can check out a few outdoor restaurants in the area before we decide on a place. I know that you said you wanted to get married on the beach, but we can work out all the logistics in due course. I assume you want to be married by a minister."

"Yes, but the problem is, I don't know one. As I do not regularly attend any church, I'll have to search for a Protestant minister who will perform the ceremony for us. Don't worry, I'll get all that done before I visit you in Dearborn. There is this restaurant called Harbor lights on the beach in Daytona that I want to check out. I hear they have a large deck and cater to parties. Perhaps we can go and have a drink there before you head back home?"

"That sounds like a good idea, but for now, what can I do to help you get ready for this evening?"

"Since you insist, would you mind peeling these potatoes, then dice the carrots, and put them in this saucepan, please?"

We busied ourselves in pre-meal chores and tidying up the place. Once done, we obliged ourselves to taste a German dry Riesling wine. It lived up to both our expectations. Now it was time to visit the pool for an hour of relaxation.

We energized ourselves by swimming about twenty laps, toweling off, and letting the warm sun finish the drying process. We lingered for another half an hour before I suggested we head on back. I had less than an hour to change and make my face up before our guests arrived. No doubt, Bruce could ready himself by just throwing on a shirt and shorts, and slicking back his hair.

Jen and Charlie were on time, and we chatted nine to the dozen. Jen wanted to be filled in on every detail of the wedding plans thus far. I told the guys to go in the living room whilst Jen and I did the finishing touches for the meal. I confessed to her that I was getting really antsy regarding the missing Sully women, and wasn't about to wait until May to see if I could find out anything else from photos or whatever else I could find at Mike's house.

In reply, Jen said, "I don't blame you, Molly, because I think I'd feel the same as you do. It must be very frustrating being this far away and wanting to forge ahead in finding more concrete results."

"I don't even know if I'll find out anything more, but want to have a look before Mike cleans out his house prior to moving to St. Lucia. Maybe nothing more will come from my investigation, but I want to satisfy myself that I have done everything in my power to get some answers. Anyway, enough of that right now, let's eat. I've avocado with crumbled blue cheese to start with, so if you can take these in, I'll call the guys."

Bruce and Charlie really hit it off as both of them were in the same general area of business, so there was no lack of conversation between them. I was thrilled, because it will be great for Bruce to have a guy friend when he moves here.

The pork and accompaniments were delicious. I had made some homemade apple sauce which really capped things off nicely. We ate dessert in the living room on our laps.

Jen said at the end of their stay, "Well, Bruce and Molly, this has been a wonderful evening. Charlie and I are very excited about your impending nuptials and happy, Bruce, that you are moving down here. I gather you've got one offer and another interview tomorrow, so be sure to let us know the outcome."

"I'll be sure to, don't you worry", Bruce replied. "I think that after the interview we are going to check out a restaurant in Daytona as a possible venue for the reception."

"I'll call you, Jen, once Bruce has gone back to Dearborn, so we can get together for some beach time."

"Sounds terrific, and again, Molly, it was a delicious meal and a lot of fun."

It didn't take us more than forty-five minutes to get everything back to normal. We headed upstairs and had some really satisfying sex. Sleep after was no problem.

Bruce was up before I had even awakened. He was ready for the interview, looking exceptionally dapper.

"Molly, I have absolutely no idea quite how long this will take, but I'll phone you when I'm done."

"Good luck, darling. I'll see you when I see you," I said, as I got up to fetch my mug of steaming coffee.

What would I do without coffee? I shuddered to even think about the consequences. The morning slipped by smoothly and stress free. The phone rang just before noon. It was Bruce to say that he was taking the job in the solid fuels division that he'd interviewed for the day before. He didn't have a comfortable feeling with the man who just interviewed him this morning, plus the other department was much more up his alley.

"I've already called Bob Hayden to accept the job and am going in tomorrow to sign some paperwork and make it official. I'll be back in about an hour, and then we can take off for Daytona Beach to look for wedding venues."

"I'm so excited for you and hope this job will not disappoint you."

"Well, the money is better than what I make in Dearborn and you are here, so what can be bad about that?"

Upon his return, we grabbed a sandwich and headed out for Daytona. Bruce was in a great mood. I guess the fact that he had solved his work problem here made him relaxed. We were both extremely happy with Harbor Lights and were able to book it for October 19th. Their hors d'oeuvres and desserts sounded wonderful. I picked out a strawberry and vanilla wedding cake and gave them a deposit. I told them I'd be in touch nearer the time.

"We need to celebrate big time this evening, Molly. I've got a job and we have a venue for our reception. What do you say we hit that French restaurant tonight?"

"You won't get an argument out of me, darling." I was feeling especially happy and secure with my life.

Back at home, I said, "I'm going in the shower, darling. Do you want to join me?"

"I'll be there in a couple of minutes, Molly."

I lingered under the shower, enjoying the warm beads that fell down my back. Bruce surprised me and washed my body, telling me how beautiful I was and how bloody lucky he was to have found me.

"Well it works both ways, my prince; don't you know?"

I decided to wear my purple silk sheathe dress with some lovely purple glass drop earrings that my mother had given me some months before she died. They complimented the outfit, and I was pretty happy with what I saw in the mirror. Bruce got dressed in casual navy pants, and a pale blue shirt and looked very dapper.

"We make a devastating pair, don't we, Bruce?"

"Yes, we do and coincidentally I adore your outfit. Those earrings are so beautiful! Where on earth did you get them?"

I told him that my mother had given the pair of earrings to me shortly before her death, and I was somewhat nervous about the possibility of losing them. They did remind me of how much I missed my mother, but I was determined to have a good time going out and did not want any sad thoughts to pull me down emotionally. For some reason, though, my thoughts switched to Brandy and how much I missed his presence, and said as much to Bruce.

He said, "I was thinking the same thing, darling. I think he's going to be happy here. As long as he's with us, I don't think he'll mind where he lives. I can't believe that in the beginning, I hesitated to take him full time. He's part of our family now. Anyway, let's go live it up at dinner.

Live it up we did. I ordered Duck a l'orange which was unbelievably succulent. Bruce had trout with almonds. For the first time in ages we didn't feel like a dessert, but we did opt for decaf coffee.

"What a perfect way to end a wonderful few days", Bruce offered. "I'm so sorry that I have to fly back tomorrow morning, but at least we got to be with each other and I happily found a new job here in Florida."

"Bruce, whilst on the subject of travel, I was wondering if you'd mind if I came up to Dearborn in the middle of April rather than waiting until May? May is usually our busiest month at the vets, and that way you could skip a trip to see me in April, and might only need to come back down once before you move here on a permanent basis. I figure you'll have a lot to do before you move here for good, and I can get everything organized at this end."

"Whatever works for you is fine with me. Naturally, I'll be driving here when I bring Brandy. I don't want to put him on a plane.

"I totally agree," I said.

When we got home, I settled into bed chatting away whilst he finalized his packing.

"I hate this long-distance romance stuff, Bruce. I'll be so thrilled when we are both under one roof for good."

"Talking of roofs, Molly, to repeat my sentiments, I would really like for us to buy a house closer to the beach at some juncture."

"Do you think we could get married first and have our honeymoon, and perhaps start looking in the New Year?"

"Sounds good to me", he said, then kissed me, rolled over, and fell asleep in seconds.

In the morning, I didn't hear him leave. I woke up to find a note on the dresser saying that he loved me, didn't want to disturb me, missed me already, and would call me tonight. This back and forth crap was getting a tad easier, I must say. Neither of us was that enchanted about all the flying stuff, but in our minds, we had little choice.

I decided to go to work earlier than usual as I wanted to get all the paperwork out of the way before we were open for patients. I arrived around eight and finished the filing, paying bills and pulling the files of today's patients. I heard John's customary whistle as he flung the door open. He looked completely startled when he saw me sitting at my desk.

"You scared the daylights out of me, Molly. What on earth are you doing in so early?"

"I thought that I could get a jump start on the paperwork, so we didn't have it hanging over our heads when we opened the doors. I've made coffee, if you want some."

"You bet, as I neglected to get my usual mug on the way in. By the way, Jessica and I really enjoyed our evening together with you and Bruce and look forward to getting together when he's next in town."

"I have good news on that front, John. He went for an interview at the Cape and got the job. Not only is he thrilled with the prospects, but he's getting paid more than back in Dearborn, which, I am sure, made it easier for him to make the decision to move down here."

"That's wonderful news. I am going to drink to that", he chuckled as he took a sip of strong, black coffee.

The day wasn't that eventful, just a steady stream of animals coming in for shots and minor examinations. One cat did need a bit of patching up. I thought it more exciting when we had to go out to a farm and tend to a horse or cow. No such luck today. Nevertheless, I always felt fulfilled by the end of the day that we had done well by our lovely animal patients. And to be even more fulfilled, I made my mind up that on the days I didn't go to the beach, I'd swim laps. I wanted to be in tip top shape for my wedding, as I had a few unwanted pounds hanging around.

"See you tomorrow, John," I said, as I closed the animal infirmary door behind me.

"Goodnight, Molly. Could I ask you a huge favor by picking up a large coffee for me on your way to work tomorrow?"

"I'd be happy to. Have a pleasant evening and say hello to Jessica for me."

For some crazy reason, I didn't feel as happy as I knew I should. There was this dark cloud hanging over my head in regard to the Sully women. What if we did discover something bad about Mike? Could I live with the knowledge that I was marrying a man whose father was evil? Perhaps it would be better to let sleeping dogs lie, but I just couldn't do that. There was more to discover regarding their disappearance. But for now, my focus had to be on plans for the wedding, reception, and honeymoon. And, of course, there was my physique to attend to.

The swim after work really did wonders for my mood. I finished my twenty laps feeling energized and ready to take on the world. I dried off and sat for a while drinking in the magnificent sky, livened by sea birds circling overhead. The early evening was quiet and positively soothing. However, it came time to disengage from nature and fix myself some dinner at home. First of all, I poured myself a glass of the wine. There's nothing like a glass of good, cool white wine to make way for food. However, I didn't have a chance to eat anything before the phone rang.

It was Bruce, as I suspected, who said, "Hello, my lovely fiancé. How are you doing in sunny Florida? Have you missed me as much as I've missed you?"

"Oh, for sure, I really, really yearn for you."

We bantered back and forth for a good ten minutes before he started to get very horny over the phone. It didn't take very long for me to climax. Phone sex was quite the most unique and exciting substitute for the real thing.

Afterwards, Bruce told me that he'd given his notice at work. His co-workers and boss were not the least surprised. They were all disappointed that he was leaving, but totally understood and supported him. In fact, management was writing a glowing reference letter to be mailed to the Cape facility.

He also said, "I've decided to hit the gym on a daily basis. I need to get into tip top shape for the wedding."

I let out a giggle when he said that. Great minds think alike!

"Molly, tomorrow night I have a meeting that will go on fairly late. I'm going to hit the gym immediately after, on the way home, so I'll call you the next night if that's all right with you?"

I replied, "That's not a problem. How's Brandy doing?"

"He's good and he had a really good time with Nick and Sally. They took him for long walks, so he slept very well at night. Changing the subject, I am asking Nick to be my best man. Have you thought about a maid of honor?"

"My absolute choice is Jen. I know a number of girls, but none is a great friend as she has been to me for so long. We are starting to get organized for our nuptials, aren't we?

Next week I am going to ask Jen to go to the mall with me to look at wedding dresses. I've decided I don't want the traditional gown, something floaty perhaps, not that I should tell you too much about it. Since we want to get married on the beach, I prefer a simpler style. This coming weekend I'm going to see about getting a minister to marry us. I can't believe all the details that have to be taken care of. It's so exciting, but in a way a bit harrowing. Well, that's my news of the day, so now it's your turn."

"I don't really have a whole lot to tell you. The main item was about the job. They are now going to have to advertise for a replacement for me. You have a good day tomorrow and the day after too, and I'll call you Wednesday evening around seven. Never forget that I love you to distraction."

"I love you even more, Bruce, and can't wait for us to be together on a permanent basis. Take care and have a good meeting tomorrow."

Wednesday night came around quickly and it was almost eight o'clock and I hadn't heard from Bruce. I was guessing that his meeting had taken longer than anticipated. The phone rang and I picked it up anxiously hoping it was him.

"Molly, I'm sorry that I haven't called you before but I did the dumbest thing, I sprained my right ankle at the gym. I was very glad that Nick was there, and fortunately there was a doctor in the gym working out, who very kindly looked at it, bandaged it up and told me it would take a couple of weeks to heal."

I replied, "Where are you now?"

"Nick and I are languishing at this really great Greek restaurant. The moussaka is out of this world. It was almost worth spraining my ankle for."

I sucked in my slight disappointment knowing that even with a sprained ankle he was being quite glib. Men never cease to amaze me as to how egotistical they are. I wanted to tell him that my cereal was really rather bland, but decided to let it slide.

"Enjoy your dinner, darling. And be sure to take care of your ankle. I guess your visits to the gym are going to be somewhat curtailed now."

"I can work out with weights, etc. I just can't walk the treadmill or anything that requires my right foot pressing down for any length of time."

"I'm going to let you and Nick enjoy the rest of the evening. Just call me tomorrow night. Take care and lots of love."

"I love you too, Molly, so until tomorrow night." He had hung up before anything else could be said. So be it. Another day had drawn to a close in a week that drifted along in leisurely fashion.

I was really looking forward to going to the beach with Jen and having some girlie time. I called her from work to confirm a time. She said she'd swing by my place around five-thirty and we could head out as soon as she got there.

I was hoping to swim a bit if the surf was not too heavy. I used to surf on a small foam-like board until a humungous fish leapt out in front of me – a tarpon, I was told. It scared the living crap out of me, and other surfers too. From then on, I've never touched a surf board, because I did not like the idea of my feet and hands hanging over the edge. Why I did not mind so much putting my whole body in the water, I cannot tell you.

I managed to get out of work on time and swung by the grocery store to get some more wine, coffee ice cream, pizza crusts, and a few vegetables to balance out all the junk food I was buying. I'd just finished unpacking the groceries and changed into my bathing suit when the doorbell rang. True to form Jen was on time.

"Hello there, Miss Blushing Bride. How are you doing?"

"All the better for seeing you, Jen, and thanks for asking. Please give me five minutes to finish up here. Why don't you come back here afterwards and grab some pizza with me? Also, I was wondering if you were free to go shopping with me next week to look for a wedding dress.

"How could I resist an offer like that!?"

The beach was fairly empty and the waves were calm. We dived straight in and swam quite a way without any waves buffeting us. Now tell me if this isn't perfection or as close as it comes to it. We'd been swimming for about twenty minutes when we both decided enough was enough.

"Tell me how your plans are coming along, Molly. I'm dying of curiosity",

"Well, this weekend I'm going to see the minister at the Episcopal Church to see if he will marry us on the beach. We've booked the Harbor Lights for the reception. It had everything we needed and the price was right. Now my question to you is, will you be my bridesmaid?"

"I am thrilled you asked me. Of course, I will. What color dress should I wear?"

"Crumbs, I haven't got that far yet. Possibly purple or red since those are your colors. Anyway, these are details that can be ironed out later on. It's really hard for me to wrap my head around the fact that in about seven months I'll be Mrs. Sully."

We strolled along the beach, rejuvenating our spirits and our lungs.

"One couldn't ask for much more, could one, Molly? I can't envision living anywhere that wasn't close to the water."

"Me neither and I thought I would miss the big city life, but I don't. The only thing I miss is being able to walk to a coffee shop and a local store, but that's not much of a sacrifice for what we have here. Are you ready to do an about turn, Jen?"

"Yep, sure am, and my stomach is telling me that it is in need of nourishment."

"There is one issue that is putting a large dent in my happiness, and that's this investigation into the missing Sully women. I'm being frightfully repetitive about it, I know. You are aware that Bruce was angry with me at first, but that he has bought into it, if somewhat reluctantly. However, I'm getting so antsy about furthering the investigation that I've decided to go back to Michigan in several weeks rather than delay it until May. The one thought that keeps nagging at me is: what if I discover that Mike had something to do with their disappearance? It'll mean that I'm marrying the son of an evil man. I can handle that, but I fear it will really take a toll on Bruce."

"Molly, it is what it is, and you can't go back now. No matter the outcome, you both will put it behind you and continue into a wonderful life together."

"I know you're right, Jen. It means so much to have your support. But enough of dire thoughts, let's go back and build us a pizza."

We had a great evening piling all sorts of goodies on the pizza crust, at the same time savoring some wonderful red wine. We laughed a lot about all kinds of crazy things and before we knew it it was ten o'clock and we hadn't had dessert.

Jen said, "I really don't want any pudding now, or I'll never get to sleep, so let's leave it for another time".

"Absolutely! I'm sure we'll do a repeat performance of this evening in the near future. Thanks a million for being you."

"Vice versa, Molly. I'll call you in a couple of days to see what's going on. Have a good weekend and good luck with the minister."

She sped off in her usual race car fashion and I walked back into the kitchen, feeling a bit of anxiety building up inside of me. It was time to get busy and clean up this mess before hitting the sack. I realized tomorrow was Saturday and the only thing I had planned was seeing the minister. The pool and reading beside it would be a good lazy addition. Suddenly a smirk came across my face as I looked at the pristine kitchen counter. It was my number two spot for rampant sex. I ran my fingers over it and smiled,

The next morning, I fixed my coffee and decided to call the minister of an Episcopalian church a little after nine in the morning.   I had found his name on the church's website.

"Hello, is this Minister Knowles?"

"Yes, it is" he replied. "So how may I help you?"

"My name is Molly Thomas. I'm wondering if you marry people on the beach, as my fiancé and I want to get married at the shore in October."

"Yes, I would be happy to, Miss Thomas. The only thing we ask from you is to donate one hundred dollars to the church funds. Perhaps, if you are free today, you could pop on over and meet me to arrange it."

"What's a good time for you Minister Knowles?"

"How about meeting me at eleven-thirty at the church?"

"That is a good time for me. Thanks for fitting me into your schedule at such short notice."

Things were really moving along in the right direction. I did some vacuuming, a load of laundry, and pondered over what I should wear to meet Minister Knowles, deciding on one of my favorite jump suits. This is not the Middle Ages, so I am sure the minister would be comfortable with my wearing pants rather than a dress, or skirt and blouse.

I arrived at the church a few minutes early, checked my makeup, and knocked on, what appeared to be, an outside office door. To my utter surprise this good-looking man in official garb opened it. He did not appear to be wearing a wedding band. My immediate reaction was, *what a waste*! I introduced myself and shook his hand. He, in turn, introduced himself as Minister Knowles.

"Please do come in and let's go to my own office."

He removed a pile of papers from a chair next to his desk the chair and asked me to have a seat.

"Now, what wedding date are you planning on, and at what time?"

"The date I had hoped for is October 19th and I was thinking early afternoon, say around two, if that works for you?"

He flicked through his agenda, lifted his head, and with a broad grin on his face, said,

"You are in luck, Miss Thomas. I have a free day, so I will pencil you in. All I need from you is your address, phone number, and the name of your fiancé. And where would you like the ceremony conducted?"

I gave him the requested info and said, "I was thinking that I'd like to get married on the beach where there are no cars. Just south of twenty-seventh street would be ideal, if that is okay for you? And please, call me Molly.

"Perfect, Molly! And we shall all pray doubly hard for a sunny day. Would you care for a cup of coffee? I've made a pot in the vestry."

"I would love a cup, thank you", I answered, following him out of his overcrowded office to the vestry which was relatively cold, and not so inviting.

We chatted about various topics. I asked him how long he'd been in New Smyrna Beach and he told me that he came ten years ago from a tiny town in New Jersey. He loved it here and couldn't think of living anywhere else.

I finished my coffee and thanked him very much for what he was going to do for Bruce and me. I knew my friends and acquaintances would say that I'd asked him to marry us because he was so dishy, and that he most certainly was.

"We'll be in touch, Molly, so if nothing changes, touch base with me a couple of weeks before the big day."

"I will do just that, and again thanks for agreeing to perform the ceremony. Have a good remainder of the weekend."

"I'll work on that, so until the beginning of October, Molly", he said flashing me a winning smile.

It would be no hardship to be married by this man of the cloth. With that thought I drove home in a really good mood. I tried to call Bruce, but he wasn't home, so I left him a message telling him the good news and asked him to call me this evening. I changed into my bathing suit and headed to the pool, with snacks and reading material in hand.

Good! There were only two other people there sitting on deck chairs. I decided that I would do my laps first. Gliding through the water gives me an incredible feeling, particularly when there are no interrupting bodies. I finished my laps in just under twenty minutes, which was two minutes less than the last time. I decided to forgo the hot tub for now; maybe experience its soothing, bubbly warmth later. Instead, I enjoyed the delicious breeze blowing off the water that kept it from being too warm. I had always wanted to live in a tropical environment, but this sub-tropical part of Florida would do well enough.

Five o'clock found me in the hot tub for a fifteen-minute session. Thereafter, I decided it was time for home and a chilled glass of white wine. One might think I had an alcohol problem, but far from it. I'd been around too many alcoholics to even want to go there. The most I ever had was three glasses a night, generally just two, or none - with rare exceptions (*After all, I am human!*). I cut up some cheese and an apple for my dinner and went up to bed. I loved sitting up in bed with my snacks, my wine, and a good book. Somehow being away from the kitchen removed me from a boring, lonely domestic scene.

I called Bruce from the bedroom phone, but he didn't answer. I had tried twice now, so it was his turn. I had videoed a couple of cheesy movies for the evening, so got stuck into the first one. It was a murder romance that didn't require my brain to work hard at all. I was half way through it when the phone rang.

"Hello, my princess, my darling fiancé. How are you this evening; miss me?"

"I miss you, if you miss me, Prince Charmless", I said in a humorous voice. "I assume you got my message about the Episcopalian minister being available and happy to marry us. He surprised me by being rather good looking and very amenable. I know everyone is going to think I picked him for his looks, which is so far from the truth, but it doesn't hurt to have something good to look at besides you, Bruce. I'm sorry, darling; I forgot to ask about your ankle. How is it doing?"

"It's coming along nicely; thanks, my love. Back to the minister; how much does it cost for his services?"

You'll never believe it when I tell you that all we have to do is give a donation of one hundred dollars to the church. In my mind that is dirt cheap for what he's doing. We agreed on the beach down by 27th street. I said I'd contact him a couple of weeks before the date just to solidify any last-minute details. Other than that, I spent the entire afternoon at the pool, which was wonderful. What have you been doing with yourself?"

"I worked late last night and today I went in to finish up some lose ends. I have a lot of stuff to do before I leave for good.   They are going to start advertising for my replacement next week, so that'll keep me busy. I stopped off at the gym and caught up with Nick, and then we snatched a couple of beers afterwards. What are you doing right now, Molly?"

"I'm sitting up in bed with my wine, apple, and cheese watching a murder/romance movie."

"Well, darling girl, if I were there, you wouldn't be watching any romance; you'd be experiencing it. I can just picture you with your beautiful body ready for me to ravage when I come back in two weeks."

"Oh, so you are coming back that soon?"

"You better believe it. Thanks to Nick and Sally for taking care of Brandy at the drop of a hat. Actually, I think they will be quite upset when I move and take him with me. They love taking him for walks. They may even be forced to get their own dog one day. I'll call you tomorrow night. Enjoy your movie and never forget how much I adore you."

"I love you to pieces, too."

The first movie was very relaxing and the next was hilarious, written by Tyler Perry, whom I love in all of his roles. I am glad no-one was with me to hear my guffaws. I took a quick shower before turning the lights off around midnight and slept right through until almost ten. Boy, do I love sleeping for such a long time.

I decided that I'd go through my entire wardrobe, making two piles of clothes to get rid of: one for the garbage and the other for the consignment store. I needed to make room for Bruce, and since I had nothing else going on today, why not? It was truly incredible how much stuff I was jettisoning. One half of the closet was now bare. *Good for me*! Just as I was wondering what to do about eating today, the phone rang. It was my friend, Angie, from the gym days. We hadn't seen each other in an age and she wanted to know if I was free for a late lunch.

I replied, "That's a splendid idea. "Do you want to meet at the hamburger place on beachside?"

"Great! How about we meet up at one-thirty?"

"That's perfect, Angie. I'm looking forward to catching up with you."

I do love surprises. This could turn out to be an especially good day. There was enough time to swim perhaps twenty-five vigorous laps to help offset my upcoming calorie intake with Angie. The pool was deserted, so I swam my laps in twenty minutes flat, got out, and spent five minutes in the whirlpool before heading home to change.

There were several really nice ladies at the gym, but I hadn't gone there in so long that I'd lost contact with them, until today. I was looking forward to catching up on the gossip and filling Angie in on my news. I got to the restaurant a few minutes early and ordered a beer. I'd barely taken two sips when Angie showed up. She looked fantastic; I also remembered how much I liked her as a person.

"Angie, over here", I called to her. "You look really great. You must be working out a lot."

She replied, "Well, you don't exactly look as if you've been sitting still since I last saw you. So, tell me, why haven't we seen you at the gym for several months now? Before you do, let me order a beer."

"I have so much to tell you, Angie, but I won't bore you with a lot of detail. Anyway, I met this old fart, Mike Sully, at the pool back in July. Mike has a son he wanted to introduce me to when he came to visit his father a few days later. And so, it happened that I met Bruce Sully, the son, who lives and works in Dearborn, Michigan. We eventually fell in love. He made several visits here, and I went to Dearborn twice. We got engaged a couple of weeks ago and are getting married in October by the ocean in New Smyrna Beach. You'll get an invitation for sure. Bruce just got a job at Cape Canaveral and will be moving down here in September. His father is not a nice man in my opinion, and may have a very dark past. Bruce is not very keen on his father either."

I went on to explain about the disappearance of Bruce's mother and of his girlfriend, my investigation into the matter, the hiring of Bri as an investigator, and my consequent difficulties with Bruce.

"Wow, you really have been busy, Molly. Congratulations to you both for getting beyond the trauma of your investigation and becoming engaged. I wish you would come back to the gym as so many of the ladies have asked about you."

"I definitely will rejoin in June, but before then won't work for me as I'm going to Dearborn in a few weeks and

Bruce will be coming down here later. Before we gossip any further, let's order. I don't know about you, but I'm starving."

"Good idea, Molly. I'm going to have a burger, fries, and another beer."

"Me too," I said, and we placed our order.

"Now, it's your turn, Angie. What's going on in your world?"

"My life isn't exciting like yours", she said. "I'm still working at the hospital as a receptionist, going to the gym about four times a week, and still dating Peter who is a radiologist in Daytona Beach. There is nothing exciting like wedding bells on the horizon, but I am utterly happy with my life right now, so no complaints at all."

We chatted on about a myriad of topics until our food arrived and we literally fell upon the burgers as if we hadn't eaten in a week

"I'm going to have a coffee and a coffee ice cream. Angie, how about you?"

"That sounds wonderful. I might as well splurge. I'm not seeing Peter this weekend as he has emergency duty, so this will set me up for the rest of the day."

We'd been sitting in the restaurant for about two hours when we agreed we shouldn't leave it so long before seeing each other again.

"Thanks so much, Angie, for phoning me, and I'm so sorry that I was really awful about staying in touch."

"I quite understand", she said. "I can't wait to meet Bruce. Perhaps when he has moved here permanently, we can double date?"

"Absolutely! Apart from my old school friend, Jen, you are the closest friend I have here. I must say, good things come out of trying to get into shape!"

We said our fond farewells, gave each other a hug, and promised to get together sooner rather than later. It felt good to know I had several friends in the area, including my boss and his girlfriend. I'd never been someone who needed loads of contacts but was feeling more and more like I belonged in New Smyrna Beach. I couldn't wait to get home and call Bruce. I got in and decided to fix myself a brandy before calling him. I barely had time to fix my drink when the phone rang.

"Hello, my darling princess, what has been going on in your world since we last spoke?"

"Hello, my handsome lover. Well, I had a pleasant surprise. Angie, a friend from the gym, whom I hadn't seen in a long time, rang me this morning to get together for lunch. And we did. It was so much fun, Bruce. When you move here we'll get together with Angie and her boyfriend. I know you'll enjoy her company. Otherwise, nothing much out of the ordinary is going on. I went to the pool this morning and worked out. How's your job wind-down going? Oh, and I should have asked you right off, how your ankle is mending?"

"It's doing much better, thanks. Work-wise, I'm very busy. Next week the first candidates for my position are being interviewed."

"That sounds promising for your being free to locate here. Don't forget I love you to pieces and can't wait for your visit in two weeks' time. Anyway, tomorrow I plan to spend a good part of my day at the pool, weather permitting, and will call you afterwards in the evening."

"I'm going to the office in the morning, in the afternoon I'll hit the gym, then Sally is cooking dinner for Nick and me, so it would be better if I called you Monday night."

"That's fine, Bruce; it'll give me more time to finish sorting out the closets. I'm almost done. I'm also going to the mall next weekend with Jen to look for wedding and bridesmaid dresses. Have a wonderful Sunday and don't forget how much I love you."

"That I won't, darling, so we'll talk Monday evening."

I did a couple of hours of sorting out the bedroom closet. It looked so neat and orderly. I had thinned out a ton of clothes that I never wear, destined for a consignment store. Bruce certainly can't complain about the lack of space that I'd made for him. The thought of him living with me permanently basis, however, left me with an odd feeling, since I've never lived with anyone outside of my mother. But enough of domestic thoughts; it was time for a decaf and Sunday night television with PBS.

Work was uneventful, which I preferred. I had the office work down pat, and once the animals started coming in the work day rapidly passed by. However, at work or elsewhere, my mind would drift to the thought of getting married in just over six months. Talk about a life change!

Although, it wasn't nearly as traumatic for me as it was for Bruce, who was changing jobs and location.   I kept reminding myself how much he must love me to make so many changes in his life.

The beach was glorious this evening.   The purple hue that hung over the water was nothing like I'd seen before and there was a blue-hull sailboat that shimmered on the ocean, looking mystical.   I was lost in my thoughts and had to pinch myself to get back into the real world.   I picked up my walking pace, finishing up by running the rest of the way back to the parking lot.   The sky had turned crimson. I lingered for several moments drinking in the beauty of it all.

Mid-morning on Tuesday I received a message from Bri asking me to call him back.   I couldn't imagine why, but did so anyway, and was lucky enough to catch him in the office.

"Molly, you will never believe what I'm going to tell you. I was doing some work for an Australian friend of mine who works at the Australian embassy office in Detroit.   As a long shot, I'd asked him to inquire if his office had issued a visa to a Valerie Pickering.   Imagine my surprise when he said that a couple of months ago she'd been to the embassy asking for a visa and immigration papers for Australia. Isn't that the most amazing news?   It seems she is alive and well and kicking up her heels down under.   I don't know for the life of me why I never thought of this avenue before, but I just didn't.   Now all we have to do is solve the mystery of Mike's missing wife.   I knew you'd be tickled to get this news."

"Bri, it is truly wonderful to know Miss Pickering is okay.   Thanks a million.   I can't wait to tell Bruce.   I'm heading up to Dearborn next month, so will be able to see you in person.   Again, thanks so much for this amazing bit of information.   If I owe you any more money, please let me know."

"No, you're fine for now, Molly.   I look forward to seeing you in Dearborn, so goodbye for now."

I put the phone down, barely believing what I'd just heard.   Was it possible that Mike's wife was alive and kicking somewhere?   I fervently hoped so, but I really didn't hold out much hope.   *Don't be pessimistic*, I told myself. *Look what happened with Valerie!*

The day couldn't go fast enough, as I was so anxious to call Bruce, but knew full well that I couldn't call him during the day. I was too edgy to contemplate hitting the beach after work, so decided I'd swim some laps that would get rid of a lot of my nervous energy before I got hold of Bruce. I was right. Twenty laps did the trick, and I got out feeling relaxed and ready for the evening.

I called Bruce, but got his answering machine, so I left an intriguing message, "Bruce, call me back as soon as you can, please. I've got some interesting news to give you."

I couldn't really settle to do much of anything except finish off the closet project. All I had to do was put consignment shop clothes into good plastic bags and the remainder into designated trash bags. I jumped a bit in surprise when the phone rang.

I picked up the receiver and said, "Hello, this is Molly, who is this?"

Bruce replied, "It's me, darling. Sorry I wasn't around when you called before. What's this news you have to tell me?"

"I had a call from Bri to tell me that he happened to ask a friend who works at the Australian embassy in Detroit if his office had issued visa papers to a Valerie Pickering. Guess what; she applied for a visa, and not only that, but also immigration papers, several months back and is evidently there now. So, you see, she is continuing her life as a newly minted Aussie! Aren't you thrilled to know that she is not among the dead or missing?"

"Yes, I am very relieved, and happy that she decided to start a new life for herself. I don't need to know anything further. Let's hope he digs up something equally positive about my mother; although, like you, I am less than hopeful.

I don't have any news for you other than to send you Brandy's love. My ankle is almost back to normal. I figure another week or two will do the trick. I love you, darling girl, and cannot wait to see you."

"I am excited to think that you'll be here soon. You will be pleased to hear that the bedroom closet is ready for your clothes invasion. I'll keep you posted on any wedding stuff, but there really isn't much else to do at this point other than think about invitations. Perhaps when you're here next we can come up with a decent wedding invitation design, and figure out whom to invite beyond the list I have in mind now. Until I talk to you again, I love you, darling; have a great night and don't miss me too much."

Bruce replied, "I'll try not to, my love, but that is asking a lot. Take very, very good care of yourself."

Phone sex wasn't on the agenda tonight. I was too absorbed with the information about Valerie to switch gears; besides, we'd have plenty more opportunities for that.

The next morning, I called Jen from work and we decided to go to the mall Thursday night. I filled her in on the news with regard to Bruce's old girlfriend. She was as astonished as I was.

"I look forward to hitting the bridal stores with you, Molly, and if we have no luck at the mall, perhaps we could head up to Ormond Beach to check out those stores. I'm sure they are opened late at night during the week. Tell you what; I'll call them to find out what their hours are. I'll pick you up around five-thirty."

"Terrific! See you then, and thanks for coming with me."

"Who knows, Molly, I might spy a bridal dress for myself, aside from a dress for your wedding."

For some crazy reason, I kept hearing in my head the song, *Nights in White Satin*, made famous by the Moody Blues. I couldn't stop humming to it, which, I suppose, was better than having dark thoughts. For two days, every time I wasn't busy the tune popped into my head and however hard I tried to sing something else, it took center stage. As soon as I got home I put the computer on and drew up the original version and played it umpteen times until I was sated. Fortunately, by the time Thursday came and it was almost time for Jen to pick me up, I'd managed to rid myself of the repetitive song and turned to the excitement of looking for a wedding dress. I had a quick shower and threw on a decent warm up suit, went down to the kitchen and waited for Jen. True to form I heard her roar into the drive way, honk the horn, and run up to the front door to pound on it.

"Come on, future bride, get your act together. We have a long shopping night ahead of us and if we are lucky we'll be able to treat ourselves to a late dinner."

"I'm ready to rock and roll, Jen," I said as I got in the car, barely having time to buckle myself in before we roared off.

It took about twenty-five minutes to get to the Mall. We decided we'd hit a specialty shop first before looking at the bigger department stores. An unenthusiastic gal at the shop asked us if we needed help. I thought to myself that she needed more help than we did. She was chewing on something and could have cared less about us. We rifled through the dresses, having a giggle at some of the most outrageous ones. Tucked in between a couple of hideous bouffant dresses was a simple sheath dress with a handkerchief hem line, in a mixture of silk and lace. It was beautiful and quite elegant.

"Jen, look at this dress. Isn't it divine? I'm going to try it on. It's even in my size, so fingers crossed. Why don't you come into the changing room with me? Our helper doesn't seem to care one way or another."

I put the dress on and looked at myself in the mirror. It was more than perfect. And to think that it was the first one I'd tried on.

"I'm not looking any further, Jen. This is exactly what I want, and the price is even better. Now, did you see anything for yourself?"

"Not really. Let's take a gander in a couple of the larger stores. I'm thrilled that you don't have to go scouring through masses of shops to find something. We definitely deserve a celebratory dinner."

Unfortunately, we didn't find a bridesmaid or bridal dress for Jen that she liked. However, there was plenty of time for future forays and at least one of us had been successful.

"Let's get out of the mall and go somewhere decent for a meal, Jen."

"What about that fish place on beachside? We've never tried that."

"I'm game if you are."

She nodded in agreement and off we went.

The food was excellent. No desserts this time around. I was determined to keep on the straight and narrow with regard to my diet and Jen also abstained. Instead we ordered another wine and mulled over the events of the day, before Jen dropped me off.

In front of my house I said, "Jen, if you have time over the weekend, we can continue shopping for a dress for you."

"Actually, Charlie and I are going to spend the weekend in Cocoa Village. He loves it down there and we have found a cute bed and breakfast near the Indian River. Perhaps we can shop one night during the week, if you're free."

"That sounds good to me, girlfriend. Thanks for coming with me tonight and driving. It made it so much more pleasurable having you along."

"Anytime! But now I must really get going. I have a busy day tomorrow. We have a convention next week and I have a lot of crap to do for that, so let's talk on Monday. Have a good weekend and don't get too lonely without Bruce."

"I'll try not to. Enjoy yours."

I had a sinking feeling come over me at the thought of being totally alone. Ah, well, I would spend a lot of time at the pool and catch up on my tanning and reading. I reminded myself that life was good and that things could be a lot worse. I took my dress upstairs and tried it on again. It was truly beautiful. It flowed magnificently and the top part was simple, but elegant. I had to admit to myself that I looked pretty darned good. I was excited about telling Bruce that I'd found a dress. He called me around eight.

"Bruce, darling, you're not to going to believe this, but I found a wedding dress with Jen's help. It is exactly what I'd been looking for. Isn't that great news? But, you shall have to wait until the nineteenth of October before you see it. I feel as if a load has been lifted. Now Jen and I shall concentrate on finding her a bridesmaid's dress, if she doesn't find one on her own.

"Naturally, I'm thrilled for you. I'm sure you shall look gorgeous when I see you in it; though you would look fantastic in a sack. For me there is not much to report, except my ankle appears healed and I'm going to try and play a game of squash with Nick tomorrow night. But we'll play at a leisurely pace. It's just to get a little exercise and a test to see how my ankle responds."

"Please do take things gingerly, Bruce, as I don't want you buggering it up again, for your sake, and mine. Men do take un-necessary risks at times."

"Yes, I'll be careful. Anyway, I've booked my flight for next Friday night, so make sure you're home early. I expect to get in around five. I must admit this back and forth travel is becoming somewhat old hat. Still, you'll be coming here next and then that is all the travel between us until I transfer for good. Or something unforeseen comes up. On to more intimate thoughts; what are you wearing, darling girl?"

"I'm actually in my underwear."

Need I say what followed? We had the most delicious phone sex ever. I couldn't believe that someone could get me that aroused through a phone, but it happened. We both moaned and groaned in unison and said that we couldn't wait until we were together in the flesh again.

"Bruce, you are an amazing man. I love you to distraction. Let me know how the game of squash went and have a great night's sleep dreaming of me, I hope."

"Just to let you know, you are in all of my sexy dreams, night-time and day. I'll call you on Saturday morning to let you know how the game went. In the meantime, you have a great evening and a glorious Friday. Until then, I'm signing off with love and kisses. Oh, I almost forgot; my father arrived in town yesterday and is staying for about ten days. Lucky, you, as you'll miss seeing him. On that upbeat note, I really will sign off now."

"Bye, darling; have a good visit with your dad", I said chuckling as I hung up.

Oh, you better believe it; I was one lucky chick not to be seeing Mike in two weeks. I don't think I'd ever disliked anyone quite as much as I did Mike. You can't choose your relatives, but you can certainly choose your friends, and lovers.

No sooner had I hung up from Bruce and I walked into the kitchen to pour myself a delicious glass of wine, when the phone rang again. I naturally assumed it was Bruce who'd forgotten to tell me something. Wrong!

"Hello, Molly, this is Mike. I'm in Dearborn and Bruce just told me the wonderful news about you getting married and I had to call and congratulate you. I am thrilled for you both."

"Thank you so much, Mike, for calling. I really appreciate that. I gather your mind is made up about living in St. Lucia. I can't say that I blame you escaping the abysmal winter conditions. Have you found a house yet?"

"Yes, as a matter of fact I have. It is two doors down from my friend's and comes fully furnished, so I won't have to ship anything out there. The development is quite beautiful and has its own pool. You'll have to visit with Bruce some day when I'm settled in."

"That would be great," I said, meaning no way in hell will I be visiting you.

Thank goodness, we still had phones without our images. Mine would have belied my words. Leave that to Skype for communicating face to face.

"Well, Molly, I won't keep you, but I'll be seeing Bruce for lunch on Saturday and I shall fill him in on all the details about the place. And he can relay that to you. Again, many congratulations on your engagement to my son. I couldn't think of anyone I'd like more as a daughter-in-law."

"Thank you, Mike. I really appreciate your saying that. Have a wonderful get- together with Bruce and a safe return to St. Lucia."

Maybe the old geezer wasn't so bad after all. He seemed to have a heart which I'd never managed to discover before. And, if I hadn't met him at the pool, I wouldn't be with Bruce. The last conversation and my resultant emotions brought on the need for that large glass of wine, along with some sharp cheddar and crackers. I wasn't in the mood for doing much of anything after downing the wine in record time, so I decided to hit the sack and watch a movie.

The one thing about waking up without Bruce that I missed more than anything was the smell of steaming coffee coming from the dresser. I moseyed downstairs and switched the pot on and stuck some toast in whilst waiting. I had all day and no plans to speak of, so I took my coffee, toast, and newspapers and headed on back to bed to wile away this Saturday morning, which I did pretty successfully. This was most definitely the *Life of Riley*. The phone rang late morning. I half expected it to be Bruce, but was surprised when I heard Jen's voice.

"Sorry to bother you, Molly, but I have good news. I went into this wonderful dress store in Cocoa Village and found a dress in chiffon in varying shades of purple that fits in with your bridal scheme. The skirt has an uneven hemline, and the top is like a tee shirt. It's beautiful, fits me like a tee, and both Charlie and I thought it would be perfect as my bridesmaid's dress. The price is very affordable as it was on sale, so I went ahead and bought it, hoping you would not be offended. I'm really calling to beg for your approval of my decision."

"How could I not approve? It sounds perfect. I'm glad you found your dress sooner than expected. Thanks so much for letting me know, which wasn't necessary, but I would have done the same thing, if the roles had been reversed. I'm really looking forward to seeing it sometime during the week. Have a great remainder of your time there. You got me thinking that perhaps Bruce and I would also visit Cocoa Village and the surrounding area when he comes next weekend. Do you like the Bed and Breakfast that you're staying in?"

"It's awesome, not overly expensive and their breakfast is to die for. I'll bring you a brochure back. Anyway, enjoy your quiet time, Molly, and I'll call you next week. Bye for now."

"Bye, Jen, and enjoy the rest of your weekend."

Another bridal task completed, and without my help! Now I could concentrate on whom to invite to the wedding and reception, another job I did not relish doing, but at least we didn't have a huge number of guest candidates. After completing a preliminary list, I got my stuff together and headed to the pool. The weather was perfect for lounging outside. There wasn't a cloud in the sky. Three other people were poolside. As per usual, I decided to get my laps over with and then relax. Although I found it somewhat boring thrashing back and forth, the feeling of wellbeing afterwards made up for the effort. I spent almost three hours topping up my tan and reading, short naps aside. By five-thirty it was time to depart for wine, and sustenance. I had rented a couple of Redbox movies, looking forward to my evening alone. Having been raised as an only child, I am very comfortable with my own company. This seems a distinct advantage under my circumstances. Many people can't stand being alone. On the other hand, being in the midst of many people can cause me to panic a bit. Crowds are not my cup of tea.

The movies were good. One was a romance and the other a cops and robbers spoof. I wasn't sure what I'd do tomorrow, but between the Sunday papers, swimming, and generally mucking around the house, my day should pass without a hitch. By the time I'd watched both movies it was well past midnight and I had no difficulty sleeping until almost ten in the morning. Bruce would have been horrified that I had slept late, but I was making the most of my weeks left of single life.

I'd decided to hit a couple of printers during the week to get samples of invitations. It really wasn't too early, as for the most part, they needed to be sent by the end of June. It took time to get them printed so my mind was made up on this issue. Jen called me during my lunch hour on Monday to see if I was up for a run on the beach. I didn't hesitate in saying yes. The weather was gorgeous at this time of the year. Most of the snowbirds had gone back up North, and although it was bad for most retail business, it was great for us locals.

We ran at a steady pace on the sand, not really fully enjoying the beauty of the ocean, but after completing a couple of miles, we looked at the waves, drank in the salty air, and agreed that there wasn't a place within miles that could improve on this. We again, for the zillionth time, agreed that life was wonderful in our little piece of the world.

We skipped going out for dinner as we both were counting the pennies. Jen, as promised, gave me a flier of the Bed and Breakfast located in Cocoa Beach. It looked like an awesome place to stay. I would ask Bruce tonight if he wanted to stay there overnight on Saturday. It wasn't as if it were a long way away, less than an hour

Before Jen departed for home, I asked her if I might drop by Tuesday or Wednesday evening to see her purchase.

She replied, "Wednesday would be good for me. Charlie and I are going out with some office people tomorrow night. I don't think you'll be disappointed when you see the dress."

"Done deal, girlfriend. I'll be over around six, if that is okay. Have a good evening tomorrow, and if I don't hear from you, I'll see you Wednesday night."

"Six is good. Why don't you plan on eating dinner with me, Molly?"

"If you're sure, I'd love to."

True to form Bruce called me around eight. We talked for about forty minutes. We were both in rather serious moods so there was no phone sex. It probably would be bloody boring, if it were initiated every time we were on the phone together. Happily, we were pretty much in sync, sexually.

I filled him in on Jen's dress purchase and my intention to see a couple of printers later in the week' and I said, "I think doing invitations is the worst task for us, but it has to be done. Oh, and before I forget, are you interested in going to Cocoa Village overnight on Saturday? Jen and Charlie stayed at a great Bed and Breakfast there. If it appeals to you, I can go ahead and book it."

"I say go for it! I could do with a change, and I'm sure you can as well. By the way, my ankle is definitely back to normal. I have no pain or swelling, so I'm pretty happy about that. Work, especially my transition, is going very well. I may get to play a game or two of squash with Nick before I leave to see you this Friday. Brandy sends you slobbery kisses, and so do I. Take care, darling. I'll talk to you later."

"Don't call me Wednesday, because I'm having dinner with Jen, so call me on Thursday after eight. I love you too, so see you in a couple of days."

Tuesday was tedious. I had to spend the better part of the day doing paper work which I'd promised John I'd do. It was almost four o'clock before I'd finished everything. I'd not seen the office so tidy in months, and had to get John in to take a peek. He couldn't believe his eyes when he came in.

"Is this really our office, Molly? Congrats to you, as I know it's a very arduous and boring job. What say I take you out to lunch tomorrow to compensate for your Herculean efforts?"

"I can handle that, John; so, if it's all right with you, I'll go out into the surgery area and see how many animals we have left for the day."

"Have at it Molly. I need to write a couple of notes, so when it's five, head on out, and goodnight in advance."

"Goodnight Boss," I said with a big grin on my face.

I only had two cats that needed spaying before the day finally drew to a close. I locked the surgery door, yelled out goodbye to John and took off for the first printer's office in

New Smyrna Beach.   They gave me several samples of invitations and I decided that instead of shopping around I'd go with them. It was less hassle and they seemed pretty competent and reasonably priced. I made a diversion to the beach and walked along the soft sand for almost an hour, which was terrific and made up for the arduous job of grocery shopping. I managed to do it all in fewer than half an hour, drove back, unpacked and put everything away except a frozen pizza which was my dinner, and pour myself a large glass of wine, all before seven o'clock. I deserved a rest! Any excuse was better than none. My rest turned out to be almost ten hours of sleep. After eating, showering, and watching the news, the combination of the wine and sea air did me in. I awoke abruptly to the loud alarm. How I missed Bruce when it came to bringing me coffee in bed. He'd spoiled me.   That would continue after we were married. It would be one of my marriage rules! I'd be sure to tell him that when he next called.

Nothing much out of the ordinary occurred at work during the course of the morning, and before I knew it, it was time to go out to lunch with John. This was the second time since I'd started to work for him that we'd had lunch together. We went to a local Italian restaurant and I splurged and had fettuccine alfredo which was to die for. John had spaghetti Bolognese which looked rather dull in comparison to mine. A lot less calories, but who was counting? We talked about books as he, like me, was an avid reader. I mentioned that my two favorite books were *The Magus*, and *The French Lieutenant's Woman* by John Fowles, although I had many other authors that I enjoyed. He was presently reading *A hundred years of Solitude* by Gabriel Garcia Marquez, and was thoroughly enjoying it.

"When you've finished with it, I'd love to borrow it, unless, it came from the library."

"As a matter of fact, I bought it at a garage sale so you're more than welcome to borrow it when I'm done, in exchange for lending me *The Magus*, as I've heard great things about that book. I'm presuming you have it, that is?"

"I do indeed. I'll bring it in tomorrow before I forget. The rest of the lunch hour was taken up talking about the wedding, Bruce's job transfer, and what the rest of the week looked like in terms of any animal patients."

"If you don't mind, I'd appreciate your coming with me tomorrow to a farm. There is a cow that has an infection in her right calf, and I don't mean her baby either." He roared with laughter at his play on words. I laughed out loud, although it wasn't THAT funny. Dear John, he was the best kind of boss anyone could wish for.

"Sure, I'd love to come with you; anything to break up the daily routine. Don't get me wrong; I love my days at the clinic, but it's always nice to break up the routine."

"Would you care for a coffee to finish off our meal, Molly?"

"Yes, please. I'll take a double espresso. And thanks again for lunch. I'm going to Jen's for dinner this evening, so I will have to swim double the number of pool laps after work."

"The pleasure is all mine," he said giving me such a winning smile.

We finished our coffees and headed back to the office to deal with two injured dogs and one cat that needed his usual shots, plus a bit of paper work thrown in. Five o'clock came around quite quickly.

"I'll see you tomorrow, John, and thanks again for a lovely lunch."

"Have a good evening, Molly. Before you leave, could you bring me in a coffee, please? I'd really appreciate it. I'll be here for a while."

"No problem, consider it done", I said as I waved goodbye.

Another work day was over; although, one could hardly call it a whole day's work. There was hardly ever a dull moment at the clinic, and never in the field. After completing my laps - less than the number I had promised, I dressed for dinner and stopped to buy a bottle of chardonnay on the way to Jen's.

Dinner with Jen was always so relaxing. She scolded me for buying the wine, but I sloughed it off, telling her to give me the opener so we could start the evening off right. The chardonnay wasn't half bad. Fortunately, Jen had decided to make a chicken salad which I was grateful for, as having had the fettuccine, I was a bit carbed out.

"Gosh, Jen, you must think me an awful friend. I totally forgot to ask you to show me your dress."

"Actually, no, I didn't think about it, Molly. I'll put it on for you after dinner. Now I didn't get a dessert, as I know you and I are both watching our calories. I did make some hazelnut decaf though."

After we cleaned up, Jen went up to change. She came down the stairs looking magnificent. The sight of her in the dress quite took my breath away.

"You look stunning, girlfriend. The dress is absolutely beautiful. It's made for you, and the colors are truly gorgeous. You must be thrilled with your find and the fact that you did it so quickly."

We laughed and hugged each other. *There is nothing like one's best friend,* I thought to myself, as she went upstairs again to put it away. Once she'd come downstairs and we'd finished our oohs and aahs over the dress, she poured us a large decaf and we went outside to her deck. One thing I really loved about her house was the deck. I knew that once Bruce and I haven't been married for a while, we would be looking for something somewhat larger, with an outside deck. My place was perfect for me, but with the two of us in it on a permanent basis, it was something else.

"Great coffee, Jen. Did you put some hazelnut syrup in this or is it straight up hazelnut decaf?"

"It's hazelnut coffee out of the can. I haven't bought it in ages. I must do it again."

"By the way, Jen, I did book Saturday night in Cocoa Village so Bruce and I could get a change of local scenery."

"Good for you", she said.

Glancing at my watch, I said, "This has been very pleasant, but I must leave as I must get up early to prepare for a trip with John to a farm to check on a sick cow. I'll call you before going to Cocoa Village, and again thanks for dinner."

"Pleasure is all mine," she said cracking up as she said it. "Boy, don't I sound like the formal madam? Anyway, enjoy the sick cow experience. I'll look forward to your call."

"I'll be sure to give the cow your regards", I giggled, as I walked to my car.

In the morning, I stopped by the coffee shop for John's coffee, and mine, on the way to work. He showed up a little later and grabbed the coffee as if he hadn't had any in days.

"Thanks, Molly. It really means a lot to me that you thought of my need for an adrenalin rush. Give me an hour and we'll head on out to Farmer Dave's."

I took care of a couple of cats, then put a closed sign on the outside door, grabbed my coffee, and proceeded with John in his rugged SUV to our appointment.

Dave is what you would call a true Florida cracker, having been born and raised in the Samsula area of Volusia County, with more cattle around than one might imagine. He reminded me of farmers in the West Country in England. I was surprised that he didn't have straw hanging out of his mouth, when we arrived. He was so friendly and grateful that we'd come all this way out to see his favorite cow. It was less than thirty minutes away, but the appreciation didn't go amiss.

"So, Dave, lead the way to the patient and let's sees what we can do", John said.

Dave grinned and imparted, "Her name is Sunny Sue, because of her pleasant disposition and seeming smile".

I'd never really thought of cows smiling, but Sunny Sue indeed grinned at us, in my mind anyway. I patted her before kneeling down to see what the problem was.

"I think she has an abscess on her leg John, but you might like to verify my diagnosis"

He made his own examination and readily agreed with me.

"This should be easy to treat, Dave. I'll lance and dress it, and inject her with antibiotics. I'll give you medicated ointment that you must apply daily, along with bandages and tape to keep it covered. One of us will come out tomorrow to check on Sunny Sue."

Dave appeared quite relieved and somewhat emotional over our care for his bovine pet as he said, "Thanks so much to both of you. I don't know how to thank you, other than paying your bill".

He then laughed out loud. John and I chortled in response.

"As I said, one of us will see you around the same time tomorrow. Just make sure she doesn't go into the fields until we have determined that she's better. And, yes, Dave, Molly will definitely send you a bill."

I could have sworn Sunny Sue smiled at us again. I never thought that I would live to see a smiling cow. I'd call

Bruce after I'd eaten and tell him about my interesting day. He beat me to it.

"Hello, darling girl, how are you?"

"Just wonderful now that I'm talking to you. How has your last couple of days been, Bruce?"

"I was rather uneventful, apart from playing a game of squash with Nick and getting my office ready for my replacement. What about you?"

"Yesterday I had lunch with my boss and in the evening Jen made me dinner. She modeled her bridesmaid's dress. It's sensational, Bruce. She looks so gorgeous in it, and to think that it was the first dress she tried on. Today John and I went out to a farm and visited a sick cow. It is the first time in my life that I've seen a cow smile. She was so sweet for such a large animal. She had an infected calf, and not the baby kind. Sorry, but that was John's joke which he thought hilarious. I didn't think it that humorous, but I laughed anyway. One of us has to go back to check up on things tomorrow, and I wouldn't mind betting it's going to be me, which will not upset me one iota. For me it's been an interesting couple of days. By the way, what time do you get in tomorrow?"

"Around seven, and I'm sorry it's so late but I didn't have much say in the matter. Don't get dinner for me, as I'll grab something at the airport. Besides, we're taking off in the morning for Cocoa, which I'm excited about, but I'm more excited about seeing you, my sexy babe.

He continued with more intimate expressions of lust and said, "I'm picturing you naked, lying on the bed beckoning me to take you, which I most certainly will tomorrow night".

"I can hardly wait, my studly prince."

And I didn't wait to have a very quick, unexpected orgasm. Just picturing my man in an aroused state had made me super horny. My groan must have set him off as well.

Finally coming down out of the clouds, I said, "Well, darling, I'm just about to eat my nearly cold pizza, so let's call it an evening".

"I'll see you around eight-thirty at your place, soon to be our place. Make sure you have a good bottle of red wine opened and breathing."

"Your wish is my command, senor. Here are some kisses to help get you here safely.

"Hugs and kisses back, and I'll give Brandy a big slobbery kiss from you, too."

I ate my pizza feeling quite relaxed, ready to hit the bed and watch TV. I really hoped that I had to go to the farm tomorrow. I was looking forward to seeing Sunny Sue again and getting that award-winning smile from her.

Indeed, at work the next day, John asked me if I could go out to Farmer Dave's as he had bills to pay and would rather do that before the weekend.

"I'd love to, John, as I've grown rather fond of Sunny Sue. I'll leave around ten-thirty."

Dave greeted me looking as if he'd been mucking out stalls, which I found out to be correct.

"How's Sunny Sue doing, Dave?"

"She seems to be doing quite well. She hasn't been at all restless, but I've left the bandage changing for you."

"That's what I'm here for."

He led me to Sunny Sue, who, true to form, gave me an award-winning grin. I never thought I could fall in love with a cow, but I just did.

"How are you doing, my beauty?" I said, as I gingerly took the bandage off.

The affected area seemed to be healing nicely. I smeared on more antibiotic cream and re-bandaged it. Sunny Sue didn't flinch a bit. I gave her a pat and told her that we'd be back again on Monday to check on the progress.

"Have you got enough bandages and cream for the weekend, Dave?"

"Yep, sure have Molly, and thanks so much for coming out. I guess you'll be back again on Monday?"

"If I can swing it, I'll be back, but in the meantime, you have a good weekend."

"You too, Molly, and drive carefully."

I stopped off on the way to grab some lunch and got back to the infirmary around one-thirty. John was out to lunch, having left me a message saying he'd be back around three and to go ahead and open the infirmary up. It was really slow and I only had two dogs that came in for routine shots. As I was finishing up with the second one I heard John enter.

"How did it go with Sunny Sue?"

"She is doing very well, the sweet thing. I'm in love with Bruce and a cow", I said with laughter in my voice, and he actually laughed back.

"Animals are quite amazing aren't they, Molly? They have such humanistic traits. I know that you'll want to go back again on Monday, so it's a done deal."

"Thanks a lot, John. I was hoping you'd say that. Do you and Jessica have any plans for this weekend?"

"We have nothing that spectacular other than going out for dinner on Saturday night. And what plans do the love birds have for the weekend?"

"We are going to stay over at a B and B in Cocoa Village Saturday night, so that will be a nice change of pace."

The rest of the day was as slow and we just talked while cleaning everything up in preparation for Monday. We then wished each other a great weekend and I went home to prepare for Bruce's arrival.

I'd bought a really good bottle of Pinot Noir, so I opened it to breathe, and tasted it after a few minutes to make sure it was good. And it was. I picked on a bit of cheese, but was not feeling that hungry for food right now. I was feeling nervous, like waiting for a first date, despite our already very intimate relationship.

The doorbell rang and I sprang to answer it. Bruce nonchalantly entered, pecked me on the cheek, and said he needed a quick shower. I had frankly imagined that he would rip off my clothes and ravage me. Instead, we traipsed upstairs for his shower, with me being sexually frustrated. It was worth the wait. He emerged from the shower stall with a magnificent erection. He grabbed me, kissed me passionately, and began to disrobe me in tantalizing fashion. When I was stripped down to my bra and panties, he led me downstairs to the kitchen counter and laid me on it. He removed my bra, then my underpants, kissing each area in turn. It made me delirious with desire. At last my lover mounted me and I pulled him into me with desperation. It was the best sex we'd had on the counter. It was ferocious, hot, and wild.

"Damn, girl, you are good; no scratch the good, you are fantastic, and good evening to you too!"

"Good evening to you, tiger man. I can't say that you are anything but tremendous when it comes to turning me on. I'm happy to have you back here again. Now down to the mundane, do you fancy a good glass of Pinot Noir? I bought it especially for this evening."

"Sounds just the ticket. Why don't we take the glasses and the bottle upstairs?"

"I won't say no to that suggestion, but give me a few minutes to tidy up the kitchen, set the coffee for the morning. I'll be right up."

The rest of the evening was spent drinking wine and cuddling. My mind did drift to the delightful ritual of being served my mug of coffee in the morning, before we both fell asleep. And so, I woke to find my caffeinated brew on the dresser, but no Bruce.

I yelled out, "Where are you, darling?"

"I'm downstairs making us a to-die-for breakfast before we pack up and leave for Cocoa Village."

Still clutching my coffee mug, I went down to find Bruce making us omelets with toast and jam. My omelet was delicious. I had no idea that he was such a good cook. Something else I've just learned about him. I enjoyed cooking, but it wasn't a passion of mine. Next to animals was my writing, and I hadn't been called in a while to do an article. If I haven't heard in a couple of weeks, I would give the paper a call.

"Delicious breakfast, darling; thanks so much. It was a treat for me not to have to think about what I was going to feed you."

"You never have to worry about me starving, or you, when I am around. That's one thing I'll say about my father, he's a great cook who taught me well."

I immediately thought about his missing mother and how I was going to do some more digging around when I returned to Dearborn in a couple of weeks.

"I suggest that as soon as we've cleaned up here, Molly, we leave. We can catch a few rays after checking in, and before we have to think about where to eat dinner."

"I'm ready, Bruce. I packed whilst you were fixing breakfast, so I'll clean up here and you can go and pack. It's not as if we have to take a ton of stuff, after all it is only one night away."

We got out of the house before lunch time and it only took an hour and a half to get to the Bed and Breakfast. It was delightful. Our room was decorated in cheerful chintzes with a striped duvet cover. It was airy and relaxing. We decided to don our bathing gear and head for the beach. It must be about five years since I'd been to Cocoa Beach. The whole area had developed considerably. The beach was so different from New Smyrna. Shells were larger and much more prevalent; the sand was considerably coarser. As we were strolling along, Bruce told me that he was surprised he hadn't had a visitor's guide to the area.

"Bruce, funnily enough I was going to fill you in on the little I know. Actually, Cocoa Beach lies between the Atlantic and the Banana River, as a thin sandy barrier of land, running north and south about six miles long. Cocoa Village is about four miles to the west separated by two rivers and two slivers of land

Cocoa Village is the historic area of the City of Cocoa, which borders the western side of the Indian River and that merges with the Banana River south of Cocoa. In the 1960's there was a woman who was a city council person who loved Cocoa and devoted herself to its improvement, especially in the historic area. Her name was Myrtice Thorpe who owned Myrt's, a popular restaurant where the restaurant, Black Tulip, now stands. It's a quaint part of town with tree-lined streets, a riverside boardwalk, and fine restaurants and boutiques. You'll see for yourself when we explore it this evening."

"I knew you wouldn't let me down. Thanks, darling, it will make this evening more enjoyable having had a preview. I can hardly wait, which brings me to the subject of restaurants. Do you have any ideas as to where we might eat this evening?"

"Since we don't want to be tied down to a time, we could see what tickles our fancy."

"Good idea. Now let's head back to the room for a little R and R", Bruce said, with that look on his face.

I knew exactly what kind of R and R he was planning, and I wasn't backing down from that. We had a few blissful hours of devouring each other until it was time to grace the historic streets of Cocoa.

We ambled up and down the sidewalks and walking streets, window shopping, and finally deciding on a little Italian restaurant on a side street. We were not disappointed in the meal. Coffee and a shared crème caramel finished it off admirably.

We were quite tired so we went back to the B and B after a short, after meal stroll. After all, Bruce had to fly back to Dearborn tomorrow evening. Plus, we had decided to select a format from the many I had brought along, and compile a 'final' list of invitees with an added number for contingencies. I said that on my coming stay in Dearborn I would write them out and mail them. But I needed to get the selected design and number to the printer before Wednesday, so that I'd have the cards before my flight. What a royal drags this commuting was, despite my excitement to get on with the investigation at Mike's house, once he had left for St. Lucia. I'd never let on to Bruce how I strongly I felt about my project.

We were both bushed and fell into bed. Bruce was asleep before I'd even had a chance to say goodnight to him. Ah, well, this was normal living.

The Sunday B & B breakfast was delicious. Afterwards, we decided to go to the beach with the selection of invitations. Bruce paid the B and B bill, packed up the car and off we went.

It was quite soothing to sit at the water's edge perusing the different styles of invitations. Fortunately, it didn't take us long. We both looked at them and the decision was unanimous.

"Well, it's a stroke of luck, Molly, which we both opted for the plain and simple one. The tougher part is your having to write them all out and mail them."

"Oh, that's no big deal, Bruce. Do you feel like a walk along the beach before we head back to the casa?"

"Sure thing, darling. I'm up for a bit of exercise before sitting down again."

We must have walked about three miles, admittedly at a leisurely pace, right at the water's edge. The sand was quite rough and the waves were high. I couldn't help but giggle at my last surf boarding experience.

"Give me a penny for your thoughts, baby girl."

"Oh, I was just thinking how great it would be to have a surf board, but then I decided it was much better having you. I didn't mean to compare you to a plank of wood."

I got the giggles and so did Bruce. It's so wonderful to be able to laugh over something so absurd. We decided to turn around and head back to the car, chuckling away. It's amazing when someone else laughs how contagious it is. It reminded me of a yoga class I took with a college friend years ago. We would all end up on the floor and someone would start laughing. Before long the whole room was laughing. Everyone left the class feeling terrific.

We took our time driving home, stopping for a snack at a little shack just outside of Titusville. Bruce's plane was not until eight this evening giving us quite a bit of time to relax before he geared himself up for the trip back. It was no surprise to both of us that we opted to make leisurely love.

"It's amazing what sea air does to a man's sex drive," Bruce said.

I couldn't help being amused by that comment and replied, "Oh, I thought it was my sensational body that turned you on, not the sea air." We once again broke out laughing.

"Darling, I'm going to get us some wine and a few snacks whilst you pack, or whatever, for your return to the semi-thawed North."

"Great idea, since I've worked up quite an appetite. I wonder how many calories we've worked off in bed."

"No clue, don't want to know, don't care," I said.

Disappearing downstairs to the kitchen, I stared briefly at the counter where some of our *encounters* had taken place. Pun intended!

It didn't take me that long to put a few snacks together on a tray along with a couple of glasses of wine. I didn't want to bring the bottle upstairs as I knew Bruce would like to be somewhat with it for his trip home, but hopefully not his home for long.

"Let's go downstairs, Molly, for the remaining hour I have left here. I tell you one thing that I am going to want down the road is a deck that we can go out on, rather like the one Jen has."

"I know, I know Bruce, you've mentioned that before, and we've talked about looking for a different home down the road. Do you think we could get married first?"

I smiled as I asked, but felt anguished at that particular moment. The book, *Men are from Mars, Women from Venus*, hits the nail on the head. Women are so much more practical.

The hour passed by very quickly. We chatted about what he was going to do in the coming couple of weeks before I landed in Dearborn. I filled him in on my week with the printer, the cow, and just generally keeping my head above water. The doorbell rang, and my heart missed a beat. Here we go again with the goodbyes.

"Have a safe flight, my darling, and call me tomorrow morning just to let me know you've arrived safely. This evening will be too late. I love you, and again will miss you like crazy."

"Me too darling, see you in a couple of weeks."

He kissed me quickly but passionately, leaving me as always feeling empty. He didn't turn around and wave goodbye. His mind was elsewhere. My mind was on doing a quick bit of housework to get rid of my nervous energy as tomorrow I had to go out to the farm to see how Sunny Sue was doing. I couldn't believe how excited I was at the thought of seeing her. Imagine a cow could do that for me! I'm lucky that the simple things in life really get me going. That said, the vacuuming didn't take me long and afterwards I felt so much more relaxed. I didn't even have trouble sleeping despite knowing that Bruce was at this moment air bound.

Whether John wanted it or not I picked up a coffee for him on route to work. He was so grateful and asked me if I could make this a daily occurrence.

"Not a problem John. Now, I figured that I'd go out to the farm around eleven if that works for you?"

"Fine, Molly."

"If John wasn't such a great boss I would have been somewhat miffed at this prospect, but nothing was too much effort for him right now. He was letting me go out to the farm, knowing how much I wanted this task, if you could call it that. I left around eleven and got to the farm just after half past eleven. Dave greeted me with much enthusiasm

"I'm really glad to see you Molly. Don't get me wrong, nothing is amiss with Sunny Sue, but I'm not really into changing bandages so will be super glad to have the day off. Let's go see the old girl then."

"Sunny Sue came walking towards me with that wonderful smile. I patted her forehead, and plonked a kiss on it.

"Let's take a look at your leg sweetheart," I said lifting it up and putting it on my bent knee.

"Oh, this looks really good Sunny Sue. I swabbed it off, put some more antibiotic cream on the area, and re-bandaged it.

"Dave, she'll only need this treatment for about another ten days. One of us will come out on Wednesday and Friday, by which time it should be good enough to heal without bandages."

"Thanks, so much Molly, so see one of you the day after tomorrow."

"Yes, you will Dave. I stroked Sunny Sue one last time before leaving and got another killer smile. My day was made. After work, I dropped off the chosen invitation to the printer who said he'd have them ready by next Wednesday. That would give me plenty of time to get the names of the people I wanted to invite to the wedding assembled before I left, which would be a simple task. I went running on the beach with Jen on Tuesday night which was, as always, delightful. She couldn't make dinner plans and that suited me fine.

"I've got a ton of things to do before I leave in roughly ten days Jen, so perhaps if you have time over the weekend and you're not busy with Charlie, we can grab a bite."

"Yes, that'll suit me fine. He can't come down this weekend as he has to work both days to prepare for a big meeting on Monday, so I'm free most of the weekend. We'll talk later in the week, but in the meantime, ciao for now."

"Goodbye to you too Jen," I said with a grin on my face. She roared off as usual into the sunset.

John had decided to leave me to go to the farm both Wednesday and Friday, knowing how much I loved that cow.

"Call it compensation for bringing me coffee in every morning," he said chuckling to himself. "

"Hey Molly, if things don't work out with Bruce you've always got Sunny Sue."

"Very funny John thanks for the great idea, which I hope will never come to fruition however much I love that beast."

My visits both Wednesday and Friday were enormously satisfying. I swear that animal smiled even wider at me. I collected the damage from Dave and told him that I'd pop in at the end of next week just to make sure she was alright, telling him not to hesitate to call if things didn't seem to be progressing properly.

"Molly I can't thank you enough for what you've done for Sunny Sue. She has taken a real shine to you so don't be shy about giving her a social visit from time to time."

"I'll do just that Dave, and thanks for the invite. I'll see you next week around the same time on Thursday. I'm flying off to Dearborn on Friday so won't be able to make it that day.

'No biggy, Molly; see you next Thursday, and have a good weekend."

"Thanks, I will, and the same to you, Dave," I said as I climbed into my car and drove off through the slush. A farmer's girl I was not. My conversations with Bruce were, as always, long and wonderful and of course we indulged in phone sex. We both had too much to do before I flew in next Friday, so were limiting our phone calls to every other day.

"I'm going out with Jen on Saturday so call me Sunday night Bruce, oh, and before I forget I took the invitation to the printer's and they will be ready in time for my trip. I know you are as excited as I am about writing them out."

"You better believe it. I'm having dinner with a few guys from work on Saturday, some I know quite well, and the others are just department people that I interact with on occasion. It's an early goodbye dinner. Nothing much else other than slobbery kisses sent from Brandy. You have a wonderful Saturday darling and love to Jen."

"Thanks, my love, and you have a great dinner. I'll look forward to hearing all about it Sunday night, and kisses back to Brandy. I know he misses me as much as I miss him."

I was meeting Jen at a local steakhouse around seven, so decided to spend a good part of the day at the pool again. The weather was settled and even though the snowbirds were dribbling back home it still wasn't too crowded. For once Jen beat me to it and was propping up the bar with a glass of wine, and one beside her.

"This is for you, girlfriend. We are going to have a lovely, leisurely dinner tonight. I wish I had lots of gossip to tell you but don't, so I'm counting on you to spice up the evening.

"Sorry, but outside of having selected the invitations for the wedding there is nothing to tell you that'll excite you, besides my having visited Sunny Sue twice. When I visit her again outside of office hours you should really come with me to see what I mean about her smile. The only other issue is that I'm so anxious to go back to Mike's house and fish around more. It is ridiculous how something like this can consume one for so long."

"Not really, Molly. I think it's having such a vacuum that's really bugging you. If you could just lay your fingers on some concrete evidence, that might help things move in the right direction. I'm convinced that you'll unearth the truth about her disappearance at some juncture. However, let's shelve this subject for now and talk about other stuff, for example what we are going to eat."

"I'll go along with that, Jen. I know that I am treating myself to a blooming onion and steak and fries, how about you?"

"I'll have the same, thanks."

We both opted for dessert and decaf coffee. By the time we'd finished and paid the check it was nine-thirty. Time always flies by when Jen and I eat out together.

I asked her, "What are your plans for tomorrow?"

"I have to clean the house, run some errands and grocery shop. It's going to be a very mundane Sunday, but I've neglected the place for a while now. How about you, what are you going to do?"

"I'm going to have a lazy morning, do a bit of cleaning, and spend the afternoon by the pool. I have a very busy four days at work before I fly out on Friday afternoon."

"It's hard to believe that this will be your last foreseeable trip to Michigan, Molly. You must feel a bit strange knowing you won't be going back."

"Oh, I'm sure we'll be going back from time to time, especially in the summer, as Bruce has no intention of selling his house for a couple of years. It's just this wretched commuting that we'll be able to forego that thrills me."

We ambled out to the car park and for once Jen didn't roar away. She was quite sedate as she took off. This would be a first for her in a long time. I waved to her as she disappeared from sight. Thank God for her, I thought as I moseyed off home.

Sunday was bliss even though I had to make my own coffee, but the quiet in the house was comforting and I actually managed to read the paper in detail for a change.

I went for a long swim and took a couple of hours relaxing, and trying to clear my mind, which I did successfully. Since I didn't have to rush back to cook dinner, I stayed until the sun was sinking into the horizon, shedding a dark pink haze over the pool. I was alone and it was beautiful. Later, I made a healthy dinner for myself and curled up with my book waiting for Bruce to call. He telephoned around nine and was quite business like.

"Sorry to be late calling, Molly. I had a bit of a hangover this morning, and have several meetings tomorrow and Tuesday. Do you mind if I call you Tuesday night and we can chat at length?"

"No darling, that's fine. I'm actually tired and have, like you, a very busy few days coming up. I'm picking up the invitations Wednesday, going out to the farm on Thursday and will be with you Friday. Tuesday is good. I miss you and love you very much."

"Miss you too, darling, so until we speak on Tuesday night around eight, I bid you farewell."

I could hear his chuckle as he hung up before I could say another word, and I crashed.

Two coffees in hand I got to work earlier than usual, as I wanted to make sure the office was cleared up as much as humanly possible before winging off to Dearborn. I worked on a very cantankerous poodle, which was a rarity, as most of the pets that came in were quite docile. I was feeling a tad stressed. It was almost as if I were trying to cram too much into my few days here. *Slow down, girl*, I kept telling myself. It worked; the pace magically slackened. John told me he'd take care of the paperwork this week and preferred that I concentrate on care of the animal. I had a lengthy conversation with Bruce on Tuesday evening. It was very perfunctory. I knew why. We were both so damn busy.

"I'll call you Thursday night Molly, but in the meantime, don't work too hard. I love you and cannot wait to see you on Friday."

"Don't work too hard doesn't enter into the equation right now. Don't YOU work too hard either, and I love you too. I'm picking the invitations up tomorrow night with the fervent hope no corrections are needed.   Bye for now, darling; talk to you on Thursday."

I stopped by the printers on Wednesday to pick up the invitations.   I felt very excited.   I had all but shelved thoughts of the wedding itself during the past week, but now reality was setting in.   I'm getting married!   The invitations were perfect and for that I was very grateful.   I went for a swim on the way home.   The effort re-energized me, but in a relaxed way.   After dinner, I called Jen to have a chat.   She wasn't home so I left a message asking her to call me tomorrow night.

The next morning, driving out to the farm, a deer jumped out in front of a large truck I was following.   *Bambi* luckily was not hit thanks to good brakes and quick reaction by the trucker.   My defensive driving was no less brilliant; though my nerves were jangled a bit.

Still a little shaken I entered the farm's muddy driveway, excited to see Sunny Sue again.   Dave, in his usual farm attire, waved to me.   He had a bag of corn that seemed to have just been picked.   He gave me a semi-toothless grin and told me that Sunny Sue was eagerly awaiting me in the barn, but she was beginning to get somewhat agitated.

"Perhaps she is claustrophobic, or at least anxious to roam about the fields again, Dave.   Let's examine Sunny Sue and her wound to see if they are ready to meet the outside world again."

We walked into the barn and sure enough she was grinning from ear to ear.   I caressed her, said pleasant nothings into her ear, and then proceeded to remove the bandaging.   She certainly was friskier than before and the affected area had progressed nicely.

"Sunny Sue, my girl, I pronounce you fit to go out into the fields again."

With a grateful look on his face, Farmer Dave said, "Miss Molly, how can I thank you?"

"Well, you might give or sell me several ears of that corn you are about to drop on the straw," I said, hardly being able to contain my laughter.

"Here, take this bagful and give some of them to John, no charge."

"Thank you so much, Dave", I said gratefully, though the weight and strong fresh smell of corn was more than expected.

"I'll see you in a couple of weeks. I'm going to Dearborn to see my fiancé, Bruce. Don't hesitate to call John should you need anything. And when I return to the office, I'll call to see how Sunny Sue is doing."

I gave him a bill I had prepared at the office and he insisted on giving me a check for the full amount.

Back at the clinic, John was pretty happy with the corn, though he only wanted a few ears. I wasn't that ecstatic about having to shuck the rest of it, so I decided to offload some on Jen.

John later offered, "Molly, since we have a slow day, I suggest we pack up around four. I'm sure you have plenty to do for your trip."

"Yes, thanks so much for being thoughtful." My mind was racing with so much to do. "I'm usually pretty good at coping with a ton of stuff, but now I feel a tad overwhelmed."

"I'm not surprised. Getting ready for your flight and planning a marriage must be quite difficult, to say nothing about thinking about a new life with Bruce", he ventured, and sounding the philosopher

"Thanks for your understanding. I'll see you tomorrow, John, and I won't forget your coffee."

I'm a clumsy clod, like my dad, and managed to trip over a stone on the way to my car. My mind then flashed back to a saying my mother loved to use, about dad in particular, which was, *He's an utter walleye.* I have no clue if that is the correct spelling, but love it anyway.

My irritability brought on by stress, and strain of the tripping variety, lessened as I drove back via the beach. I didn't have time to walk tonight, but just smelling the sea air helped calm me.

The next two days were frantic, catching up with paper work. The clinic office looked almost like a funeral parlor; it was so bereft of the usual paperwork clutter.

On the last day of work John said, "Have a wonderful two weeks Molly; although, I know you'll be very busy with your wedding plans".

"Thanks John, I'll send you a postcard."

I gave him an unexpected hug. He was more than taken aback, but I could tell that he wasn't unhappy.

"Give my best regards to Jessica, and don't work too hard. I'm glad I managed to find you a hard-working assistant. I realize she doesn't have a lot of personality, but she is very clever. Don't hesitate to call me if you have any questions."

"Will do, Molly," he said giving me a winsome smile.

Once home, I went about cleaning up kitchen stuff until Jen arrived and poured herself a glass of wine. She was to take home whatever was perishable in my fridge, and agreed, as usual, to check my mail every few days for anything that might need my attention. Before I returned, Jen said she would tidy up the place, and restock my fridge. We had this unspoken rule that we'd had for years, *do for each other.* After a ten-minute chat, Jen backed out the door and said she'd see me in the morning. As promised she picked me up in plenty of time to get the plane.

"Thanks, Jen, for being you. I'll call you tomorrow night to chat, but will e-mail you at work to let you know that I've arrived safely. Apparently, it's sixty degrees in Dearborn. I guess they are experiencing a heat wave."

"You're chronic about the cold, Molly. I know you'll survive with Bruce keeping you warm. Don't forget that I want a progress report on how the investigation goes."

"I promise to keep my bridesmaid abreast of things."

I jumped out of the car, grabbed my luggage, and blew kisses at her as thanks. Jen had to leave abruptly as she was blocking a large bus. We each waved goodbye and I turned to hit the tarmac.

I was flying Delta which had satisfied me well enough on previous flights, but had to chuckle at a friend's take on the initials, *Divine Elephant Leaving Trails Aloft.* It amused me, because elephants are my favorite animals.

As luck would have it, I had successfully requested an outside seat and didn't have to move. No screaming babies, drunks, or loud mouths were on this flight. I ordered vodka and tonic and a very mundane ham sandwich. I dozed off, awakening just before touchdown. My heart was racing. I couldn't wait to see Bruce. I only had a small carry on suitcase and an oversized handbag so didn't have to go to baggage claim. I saw Bruce waving enthusiastically at me. I ran straight into his arms like a teenager.

After a steamy kiss, he said enthusiastically, "Well, my bride to be, I can see you haven't lost your killer looks. Am I ever glad to have you here with me!"

I replied, "Imagine spending two whole weeks with you and Brandy, seeing Nick and Sally, meeting some of your office and gym friends, writing invitations, and undertaking some naughty, intimate stuff".

Bruce grinned in his winning way that had melted my heart right from the first moment that I'd set eyes on him.

"Well let's get going, dear heart. We mustn't waste a minute of our time together; besides Brandy is chomping at the bit to see you. I really think he has been having withdrawal symptoms since the last time you were here. Don't forget that I have to work four days a week."

"Only four days?"

"Yep, I managed to get a three-day weekend while you're here, so let's get moving, my princess. The kitchen counter awaits you."

I couldn't help but burst out laughing.

"I know exactly what you have in mind, but won't Brandy interfere with our plans?"

"Nope, he won't, because I'll let him out, feed him, and now that the weather is improving, I'll stick him in his outdoor pen. That's, of course, after he's licked you to death."

Funnily enough driving from the airport to Bruce's house, I felt almost at home. The weather was beautiful, and the city shone with of daisies and newly flowering shrubs. *Could I live here*, I asked myself? *No, I could not.* I suppose for five months of the year it would be okay, but bouncing from house to house at such long distances, was not my thing. My immediate roots were in New Smyrna Beach, at least for now. I dozed off and before I knew it, Bruce gently tapped me on the shoulder.

"Wake up! Brandy is anxious to see you and I'm doubly anxious to ravage you."

Both events happened in that order. I thought Brandy would wet himself with excitement and the kitchen counter experienced some urgent, quick, but satisfying, sex.

"Whew Molly," Bruce said having taken me at a pace that I'd not witnessed before.

"Next time I promise to be slower."

"That's fine with me, darling. I needed you desperately too, and as you have said, we have a week to pleasure ourselves in leisurely fashion."

Later that evening I was feeling quite comforted to know where everything was. And that we would be coming back from time to time, when I had unpleasant thoughts. The job he'd secured at the Space Center might not pan out; our marriage might collapse. I admonished myself for having dismal thoughts, and was snapped into a positive mood by the appearance of Bruce, who walked into the bedroom with a tray holding wine, glasses, and cheese. He put the tray down and looked at me. Neither of us spoke. It took us only a moment to throw off our clothes, take a large sip of wine, and drop into bed as one entwined sensual form.

His majestic body enveloped me, with his hands and lips caressing me, while his enormous *member*, as my mother used to call the male appendage, pressed up against my belly. I finally could not withstand the urge - so much for leisurely foreplay! I pulled him into me. His slow, rhythmic thrusts drove me crazy, and I dug my nails into his back. We at last climaxed with such intensity that the tray on the dresser shook. When we'd both come down to earth, Bruce got up, and brought me a hunk of cheese and some wine.

We decided to take turns showering, me first. Once done, I threw on sweats and went downstairs to let Brandy out.

"Poor baby, I know that you're bursting at the seams."

With a grateful expression, Brandy ran out, did his business, and then tore around the small fenced in garden until he'd totally exhausted himself. Back inside, he nuzzled up against me, giving me the largest doggie smile ever.

"Brandy, I love you so much. I can't wait to take you for long walks on the beach. We are going to have so much fun together."

He gave me a dog's grin and wagged his tail in agreement. Life was good to me now.

I made French toast in the morning and took it upstairs, to find Bruce sitting on the edge of the bed in the most fetching pair of briefs, reading the local rag.

"So, what gives in downtown Dearborn today, darling?"

"Oh, nothing much outside of the usual trade union disputes, a few rapes and a large exhibit at the Arab American Museum. I would imagine you'd like to go over the invitation list today and finalize who we are inviting.

Fortunately for me I've only got sixteen people on my list and I would imagine none of them will be attending, except Nick and Sally who have made it a point to combine our day with two weeks' vacation in New Smyrna Beach."

"That's awesome, Bruce. I had no idea they would be coming. I have about twelve people, making it a select group. Who are you having as best man?"

"Nick, of course," he said, giving me a look that said, *naturally, dummy.*

We ate our French toast with little conversation. Once finished I took the tray downstairs. I'd no sooner put the dishes in the dishwasher when I felt what seemed like a rod poking into my thighs. Some rod it was and the kitchen counter experienced another wild encounter.

"Phew, I need a nap now", he said carrying me into the living room, and gently put me on the sofa. Three blissful, uninterrupted hours of sleep washed over us until we were awakened by the phone ringing. It was Sally confirming dinner tonight at six. They'd come over for drinks first. I was feeling very alive, well rested and sexually one hundred percent fulfilled. Bruce noticed that there was a message on his answering machine. It was his dad informing us that he wouldn't be able to make our wedding. It seems there was so much legal red tape that the house closing was put off until the day prior to our big day. Was I really sad that he'd be missing our big day? Honestly, no.

Tuesday was my day to see Bri. I had talked to him briefly before I left New Smyrna Beach and he suggested that we both examine Mike's house later in the week. I'd mentioned that I had a key and it would be better if Bruce didn't know what we were planning just yet. After our first meeting, I'd clue Bruce in, but not right away.

Nick and Sally were always punctual and it was great being with them. They were two people whom I felt I'd known for much longer than I had. We chatted away, the guys about work and the gym, whilst Sally and I stayed in the kitchen gabbing about the wedding.

"I can't believe that you are actually coming all the way south to New Smyrna Beach for our big day."

"I wouldn't miss it for the world; besides, it might put a few ideas into Nick's head. We live together and act as if we're married, all but in name. Some men just need a revelation, or a push, to pop the question, don't you think?"

"Well, in Bruce's case he was quicker in that department than my wildest dreams could imagine, but in general, I absolutely agree. My own experience is limited to two real romances. Before Bruce, I was engaged to David, a lawyer and wonderful man, who was tragically killed in a car accident. Of course, I had a few casual flings and teenage crushes in my younger years."

"I'm so sorry about David, but am I ever glad you met Bruce. I've lived here for three years and can honestly say you are the first female that I feel a real bond with. I'm pissed you two will be living permanently in Florida, but in consolation, we do have Skype and the phone, and I know you'll travel here on occasion. Now, since you're here for two weeks and Bruce is working four days a week, will you make time for me? I'd love to go to lunch or shop with you, or even take a trip somewhere."

"Sally, I was hoping you'd feel that way. Outside of writing out the invitations, which is *hanging over my head like a widow's veil*, and a few business errands, I'm free as of Wednesday.

Sally smiled at my use of the *widow's veil* phrase. I frequently reminded myself that no matter how long I lived in the States, my heritage was European, and even being a citizen sometimes didn't help my inward restlessness for Europe. Perhaps Bruce and I could travel across the pond one day.

Our conversation was interrupted by our men asking us if we were ready to eat. A unanimous, *yes*, spouted out of our mouths. We giggled like two stupid schoolgirls and joined the loves of our lives for the short walk to the local steakhouse.

Dinner was as wonderful as I'd remembered from the first time I'd been there. There was no lack of conversation as we dined. Sally and I made plans to meet at the local corner café on Wednesday morning and she said she'd arrange for us to take a cruise on the Diamond Jack. We'd agreed the weather was perfect for that. Last time Bruce and I were on the boat, it was in the company of Mike, and it was damn cold.

After we said our *good nights*, Bruce took my arm, but for some reason a chill came over me, and I suddenly felt as if I never wanted intimacy again. He sensed my mood, letting go of my hand as we walked back to his house. I couldn't call it my house and probably never would. We went to bed exhausted and a bit wined out. Sex was not on the cards tonight and that was fine too. Life isn't one hundred percent full of rose buds; sometimes it has its thorns.

The next morning was like most mornings that I'd shared with Bruce. We had great sex, no *thorns*, and he delivered coffee on a tray. The only thing missing was my flower, but that was low on my list of requisites.

"What shall we do today, Molly?" Bruce asked, but before I could answer he said, "I know, I know. We've got to complete the invitation list then we can work on our leisure day".

Once downstairs, we knuckled down to fine-tuning the list of invitees. I had twelve people and Bruce had sixteen, which was a really manageable number.

"Oh, we'd better include Minister Knowles so that makes it twenty-nine." I'd pared mine down to my best friend Jen and several girls from the gym whom I hadn't seen in a while and John and Jessica. Most of my really close friends were in Spain, London, and Hungary and they knew they were invited. Bruce's situation was pretty much the same outside of inviting his dad, whom I fervently prayed would decline. Deep in my heart I was convinced Mike was evil, and I was going to prove it one way or the other.

"Now, my bride, think what you want to do for the rest of the day while I let Brandy out.

I thought, and knew, that all I really wanted to do was take a walk in the neighborhood, pick up a few groceries, and have a cozy night in. I told Bruce my idea and he was agreeable. The weather was beyond perfect. We dressed in sweats and strolled down Blakely Street and several other flower lined streets whose names I'd forgotten, but everything looked breathtaking. However, my mind drifted back to the fact that I never wanted anything more than to get married and live back in New Smyrna Beach. Then images of England snuck into my mind. Attempting to get my attention, Bruce's voice interrupted my reverie.

"Sorry, darling", I apologized. "For some strange reason, the flowers here reminded me of my home town and I guess I was in a trance, thinking on it."

"I had thoughts you were getting pre-marital nerves and wanted to change your mind. Also, I know how much the business with my father is eating away at you.   Frankly speaking, I am having a harder time dealing with it, than I thought I would. The sooner your head is cleared and your business with Bri and all this garbage is finished, which I know you cannot wait to do, the better off we'll both be. There, I've said my piece and we can get on with enjoying the rest of the day."

"Wow, that was heavy, Bruce. I never realized you still feel agitated about my involvement. But you are surely entitled to, since it's to do with your father. No matter what, *blood is thicker than water*, and I've been somewhat out of place with my delving. You cannot possibly imagine how many hours of sleep I've lost just feeling such guilt over my inquisitiveness. But I am who I am, and my journalistic bent has made me pry. When you think about it in a less serious vein, it is really Brandy's fault. If he hadn't dug around so much, my imagination might not have been sufficiently piqued."

I added in a hopefully humorous tone, "Now I feel better, darling. Let's have some lunch and walk in that beautiful square that you took me to when it was covered with snow and I was one frozen puppy."

"Sure thing, kiddo", he said in a better mood.

He squeezed my hand and gave me that killer smile that convinced me more and more that I was not about to let anyone take this hunk of a man from me. The rest of the day floated by gloriously stress free. We ate at a tiny Greek hole-in-the wall restaurant that turned out to be a real find. When the pleasant meal was over, Bruce gave me that, *let's hurry back; I'm hungry for you*, look.

He paid the bill and we ran the entire distance back to his house. Need I say more than the kitchen counter was rapidly cleaned off; the rest is left to one's imagination!

"You are one hell of a lover, and on top of it I really love you, so let's go ahead, and get married. Oh, yes, I forgot we already agreed to that", he said facetiously.

We stood up laughing away and headed upstairs. Around two in the morning I felt something prodding my buttocks. Yippee, Bruce was hot to trot for a quickie, which it was. No complaints from me though. *I'll take it whenever I can get it*, I thought, as he turned me over abruptly and sunk into me as I wrapped my legs around the small of his back. It was sublime. Bruce knew that I wasn't keen on anal sex, trying it once with poor results. He never complained that I was prudish, which I don't consider myself to be, and he never tried that position again, though that didn't stop us from other unique figurations.

I woke up around nine to the usual smell of coffee and Brandy nestling on the empty side of the bed.

"Hey, buddy, it's good to see you", I said jumping up to retrieve my mug of tepid, but strong coffee, which I downed in a few swigs.

"Don't go anywhere, Brandy, I'll be right up", I said, ambling downstairs to pour myself more caffeine to aid the wakening process.

He had no intention of moving, so I imagine Bruce had let him out earlier on. I gradually came too, thinking how lucky I was to have two great males in my life. I threw on a better than average looking pair of sweats, shoved Brandy off the bed so I could make it. He was informed that we were going over to Mike's house, then we'd come back, and he would guard the house whilst I went to see Bri. I'd made a two-pm appointment with Bri when I was up north. I'm sure it would be abortive, but at least I'd ease my curious mind.

I downed three slices of toast loaded with butter and apricot preserves to take care of my empty stomach. It was in my mind to actually run to Mike's house to make up for my gluttony, and wear Brandy out so he'd laze around or sleep through my appointment with Bri. After finishing my final cup of coffee, I spent some time cleaning up the kitchen, and then ran upstairs to put on my makeup. I was good to go.

"Brandy, are you ready to hit the pavement?"

He wiggled his tale and gave me a beautiful doggy smile. It usually took about a half hour to walk to Mike's house, but this time it took just under twenty minutes as I jogged the whole way there, Brandy happily trotting beside me.

I checked Mike's mailbox first. I doubted there would be much. Supposedly he had made provision to forward his mail to the house in St. Lucia. There were a couple of flyers and that was the sum total of the mail. I chucked them in the garbage, knowing full well he wouldn't want them. I decided to dig out more photos to see if I could shed any lighter on his mother, but to no avail. All I came across were loads of photos of Bruce, Mike and his mother, and an assortment of pictures of people I didn't know. Damn it, I thought. I guess we might never know where she disappeared to. I was lost in gloomy thought when Brandy came up to me, giving me the hint that he wanted to go out and pee.

"Off we go Brandy; it's time for another dose of fresh air. I had three hours before my appointment with Bri. It was gorgeous outside. I reckoned it to be in the high seventies. Brandy rushed out the door, peed, and charged around the garden a few times before closing in on his favorite spot, where he started digging away. My mind was on my meeting with Bri, so I hadn't paid much attention to Brandy, until he began to bark frantically. I turned around to find, to my utter amazement, that he had exposed bones which didn't look animal-like to me.

"Alright, alright buddy, that'll do; let's go inside now."

He was more than reluctant to stop digging, so I pulled him indoors after cleaning his paws. I decided to get a spade from Mike's garage and continue the excavation process. To my horror, when I cleared away more dirt I found what appeared to be arm-like bones partially covered by skin. What on earth had Brandy and I stumbled on to? I called Bri in frenzy and asked him if he could possibly come to Mike's house to see what exhumed.

"Bruce is working and I don't want to get him involved until I know what I've found", I said, still in shock.

"Sure thing, Molly, it's just between us for now. I'll be over just after two."

"That will give me time to grab a bite to eat at a café nearby. Mike's house is devoid of any kind of nourishment, and I'll be better off with a something on my stomach to steady my jitters."

I put a leash on Brandy who wasn't a happy camper having been shut in, but rules were rules. We set off to the café about two blocks away that evidently allowed pets. It was a typical down-home diner. The coffee sucked, but I had a double hamburger and fry that more than made up for the coffee. Brandy slept whilst I ate, which wasn't such a bad thing. The whole dining experience lasted half an hour. The server went to fill my cup, but I gave her a sickly, no thank you, smile.

"Just the check, please", I said, slurping the last of the dark colored water.

I paid up, woke Brandy, and decided to walk around a bit before returning to Mike's. I stopped at a local convenience store and bought a can of coffee, some chocolate biscuits, dog biscuits and a large bottle of apple juice. We walked several blocks until Brandy started to visibly lag, so we turned around and headed back to the mystery. Brandy wanted to revisit the garden, but I didn't want him to go out there until after Bri's visit.

"I know, Brandy, that you think I'm so unfair, but you'll just have to bond with me in the house for now", I said soothingly.

I busied myself putting all the photographs back in the musty old box and took them back upstairs to the loft where they belonged. Bri rang the doorbell fifteen minutes earlier than his expected time of arrival.

"Coming," I yelled out, as I ran down the stairs two at a time. "Hello, Bri, thanks awfully for meeting me here. If you want to come out to the garden, I have a few strange findings that I'd like to show you."

"Lead the way, Molly. So, what's the big discovery?"

"Well, you see where Brandy and I have dug? It's exposed bones that don't look like animal remains to me."

He agreed, took the shovel, and gingerly dug some more, while I directed my eyes elsewhere.

"Holy shit! I found a disintegrating rib cage", he exclaimed.

I gazed in horror at what he was directing my attention to. It certainly looked human. I felt sick and turned my head away to throw up.

"What on earth are we going to do about this, Bri?"

"I'm going to call the police. This is serious and we can't procrastinate. And for certain we cannot do any more digging. This is probably a crime scene. Now, the other big question is, are you going to call Bruce at work, or wait until we find out more details?"

"He knows I'm seeing you today, but I haven't told him of Brandy's discovery. I should have told him, I guess, so now I might as well call after the police have investigated. I dread telling him for fear of how it might affect our relationship. But most importantly I would hate for him to possibly witness his mother's remains being dug up. Besides he has some important things to do today and there is nothing he can do here at this point.

"I understand. Once the police are on it, I think you, and I, will feel a little more settled. Anyway, I could use some coffee to settle my nerves. My investigations have involved following paper trails and people, not exhuming dead bodies."

"I brought some over earlier, as I knew the house was totally cleaned out of any kind of food or drinks. Give me a second to brew it. Do you mind looking after Brandy?"

"No problem. I'm dialing the police right now," he said.

Whilst I was making us coffee, I nervously ate two donuts without even tasting them. I kept going over and over the gruesome discovery and its consequences for Bruce and me, and our life together. But there was no going back. As soon as the coffee was ready I found a tray, grabbed the creamer, some sugar, and several more donuts, and went outside. Brandy was lying quite peacefully on the bit of manicured lawn that was left.

Bri said, "Thanks for the coffee and donuts. The police should be here shortly, including a crime scene investigator, I imagine. I think we can hang up doing anything further until they get here. Are you going to call Bruce as soon as we have a more complete picture?"

"I think I'll wait until he gets home from work to clue him in on the day's findings. Telling him then won't make it any worse."

"It's your call", he said, just beginning to work on the second donut. "Damn, these donuts are good. Where did you get them?"

"There's a coffee shop on the corner of this street. In fact, if you turn left when you leave, it's on the same side of the road. You can't miss it. I haven't a clue what it's called. It's a hole in the wall place, but their donuts are to die for."

A few minutes later the front door bell rang.

"That'll be the coppers," I said in my English vernacular. "Hi, I'm Molly Thomas, the owner's future daughter-in-law, and you are?"

The closest man addressed me, with his badge held high, "I'm Detective Andrews, this is Detective Clifton, and Crime Scene Investigator Brown.

"Nice to meet you, detectives, and you, Mr. CSI. I assume you know Bri."

Bri and the police said their hi's and shook hands.

They all looked to be in their thirties and all three were not hard on the eye. The detectives were dressed in suits while the investigator was dressed in dark blue overalls with a CSI logo on the front. If I hadn't been in love, I could I see myself really flirting with all of them, individually of course!

I volunteered that the house belonged to Mike Sully, and that I was checking the house for my fiancé, Bruce, Mike's son. I explained that it was really Brandy that made the discovery of the body, and that I called my friend, Bri, to confirm my suspicions.

Bri led them to the backyard, where they examined the skeletal remains already exposed. CSI Brown then proceeded to cordon off a considerable area around the disturbed ground with the help of the detectives, using CSI tape. He took photos and then borrowed my spade and began to carefully remove the soil.

Watching him exhume a skeletal body wasn't my thing, so I decided I'd give a quick call to Jen at work. She was out of the office, so I left her a brief message saying that I'd call her tomorrow evening. All of a sudden, I heard CSI Brown shout that he had a skull and it was definitely human, and most probably female. With that, he said he and an assistant would have to meticulously sift the soil in the immediate area and exhume all of the bones for examination back at his lab.

Detective Andrews asked me if any females lived at the house, so I told them about Mike's wife, and that he was in St. Lucia. At their request, I gave them Bruce's home address and phone numbers. I begged them to let me call him first, explaining that I had not wanted to bother him at work, but should have called him. Because the investigation was in such preliminary stages, the detectives agreed they would call him tomorrow for a deposition.

Detective Clifton asked, "If you don't mind, Miss Thomas, we would like to briefly tour the house. Bri can accompany us. A thorough examination might come later. Also, would you happen to know if there is any female clothing in the house? It will help in comparing the size of the skeleton to the size of the clothing."

"Of course, you may look around. As for clothing, there are several items in a wardrobe upstairs that belong to Bruce Sully's mother, I am pretty sure. While they nosed around, I found a dress, a pair of slacks, and a sweater that I put into a plastic bag. We met at the stair landing.

"These should help with your investigation, Detective Clifton", I said, as I handed him the bag of clothes. "When do you think you'll have a more concrete idea about who it is and how she, or he, died?"

"Well, first of all, CSI Brown has to completely process the crime scene. Then he has to examine the remains in detail at the lab, determine the cause of death, and develop physical details in order to come up with a lifelike description. Meanwhile, we'll get a court order to do a thorough search of the house. Of course, we need to interview Bruce Tully and ask him to provide us a DNA sample to compare with DNA from the body. That study may take some days. We also ask you and Bri to be available for a more formal statement tomorrow. But right now, we are just drawing up in our minds a preliminary picture of the case, enough to make a written report."

Detective Andrews added, "We'll keep you advised as much as we deem appropriate, and if you don't mind, we might do that to some extent through Bri, whom we can advise in a more shorthand fashion. He can explain to you where we are with the investigation.

"Thanks for giving me the frank reality of what has to be done. I shall help however I can, including answering questions tomorrow", I said in reply. "I have had this gut feeling for several months that there was something weird here, ever since Brandy nosed around this area in the snow, the last time I visited to pick up the mail."

"Well, you can tell us more about that tomorrow. For now, there is nothing you and Bri need to do here. You might as well take off after you lock up. Please don't remove anything that belongs in the house. We'll let ourselves out the back gate", Detective Andrews said. "We'll get a key from your fiancé once we have the court order."

Bri agreed to make a formal statement as well, and that he'd certainly convey whatever the detectives told him about developments, that hadn't been passed to Bruce or me already. He left to go back to his office, while I re-entered the house to clean up whatever mess there was, and retrieve Brandy.

It didn't take me long to walk back to Bruce's. I called him at work to find out what time he planned on being home.

He said, "I'll be back around seven, darling; so why don't we run out for a bite?"

"Oh, that's okay, Bruce. I thought I'd cook us a couple of steaks. Maybe we can go out tomorrow night."

"Whatever suits you is fine with me. By the time I get home, I probably won't want to go anywhere either."

I thought about the bombshell that I was going to drop in his lap. I didn't know how he'd react. He'd probably be furious, but that was the risk I had taken. It wasn't as if he didn't already know about my probing for answers, but not even I would have guessed it would come to a body, possibly his mother's, in his father's backyard. I busied myself making some snacks, opened a bottle of merlot, and helped myself to a glass whilst preparing dinner. I was deep in thought when I felt something pinch my bum. I hastily turned around to find Bruce who had successfully snuck up on me. I pushed him back, and then leaped forward to plant a passionate kiss on his ready lips.

Trying to be nonchalant, I informed him, "No sex right now, my gorgeous man. I'll fix you a drink as a substitute. Let's go and sit down in the living room. I've got something I have to tell you."

"That sounds ominous. You *have* to tell me?"

"Well it's about the findings at your dad's house. I was going to meet Bri at his office today but I called him over to meet me at your dad's house instead. You see, I left Brandy out to pee and he started digging around in the same place he did months back and exposed some bones that looked human to me. I got a spade and dug around to find what looked like human arm bones. I asked Bri to take a look so he came over and he discovered a rib cage that was most certainly human. At that point, he insisted he call the police. They made it a crime scene and found a skull, most likely female."

He interrupted my story with, "Why didn't you call me when all this happened?"

I profusely apologized and told him about my reluctance for him to be here to view the exhuming of remains that were possibly his mother's. And, there wasn't anything much he could do at the time, as well as he was busy with work. Before he could respond, I filled him in on the details about who was there, what they were doing, and that the detectives would be calling him tomorrow to make arrangements to interview him, as well as Bri and me.

Bruce looked at me with a shocked look, as if he were just realizing that it really could be his mother. He didn't say anything for what seemed like ages, and then he got up and paced around the living room. I waited anxiously for him to say something; anything other than stare at me with a look I'd never seen before.

"For God's sake, Bruce, please say something. Cursing me out is better than this silent treatment and the look you're giving me. You know that I adore you and this whole scenario has gotten out of hand, but everything I've done is because I care; despite the fact that I'm a nosey, interfering bitch."

Bruce continued to pace around, but suddenly he grabbed me, kissed me with fervency, then looked at me with another look that I knew so well.

"Molly, my darling, it's just so disturbing to know that it well might be my mother's remains that are sitting in a police lab. It has hit me hard. I don't want to dwell on the worst possible outcome, but I have to face reality. It chills me to think that my father may be involved."

I tried to lighten the moment just a bit with, "If only Brandy were not such a curious dog. I knew from the moment I met him that we had a lot in common."

Bruce took my hand, a tentative smile on his face, and led me upstairs without any need for words. I think the stress of everything made our lovemaking all the more intimate and in effect dissipated that negative tension. Eventually Bruce said that he was starving, and not for me this time! I said that I'd fix us a tray and bring it up. I went downstairs stark naked and in a much happier frame of mind. I threw some edibles together plus the essential wine and proceeded cautiously up to our love nest, not feeling quite as relaxed as I thought I'd be.

Welcome to reality, Molly, I said to myself, as I told Bruce to move over and make room for the tray. He budged, but barely, and we both caught the tray as it was about to fall on the floor. Laughing hysterically, we replaced it and quietly ate and drank. Once we'd finished our snacky meal, Bruce pecked me on the cheek, sprung up, put the tray on the sideboard/dresser, and started fiddling with the sofa. He turned around with a severe look on his face and told me that the beading was crooked on the sofa.

"What on earth are you talking about?" I said, trying hard not to laugh. "How sloppy of me, darling. I'm sorry."

"Don't be so cavalier about it," he said peevishly.

I slammed my glass on the tray and burst into tears as I went downstairs, tray in hand. Thank goodness, we'd had sex, because he, or I, sure as heck wasn't getting any more for a while. I took Brandy out for a pee, grabbed a blanket, and decided to sleep on the sofa all night. *Wow! Our first real spat.*

At first, I slept fitfully, thinking about the gruesome discovery and where it might lead us. I doubled my resolve to see the investigation through to the bitter end, and if Bruce decides not to marry me, then it just wasn't meant to be. I finally fell into a deep sleep only to be awakened by a rod poking at my backside. Evidently, I had not taken up the whole sofa. So much for celibacy. My front turned to his and we engaged in sex until I faked an orgasm, so I could return to sleep, which I did until nearly ten the next morning. I awoke to the aroma of coffee, a flower, and a lovely note that made me feel that we'd make it to the altar (well, to beach sand anyway).

He was long gone, which I thanked the lord for; as I knew Bri would be contacting me at some juncture. I'd no sooner emptied my head of the negative vibes floating up and down my body when the phone rang. It shook the heck out of me. I rushed to get it, knocking into Bruce's antique dresser whilst stubbing my toe.

Answering the phone, I said, "Hello, Bruce Sully's residence".

"Molly it's me, Bri. The detectives would like to interview us on a more formal basis this afternoon, say around two, now that they have a better picture. Evidently the remains are definitely female and represent the approximate build of Bruce's mother. We'll be interviewed separately, of course. I also understand they are calling Bruce at work. Anyway, I'll no doubt see you at the station."

Shortly after we hung up, Bruce called to inform me that he was going to the police station in a half hour to answer questions and provide a DNA sample. Later in the morning he called back to tell me about the meeting with the detectives. He told them when he had last seen his mother, who she had been seeing and the address and phone number of his father in St. Lucia. Also, he wasn't aware of any females staying at his dad's home; although, he couldn't be sure about lady guests for drinks or staying overnight.

As for a DNA sample, they swabbed the inside of his mouth and informed him that the testing would be a high priority. Further, they asked for a key to his dad's home after they showed him a court order. It was their intent to do a thorough search of the home tomorrow.

Bri and I arrived at the police station at about the same time that afternoon. Bri was interviewed by Detective Clifton. Bri explained about looking for the former Mrs. Tully, but that there was no evidence of any foul play, so it was not yet a matter for the police, that is, until Brandy's discovery. We were just operating on my uneasy feelings.

Detective Andrews questioned me after I gave my summary of all that had transpired since I first met Mike Tully. That's when I told him about the photos and the scribbling on the back. I also revealed my interest in what happened to Bruce's girlfriend, who, however, was found alive and well by Bri. And, that revelation had made me feel that I was probably on a wild goose chase with Greta Folly.

In the parking lot, Bri and I shared thoughts on our sessions with the detectives. We didn't seem to have any discrepancies between our stories, which made sense, since we were being truthful.

However, Bri said, "You know, Mike is not the only possible suspect. As far-fetched as it seems, Bruce cannot be eliminated at this time. Greta's boyfriend, if there is one, also would be a person of interest."

I shouted, completely flabbergasted, "No way Bruce could be involved; it's not possible!"

"Of course not, but you have to understand the position of the police, who must look at all possibilities, until they find evidence to the contrary. Naturally, Mike Sully is the most logical candidate. At this point they still have to discover for certain just who the victim is, how long she has been dead, and by what means."

Bri and I wished each other a good evening. Then I returned to Bruce's home completely flustered. Bruce was naturally upset and had left work early to greet me, anxious to hear about the afternoon interviews and compare notes.

I outlined my session and what I could of their time Bri.

In reply, Bruce said, "We all seem to be on the same page. I will say that the detectives are anxious to bring their investigation to a close as quickly as they can, before it becomes a *cold case*. I believe they are trying to communicate with my dad, and to get him back here, if they can, without resorting to the extradition process."

The evening meal for us consisted of warmed leftovers and a little wine. We were mentally exhausted and retired to bed to comfort one another with gentle strokes using our hands, lips, and toes. And then we entwined our bodies.

Bruce went to work early to catch up on the projects that would bring him closer to being able to come to me in Florida. I straightened the house, drank too much coffee, waiting, I guess, for another shoe, or clue, to drop.

And so, it did. Bri called me in the morning to say, "The crime lab ascertained that the victim had evidently ingested ethylene glycol that was found in what remained of the blood and digestive system. DNA results should come shortly. The detectives are at the house now, no doubt very interested in the photos."

It was in two days that the police came back with the DNA test that we were dreading. Detective Clifton arranged to meet with Bruce at his home. Bruce insisted that Bri and I be present.

"I am sorry to have to inform you, Mr. Tully, that the DNA testing confirms that it is your mother, Greta Tully, who was found in your father's back yard."

Bruce let out a great sob, while I gasped and Bri hung his head in deep sadness for Bruce. We all expected the outcome, but the fact overwhelmed us all. Again, my mind seized on the thought, *our wedding is less than three months away. How can we reconcile that with his mother's death, most probably by the hand of his father?*

It was heartbreaking to see Bruce in such a shattered state. I pulled him to me on the sofa and caressed his face, offering my feeble expressions of support and understanding of his sorrow. Detective Clifton evidently felt it was not appropriate to go into any further details about the case, so he excused himself. Bri offered his solemn condolences and seemed to be somewhat uncomfortable intruding further on Bruce's grief and my consoling attempts, and said he should be going. Bruce in his grief did not respond, so I escorted Bri to his car to have a quiet conversation.

"Thanks, Bri, for being here and giving us you support. I'll call you in the morning and give you a heads up on what further, if anything, we might want you to do. May I settle with you a little later, when we have reached an end to this mess, or we decide on a continued retainer?"

"No worries, Molly, I'll just calculate everything when the case has simmered down. I look forward to your call and what's next on the agenda, if anything."

"Will do, Bri, and again, I can't thank you enough for everything you've accomplished. I'm remembering back to how I randomly picked you out of the yellow pages, when I was being my usual inquisitive self. Fate was definitely on my side finding you. Anyway, I hope you enjoy your evening. By the way, I assume I should call you at work."

"Sure thing, but call me any time after ten-thirty until around five. I have to run out and meet a prospective client between noon and one-thirty. I hope you have a decent night's sleep and that Bruce recovers quickly from the shock about his mom, and his dad."

"Bye, Bri", I replied.

When I returned, Bruce had already raised himself from the sofa and was walking back and forth, not looking dazed anymore, but rather that he was thinking hard.

"Molly, my mother's death is hard to take, but that it was my father who probably murdered her, gives me chills. But facts and circumstantial evidence make it an almost sure thing. Perhaps we should keep Bri on to keep in touch with the police on our behalf. I think they might be more forthcoming with him, since he speaks their lingo and they seem to appreciate his abilities. In fact, I'll call the detectives tomorrow and let them know we would like them to keep Bri advised of developments, or respond to his phone calls when feasible.

"My darling Bruce, I feel so awful for you, but I'm glad to see your having such a practical view of the situation. I've already told Bri I would call him tomorrow. Anyway, try not to dwell on it now. Let me fix you something to eat, and bring you a glass of wine.”

“A red would be nice and thank you for being you”, he said. Now to heck with all this crap, come here my sexy bride.”

Without hesitation, I obeyed my master and we had sex on the living room floor. The animal inside of Bruce let itself free and boy did we have rough sex. It was fast and furious, but it unleashed a ton of emotions that were bottled up inside of us. We looked at each other with nothing but adoration and from this moment on I knew that everything in my world was alright.

The next morning, I awoke to coffee on the dresser and a note from Bruce saying that he adored me. I didn’t even hear him leave, thankful that I’m a pretty deep sleeper. Brandy curled up beside me on the bed amidst the daily papers which weren’t particularly interesting. By the time I’d inhaled a day-old donut, drunk my third cup of coffee, and let Brandy out, it was well past ten-thirty and time to telephone Bri.

“Hello Bri, this is Molly. We’d like to confirm that we want you to stay on the case and act as our contact with the police when it makes sense. Bruce is making them aware of our wishes.”

Bri replied, “It will be my pleasure to continue working for you. Really, I have a profound interest in seeing this drama to its conclusion. I’ll be very fair in my charges and it’s not necessary to pay me a further retainer at this time. I’ll give the detectives a call towards the end of day. If there is anything to report, I’ll let you know.”

I said in closing, “Too bad you don’t live in New Smyrna Beach, Bri, because I’d love you to come to our wedding. You’ve become a real friend”

“As a matter of fact, Molly, I’ve got two weeks ‘vacation and it occurred to me that if you’re really serious about this, add me to the wedding list.”

“Fabulous, Bri! You are on our list of invitees, then.”

We said goodbye and I called Bruce and told him of my conversation with Bri.

Bruce then said, “That’s good about Bri’s continued involvement and his intention to join us on our wedding day.

I was able to contact Detective Andrews. They are okay with it, but when it suits them, of course. He did tell me that they were going examine the house, and particularly the photos you talked about and where they were located. Anyway, I've decided to take the day off tomorrow, but right now things are really hectic here. In fact, I'll be very late this evening so eat without me."

"I'm sorry I'll be dining alone, but I quite understand. See you later on this evening."

"I am delirious with great expectations to see, my bride-to-be", he said in a rather lecherous tone.

I chuckled and hung up. I knew what he had in store for me! I felt quite horny just thinking about what we would get up to later on tonight.

Bri called late in the day and said he had an update, suggesting he stop by around two in the afternoon, and that Detective's Andrews and Clifton were coming as well. I told him that would be a good time. *There must be a break in the case*, I told myself, but resisted the temptation to question Bri about it. Bruce should hear it first hand, and not from me.

I busied myself making gnocchi in a drop-dead cream sauce and sat in front of an atrocious reality show just to pass the time of day. Fifteen minutes of this crap was enough to make me crave large bourbon. It wasn't even five and I'd already eaten, let Brandy out and I was feeling excessively restless. There was one solution to appease these feelings and that was chocolate, after the bourbon naturally! I remembered I'd bought a box of Cadbury's milk chocolate and stuck it in the top of the kitchen cupboard. After downing about six caramels and a few cream ones my bad mood disappeared. Now I felt bloated but happy. Brandy was restless to go out. I combed my hair, threw on my walking sneakers, and decided a tour around the block would be really therapeutic for both of us. Sure enough, we enjoyed the quiet, warm streets that smelled of jasmine. We walked for about twenty minutes and Brandy was ready to head back. He knew the route and was tugging me in the direction of Bruce's. I decided that having taken this walk I deserved a few more chocolates. I had four more then put the box back on the top shelf. Secretive eating was wonderful! I would take a shower and wait for Bruce in the pre-bridal bed. Boy that sounds really hokey! I heard him come in around nine and yelled down to him that I was waiting for him. I asked him if he wanted something to eat.

"Just you", he immediately answered.

Before I knew, it he disrobed, hopped in and out of the shower, and stuck to his word. None of the past twenty-four hours had affected our desire for each other, which was a good thing. After we'd come down to earth, we lay together and talked about the weirdness of what has transpired so far and the pending visit in the morning.

"I've been trying so hard, Molly, to wrap my head around the possibility that my dad is an evil man. I don't feel close to him, but I never in my wildest dreams imagined him to be a killer."

"Bruce, don't torture yourself with such thoughts. We've just got to wait until the facts come out."

"You're right, darling, as always," he said as he fell into a deep sleep. It wasn't long afterwards that I joined him.

I loved our mornings. I jumped out of bed feeling happier than I probably should be, and said that I was going down to make us pancakes.

"Sounds perfect, darling," Bruce yelled back as I ran downstairs, coffee in hand, hotly pursued by Brandy wanting to go out. He wasn't too long in the garden, thankfully. He probably found his backyard dull compared to Mike's, and thank goodness for that. I made our pancakes, threw some syrup on them, and went back upstairs. Bruce ate quietly and quickly. I guessed he probably didn't eat much yesterday.

"Boy, the cakes are really good, or rather they were good, Molly", he said giving me that winsome smile.

"There's plenty of batter; I'll run down and fix you some more."

He ate the next batch almost as fast as the first, but declined a third helping. Now that he'd finished his, it was time to finish mine. I broke off a piece and gave it to Brandy who naturally downed it in one gulp. How anyone could be upset with this lovely doggy?

Bruce said, "I guess it's time to get dressed and see what the day has in store for us."

I put on a tight pair of grey leggings with my favorite tortoiseshell top, matching earrings, and quietly admitted to myself that I looked pretty hot. When Bruce stepped out of the shower my opinion was confirmed,

"You look sensational, Molly. We must have more investigations, if this is what it takes."

"Oh, so I don't usually dress well enough; is that it?"

"Now you're acting dumb. Not only are you beautiful, but it's the core of you that is doubly exciting. So now that I've cleared that up, let's go downstairs and make some fresh coffee for our visitors.

I diligently made a large pot of strong coffee, got out five cups and saucers, found a pretty china plate, and put a bunch of assorted cookies on it.

"Five cups and saucers, what the heck," Bruce exclaimed. "This isn't a tea party, is it?"

"No, darling; it's not," I said acerbically. "It's for Bri, the two detectives, you and me. I'm just trying to be a good hostess and make it a pleasant meeting."

"Oh, of course; forgive me. I'm just a little anxious", he admitted.

I sensed the tension in his voice, and hoped it would not get any worse as the day wore on. At least now we were almost at an end of this whole affair. We both prowled around the house like two caged tigers, not even tempted to have a bite for lunch. Finally, the dreaded sound of the doorbell sent both of us charging to open it, but Bruce did take a step back to allow me the honors of welcoming our visitors.

"Hello Bri, Detectives, Clifton, and Andrews", I said ushering them into the foyer in that order.

They greeted us in return. Bruce led them into his living room and I brought the tray of coffee and cookies, and gingerly put it on the coffee table. The cups, saucers, spoons, and condiments had already been laid out. Not being the upmost hostess, I did ask them to fix their own coffee, and offered tea if they wanted it. All were coffee drinkers, thank goodness.

"Let's cut to the chase, if you don't mind", Bruce said solemnly. "It's not exactly exciting thinking that one's father might be a murderer, so the sooner you tell me just what your findings are, the sooner we can get this whole ugly mess sorted out, and the better off we'll be."

"Alright then", said Bri, "But rather than hear it from me, the detectives will tell you their observations and decisions on proceeding with the case. I'll fill you in on the details I was able to glean about your mother."

Detective Andrews started, "First of all, you realize that your mother was probably fatally poisoned by ethylene glycol. The coroner did find a tiny fracture of the skull after a full autopsy, but he did not think the blow would have been fatal. Death may have been about a year ago, based upon empirical evidence. Of course, you know DNA comparisons positively identified your mother. To add to that, one our junior detectives located her dentist and brought in her old dental records. She was also identified by that method to corroborate the DNA testing."

I nervously watched Bruce tear up. My heart was breaking into so many pieces that I wished briefly that I hadn't started this investigation, but reality kicked in and I knew I had done the right thing.

Bri said, "Molly, I had said there was a possibility of a boyfriend being involved, if there was one. I had started inquiries to see if what Mike said to you and Bruce was true. Yes, there was a Philip Glaston and he did die of a heart attack before her estimated time of death. Bruce, I can only now confirm that he bequeathed your mother considerable money, and that he had prepaid for an apartment in his name, which she used after his death. The apartment manager and tenants did not see any man, or woman, enter the premises after Mr. Gaston's death. Your mother was frequently away, so there was no definite timeline as to when she was last seen."

Detective Clifton continued, "We strongly believe from the circumstantial evidence that your father, Mike Sully, is guilty of murder. However, until proven guilty he is our prime suspect. We'll have to arrest your father, and to do that we need an extradition order for St. Lucia authorities, in order to have him arrested and released to our custody.

Andrews added, "We have not contacted him for fear of his fleeing elsewhere, if he feels threatened by us. Please don't let on to your father, if you make contact with him. Quite frankly, we don't understand why he would leave his home and backyard for others to explore, accidentally or otherwise. But people don't always react rationally, for many reasons."

Darling Bruce looked as if the bottom was falling out from under him, and it was partly my fault.

"I feel so responsible for all this," I said bursting into uncontrollable tears. "If only Brandy hadn't dug the bones up and if only I hadn't been so nosey all this would never have surfaced."

"Are you kidding me", Bruce said still holding me. "Don't you think I've been eaten up for the longest time wondering what happened to my mother, and even Valerie's disappearance seemed a trifle odd to me. I'm glad that my father can be brought to justice, if he is guilty. Quite frankly, I think he is."

Sensing the meeting had become so personal between Bruce and me, Andrews and Clifton excused themselves, saying it was necessary to get on with the extradition paperwork. Bri, too, felt it was time for him to leave. Bruce ushered them out, thanking them for their efforts to explain where they stood in solving his mother's murder.

We mutually agreed that a little wine would fortify us, while we sat on the sofa to unwind. We finished a whole bottle rather quickly before heading back out to the kitchen to forage for some real food. But then I broke down, yet again despising myself for this catastrophe and the strain it had caused us. I guess my wailing touched a chord as Bruce grabbed me and told me to stop crying immediately. He gave me *the look*, which I knew only too well. From crying and feeling ghastly, I suddenly felt loved and very horny. What followed was the wildest sex we'd ever had on the kitchen counter. It seemed the tension we'd been feeling was totally channeled into our deep desire and love for each other. I know now more than ever that besides an immense sexual attraction for Bruce, I admired and respected him deeply, and knew that we could get through all of this ugliness together.

While I was straightening the counter, Bruce said, "Well, honey, what say we grab a bite to eat and head upstairs? The bed appeals to me more than the living room right now."

My mouthed dropped at being called *honey*. I disliked being called that, so once I set him straight, he reverted to plain *darling*.

"I'm with you on that idea, Bruce. I'll make us a couple of ham sarnies accompanied by some old-fashioned fruitcake I bought a couple of days ago and meet you upstairs."

"Sounds fabulous, but what's a *sarnie*?"

"That's British vernacular for sandwich", I replied.

Good to know! I'll see your highness in our love boudoir," he said with a grin.

Amazing what love making could do for the human spirit. Once in bed with the tray of food, we settled in like a very comfortable couple who'd been together forever.

"Molly, I've been thinking; since the police have the investigation in hand, and since I have Friday and Monday off, why don't we hive off to Harbor Springs? It's a little over five hour's drive away on the north shore of Little Traverse Bay, north of here on what is called the Upper Peninsula. I haven't been up there since I was a child, but the scenic ride through the tunnel of trees is magnificent. It's a perfect spot for us, as it's small and we could really have a mini vacation. What say you?"

"I say it sounds too good to pass up such a relaxing time for both of us, and for you in particular, darling. If we stayed here we'd probably end up getting antsy with each other."

"That's settled then", Bruce said and added in humorous fashion, "Of course, we'll be taking Brandy, the *Curious Cur.* He needs a break too. I'll get right on it and find a pet friendly hotel for three nights. I'll also let Bri know where we'll be and have him inform the detectives.

Oh, yes, I vaguely remember going to the Thorn Swift Nature Reserve up there. I know you'll love it."

 We proceeded to eat our pieces of cake in record time, and then leaped out of bed with renewed enthusiasm.

"I forgot to mention, there are some interesting stores and a farmers' market in Harbor Springs, from what I've been told," he said.

Picturing our pending trip as a pre-honeymoon holiday, I walked around with the gait of a teenager. *You one lucky broad,* I told myself.

"What would you like to do for the rest of the day, Molly?"

"Well, we could go for a long walk with Brandy, which will invigorate us all. What do you think about going out for dinner? I know that we are going away Friday, but since you took the day off, why not spoil ourselves. After all, this is my holiday time."

"I think that's a great idea, as the busier we are the less we'll dwell on the reality that you, my darling girl, might be marrying the son of a murderer."

"Oh, for heaven's sake, Bruce, no more negative thoughts. This is your day off."

We put the leash on Brandy to begin our walk. It was the most beautiful late afternoon. The temperature was in the low eighties and the flowers lining the city streets were in full bloom. How could anyone not feel high on life in this setting? We walked at a pretty swift pace down streets that I'd never been down before, or at least if I had, I didn't remember them. We walked about three miles in total until Brandy was lagging and obviously dying to get back and curl up in his bed. Now that's a thought, but having had some good sex earlier, I wasn't sure either of us would be up to another romp. Wrong! We stayed in bed until almost seven when our stomachs started to growl. We returned to the local steak house, which didn't disappoint us. Anyone who saw us devour our steaks would think we had not eaten in days. Sex and long walks certainly make for a healthy appetite.

"That was so yummy, Bruce. What a perfect way to end what has been a roller coaster day."

"You better believe it. If you don't mind, let's go straight home as I have a very early start tomorrow. Oh, I have very good news that I totally forgot to tell you about. I guess with all this drama that's hit us, it kind of took the back burner."

"What is it, Bruce? I can hardly wait to hear."

"I received a letter from Cape Canaveral confirming my starting date as August first, but the real highlight of it is that they went well over my salary demands, which translates to my making two thirds more than I make now."

I screamed with delight, hugging my future husband as we undressed for bed.

Bruce was gone when I woke up, but that was fine. I had plenty to occupy myself with, beginning with sorting out my clothes for Friday. I decided to walk Brandy to my favorite diner on the corner for a waffle and eggs. Life was pretty good, well more than plain good. It was bloody marvelous, if you discounted the reality of murder that lay upon our shoulders.

Once back from the diner I'd call Jen at work and give her an update. The diner never failed to produce the best breakfast that I'd had in Dearborn and the best part was that I was allowed to bring Brandy. Fortunately, he slept the entire time whilst I ate. The owners recognized me, which was heartwarming and made me feel at home. Next time I came in I'd be chattier and ask their names, but for now I'd content myself with anonymity. As soon as I got back I called Jen, but she didn't answer her phone, so I left her a message asking her to call me back anytime for the rest of the day. I was feeling very restless, so my decision was to do a major clean of Bruce's house and prepare a few good dishes to put in the freezer. I felt quite good after about three hours of wielding a vacuum and bending and stretching more than I knew I was capable of, plus I was cooking enough dinners for five nights. Bruce would have something to pull out and heat up with little effort, after I left for Florida. My food preparation was interrupted by the phone ringing.

"Hi, Molly, what gives?"

"Hello, Jen, I'm not sure where to begin, but it's as I suspected all along. The remains were those of Bruce's mother, as ascertained by DNA and dental records. As for the method, it seems ethylene glycol was the poison of choice. Now I feel dreadful, yet vindicated in my suspicions. The prime, and only, suspect is Mike Sully, Bruce's father. There is little doubt he did it. Bruce has accepted that it was his dad, but Mike, of course, would have to have his day in court before being convicted. It's tough on Bruce, but he wants justice for his mother. The police are in the process of extraditing Mike.

"Molly, don't put the onus on yourself, for goodness sake. You knew that once Brandy started sniffing around and you dug through all the old photos, your investigative antennas would kick in and there would be no going back. I'm sure Bruce will feel much better when he has permanent closure on the death of his mother. And so will you. It will be a new beginning for both of you."

"Thanks for your support and understanding, Jen. But enough about the grim circumstances here in Dearborn. The upbeat news is that Bruce and I are driving to a place called Harbor Springs on the Upper Peninsula of Michigan for a long weekend. Now on the romantic side, what's with you and Charlie?"

"Nothing much new really, but we are definitely in it for the long haul. Neither one of us has brought up the subject of marriage or living together. I'm sure in time we'll live together, but for now we're content to be just as we are. I'd love to natter on; however, I've got to get back to work, unlike a certain person I know who has two weeks holiday."

I chuckled and said, "Right! Some holiday this has turned out to be. I'll talk to you next Monday, Jen, and thanks for being you and for all the great advice you've given me."

"Girlfriend, it's a two-way street. You are my best friend and I'm so lucky. I've got to dash. Enjoy your Harbor Springs getaway."

Before I had time to say anything else, she'd hung up. I felt in a really upbeat mood and ready to face another day, or at least the rest of this one. Bruce called to say that he'd be back around nine in the evening, and was terribly apologetic, but in light of taking off Friday and the following Monday, he had an important project to finish.

He concluded in a deliciously wicked tone, "Don't fix dinner because we're ordering food to be delivered. See you later, Miss Molly; hopefully you'll be awake to greet me".

"I'll do my best. In the meantime, I'll keep the home fires burning."

He mumbled something which I didn't catch and hung up before I could say goodbye. I'm sure he was working his butt off to clear his workload enough to spend four days with me.

I was not unhappy to have a quiet early evening alone, so I curled up on the sofa with Brandy. Hunger pangs made me demolish a small block of cheddar cheese. As I munched, my mind flashed back to a comment my mother used to make, *if you're going to indulge then go big.* Golly we'd had some feasts together. In times of tragedy Mum would always buy my favorite sugar-coated bonbons accompanied by creamy coffee. "Where are you now, Mum?" I cried out. "You left me at too young an age."

I sprung up to let Brandy out for a quick tinkle. Back inside, he ate his food and settled in his bed for the night. I cleaned up the kitchen and climbed the stairs to bed. Sleep came rather quickly and before I knew it, the smell of coffee jolted me awake. Heck, I hadn't even heard Bruce come in last night. I rolled over and he wasn't in bed beside me. I went to the dresser to find a note saying that I looked so peaceful that he didn't want to disturb me, so he slept downstairs with Brandy. Also, he needed an early start, expected to be back around five, and would make it up to me.

I could hardly wait for his return. Today I decided to sort out my wardrobe and generally indulge myself, after Brandy and I went to breakfast. I put his leash on and strolled to my diner. This time the owners introduced themselves to me. I didn't fully catch their names, but gleaned they'd emigrated from Greece some thirty odd years ago. I introduced myself and Brandy, and ordered pancakes. Their being from Greece made me wonder why they left such a picturesque country. But I didn't know them and who was I to wonder. I wasn't living in Europe myself, though Greece was a lot sunnier and warmer than the British Isles. The pancakes were, as usual, to die for and Brandy enjoyed the crumbs. I boxed up the remainder of my brunch, and headed back to the house. No matter how hard I've tried to feel totally comfortable here, I cannot. I pray that Bruce sells his house after we get married. I really wouldn't care if I ever came back here, particularly in light of current events. The day was spent organizing my clothes, reading, going on another walk with Brandy and fiddling around to bide my time before Bruce got back. He called to say he'd be back around six and that he was bringing back left-over pizza from lunch.

"There'll be plenty for the two of us, my darling" he assured me.

When Bruce returned home, we weren't as passionate as one might have expected we'd be. Nevertheless, he kissed me with the hunger of a lion just released from his cage, then pulled back, got two plates out, divided the pizza and poured us wine, pointing upstairs. *No kitchen counter, it wasn't your turn tonight to be used in the non-traditional way!*

"I'd better let Brandy out, darling, so I'll see you upstairs. I won't be a jiff", I said.

Brandy did his thing, didn't linger, and came back into the house to give me a wonderful slobbery kiss, and fell into his bed. He wasn't the only one tired from the day's activities. I put the tray on the dresser after Bruce and I made short work of the pizza. He beckoned to me with that killer smile and what we did next lasted longer than I expected.

"I adore you, Molly", he said when we had returned to planet Earth.

"Likewise, darling. You're my only thing."

He smiled, rolled over, and closed his eyes, asleep. I lay there in a pool of delicious sweat and closely followed him into a deep slumber.

We woke up to the morning with great enthusiasm, realizing that we were heading out the door for three glorious days away from here. We enjoyed a breakfast of cereal fruit, and coffee, naturally.

"Have you got all your clothes together, Molly? I have yet to pack my stuff, but it shouldn't take long."

"Yes, I'm good to go. All I have to do is put everything in a suitcase. Oh, darn it, I forgot about Brandy. We are taking him with us, aren't we?"

"You mean you'd forgotten that I said I'd book somewhere that was pet friendly. I guess your mind isn't fully on the job at hand, is it?"

"Well there have been many extenuating circumstances, but, of course I remember. Otherwise, we would have organized to leave him with Nick and Sally. I'm just testing to see if you remembered. Now we've got that settled, what time are we leaving to go to Harbor Springs?"

"I thought we'd head out around nine-thirty, he answered. "I'm off to pack now."

I'd cleaned the house yesterday, so all we had to do was set the burglar alarm, make sure we had enough food for Brandy, throw his bed and our luggage in the trunk, and head out the door. I had no clue how long it took us to get to Harbor Springs, since I slept most of the way. The hotel Bruce had booked for us was on one of the main streets of this delightful, laid back town. The name escapes me, but it was pet friendly. The room was adequate, not luxurious for sure, but had enough space to put Brandy's bed in one corner. It had a king size bed which was great, but the room was lacking in atmosphere. We'd create our own.

"Sorry that it's so utilitarian", he said.

"Bruce, we're not going to spend hours in here, so no big deal. Our honeymoon suite shall make up for this in spades."

"But for now, let's put any grim thoughts aside and enjoy these few days away. First of all, food!" he exclaimed. "Where would you like to go?"

"You're asking me where to eat when I don't even know the place? I am going to be led around Harbor Springs by you, my tour guide."

He replied, "I haven't been here since I was a boy, but I did pick up some brochures in the lobby. I also did a little research on the internet while at work."

We were still sitting on the bed looking at brochures, when Brandy jumped in between us and started his wet kiss routine. I got the giggles, and Bruce guffawed, to the point that Brandy was jumping all over us in his own way of being silly. Finally, we calmed ourselves and Brandy down. We fed him, took him for a walk around the block, and then settled him in the room to take his afternoon snooze. We'd be sure to be back in a couple of hours.

Bruce kissed me lightly on the cheek as we took off for a late lunch.

"Let's head to the main street, Molly. It's been years since I was last here, so I'm sure that it's changed a lot."

"Great, Bruce, I'm ready to hit Harbor Springs' *High Street.*"

He smiled indulgently at my English terminology. The main street was quite enchanting. I felt as if I were in England. The road was cobblestoned with sidewalks that were smooth for walking on. It had twinkling lights hanging from all the trees. It was very festive, if a tad over commercialized, but nevertheless presented a very pleasant atmosphere.

We entered the first café that served breakfast and lunch. It was open until three in the afternoon. Unfortunately, it turned out to be less than stellar by a good margin. But who knew? We filled our bellies with mediocre pancakes, overdone eggs and watery coffee, eating somewhat faster than usual, to be done with the place.

"Sorry about the meal", Bruce lamented over his last sip of coffee.

"It's not your fault, good sir. Neither one of us knew what it'd be like. We'll remember not to come back here again, ever!"

Bruce paid the bill and left a minimal tip. We thanked them with bleak smiles as we left.

"Did you want to look at that famous consignment store now, Molly?"

"To be honest, I'd rather do that tomorrow, because when I shop, I shop."

He gave me a knowing smile and said, "Let's walk down the street, a good ways, checking out stuff. We may even find a decent restaurant for this evening."

"Great, let's do it" I replied.

Despite a dreadful late breakfast, I felt wonderful. This part of town was quaint and quite sophisticated. About three blocks down, I spotted a couple of high-end consignment stores.

"Wow, Bruce I've suddenly changed my mind about shopping. How about you continue investigating down the street whilst I take a quick look?"

"I might have guessed you'd change your mind, and that's fine. I'll come back in about half an hour. That should give you time to do some damage."

He laughed out loud as he disappeared down the street. The first store I hit was wonderful, very retro. I found three 1940's style blouses and four pairs of skimpy tights in black, purple, orange and pink.

"Thanks very much", I said to the rather tawdry assistant who looked as if she belonged in a low-end gentleman's club rather than in this quiet, lovely town.

"You're welcome; come again", she said, abruptly turning her head away from my smile.

"If I ever get back to Harbor Springs, I'll be sure to come in", I said in an exaggerated fashion.

I guess she finally heard my accent, because she asked me, in an excited voice, if I had contacts in England, as she assumed that was where I lived. She was planning on moving over there as soon as possible, but knew no-one.

"As a matter of fact, I haven't lived in England for ages, but if you are really that interested in going, I can stop in before I head back to Dearborn. I have a cousin who lives in the Soho area of the London, which, judging by the way you dress, should suit you perfectly. By the way, my name is Molly Thomas. What is your name?"

"Oh, I'm Lucy Skinner, but my friends call me Luce Goose."

"I'll come by over the weekend, Luce Goose, and thanks for your help."

Help was hardly what she had given me, but I surprisingly liked her and really wanted to give her a break.

It also helped dilute my guilt over the grief that I had stirred up for Bruce. My momentary thoughts were interrupted by the welcome sight of Bruce opening the door and asking me if I'd finished shopping.

"Yes, darling, it's been very successful", I said, as I waved goodbye to Lucy and struggled out the door with my bargains.

"I can see that. Here, let me take those bags", which he did, as he also planted a kiss on my right cheek.

"I've been successful, too! Found us a charming restaurant that serves steak and lobster, which I know are your favorites."

"Super! I'll wait to tell you about Lucy, a clerk in the store who sort of waited on me. But right now, I'd really like to retreat to the motel for a nap", I said, while giving him my lousy attempt at a wink.

We did do some napping after I'd recounted my tale of Luce Goose, and Bruce had told me of his long walk. Otherwise, we did what most lovers do. It was glorious and steamy, and I openly marveled at Bruce's stamina.

"I'm making up for the lost time. Please don't expect anything more from me today. That means I can have a few wines and not feel pressured to please my lady again."

"Your request is granted, my good sir", I said, then both of us roared with laughter, before promptly falling asleep for a few hours.

It was a beautiful, clear evening, so we energized ourselves to get dressed up, in a very good mood. I'd brought along my red satin pants outfit that went admirably with my red hair.

Bruce remarked on seeing me in my finery, "You look utterly amazing. No, expand that to drop dead beautiful, sexy, and mine to marry."

He kissed me lightly as we said goodbye to Brandy, settling him for the night and set out for dinner, which turned out be delicious. However, on the walk back to the motel, we inexplicably got into a rather heated discussion over all that had happened and was yet to happen concerning his mother and father. I burst into tears and told Bruce I'd see him back at the motel and I ran all the way back feeling miserable, to fall on the bed devastated. It was our life in the raw, but a little too raw for me right now.

He entered the room soon after and laid himself beside me to hold me tight.

"I'm so sorry, Molly, really I am, but at times I'm not good at dealing with this mess. I just took it out on you, when it's not your fault."

"I'm not so good at handling it either, and still blame myself", I replied.

He assured me that it was a rightful discovery that I had made with Brandy. We just needed to deal with it objectively. He certainly would from now on.

Brandy interrupted us in an effort to his need for the outdoors. Bruce leashed him and left. I didn't stay awake for their return. I guess my mind wanted to escape the unfortunate part of our evening.

In the morning, I woke up rather out of sorts. It could have been the wine, or dreading events to come. Bruce wasn't in bed next to me, neither was Brandy. Now I really felt alone. I turned over in bed and cried until I felt somewhat better. Suddenly the door was flung open and in breezed Bruce, followed by a very happy Brandy. Bruce had two cups of coffee in his hands, plus donuts and a large bunch of pink and white daisies.

"Oh, Bruce, you're amazing. Thank you, darling. I feel so horrible about my childish behavior last night."

"Your childish behavior? You had every right to behave even more childlike than you did, because I acted like a thoughtless schoolboy. Anyway, we should put last night behind us and recognize that we are under more stress than we bargained for. In spite of the stuff going on with Dad, it is wonderful that I'm changing states and moving in with you. Then we are getting married! So, let's put all the drama on the back burner until we have to on our return to Dearborn", he said, as he gave me his winning smile.

I nodded in agreement, whilst munching on a chocolate coated donut, to be washed down with delicious coffee.

I wasn't about to mention that my least favorite flowers are daisies, a petty detail right then. Freesias and carnations, except red, were my favorites. Any flowers are better than no flowers; my mother and I always called them *divine*, when we encountered them alongside the roads we travelled in Spain and France, especially the large sunflowers.

I mapped out a plan for the rest of the day. It included a trip to the beach with another stroll down Main Street, starting off with a visit to Luce. She was there looking even more eccentric, yet quite exotic and beautiful. She hugged me and thanked me for my cousin's address and gave me a pair of leggings as a thank you.

"I don't need anything, Lucy. I've already e-mailed my cousin Ian who, along with his wife, will welcome you into their home whenever you decide to take the plunge."

"You hardly know me, but you're willing to do this for me, Molly? This is awesome. I barely slept last night thinking about my new adventure."

"I'm sure you didn't. I checked with your boss and she vouched for you, so on that note, keep me posted and the best of British luck to you. The weather is quite dreary in winter, but considering where you live now it'll be like summertime. Stay in touch and thanks again for the leggings."

I left feeling quite good that I could help someone do something with their life.

The beach was more like a cove. It was quaint and scenically magnificent, but was very crowded, so we decided to take a short walk then drive to a local winery or two. The *short walk* turned into almost two miles and I thought Brandy was going to conk out as we neared the final quarter mile mark from the car. But we all made it, feeling marvelously invigorated by the fresh air. Brandy jumped into the car and fell asleep instantly. Next stop was a local winery. How bad could that be? We stopped at one place - its name escapes me - where the wine was low in sulfites, and to my liking. We bought a case of the red and decided that was enough wine buying for the day.

We had already become staid in our ways, and decided to go back to the same restaurant as last night. The meal, as before, was delicious and this time we cooled it with our wine intake. We wanted to have sex later. Back at the room Bruce tended to Brandy's needs, and then we spent much of the night making raucous love.

Another day of excitement dawned. We decided to go to the Hramiec Hoffman Fine Art and Craft studio. We were not disappointed. A large carved robin graced the outside of the gallery and inside was a mélange of wonderful paintings of mixed media and some students' paintings.

We really enjoyed the artwork, but were not in the mood to purchase anything, other than a few post cards.

By the time we'd walked around town, had fish and chips at a place near the water, it was time to head back to the room. We watched some tele, drank some low sulfite wine, and called it a night. We'd agreed that we'd leave around ten the next morning and flipped a coin as to who would take Brandy out. I lost!

Mornings were most definitely a superb part of the day. Waking up to sex, coffee, and Brandy nuzzling between us was beyond awesome. Today we couldn't linger as we had to pack up and head back to Bruce's.

Back in Dearborn, the weekend flashed before my eye like a dream. It had been a terrific respite from the everyday life. It was back to work on Friday for me, which I was much looking forward to. We didn't talk very much once back at Bruce's other than to decide about the mundane necessities of life.

"I think I'll make lasagna, darling", I said.

He looked at me with a sudden guilty expression, and replied, "Damn! Don't be mad, but I've just remembered that I promised to swing by work if we were back in the afternoon. I have a big meeting tomorrow and we've still got a few matters to finish up. It's all very boring, but necessary."

"That's all right, my love. I understand and I'm happy you are as enthusiastic about your job as I am about mine."

"I bet you're itching to get back to those four-legged friends, Miss Molly", he said and gave me that killer smile which led to a sex-filled rumble on and around the sofa.

"Well, I didn't expect that, you lecherous brute," I said, grinning as I got dressed again.

"You are one extremely desirable Brit, so I decided to seize the moment," he said as he donned his shirt and elegant tie. "See you around seven, my femme fatale", he said, as he turned to leave.

Onwards and upwards, I said to myself. Since it was lovely outside, I asked Brandy if he wanted to go for a walk. He enthusiastically barked in agreement. We trotted at a decent pace for half an hour down the familiar flower lined streets until Brandy was pulling on the lead to return.

"Okay, buddy, I'm done too, so let's go home."

There, I had said it, *home*. Maybe I've finally dispelled some more demons lurking in my head.

The answering machine was blinking. It was a call from Bri who wanted to meet with us the next day, Tuesday, possibly with a detective in tow. Well, we wanted progress, and here it possibly was.

Bruce got back around eight, having phoned me to say he was running late. We briefly discussed the meeting with Bri, ate around nine, and headed upstairs, somewhat tense thinking about tomorrow. I'd said I'd call Bri around nine to fix a time for the troops to come around. I'd decided, after talking it over with Bruce, that I'd call Sally afterwards for some moral support. It was an effort to get a good night's sleep. After tossing and turning until around one in the morning, Bruce got up to retrieve two sleeping pills. Thankfully, they worked for both of us.

The morning was not exactly delicious, like most mornings. We arose at seven, dressed, and trundled downstairs. I suggested Bruce take Brandy out whilst I got coffee and breakfast. Bruce's foray outside lasted long enough for me to fix eggs, bacon and toast, while the coffee was brewing. I called Bri after breakfast and set a time of about eleven this morning for the meeting here.

I relayed the information to Bruce, who said, "Well, it's better to get this ordeal over earlier rather than later".

A perfunctory dusting and mopping by me made the place gleam. Afterwards, I yelled out that I was going to take a shower and change into something more presentable. Despite my rational being, I felt like a guillotine was about to come down on me. Bruce followed me for his shower. After dressing, we both looked very professional.

The doorbell ominously rang at eleven. Bruce ushered in Bri, accompanied by Detective Andrews. I had no coffee or juice for them, as Bri had told me over the phone that the meeting would be brief, and not to bother. We said our hellos and then Detective Andrews asked to speak.

"First of all, I wanted you to know personally that we have still been looking for other possible suspects."

Bri chimed in, "I have, too, in my spare time and on my own dime."

Andrews continued, "There have been no further developments along that line, by us or Bri. However, we neglected to tell you that we found a can of anti freeze containing ethylene glycol that was stored somewhat hidden in the garage. Interestingly, it had been opened, but only a relatively small amount was missing, but enough to be fatal to a human being. We have just found that its manufacture date was not that much before the estimated time of death of your mother."

Bruce, rather subdued, asked about progress the police were having with the extradition papers.

"Yes, I was getting to that", Andrews responded. "The document has been received by the authorities in St. Lucia and it will take a week or two from now to process. However, in a phone call with the local police, we were assured that your father would not be able to leave the island, and he is under fairly close watch. Once we have permission from their justice department, we'll be able to travel there, interview him, and ultimately bring him back under arrest."

Bruce said, "My father has a weak heart, and despite the fact that I don't particularly like him, that doesn't keep me from feeling desperate to preserve his life. Although, I am even more strongly desperate to see that my mother's killer is brought to justice."

I went over to Bruce, trying to comfort him the best I could.

The detective added, "We'll try not to be aggressive in our interview with your father in light of his heart condition. And, again, if you do have phone contact with him, don't advise him of the investigation. It would put him under a lot of strain, if he knew in advance we were coming for him. Of course, we are not too worried about him fleeing now."

We sighed and shook our heads acknowledging his comment and request. Bruce told Detective Andrews that we understood, and to please let him know when he'd be able to have a conversation with his father.

"Sure thing, Mr. Sully, and if there is nothing further I can tell you, I'll be off. However, I think Bri wants to have a word with you. Goodbye for now."

After Andrews left, Bri expressed his sincere sympathies and told us that he would not even think about any form of payment until after Mike's return and the dust had settled.

I said, "Thanks so much, Bri. You are a good friend, as well as a great investigator. Say, would you fancy a glass of merlot and some killer cheddar cheese."

"If you've got the time, I've got the palette", he said, with a straight face that turned to a smile at his own joke.

I went about pouring three large glasses of merlot, cut up chunks of cheese and threw a few crackers on a plate. I set the tray down on the living room coffee table. We chatted nervously about this and that, mostly news topics which idled away the best part of an hour.

Finally, Bri said, "Well, thanks much, Bruce and Molly, for your hospitality. If I hear anything, I'll give you a call."

I replied, "Thanks again, Bri, for everything. What luck to have tumbled upon such a wonderful private eye. You and I had an instant rapport from day one. Naturally, if I've gone back to New Smyrna Beach, call Bruce, who'll keep me posted on any developments. If necessary, I'll arrange for a leave of absence from work, should I be needed back here as a witness."

"That's good to know, Molly; let's hope it doesn't come that. But now I must be off. Take care and enjoy the rest of your time here together, you two. Don't forget, you can count on my being at your wedding." He gave a brown, toothy grin and left.

Oh, my God, the wedding. I couldn't see a white dress, warm sand with peach and white flowers right now. All I saw in my mind was a hangman's noose. I felt almost as low as I'd felt after my mother died. I didn't much care for Mike, but he was my future father-in-law, whatever way one sliced it. *Get over it Molly*, I told myself, pacing around the living room.

At my suggestion, Bruce had taken Brandy out for a walk. I felt he needed to clear his head too. I sat down on the well-worn sofa, closed my eyes, hoping to drift off. No such luck on that score, but I did rest my eyes for a time. Bruce returned about an hour or so later in better spirits, carrying a pizza box in his hand, along with a container of my favorite chocolate chip ice-cream.

"Yummy, darling; thank you so much. You couldn't have got anything better. Let's save the ice cream for much later. I'll open one of the reds to go with the pizza and to cheer us up."

We ate the pizza and got through the bottle of red in leisurely fashion.

After our meal, Bruce asked, "Do you want ice cream now, or shall we save it for later tonight?"

"Later tonight sounds good to me. The bed is calling us. We just need to quickly clean the kitchen."

I gave him my smile that he knew too well. We passed several hours making slow, but torrid love until we were physically and emotionally spent. We passed out until around ten.

"I'll go down and get the ice cream to cool off my sexpot", Bruce said, as he stumbled out from under the bed covers.

He was back in a jiffy and said there was a message on the answering machine, "Sally called and said to call her tomorrow at work".

I said that I would and proceeded to enjoy my frozen dessert. Having been sexually sated, I could devote all my attention to its creamy texture and the joy it gave to my taste buds. Bruce also did a number on his ice cream, slurping noisily away to demonstrate his enjoyment of the guilty pleasure. *Calories be damned*, I say!

Bruce said, after finishing his bowl, "Reality is setting in that you return in three days to New Smyrna Beach. We must definitely make the most of it to the hilt, my sweet pea."

I looked at Bruce askance and said, "Please don't call me that, darling. I'm not in to being called a flower".

"Sorry about that. Won't happen again - until the next time, anyway", he replied humorously.

 The morning wasn't much fun. Bruce was called to work on some super emergency job. I understood, but it still didn't make matters any easier. I was getting restless myself to get back to work, to see Jen and my beloved animals. Another day pottering around here with only Brandy for company didn't sit too well. Bruce said he'd be home around six, but was so distracted, that he left with barely a goodbye.

Mid-morning, I called Sally and fortunately she had a slack day and was able to talk. I filled her in on what had transpired. She suggested if we were free tonight that we all meet at our favorite steak place around seven-thirty. I willingly agreed, without asking Bruce. I'm sure he'd be happy to have a fun night out.

After talking to Sally, my mood improved. I took Brandy for a walk and a late lunch at our favorite diner. The omelet I ordered was delicious; however, the owners were on their holidays, so there wasn't the same jolly atmosphere. I didn't waste any time lingering, as I knew Brandy was eager to continue our walk. It really was quite enchanting to walk around these streets, but I still felt like a stranger. Come to think of it, even back in New Smyrna Beach I never felt one hundred percent at home. I suppose once a European, always a European. I adored my life in Florida, but there was a piece of my heart back in the British Isles, and especially in a Spain that my mother so dearly loved.

Once back at Bruce's, I called to let him know about our evening plans, then I wiled away the hours by cleaning house and reading until it was five-thirty and time for me to gussy myself up. I threw on a cute two-piece shocking pink outfit that I'd brought in Harbor Springs.

Bruce got back on time, and yelled up to see if I was ready. I shouted back that I was and ran downstairs to see him.

"Now I know one reason why I'm marrying you. You look beyond magnificent, but I happen to quite like your personality too", Bruce said; then he grinned, pinched my bum, and ran up to take a shower.

I'd arranged for us to meet Sally and Nick at the restaurant. We were too beat to walk, so as soon as Bruce was ready, we drove over and happened on a parking spot close to the restaurant.

It was exciting for me to see Sally again. We had struck up an instant friendship and it was rather sad that we would be living so far apart. But as she'd pointed out a while back, there was good enough reason for us to visit each other.

Our miscellaneous conversation flowed easily. It turned serious when Bruce filled them in on the sad situation regarding his father, Mike. Nick was pragmatic about the whole sordid affair, and confirmed what we both felt, that it was better to know than not to know. That said, we reverted to having a fun evening with a bit too much wine.

"Well, Molly, I guess this really is goodbye until the wedding", Sally said, hugging me as she teared up.

"I suppose it is, Sally, unless for some reason I'm called back to give evidence, once Mike is returned to the States. I'll call you next week."

I kissed Nick and quickly climbed into the car not wanting anyone to see me have a mild case of hysterics. Once home, we plodded upstairs, dead beat and emotionally drained.

The next morning coffee was brought up as usual, and it suddenly hit me that I was flying home the day after tomorrow.

"Darling, what's on the agenda for today?"

Bruce answered, "Well, how would you like a trip on the river, followed by dinner out? After all, it sure beats walking around here all day. We need major distractions to help avoid thinking about my dad, and mom."

"I agree, even though you're spoiling me, Bruce."

"You deserve it, so let's head out with Brandy for a late breakfast and a walk afterwards to tire him out."

I blew him a kiss as I threw on a black pair of shorts and a pink top. I looked good, and it didn't go unnoticed.

On the way to the café, Bruce asked, "Since you are so fascinated with facts, did you know that Michigan has the longest fresh water shoreline in the world?"

That's quite something; I didn't know that. I'll put that in my memory bank", I replied.

Breakfast was as good as ever, and Brandy lucked out with the leftovers. The owners were still away, so we didn't stay that long. We were all itching for fresh air. It was a pleasant stroll, until halfway home I suddenly felt a bit sick and suggested to Bruce that we might shelve the idea of going on the river.

"I'd rather be fit for dinner tonight, so if it's all right by you, I'd like to rest up this afternoon?"

"That's perfectly fine with me", Bruce replied. "I'm just sorry that you are feeling ill."

"An afternoon of chilling should do the trick, darling", I said.

I managed the stairs at Bruce's, threw my clothes on the dresser, and hopped into bed. The afternoon flowed into early evening. I felt so much better, but neither of us wanted to go out, so Bruce called the pizza place and ordered my favorite, which is with anchovies, mushrooms, and red peppers. One of us had to take Brandy out, so

Bruce gallantly threw on sweats and let him out for a quick pee break.

"I'm staying downstairs until our food arrives, Molly," he shouted up the stairs.

This was decadence that I was going to milk for all I could.

The pizza looked and tasted super, so much so, that we finished the entire pie. After letting our meal digest, a while, I took the tray with its remains downstairs to the kitchen. Upon my return, I found Bruce sitting up in bed with a rather large erection, accompanied by a sheepish grin. It was time for me to rise to *his* occasion, which I did, with great abandon. We didn't take long passing out.

I awoke around six-thirty the next morning with my mind whirring. One more day here, then back to reality. I was really ready to get back to work, but having to say goodbye to Bruce was something I was dreading, particularly since I would not be by his side if he experienced depression or received more disturbing news.

Since I woke up first, for a change, I crept down to make coffee, let Brandy out, and prepared a quick bite to take upstairs. There were four croissants in the freezer which would do the trick. Bruce was still sound asleep when I took up breakfast. I was thrilled for his late morning, because he'd been putting in long hours recently. I assumed that with the move, he was training someone else to take over before closing the door for good in less than two months. I'd already drunk two cups of coffee and had dunked the warm croissant in my coffee, before Bruce finally came to. He sat bolt upright and exclaimed how pissed he was for not being up first, since it was my last day here for a while.

"Bruce, it's fine, my darling man. You needed your rest and I'm thrilled that, for once, I can return the favor."

He had that smile on his face; the one that had won my heart after our first date. There was absolutely no getting away from the fact that I was head over heels in love with him. Nothing was going to get in the way of our wedding.

Then he said, "I thought that we could go for a ride later this morning and have a late, exclusive lunch somewhere. Since you're flying home tomorrow, I thought a fancy lunch would be better than dinner."

"That sounds marvelous," I replied with enthusiasm.

For a good bit of the morning, we lay cozily wrapped in each other's arms discussing our wedding and where we should go for our honeymoon.

"I'd like to go to Wales and show you where my mother was born, and then we could go on to London. The weather should still be decent. But if you have any other ideas, let's discuss it."

"Molly, I think that idea is perfect. I'm going to leave it up to you to book the flights, hotels etc., since it's in your neck of the woods. Of course, I'll lend a hand if necessary. I'm glad that we have settled on our honeymoon plans. Now all that remains is to get married. Is there any more coffee and a chance of another croissant?"

"There are two left and I'll make a fresh pot of coffee," I said as I took the empty tray downstairs.

I made the next pot of coffee extra strong, and headed back upstairs. I had two males to feed as Brandy had snuck up onto the bed.

"Okay, buddy, here you go", I said, breaking off an extra-large piece of mine.

This was beyond cozy and neither one of us was eager to move. Finally, around eleven we were forced to get up and let Brandy out.

"I'll hop in the shower, darling," I said, while Bruce threw on his sweats. Where did that expression hop in the shower come from? Perhaps it came from some ancient Easter celebration. Who knew? By the time we'd both got appropriately attired for a late lunch and settled Brandy, it was almost one-thirty.

"To be truthful, Bruce, I'd prefer a steak and fries over some ritzy place. Can't we leave that until another time?"

"Whatever you say, Molly, as I'm up for anything."

Bruce drove around parts of Dearborn that were totally unfamiliar to me. We happened upon a steak house that was rustic and quite romantic inside. We had forgotten about Mike, or at least if we hadn't, we did a darned good job of concealing our concerns. We were both too full for dessert, but ordered two crème caramels to go. All in all, a great late lunch and we still had the better part of the afternoon and evening ahead of us.

Our bubble burst rather rapidly upon returning. There was a message on the machine from Mike asking Bruce to call him as soon as he got in.

"Hi, Dad, so what's up? I'm sorry I haven't called you sooner, but Molly's been here for the past two weeks and we've been busy having fun and working on our honeymoon plans."

"No sweat, Bruce, I just wanted to touch base and tell you how great my new house is, or will be, once the mortgage and legal papers are signed. I can't wait for the two of you to see it."

"Right, Dad, me too," Bruce said, with a distraught look on his face, but nevertheless doing a good job of concealing his emotions.

Of course, we'd been more or less sworn to secrecy regarding the discovery of his wife's remains, the evidence gathered, and the resultant involvement of the St. Lucia authorities. The next days were going to be difficult with increasing tension.

"Well, son, nothing much else to report, other than I had a physical with a new doctor here, and he isn't too thrilled with my heart. I'm going in three weeks to have a battery of tests. On the other hand, I've met a few old geezers here whom I'm sure I'll be seeing more of. Am I ever glad I finally left Dearborn. Be sure to give my best to Molly and take good care of yourself, Bruce."

"Glad you're happy, Dad. In a couple of months, I'll be in New Smyrna Beach myself. Quite the end of an era, wouldn't you say?"

"Certainly, son, but life moves on and change is good. I must say bye for now. I'll be talking to you real soon."

"That was really tricky, Molly, not being able to say a word to Dad about anything."

"I know, darling, and I'm so very sorry for this unholy mess."

"It's just a reality we have to deal with. On a lighter note, what do you suggest for our agenda today?"

It was agreed to loaf around and read the papers, which we did until I jumped up and said that I had the urge to pack. I was finished in under half an hour for all but the last-minute stuff. My plane was at ten thirty-five in the morning meaning I didn't have to get up at the crack of dawn. Bruce would drop me off and carry on to work.

For dinner, we had a light snack and our guilty delight, the crème caramels. Then we headed up to bed to watch a corny movie. I woke up around five and couldn't relax enough to get back to sleep, so I crept downstairs and made a pot of coffee. I was deep in thought when I felt a pinch on my bum that startled me.

"Good morning, darling", I managed to say, turning around abruptly

"What's so good about it, Molly? You have to leave me yet again. Let's hope this is the last time you have to fly away without me."

"I'm sure everything will work out for us, my prince. I feel it in my waters. Here's a strong cup of coffee to jump start your morning."

"Thanks, my love", he said, then ran upstairs to get ready.

I felt quite sick with dread. I loathed flying, and each time it seemed to get harder for me to remain calm until I had touched down on the runway. Breakfast for us consisted of croissants with butter and jam. Between mouthfuls I said my tearful goodbye to Brandy, with an ardent promise of being with him again very soon. He was such a smart dog that I was pretty sure he knew I was leaving and cried in his doggy way.

We got to the airport in good time. Bruce knew that I disliked long goodbyes and agreed to my request.

"Go, darling, please", I said, as I started to cry. "I'll phone you tonight. Take care of yourself and Brandy, and don't work too hard."

I love you so much, Molly. Have a safe flight."

He gave me a sweet, soft kiss, and was gone.

I bought myself a large coffee and called Jen, who said, "About time I heard from you again. How about I pop over this evening? Charlie's out of town and I'm sure you could use a shoulder to cry on. I made a killer lasagna, so I'll bring it over. I'll be there around seven. The weather is perfect so perhaps we can resume our runs on the beach."

"Terrific, Jen. You're amazing. Can't wait to be home again and see you, hopefully this time to stay."

The flight was smooth and I slept through most of it. I didn't talk to anyone other than the usual flight attendants. On arrival, I went to the designated baggage carousel. Bruce had insisted on ordering me a cab, so after collecting my luggage, I found my driver. The ride home was quick, and quiet. The cabby wasn't chatty, thank goodness. I'd have enough of that later on.

It was great to be back. I went upstairs and unpacked before deciding coffee and a quick snack were in order. But first, I telephoned John to let him know I'd be at work as scheduled, and that I could come in tomorrow, if needed.

"Boy, will I be glad to have you back, Molly. I've been mighty busy. Hope your trip was fine. I would appreciate your working tomorrow, even though it's a Saturday."

"No problem, John. I'm really anxious to get back into the swing of things. I had a great time, mixed in with a lot of tension. Enough said for now, so I'll be in around eight-thirty with coffee in hand for you."

"You're the gal, Molly, so until tomorrow."

I could hear the enthusiasm in his voice. It was great to be so appreciated.

I spent the better part of the afternoon catching up on my mail. I paid all the outstanding bills, read a couple of magazines before deciding that I needed a quick nap. I woke up about half an hour before the alarm went off, which gave me time to dress up a bit before Jen came. I opened a bottle of our favorite dry white wine. I was really excited to see her. We were bloody lucky to have each other as friends. From the moment we first met, it was an instant clicking of personalities and I was certain that our friendship would endure. True to form she was on time. We hugged each other until the lasagna became too awkward for Jen to hold.

"I've missed you, Molly. It just isn't the same without you here. I often think that what it'd be like if you lived in Michigan full time, and it's not something I could take if it became a reality. Pour me some wine and throw this in the oven. Before I give you the mundane news from here, I'm dying to hear the scoop regarding Bruce's father."

Having filled her in on all the ghastly details about the case, I mentioned the wonderful mini vacation we'd had in Harbor Springs.

I went on to say, "In fact, I met a hippy shop assistant in one of the consignment stores who is going to England for a while, so I gave her my cousin's address in Soho. Anyway, I had days when I really liked it in Dearborn, but I very much missed your company, my fabulous job, and our familiar beach. So, I'm delighted to be back, despite being away from the love of my life. Now tell me about Charlie. How's that relationship going?"

"Molly, I'm happy to say nothing has changed. We are definitely going to tie the knot, but neither of us is in a rush. Frankly, I sort of like the fact that he travels a fair amount. I've been alone so long that the idea of having someone around all the time is hard to envision. Taking it slowly suits us both. He's kind, very thoughtful, and very sexy. Don't worry, when we become officially engaged, you'll be the first to know."

"Your life is so uncomplicated, Jen. I got Bruce and me in a right mess, but upon reflection we have to deal with reality. *Mustn't grumble*, as my granny used to say."

We chuckled, chugged down some more wine until the oven bell dinged, when I bellowed, "Chow time!"

I'd totally forgotten that Bruce said he'd call around eight and it was almost eight-thirty. He'd probably got caught up in some project at work and wasn't paying attention to the time. He would call when he could, so I wasn't too worried. We finished off the lasagna, chatting about work, the wedding, and goings on in town.

Nine-thirty was upon us and Bruce still hadn't phoned, so I asked, "Jen, do you mind if I give Bruce a quick call?"

"Go for it, I'll clean up whilst you're doing that." He wasn't home, so I left him a message to call me up until midnight.

"He's not there, so he's probably doing an all nighter, knowing him. And he's wound up like a tight ball of wool over his dad. I don't blame him one bit, but I've spent so many hours feeling immensely guilty that I'm burned out and have to focus on our wedding and living my life as close to normal as possible."

"You're right, Molly, so towards that sense of normalcy in your life, how about dinner out and a run on the beach tomorrow evening?"

"That's a great idea. What time, since I'm working tomorrow?"

Jen replied, "How about I meet you at five-thirty before dinner? We won't be too sweaty afterwards, so we can grab a hamburger."

"Terrific, Jen, and thanks for bringing the lasagna over and for your friendship." "My extreme pleasure, girl friend", she said, with that twinkle in her gorgeous deep brown eyes. "See you tomorrow and hope you make contact with Bruce."

Jen, as usual, roared off in her inimitable race girl fashion. I called Bruce and luckily, he was home.

He offered his apologies with, "I'm so sorry, darling, but I got tied up in a long, rather tedious meeting, details of which I'm not about to bore you with. I thought it was too late to call you. Unfortunately, I would like to make this conversation brief, since I have to attend another meeting at eight in the morning and I haven't eaten yet. I just want you to know that I love and miss you very much. Because I'll be working until late in the evening tomorrow, if it's okay, I'll call you on Sunday morning and we can have a proper conversation."

"I love you too, Bruce, and I understand", I said, a little disoriented.

"So, until then, Miss Molly, hugs and kisses from your man who adores you."

I started to respond, but then I heard the click of the receiver, a sound that left me feeling cold and alone. I set the alarm for work and slipped under the covers, missing my two males, Bruce and Brandy, a bunch.

The alarm sounded, and I bounded out of bed in decent spirits, a good thing. I thanked God that I was going to work today. I wasn't normally a churchgoer, but I did have strong spiritual beliefs, particularly regarding angels. I suppose my Anglican Church upbringing, plus both my parents having sung in various choirs, had rubbed off on me. The beliefs I had through various tough times had helped enormously. I'm not sure I would be weathering the effects of the murder nearly as well, without my faith.

Now I really had to get back to reality. I picked up two strong coffees and two donuts before descending upon the clinic. The animal smell and noise of the residents was nirvana. I really was home in every sense of the word.

"John, it's me, Molly," I said over the sound of a squawking bird.

"About time, as I'm getting a caffeine withdrawal headache"; he said giving me a hug. "Am I ever happy to see you! I'm afraid gossip will have to wait until lunch time, and that will probably be around two. Oh, a confession. I have a tame parrot in a cage in my office. That's the source of all that jungle noise. His name is Sammy and I promise not to let him fly around you, as I know you detest birds flapping around indoors. Now let's get down to the nitty-gritty."

The so-called nitty-gritty was a busy, but invigorating morning, giving a dozen dogs shots of one kind or another. And two large Cheshire cats with chronic arthritis needed oral medication. One of them had such a pug like face that I couldn't stop laughing. He was very good at taking the medicine and a whole lot better than the majority of humans; that's for sure.

I checked in John's office to take a look at Sammy, who, true to form, squawked his head off.

"Screw you, buddy", I said, mischievously.

Suddenly out of this greenish, brown eyed bird came a chorus of "screw you, screw you", repeatedly. I was in hysterics when John walked into his office.

"Well, I can see you and Sammy have already formed a bond, Molly. I knew it wouldn't take you long to warm to him."

We both sat down laughing to the point of silliness. It felt good, and that damn bird still continued to mimic, "screw you".

I went up to the cage and said, "Lovely bird".

Thankfully, he changed his phraseology.

"Molly, in ten more minutes let's do lunch, unless you're going to look for a job as a bird trainer." He winked as he walked out. "See you at my car in ten".

"Right on, John."

Lunch was a huge BLT sandwich. I filled John in on the calamitous goings on with Mike. John knew the beginnings but was horrified for Bruce and me, knowing what the next few weeks would be like. Then he filled me in a bit on his current life.

"I've got some good news. Jessica and I got engaged. We've decided to wait until next summer to get married and we want you to be our matron of honor. Outside of that the business is increasing, and I'm thrilled that you're not chucking your job in to be a stay at home housewife."

I almost choked on my sandwich.

"Do I really look as if I'm the type that would crochet doilies, John? I must admit I'm bad at knitting and the like. I'd much prefer to train a parrot." We ordered more coffee and splurged on chocolate éclairs.

"This is my treat, John. It's an early engagement gift. I'm delighted for you both and can't wait to tell Bruce."

After devouring the scrummy éclairs, we made our way back our version of a menagerie. There was a message from Jen. I called her back to find that she he had to cancel our plans for tonight, so we rescheduled for Sunday at the same time.

I looked in on Sammy again. I was convincing myself that I could overcome my terror of flapping birds. Sammy and I were beginning to have a friendship, or so I felt. I said, *hello Sammy*, and by golly he said *hello Sammy*, sixteen times back.

"All right, that's it for now, buddy", I said in return.

Mistake number two. As I walked out I heard *buddy* repeated too many times to count. Lesson of the day for me was, *silence is golden.*"

Five o'clock closing arrived much more swiftly than I had imagined. John told me it was time to leave, especially since it was a Saturday, and to enjoy the rest of the weekend. He would see me on Monday.

"Thanks, John, for everything, and again many congrats to you and Jessica. When Bruce comes down, we'll have a celebratory bash together. Have a great Sunday too and take good care of Sammy", I chortled.

When I arrived home, there was a message from Bruce asking me to call him as soon as I got in. I excitedly threw my bag down and dialed Dearborn.

"Oh Molly, you're finally home."

There was a hint of sarcasm in his voice which I chose to ignore, other than to tell him about my day at work, figuring that he was unaware of that fact. I also slipped in that I was happy to hear from him sooner than Sunday, when he said he would call.

Thankfully, we reverted to our normal, in love, selves. We talked for half an hour about his job and mine, and I relaying my beginnings of a love affair with Sammy. The preliminaries over, we proceeded to the main event that we had been building up to, terrific phone sex. Our imaginations ran wild until we both exploded, releasing our hormonal frustrations.

At last Bruce murmured, "I adore you, but I'm ready to crash. I've got to get up at five for an early breakfast meeting. Sleep well, my princess. I just wish you were putting you head on a pillow next to mine. I'll call you tomorrow evening between eight and nine."

I chuckled, told him I adored him too, and looked forward to his call tomorrow night. Very shortly afterwards I crashed.

Sunday seemed to evaporate. It was already five in the afternoon when I met Jen for a casual jog on the beach. We enjoyed our measured strides both against, and with, refreshing breezes. We had a great chatty time along the way. Jen suggested that she come over Monday night just for a wine and another chat. It was agreed, and then we parted for home.

I'd almost forgotten it was a work day when the alarm went off. After early morning coffee and heated up leftover pizza, I drove to work, feeling refreshed and ready to further my bond with Sammy. On the way, I made a quick stop to get John his coffee. The morning went along in usual fashion. During lunch break, I enticed the parrot to say *I love Molly.* Thirty repetitions later I wished I'd taught it to say, *I love John.* We were slow in the afternoon, so John suggested I clean up the office. It was overflowing with papers, so I devoted two hours to filing, in between occasional appointments, to get it back to being tidy. That was after I had to remove the talking bird to a vacant examination room. By the time I'd finished, it was almost five, so I re-located Sammy, and said good evening to John.

I changed into sweats when I got home. For some reason, I was too nervous to eat anything healthful. Candy kisses and chips were my choices for calorie intake. It was not much after six, when the phone rang. I could see it was Bruce, from the caller ID.

I answered with "Hello, how are you, my future hubby? I didn't expect your phoning so early."

I heard him take a deep breath, deeper than normal.

"How am I? Quite frankly I am very upset. Bri just called to tell me that the police in St. Lucia have arrested my father and put him in a holding cell. Evidently the paperwork for extradition has been approved already. Sorry to have been so curt, but he's my father, whichever way you slice it. I don't really have energy enough for niceties. I don't blame you for this development, but now I need to come to terms with it in my own way. I just want to sit by myself and think, even though I'm mentally exhausted. Of course, this has taken a toll on you as well."

"My heart goes out to you, my love", I offered. "It is hard to shake my feeling of guilt about my role in the affair. I must admit it has worn down my mental state, but let's talk tomorrow. I realize you are distracted and I'm not much better off."

He said he'd call me tomorrow night, then the line went dead and so did my heart. Another sleeping pill night, this was going to be. I ran up and down the stairs at least twenty times to exhaust myself, took a pill, and slept until the bloody alarm rang. I'd left it accidentally on buzzer, not music, and that was a shock. I got ready for work, glorious work. But it wasn't a particularly great morning. Rain bucketed down, as it often did in Florida during the summer months. Not the gentle spring rain of Spain or France, but a torrential downpour. My body craved a triple caffeine dose this morning, so I pulled into the take-out coffee place to order two extra large espressos; two egg filled croissants, and drove slower than normal to work.

"Hi there," John said, grabbing his espresso to take several hearty swigs. "Goodness knows I needed that, between nursing Jessie, who has the flu, and getting only about three hours of deep sleep last night."

"Sorry to tell you, John, but I actually slept well with a little help from a pill."

We both laughed as we entered the surgery for another fun filled day. It was hectic. We had six spayings, one cat to be stitched up, and then we grabbed a quick sandwich around one. Sammy was at John's house, so I really missed his cheery squawking.

I hadn't given too much thought about poor old Mike, who was no doubt very worried, sitting in a jail cell. The work soothed my mind and uplifted my spirits, leaving little room for dire thoughts.

John had asked me to catch up on some more paper work, a necessary, but less rewarding, part of the job. The quiet began to disturb me, so I put a soothing disc on and hunkered down to the task. I'd finished everything by almost five when John came in.

"Gosh, you've finished, Molly; I knew I could count on you. Now buzz off home. "Thanks John, have a great evening and tell Jessica I hope she feels a whole lot better."

"I'll do just that, and goodnight to you, Molly."

My evening meal was fairly sensible as I knew full well, when under stress, I needed to control my diet. The phone rang at around seven and I jumped out of my skin. I picked it up, hoping it would be Bruce, but no such luck.

"Hi Molly, it's Bri calling. How are you doing this clement evening?"

He always was a bit of a ham, but I really liked him, at least as far as a "pick out of the yellow pages" private eye goes.

"I'm hanging, Bri, and thanks for asking. Now if you don't mind, could we cut to the chase, please, and tell me why you are calling. I assume there are developments on the case."

"There certainly are. What we did not know was that Detective Clifton flew down to St. Lucia as soon as their authorities informed the Dearborn attorney general that the extradition papers were in the process of being signed. Mike Sully was in such an agitated state that he readily confessed to the murder of his estranged wife, Greta, to Detective Clifton. Detective Andrews relayed this to Bruce and then to me. Quite frankly, Bruce was in such turmoil that he asked me to relay the outcome to you. He would call you later, once he was able to absorb the reality of it. The Dearborn police felt that, considering how poorly Mike tried to cover his tracks, it's as if he wanted to get caught."

After a huge sigh, I said, "Thanks for letting me know, Bri. Of course, I'm surprised, but I am truly relieved that Mike has confessed. Unfortunately, it's a more devastating revelation for Bruce. I can't say I am feeling vindicated. Truthfully, my overwhelming feeling is sadness for Bruce." My mind, however, was flashing with all sorts of conflicting emotions.

After a few minutes of meaningless conversation, Bri said, "Why don't you get some rest. And perhaps a sleeping pill might be in order."

With that, we said goodnight to each other. I decided to call Bruce, even though he was supposedly going to call me. But he wasn't there, so I left him a message, asking him to call me back as soon as possible. I couldn't settle to anything and wished I had Brandy here with me to calm my frazzled nerves. A half hour later, the phone rang and I almost knocked over the phone, because my nerves were so jangled. It was Bruce.

His first words were, "Molly, darling, how are you? God, I miss you so much."

"Me too, Bruce; I miss you more than you can imagine. But just to let you know, Bri called me about your dad's confession."

There was a long pause, too long, it seemed. Then there was a break in his voice as he attempted to speak.

"Bruce, are you okay? You sound terrible."

"No, I'm not alright. But I'd be a lot better with you by my side. I'm not going to beat about the bush. Detective Andrews told me that my father handed Detective Clifton a written confession that was addressed to me. It was faxed to the Dearborn police and a copy was given to me. Are you ready to hear the culmination of your detective work, Molly?"

"How many times can I apologize, Bruce, darling? But go ahead and give me the sordid details."

"Here are my father's actual words,

Bruce, my only son, I'm an absolute coward of the worst sort, but I'm not a murderer. Your mother returned home after a considerable absence and we got into another one of our endless arguments. I knew she had been unfaithful to me for a long time, but I couldn't come to terms with it. She started screaming and threw a book at me, so in a moment of extreme anger, I shoved her across the room. She hit her head on the antique chest of drawers and fell down.

There was blood everywhere. She had difficulty in breathing, and was moaning in pain. I just knew I'd lost my Greta forever, so in a panic, I decided to end her misery. I mixed water and a strong dose of ethylene glycol coolant and encouraged her to drink it. I must admit over the years I had thoughts of doing her in with ethylene glycol. Anyway, she quieted down, and eventually stopped breathing. I dragged her outside and buried her. I never really intended to kill your mother, but I didn't want to rot in jail either. Besides, if I'd called the cops they would have arrested me. You wouldn't, along with the authorities, have believed my plea that it was an accident. What I did was so wrong and irrational, that I don't know how I could ever make it up to you. I adored her, but it led to despising what she had done to me.

There you have it. What a double-edged sword jealousy is. I'm going to be charged for murder. At least I won't last long in some filthy jail at my age. I will die loving you. Perhaps one day you'll see your way to forgiving me, your dad.

So, there you have it, Molly. There isn't much more I can say, other than I was told it would take anywhere from one to three weeks before he'll be flown home to be arraigned. All I can do is pray for him."

"Oh, my poor darling, would you like me to see if I could take time off to be with you?"

"Absolutely not, life must go on. Of course, I'd rather you were here with me, but as soon as my job is finished in Dearborn, I expect to be with you, with his fate decided. But nothing and no-one will get in the way of our wedding. I adore you and don't blame you one bit for starting the investigation into my mother's disappearance. When I found out, you know I was pissed for your meddling without my involvement. Thankfully, I soon understood your motive and realized I'd rather know what happened to my mother than live forever wondering where she was. So, you see, my love, out of evil and uncertainty come clarity and truth."

He added in amusement, "Boy, that last line was almost poetic".

"Darling man, I can't begin to tell you how much I adore you. And thanks for being positive. Let's hope Mike is flown stateside as quickly as possible so you can see him. Is he going to remain in jail whilst still in St. Lucia?"

"No, I forgot to mention that's he's been put under house arrest and has to wear an ankle monitor. I'm pleased about this as the mere thought of him being in an alien jail seems ten times worse than being in a jail over here. Enough said, I'm beat, as I'm sure you are. I'll call you tomorrow. Work is crazy, but fun. Give my squawks to Sammy, and Brandy sends you slobbery kisses. Bye, my beautiful bride, until we talk again."

I giggled in response, more as sense of relief that we both were regaining our humor.

"I love you, Bruce. *A demain*" ('until tomorrow' in French).

He was learning French phrases from me faster than I had expected. Not just a techy genius, but a bit of a linguist too. In general, I found the two didn't mix that well, but I knew that I was marrying someone out of the ordinary.

I was wiped out. I grabbed a snack and slept like a baby without a sleeping pill. I'm not a medicine addict, but learned the hard way via my mother's lecture. Never let yourself get sleep deprived. It's the road to ruin. I'd had a mini breakdown after she died, trying to cope without help. I learned fast. I give myself an hour and if I'm still wide awake then I'd pop a pill.

I woke up an hour before the alarm was due to ring and realized that in less than two months I'd be a married lady. Shivers went down my spine. I'd lived alone so long that I was nervous about too much togetherness. *What a ridiculous thought,* I admonished myself. We both worked, and Bruce wasn't one of those chauvinistic types like a lot of men. Besides, we had good jobs and wouldn't be closeted together like couples in retirement (*Retardment,* my auntie Rose called it).

Before I walked out the door to work, John called to tell me that he was staying home for perhaps the rest of the week as Jessica was quite ill with severe flu, and so was he. A retired vet, Dr. Ralph Samuels, would fill in for John, as best he could. He assured me that I could cope and not to worry about fiddly office work, as long as our patients were taken care of.

He finished with, "Besides, I figured you'd rather be busy than twiddling your thumbs. So, thanks in advance, Molly. I couldn't run the clinic without you. Before you hang up, I'm upping your pay by twenty-five percent. I hope that's agreeable with you".

"Agreeable, John? It's more than agreeable! Thanks a million and I promise to run the shop smoothly. Tell Jessica I hope she gets to feeling better really soon, and you too."

"Will do and call me Wednesday morning for a head's up, or sooner, if needed. Take care and again, thanks for being an ace at what you do. We sure lucked out with each other, didn't we?"

"We certainly did, and again, thanks so much for my raise, John. I'll talk to you sometime on Wednesday."

I couldn't be happier right now. I was getting a raise, marrying Bruce, and distancing myself from Dearborn. Nothing would blight my spirits now.

Work at the clinic went well, even though Dr. Samuels was a little slow, though very thorough. Bruce was as busy as I was. But we managed to speak with each night. Of course, he was thrilled about my raise. He had heard nothing new about his father. His main effort at work was training his replacement, a bright young man from New York. Apparently, he was too cocky for words, but it was easy to overlook that side of him. He was definitely the man for the job, but at a more junior level. With a name like Damian LaCroix, how could he fail?

Calls to and from John during the week were inconsequential, as there were no hiccups with work. I had quick chats with Jen, who was frantically busy and was leaving Friday morning for a long weekend in Jacksonville.

Thursday during work Jen called me to say, "Wish we could have gotten together this weekend, but my trip is part business, part pleasure, as you know. I promise we'll hit the beach next week. In fact, what about making a date for Tuesday at five at the usual beach car park?"

"Sounds great, Jen; see you then and have a good weekend. Say hello to Charlie for me."

"I'll do that. Bye for now, from your bridesmaid to be."

Arriving Friday morning at work, I felt as if the week had gone by in a day. My nightly chats with Bruce had consisted of little intimacy and no phone sex. I guess we were consumed with work and the upcoming arraignment for Mike. The days were busy with our animal patients, but at John's direction, we had limited our appointments so that we could shut up shop around four, which we did. I tended to some paperwork until four-thirty, as I did not want to leave a complete mess of the office. Then I stopped for a burger and fries on the way home.

Bruce called around six to say, "What are you doing this weekend, Molly darling?"

"I'm going to rest, walk the beach, and miss you. What have you got planned?"

Bruce responded, "Nothing much besides taking care of Brandy and working out at the gym. I've got a business meeting Sunday afternoon. I can't wait to lead a normal life with you darling, if there is such a thing as normal.

Staying super busy helps a lot. Tell you what, I'll call you Monday night, and we'll have a long chat. Oh, I just realized that they're having a guys' night out Saturday as a sort of an early farewell and a welcome to Damian."

"That sounds like fun. By the way, I'm meeting Jen on Tuesday evening for a beach run and dinner. Have a great weekend, darling."

We hung up, and that was that. The weekend went swiftly enough. But I felt as if I were going through the motions. I relaxed as much as I could by going to the pool and lazing around. I read nothing, ate junk food, and slept more than normal. I couldn't wait to get back to work, but admitted to myself that I enjoyed being alone, which stems from being an only child. John called me Sunday whilst I was at the pool saying he'd be in around eight tomorrow and could I pick up donuts and coffee, which I willingly agreed to do.

When I got to work, coffee order in hand, John was sitting in the office looking as pleased as punch.

"Morning Molly, do you think you might come and clean up my office at home? This is amazing to come back to such order. Thanks a million", he said as he slugged down the coffee and ate two donuts in record time.

"No problem, John. You look good. How's Jessica?"

"Almost back to normal, thank goodness. Now catch me up on last week's goings on."

I did as he requested, then asked "Do you think you could bring Sammy in tomorrow? I've grown quite attached to the squawking one".

"Yes, you've taught him some choice words. Jessica has an even worse phobia about birds loose in the house than you do, so he's all yours the work week."

He burst out laughing and almost choked on his third donut. I realized I was ravenous and I proceeded to down my own donuts in record time, before turning to the animals. The morning was slow but steady. Around ten-thirty the phone rang. John answered it and said it was Bruce. He cupped his hand over the phone and told me Bruce sounded mighty agitated.

"Take it in the office, Molly. You'll have more privacy there."

"Thanks", I said, as I ran into the office and picked up the phone.

"Hello, darling; what's going on?"

All I heard were sobs, then nothing.

"Bruce, what is it?"

"I just got a call from Bri. Dad had a massive heart attack late last night. He was rushed to hospital where they discovered he had severe blocked arteries. While under sedation, awaiting surgery, he died. They figured that even without all the stress of the upcoming legal proceedings, he would have had this heart attack sooner or later. He'd never had regular checkups. At first, I couldn't believe what I was hearing, but truthfully, Molly, his dying is a thousand times better than wasting away in some overcrowded prison. They're shipping his body back after the coroner's report is finalized. Detective Clifton has already returned."

"I don't know what to say, Bruce. I'm stunned and so sad. I insist on taking a leave of absence to help and give you support. I guess, in retrospect, this was a better way for Mike to go, but I still feel terrible for you. I'll come up as soon as I've told John and booked my flight, darling."

He was too distressed to argue, and said, "That would be wonderful of you, Molly. Your being with me will greatly lessen my personal pain. Truthfully, I'm really relieved for the resolution to my mother's disappearance and the reason why, devastating though it is. As for Dad, he was not that old, but I realize his health was failing, because he was stubborn, and refused to have regular checkups, despite my urging."

"I just want to fold my arms around you to give you comfort. I'm just sorry I can't right now", I said with all the emotion love could give me.

"Oh, Molly, I feel as if you are with me now."

After a few moments of silence, Bruce managed to calm himself and then said, "I'm calling a funeral home in the morning to make initial arrangements for my dad's cremation. That had always been his request.

Incidentally, I found that Dad had put a down payment on the house in St. Lucia, but the paperwork had not been finalized, so I'm going to track down the owners to hopefully void the contract. The death of one party normally does that, or so I believe. Well, not much else to say, darling. Do you think you could make it by Wednesday?"

"I'll get off the phone now and, tell John, and then I'll work on finding a flight, and call you tonight."

I went back to the surgery unit where John asked me what was up and telling me that I looked like a ghost had just haunted me.

I summarized the conversation and asked John if there was any way I could leave tomorrow afternoon. Naturally it's unpaid leave. I feel awful asking this of you, since I've just got back from two weeks paid holiday."

"Don't be ridiculous, Molly. You're off as of this evening and take as long as you need to. It coincides with Jessica's vacation weeks, so I'll ask her to come in a couple of days a week to take care of the office, and we have assistants on call, which can help with surgeries and the like. I'm not about to replace you. As long as you are living, the job will always be yours."

I cried and rushed over to hug him.

"You're the best boss ever. Thanks, John."

We worked in unison until around six, because of a collie who was slightly injured in a car crash. I finished cleaning up the operating area while John dictated the surgery details into his recording machine. Finally, it was time to take my leave.

"I'll let you know my flight details, John. I promise to call you from Dearborn. Hopefully, my stay should not be longer than a week. I'll more than likely return on Saturday which will give me Sunday to come down to earth, yet again."

"Take care, Molly. I'll look forward to your call. And don't worry, we will survive well enough in your absence, but know I'll miss your wonderful self."

The first thing I did upon getting home was to call the airlines. I got a flight that left around noon, returning Saturday at four in the afternoon. It was not an expense that I had budgeted for; however, Bruce would insist, no doubt, on reimbursing me. I called Jen and filled her in on everything, and said how sorry I was to have to cancel tomorrow evening.

"That's a bummer, but a blessing in disguise, if you ask me", Jen said. "Call me when you know your time of arrival back here. Charlie and I'll pick you up on Saturday and we can have dinner together. I think you'll need some light relief after what you will have gone through."

"Thanks. You're the best friend ever, Jen. I'll call you tomorrow night from Bruce's."

A sleeping pill was a necessity for a decent night's rest. My mind wouldn't calm down without it. The pill did its job. I arose fairly refreshed, packed and had a light breakfast. The van service I had called to pick me up at nine in the morning arrived on time. The flight was good and I slept through most of it. Bruce met me just the other side of luggage claim, running towards me and picking me off the floor to hug.

He declared, "Am I ever glad you're here, Molly! I realize more and more how very much I adore and need you."

"Likewise, Bruce", I said, locking arms with him as we went to his car.

We nervously chattered the entire way back to the house. He made one revelation, that his mother's remains had been released to him by the authorities and that he was having them cremated. That's all he wanted to say about it at the time, so I honored his wishes.

Once inside his home, he dropped my bag on the living room floor and led me upstairs. I'd forgotten how much I'd missed sex with Bruce. There was no time for small talk. We took a quick shower together, and then he took me quickly and fiercely.

"Wow, if ever I needed you, it was now, Molly. Welcome back to *my* neck of the woods!"

I lay comfortably in his arms whilst he told me about the cremation service.

"It's Thursday noon at Nelson's Funeral Home for my father. I hope you don't mind coming with me.

"Why should I, Bruce? I'm your partner for life and, after all, he would have been my father-in-law. By the way, where is Brandy, my other male love?"

"Nick and Sally took him for me and they're keeping him until Friday morning. He was happy to go there and have more company in the daytime. By the way, are you hungry? I thought we could walk to the diner, and perhaps we could pick up a few things from the grocery store on the way back. Man cannot feed on love alone."

I nodded an emphatic, yes, and laughed with him, before we got ready for a very late, but much needed lunch.

I missed Brandy being with us on our walk to the cafe. It was the first time to be there without him, and I couldn't wait to be with my canine buddy.

While I devoured every bit of my omelet, hungrier than I had imagined, Bruce filled me in on various details.

"Dad wanted his ashes scattered in my back garden, so that's what I'll do. Actually, come to think of it we might as well do a two for the *price* of one and scatter my mom's ashes next to him. After all they did love each other once upon a time. As for the house purchase in St. Lucia, the sellers of the house, under the circumstances of my dad's death, agreed to close out the contract and return the down payment, minus costs they had incurred. I'm not sure what their obligations were under local law, but it sounded fair to me. Needless to say, I am not looking forward to tomorrow's viewing, but at least having you by my side will ease the pain.

"I'm so happy that I'm here with you, darling. Thank the Lord for giving me such a wonderful boss. We'll have to take John and Jessica out for a scrumptious meal when we are finally together in New Smyrna Beach."

"I certainly agree. Now, do you want dessert or shall we buy a cheesecake for later?"

"The latter choice appeals to me", I replied.

We ambled quietly, each of us in deep thought, to a locally owned grocery store to pick up a few basics and one of its small homemade cheesecakes. Back home we watched a couple of movies, splurged on our cake purchase and slept like babes until almost nine-thirty the next morning. Bruce beat me to the kitchen to return with our usual coffee and donuts. It was followed by great morning sex.

The official viewing was set for noon. We busied ourselves tidying up the place and dressing in a sober fashion. I'd never been to a viewing and wasn't looking forward to it. Frankly, I think the idea of seeing a dead person, gussied up is somewhat barbaric, but that's my humble opinion. We got to the funeral home around eleven-thirty, the first to arrive. I held onto Bruce's hand, tighter than I probably should have. We were ushered into the viewing room, where I almost passed out when we were shown the casket with Mike lying there, dead for sure, looking like a candidate for a wax museum. I touched his hand and prayed for his soul. Bruce kissed his father's cheek and whispered something in his ear. There was a hint of hint of tears when he turned to me.

"Let's go into the greeting room, Molly", he said when he'd collected himself. "That was a thousand times worse than I'd anticipated. It was the finality of it that got to me, plus seeing him so formally dressed. It seemed so unreal." In a lighter tone, he said "I guess this is my final goodbye to the old fart."

We both laughed nervously and went to mingle with many well wishers, most of whom I didn't know. Nick and Sally were there, plus a lot of Bruce's friends from work and the gym, along with Mike's acquaintances.

"It's great to see you, Sally and Nick, even under such macabre circumstances. Thanks for coming and thanks for taking such good care of Brandy", I said on our behalf.

Sally replied, "No problem, guys. We adore Brandy and will miss him as much as you two when you're settled in New Smyrna Beach permanently. We are psyched to have two weeks there in October for the wedding. That'll be a great vacation for us."

"Now, I've tentatively booked you into this great bed and breakfast, subject to your approval, for the time Bruce and I are around. And since you are dog sitting, we insist you move into my place – well *our* place, when we go on honeymoon", I said.

Nick chimed in, "If you're sure, Molly, that'll be wonderful; plus, it means we'll be able to eat out more".

"Absolutely! I guess we'll see you Friday morning when we pick up Brandy."

Bruce interjected. "You wouldn't feel like a late lunch with us, would you? I for one could do with some laughter and a good meal after all this."

"Sure, we'd love to," said Nick, who got a positive signal from Sally. "How about we meet you at one-thirty at our favorite steak place? That should be enough time, shouldn't it, Bruce?"

"Of course, and again, thanks for coming here. It means a lot to me", Bruce replied, who then got attention from a number of work mates wanting to pay their respects.

During a lull, Bruce said, "I'm picking the ashes up on Friday morning and I am really glad you'll be there with me".

"Well, it's the least I can do, Bruce. I'd be there for that part, no matter when it happened. I'm feeling more at peace now and hope you are too."

"Funny enough, I am. There is closure at last. I feel I can really move on with my life now."

Lunch was wonderful. We ate a lot and drank more than usual. It was a fitting, if gluttonous, way to end a somber occasion. In fact, we had the best time we'd ever had together, and left feeling no pain at all. We'd been in the restaurant over three hours and decided it really was finally time to leave.

Before parting, Nick and Sally accepted our invitation to mark the occasion of the spreading of Mike's and Greta's ashes.

We retreated to Bruce's home to jump into bed and watch TV, until we rolled over to sleep from about ten right through to six the next morning.

Coffee was served earlier than usual, but the routine was the same. *I'd hate for it to change,* I thought to myself.

"Well, my bride-to-be, we have a free day today. What would you like to do?"

"I'd love to take a boat ride, if possible."

"Your wish is my command. I'll get on the phone and reserve two tickets."

The cruise was an exercise in decadence. We sat on deck, drank champagne, and snacked on cheese, pate, and crackers. It was the perfect escape from reality. By the end of it we were flushed from the sun and two bottles of bubbly that we'd consumed.

We got off around five and stopped at a family owned Greek restaurant. Bruce ordered Moussaka for two and coffee from a rather perfunctory waitress. The food made up for the mediocre service.

Once back at Bruce's he switched into a very different mood.

"I've got to make some business calls, darling, so if you can amuse yourself, I'll be a couple of hours."

"Sure can," I said, deciding to call Jen for a chat on my cell phone. She was home so I filled her in on the events of the last few days.

"Oh, Molly, what a nightmare you and Bruce have been living recently. At least it'll be over Friday, and you can come back to concentrate on your wedding plans. It'll really keep your mind off the past few months. Things are now on the upward turn, so I'll pick you up on Saturday. Keep Sunday free for the beach, as I know you'll need it."

"I'll do that Jen. You're the best, as you well know, so until Saturday. Once we've gotten through tomorrow, things have to improve. How could they not? Say hello to Charlie for me."

Jen replied, "Hello to Bruce too. See you on Saturday."

I had a long shower, pampered myself to smithereens, went downstairs, and made a decaf. I peeped into the office and told Bruce what I was doing, and he said he'd be up in under an hour. The hour was much more. I never heard him come to bed. The next thing I knew, the alarm sounding. He wasn't in bed and there was no coffee or note.

I went down to the kitchen and made a large pot of coffee, nervously wondering where the heck he was. It suddenly dawned on me that he'd probably gone to pick up Brandy. I'd barely downed one mug of coffee when I heard a car door slam. As I opened the front door, in rushed Brandy, panting with excitement, closely followed by Bruce and a large bouquet of peach roses.

"I panicked for a second, wondering where you were before it came to me that you were getting Brandy. I have the makings of an omelet ready for us, knowing you'd be hungry.

I was right. After I served him, Bruce used his knife and fork with quick precision, barely looking up from his plate. My pace was a good bit slower.

"Thanks, darling, I feel more prepared to face the world. Nick and Sally are coming over around five and then we we'll have the ceremony. Fancy taking a walk with Brandy in about an hour? Oh, another item I'd forgotten to mention was that I'd spoken to Bri and said I'd mail his check for five hundred bucks within the week."

"Darling, that's my bill and I'm paying him. I'm the one that started this investigation."

"What difference does it make, Molly? Once we are married, we'll be pooling our funds anyway."

I swallowed hard and realized that I didn't want to pool everything. It was too much like totally giving up my independence.

"No, I'm sorry, but I stand firm on this issue, Bruce. I started this investigation and I'm going to pay Bri. Please don't argue with me."

"Fine, fine, since you feel so strongly about this, I'll give you his bill. Once we are married, we'll work something out about finances. One thing I'm going to insist is that you keep your entire salary, since we're going to be living in your house, at least for starters."

"Very well, darling, I'm not going to arm wrestle you over it", I said feeling an enormous tidal wave of relief wash over me about having some independence. Bruce knew me better than I thought.

We took Brandy for a long walk and busied ourselves whiling away the time until the final hour was upon us. Nick and Sally were punctual as always, bringing a couple of bottles of champagne and a large wheel of brie.

"Yummy! Sally and Nick, you know our weaknesses. Thanks so much", I said.

Without delay, Bruce said, "Well, everyone, I suggest that now is the time for our little ceremony. Let's go outside, shall we?"

Bruce gave a short, but touching speech as he scattered Mike's and Greta's ashes in the garden, away from the house. There wasn't a dry eye amongst us. Nick popped open a bottle of the bubbly and we toasted to the well being of his parents in the afterlife. This occasion was another first for me, deeply moving, but rather macabre.

Their only son ended the ceremony with, "Rest in peace, Mom and Dad. You've both had quite a life, and now you can really start afresh. Goodbye and God speed."

After more tears and more champagne, we silently gathered our thoughts. Personally, I now felt completely at ease with what I'd started. Bruce had closure, and in a way so did Mike and Greta.

"Who's for more champagne?" Bruce said, switching from a somber tone to one of joyful relief.

We all nodded in the affirmative, glanced back at the garden, and went inside.

"Won't you stay for pizza, Sally and Nick? It's frozen and not exactly gourmet, but we'd love for you to join us, wouldn't we, Bruce?"

"Yes, we'd love you to", Bruce affirmed.

"Thanks, it would be our pleasure", Sally said

After finishing off the brie and bubbly, Sally came into the kitchen to help with heating and serving the pizza.

"What a day, Molly. I think despite the past it was a beautiful ceremony, and now the two of you can get on with living the good life. Have you got everything organized for the big day?"

"Yes, pretty much. The minister is booked and the service will be held on the beach, a free venue. I'll smooth out all the last-minute details when I return. My best friend, Jen, is my only bridesmaid. We've known each other forever and I'm not sure how I'd cope without her. Anyway, I'm excited and as nervous as can be. I've lived alone for so long, but I do feel as if I've known Bruce forever."

At last, the pizza was ready and loaded on a tray along with plates. Jen and I found the guys nodding off on the sofa.

"Dinner is ready, guys," Sally said.

I was thinking to myself how easy it is for men to fall asleep. Women, on the other hand, have a much harder time napping, particularly in times of stress.

We munched on pizza and drank red wine, while chatting about the wedding and Nick and Sally's visit to New Smyrna Beach. Suddenly it dawned on me that I had to fly back.

"Sorry guys, but I'm going to have to kick you out. I'm flying back tomorrow with a number of loose ends to tie up, plus packing, before I leave, so I need my beauty rest."

Sally, replied, "We understand totally, Molly. We'll see you in October. Have a safe flight."

Bruce jumped up, gathering up the plates before ushering them both to the door. "Thanks for the bubbly and cheese, and being with us today. It meant a lot to Molly and me. Anyway, I'll see you, Nick, on Tuesday at the gym."

After final farewells, Bruce and I quickly cleaned the kitchen and headed upstairs to bed and then an early, hectic morning.

The events of yesterday had wiped us. We barely spoke whilst I packed up the few things I had for the flight back. It was hard to believe that I not would be returning to Michigan as a single girl.

"Bruce, here's my check for Bri. Please mail it for me, whilst I make us brunch. I don't have to be at the airport until two. Also, I want to say that your little ceremony for your parents yesterday was quite moving. It was a beautiful send off for them."

God rest the bastard's soul, I said to myself, thinking about Mike. There was much more sorrow in my heart for Bruce's mother, Greta. May she now really rest in peace.

Bruce interrupted my momentary thoughts with, "I could wax poetic right now, Miss Molly, but I'm just going to say that I'm the luckiest man alive. I know I've said this many times, but I adore you, your humor, your spirit, and your sexy self."

"Likewise, the compliments are returned, but even if it breaks the spell, I must finish the pancakes; otherwise, we'll never eat."

We ate quickly in order to get to the airport on time, and we did. Bruce knew full well now much I hated protracted goodbyes, so our parting was brief, but filled with emotion, and my tears.

After a smoldering kiss, I managed to say, I'll call you tonight when I get back from dinner with Jen. It'll be around ten, if that's not too late?"

"That's fine. It'll give me a chance to clear my desk. I've got a ton of stuff to do before leaving here. At least I made the right decision not to sell my house just yet. I think that would have been way too much to cope with. I adore you, Molly, have a safe flight, and love to Jen."

"Will do, Bruce", I said, as I turned my back on him and headed for the plane.

I slept the entire way to Orlando. Jen was there waving away as I went through the arrival gate.

"Hello, Molly. I'm sorry, but Charlie had to stay in Jacksonville, so it's just you and me this evening."

"That works for me. We can have undivided girlie talk, and I'll fill you in on the viewing and ceremony."

"There's this great crab place on the way home. Do you want to try it, girlfriend?"

"You bet; lead the way", I replied.

While we picked crab meat from the shells we cracked open, and devoured the delicious contents, I filled Jen in on the past two days' events.

"I'm so thrilled it's behind me, Jen. It's as if a tidal wave has washed over me and cleansed me of any wrong doing. Now I can really look forward to the wedding."

She drove fast, as usual, the rest of the way home, careful not to overshoot the speed limit enough to guarantee a ticket.

Jen said, as we arrived at my place, "I won't come in, as I didn't get very much sleep last night. Perhaps one-night next week we can go over all the wedding arrangements?"

"Sure thing, and again, Jen, thanks for picking me up and being here for me."

"Works both ways, bride to be," she said, as she left.

I called Bruce around ten that evening without luck, so I left a message that all was good, and I'd call him tomorrow evening.

 Sunday morning was gorgeous, so I decided to go the beach around noon. Before a late breakfast, I called John to say I was back and that I'd be in Monday morning.

"Hope all went as well as could be expected, Molly."

"Thanks, it did. To say the least, I'm glad to be home. I'll give you the full story Monday. And be sure to give Jessica my best regards."

"Will do and have a happy Sunday. Until Monday, then."

Today would be a total goof off day. I needed sea air and time to regroup. After a quick breakfast and several cups of coffee, I drove to the beach, parked, and set my things down on a large towel. I then proceeded to run along the sand with long flowing strides and let my mind wander to what was ahead for me and Bruce.

Once wed, our lives would irrevocably alter. There'd be no more usual back and forth to Dearborn. The transition wasn't going to be a walk in the park, and we'd known each other for just months. However, we were attuned to each other as if it were much longer. I was more than prepared to take the gamble, and so was Bruce.

I stopped to take in a large breath of sea air, look up at the beautiful blue sky, and eagerly awaited the arrival of *MY* Michigan Man.

www.ingramcontent.com/pod-product-compliance
Lightning Source LLC
Chambersburg PA
CBHW080847190726
48292CB00010B/2904